DOC

Doc Savage—born Clark Savage, Jr.—was raised from the cradle for his task in life—his job of flitting about the globe righting wrongs, helping the oppressed, smashing the guilty. He is a physician and surgeon—and a mighty good one, the tops in his line. He has the best and most modern equipment at his command, for he has limitless wealth. His main headquarters are in New York, but he has his Fortress of Solitude at a place unknown to anyone, where he goes at periodic intervals to increase his knowledge and concentrate. He's foiled countless crooks, and changed many of them into honest, useful citizens. The world would be a great place if there were more Doc Savages. But there's only one.

Four Complete Adventures in One Volume

THE INVISIBLE-BOX MURDERS
BIRDS OF DEATH
THE WEE ONES
TERROR TAKES 7

Kenneth Robeson

BANTAM BOOKS
NEW YORK · TORONTO · LONDON · SYDNEY · AUCKLAND

*This edition contains the complete text
of the original hardcover edition*
NOT ONE WORD HAS BEEN OMITTED·

DOC SAVAGE OMNIBUS #9
*A Bantam Book / published by arrangement with
The Condé Nast Publications, Inc.*

PRINTING HISTORY

The Invisible-Box Murders was originally published in Doc Savage
magazine, November 1941. Copyright 1941 by Street & Smith
Publications, Inc. Copyright renewed © 1969 by Condé Nast Publications, Inc.

Birds of Death was originally published in Doc Savage magazine,
October 1941. Copyright 1941 by Street & Smith Publications, Inc.
Copyright renewed © 1969 by Condé Nast Publications, Inc.

The Wee Ones was originally published in Doc Savage magazine,
August 1945. Copyright 1945 by Street & Smith Publications, Inc.
Copyright renewed © 1973 by Condé Nast Publications, Inc.

Terror Takes 7 was originally published in Doc Savage magazine,
September 1945. Copyright 1945 by Street & Smith Publications,
Inc. Copyright renewed © 1973 by Condé Nast Publications, Inc.

Bantam edition / July 1989

ISBN 0-553-28000-7

Published simultaneously in the United States and Canada

PRINTED IN THE UNITED STATES OF AMERICA

O   0 9 8 7 6 5 4 3 2 1

Contents

THE INVISIBLE-BOX MURDERS

Contents

I

FEAR OF BOXES

It was a cellophane box, so it was not invisible.

Being made of fairly good cellophane—ten cents a sheet in the dime stores—it was transparent. Not as transparent, perhaps, as good window glass, but you could see through it without trouble.

It was approximately half the size of a shoe box; as wide and as high as a shoe box, but only half as long. Otherwise, it bore no resemblance to a shoe box. The lid was not the same. This lid was a kind of flap.

It looked, as nearly as Doc Savage had been able to make it look, exactly like the newspaper photographs, and the police photographs, of the other boxes.

So it looked like the invisible boxes. Not like the invisible boxes, exactly. But at least like the invisible boxes looked before they became invisible. Those that had been photographed.

It was a little complicated. Or more specifically, baffling. Baffling was the word.

Doc Savage was putting the box on a man's doorstep.

It was a little more complicated than that, of course. Getting into the building had not been entirely simple. It was an office building, the time was near the noon hour, and the place was crowded with people who might recognize Doc Savage. He knew this. The people were not personal acquaintances and no one he had met, but there just might be someone who might recognize his picture from the newspapers. So he had come in through the freight entrance and walked up eleven flights of stairs.

He had stood on the eleventh floor, in the hall, for twenty minutes. Rather, he had occupied a broom closet, with the door opened a crack, for that long.

J. P. MORGAN
Investments

That was what it said on the door.

It was not *the* J. P. Morgan, however. This one's middle

5

name was not Pierpont, and he was not an international banker, or a private banker at all. He was just a buyer and seller of cheap securities of the type called cats and dogs. And he was not very prosperous.

Some detective work by Andrew Blodgett Monk Mayfair, associate of Doc Savage, had unearthed that much about this J. P. Morgan.

Finally, the secretary had gone out to lunch.

Monk Mayfair had explained that the secretary wasn't very pretty. That undoubtedly meant she was as homely as a mud fence with the hide of an octopus tacked on it. Monk Mayfair was easily affected by women; and when he thought one was homely, she was homely indeed.

This was right. The secretary wasn't attractive. She looked hungry and in a hurry. She hadn't locked the office door behind her, which indicated that J. P. Morgan was in.

Doc Savage had wanted Mr. Morgan to be in. He walked to the door, opened it and entered, careful to make no sound.

The reception room was furnished with a desk, an uncomfortable chair, a telephone—these for the secretary—and a seedy and once-luxurious divan for clients.

Doc put the cellophane box on the desk. He picked up the telephone, connected it to the inner room, pressed the key and got a man's voice in answer. Presuming this was Mr. Morgan, Doc Savage spoke rapidly. Doc was a man of many unusual capabilities, and one of these was the ability to imitate voices, even a woman's voice after a fashion.

Because, being quite masculine, he could not exactly duplicate the secretary's voice exactly, he used a whisper instead.

He said, whispering, "A package just came for you, Mr. Morgan."

The voice said, "Bring it in."

"You better come out and get it," Doc said.

Then he got out of the office, closed the door to a half-inch aperture and waited to see what would happen.

He had put the cellophane box on the stenographer's desk; so he hadn't literally left the box on the man's doorstep.

J. P. Morgan came out of the inner office almost immediately.

In looks, Mr. Morgan was an old gentleman of surprising benevolence. He was of less than average height, more than average width. His hair was very white, his whiskers very silky and as white as his hair. He had fawnlike brown eyes with little crinkles at the corners.

Peace and good will; I love my brother. That was Mr. Morgan.

Mr. Morgan looked around the office, then saw the cellophane box.

He proceeded—if one should want to put it humorously—to have kittens.

His eyes seemed to be trying to get out of his skull. That was the first thing, as he looked at the box. Then he made a noise. It was the noise of a man caught under a freight train.

He jumped backward wildly. His eyes hunted for a weapon. He snatched a fire extinguisher off the wall and squirted the extinguisher contents at the box.

He did not go near the box, or try to put it on the floor. He just squirted the extinguisher stream at it. The pencil of tetrachloride—or whatever was in the extinguisher—knocked the cellophane box off the desk, and it fell to the floor.

The scared Mr. Morgan kept squirting until the extinguisher was empty. He threw the extinguisher at the box, missing it.

Then he proceeded to try to burn the box. He dumped the contents of the wastebasket on it, struck a match and applied it to the paper. He didn't seem to give a hoot about whether the shabby rug got a hole burned in it or not.

Fortunately or unfortunately, the stream of fluid from the extinguisher had soaked the contents of the wastebasket, so the paper wouldn't burn.

First he had tried to extinguish it; now he was trying to burn it. This was rather silly. It showed only one thing: Mr. Morgan was so scared he didn't know whether he was standing on his head or on his feet.

Then it dawned on him that the cellophane box was empty. He bent over, staring at the box. He looked utterly relieved. He sank back in the stenographer's chair so loosely and so helplessly that the chair upset, scooting out from under him and depositing him on the floor. He sat there on the floor like a man who had been nearly knocked out.

Doc Savage walked into the office.

"It might be advisable for you to tell me why seeing that box excited you so," Doc said.

Morgan stood up so straight that he seemed to lift an inch off the floor. He looked at the window as if he wanted to jump out of it.

"Oh, hello," he said vaguely.

Doc Savage moved toward him, saying, "Mr. Morgan, I presume."

This was purely a conversational statement because Monk Mayfair had described Mr. Morgan, and this was he.

The old gentleman looked at the doors as if he wanted to dash out through them, and at the stenographer's desk as if he wished to crawl under it.

"I . . . er. . . beg your pardon," he said.

Doc Savage took him by the arm. He did not resist. Doc led him into the inner office. The place was furnished with a desk, filing cabinet, an uncomfortable chair behind the desk for Mr. Morgan, and a less comfortable one in front of the desk—exactly the reverse, in comfort degree, of the arrangement in the outer office. Doc sat him down in the chair.

The bronze man went to the outer office, then returned with what was left of the cellophane box. He put this on the desk in front of Mr. Morgan.

"Why did it excite you?" he asked.

Morgan swallowed, and the ends of his fingers twitched as if they were in cold water.

He was not going to talk.

Doc Savage was a big man, so big that his real size was startlingly apparent whenever he stood close to an ordinary object, such as a chair or a desk. His skin was deeply bronzed, and his eyes like liquid gold under narrowed lids. He was, in whole, a striking figure. Strength seemed to flow like molten metal under every square inch of his skin.

Doc said, "Four men have died. Four that the police know of, and there have been many others."

Morgan began turning white.

Doc continued, "The deaths have mystified the police. There seemed to be no reason for any of them and no connection between the four deaths."

Morgan started trembling.

"They were not natural deaths," added Doc Savage. "Each one was mysterious, unexplained—and are still unexplained. The leading scientists of the police department were baffled, and the consulting experts called in on the cases are baffled."

The white-haired man's breathing now became audible. It was a sound like cloth tearing deep within him, a soft and low sound, but disturbing.

Doc said, "A box was found near each dead man. In each case, it was a box, presumably made of cellophane."

Morgan opened and closed his mouth.

"The boxes later vanished," Doc said. "They disappeared completely and inexplicably, and no one seems to be able to explain just what did happen to them. It is very mystifying to the police."

Morgan took hold of his lip with his teeth, very tightly.

"The newspapers are referring to them as invisible boxes," Doc added.

Morgan's paleness, trembling and strained breathing had all combined until he now looked and acted like a man about to fall into fragments.

Doc Savage made what was obviously his final statement in his summary.

"All of the mysteriously dead men," he said, "happened to be acquaintances of yours, Mr. Morgan. That is a matter which the police were not fortunate enough to discover."

The white-haired man broke.

For something more than five minutes, he alternately sobbed, clenched and unclenched his fists, or pounded wildly on the desk in front of him. He jumped up, or attempted to do so several times, as if he wanted to run screaming from the place. In each case, Doc Savage restrained him.

But finally, he said, "I am only Uncle Joe Morgan. Why should anyone want to do such things to me?"

Doc Savage took a chair, the uncomfortable one. His eyes, which had been narrowed, seemed to relax, so that the lids widened. His eyes were like pools of flake gold stirred by tiny winds.

"So you *do* know something about the affair," he said.

Uncle Joe Morgan shuddered. It was the fifteenth time, at least, that he had shuddered. But this time he did it violently.

"I am a gentle man," he said. "I have no enemies because I am not an ambitious man." He moved a hand vaguely, indicating his office. "I make a very modest living, dealing in low-priced, but sound, stocks, bonds and commodities. I have no bad habits. My only hobby is boating, and practically my only piece of property is a small schooner which I own."

Doc Savage studied him.

"Which is all preliminary to your saying what?" he asked.

Uncle Joe Morgan swallowed with great difficulty. "I have realized the coincidence of each of those men being an acquaintance of mine," he said. "And it has frightened me. As far as I know, those men who have died have had no connection with each other, *except that they knew me!*"

"Which means?"

"I . . . I would give everything to know. All I own." Uncle Joe Morgan clenched his hands. "I mean that."

Doc Savage indicated the cellophane box. "Seeing that box disturbed you a great deal."

The other man bowed his white head. "I know. I have just told you why."

Doc Savage said nothing. His metallic features, rugged and well-molded so that they were handsome without being in any sense pretty-pretty, showed no expression. His face gave an impression of controlled power.

"You seemed *very* scared," he said.

The other straightened. "You do not believe me?"

"You were unusually disturbed," Doc said.

Uncle Joe Morgan took out a handkerchief, wiped his face.

"I give you my word I know nothing about this," he said. "I am just unnerved by those deaths. Those men were not extremely close to me, but I knew them quite well. They have died one after another, in that weird fashion, and it has terrified me. *Just the men I know are dying?* Why is that?"

"You cannot explain it?"

"No."

"You might try to think of something."

Uncle Joe Morgan's lips were paper-white and his breathing had, all during their talk, become more and more like cloth tearing. The tearing had started, seemingly, deep in his lungs, so that it was barely audible; now, it was up in his throat, and loud.

"I have thought about it," he said, "for four straight days and nights. I have not slept."

Doc Savage arose. There had been no sound audible to normal ears. But the bronze man went to the reception room door, opened it; and the homely secretary was there. She looked up curiously at Doc Savage and then, fascinated by the unusual power which the bronze man radiated, as people always were, kept staring at him.

He closed the door and went back to the desk. He put both hands on the desk. The sinews in the backs of the hands stood out like steel pencils.

"What about Ted Parks?" he asked. Then, when the old man seemed to melt in his chair: "So you've thought of that, too?"

"You mean—Ted Parks also knew the men who have died?"

"Yes."

"I . . . I knew that."

"We had better talk to Ted Parks," Doc Savage said.

"He . . . he has disappeared."

"Yes," Doc said. "So we discovered."

"Look." Uncle Joe Morgan reached into his desk and brought out an envelope. From the envelope he took a paper, which he spread on the desk. "Look," he repeated.

It read:

I am coming to see you at four o'clock Friday.
You better be there, and you better not tell anybody
I am coming. AND I MEAN NOBODY.   Bughide.

"Ted Parks wrote that. Today is Friday. So he is coming at four o'clock today." Uncle Joe Morgan drew in a deep breath. "That name he signed to it, Bughide, is a nickname I called Ted one time. I think he has always resented it. I called him the name because he is so easily offended. I think I referred to him having a hide no thicker than a bug, at the time."

Doc Savage looked at the note in silence for a while.

He asked, "Have you any objections to my being present at four o'clock this afternoon when Ted Parks pays you this call?"

The white-haired man sat up straight.

"I would be delighted," he said.

"Have you any idea why the note has this violent tone?"

Doc asked. "The reference, in particular, that you had better not tell anyone."

"I have no idea."

"Expect me shortly before four o'clock," Doc Savage said.

Doc Savage left the office building and stepped into a nearby restaurant. He took a seat in a booth in the rear, a booth with high wooden partitions in front and behind.

A man was already seated in the booth. He was a short, wide man covered with rusty-red hair. He had sloping shoulders, no forehead worth mentioning and a face that was something to start dogs barking.

This pleasantly apish fellow had a pig under the table. The pig was sitting there in comfort, one eye on the proprietor of the restaurant, who did not look happy.

"Well, did he admit getting the note from Parks?" asked the man.

"Yes, Monk, he admitted that," Doc Savage said. "But he admitted to very little else."

Monk Mayfair grinned. "That's a point in his favor. I don't reckon he could have known I went through his mail and gave that letter a go-over with Long Tom's pet portable X-ray machine."

Doc Savage asked. "Is Long Tom on the job?"

"Yes," Monk said. "He has tapped Uncle Joe Morgan's telephone line and put a recording instrument on it."

"And Renny?"

"Renny has rented an office across the street. He is sitting there with a pair of binoculars, watching the inside of Uncle Joe's office."

"Ham?"

Monk sniffed, as if he did not care for Ham. Ham was Brigadier General Theodore Marley "Ham" Brooks, noted lawyer, one of Doc Savage's five assistants. Monk's sniffing about Ham was misleading. They were like brothers, and they never let a day pass—and seldom an hour—without a quarrel.

"Ham," said Monk, "has gone to hire a good, trustworthy lip reader to sit in the office with Renny and read the lips of Uncle Joe Morgan, or any visitors he has, with the binoculars."

"The situation seems to be taken care of," Doc Savage said.

"From this end, it is."

The bronze man arose. "Contact me at headquarters if necessary."

Monk nodded. "O. K. By radio. Right."

Doc Savage left. The restaurant proprietor was wiping his hands on his apron and glaring at the pig under Monk's table.

It was then one o'clock.

II

GIRL BRINGING TROUBLE

At two o'clock, the frantic girl came to Doc Savage.

He was, at the time, on the eighty-sixth floor of a midtown skyscraper. The floor was divided into three rooms—a reception room, a library and a laboratory. Doc was engaged in preparing plates of nutrient media for a bacteriological research he was conducting.

One of his assistants was presiding over the reception room. The assistant was Brigadier General Theodore Marley Brooks, called Ham by everyone because he hated pork, hogs, and anything swine, wild or tame. Ham was an eminent lawyer. The Harvard legal alumni were very proud of him. He was considered one of the great legal minds.

He was not engaged in a deep legal problem at the moment, however.

He was teaching his pet chimpanzee, named Chemistry, to tie one end of a string to an object, then tie the other end of the same string to a different object. Ham was getting a great deal of glee out of this teaching, chuckling as if he had something devilish in mind.

The frantic girl arrived suddenly. She began beating on the door and screaming!

Like that. Suddenly. One moment Doc was tinkering with nutrient media and Ham was teaching his chimp to tie strings and there was an amiable silence. Then the screeching; the pounding of fists on the door.

Ham bolted to his feet. Chemistry, the chimp, made a

brown streak to safety under the nearest desk. In the lab, Doc Savage put the slide of nutrient media in a temperature-controlled vacuum case as if nothing had happened.

The girl's words were mostly garbled.

But she was telling someone to, "Get away from me!"

Ham Brooks had been associated with Doc Savage long enough to know better than to take chances. He leaped to an inlaid desk, jammed a finger against an inlay which was a concealed button and caused a sheet of bulletproof glass, as clear as any plate glass, to drop between himself and the door. He punched another button which opened the door.

Wasted precaution. The girl was actually in trouble. If not, it was a very real imitation because the man who was fighting her seemed to be doing his best to get his knife into her throat! The knife had a blade the size of a razor, somewhat the same shape.

Had he been a larger man, the girl's yelling and struggling would have ended by now. He was not large. The two were, in fact, about a match in strength, and the girl had hold of the knife arm with both hands.

Ham leaped forward. In his chivalrous haste, he forgot all about just lowering the glass panel. He got his nose flattened. He went around the glass, pain twisting his face, and charged.

The small man saw Ham coming. He dropped his knife, so the girl would release his arm. She did so. The man ran. Ham galloped after him.

The man realized he would be overtaken. As soon as he understood that, he whirled, drawing a gun. It was an automatic, huge and flat, with dark bulk.

He aimed the gun at Ham and fired. And part of the top came off *his* head, not off Ham's head.

The girl—she was not bad to look at, at first glance, and she improved on acquaintance—made a mewing sound and closed her eyes from the bottom up. She fell loosely and lay on the floor, beside the knife.

Doc Savage came out of the reception room into the hall. He took one glance. Then he went back inside the reception room, leaped to the inlaid desk and pressed several curlicues of inlay which were buttons.

As a result of the buttons he pressed, all elevators in the building stopped, the stairways were flooded with a gas—not tear gas, but one that would produce unconsciousness through its ability to be absorbed by the skin pores—and the armed elevator starters in the ornate lobby received a warning flash of signal light.

Then Doc returned to the hall.

Ham was bending over the body of the small man. He had picked up the gun, what was left of it.

"Really," he remarked.

Doc Savage took the weapon. He picked up several fragments which had blown off it and examined these.

"The gun was fixed to kill the man," he said.

Then he sank to a knee beside the small man.

"Dead?" Ham asked.

Doc nodded. He went to the girl.

"Just fainted, didn't she?" Ham asked.

Again Doc nodded.

"I never saw either one of them before," Ham said. He got down and went through the pockets of the dead man. They were empty. He looked inside the clothing for labels. There were no labels. He searched for laundry marks. None of those, either.

"That's strange," Ham remarked. "You hear of murderers taking the labels out of their victims' pockets so they can't be identified. But I never heard of a guy walking around with the labels out of his clothes. He sure didn't want to be identified in case we caught him."

A purse lay near the girl. Doc picked it up, went through the contents. there was the usual woman stuff. No name, however, on anything.

The girl had brown hair, brown eyes, nice mouth, a turned-up nose. Faces of women who have fainted are usually loose, colorless and unlovely. But this face was firm, composed, even beautiful.

There was no question but that she was in a genuine faint, not faking. Doc made sure of that.

"Certainly strange, these labels missing," Ham said again.

Doc Savage indicated the remains of the gun.

"This weapon," he said, "had been deliberately tampered with so that it would kill anyone who fired it."

Ham's eyes widened.

"Say, Doc, that makes it look as if someone gave him the gun so that, if he got in a jam and tried to use it, he would kill himself. Kind of an automatic elimination, as it were.

The bronze man nodded.

They carried the girl inside, and Doc worked over her with resuscitating materials.

Ham went to the big inlaid desk, pulled out a drawer and examined an array of signal lights. He used a telephone which connected with the elevators and the elevator starters on the ground floor.

"This fellow doesn't seem to have had anyone with him," Ham reported. "At least, we caught nobody."

The girl opened her eyes.

"I don't know why they took my brother," she said.

Ham Brooks was aware that he jumped and that Doc Savage showed no emotion. Doc's self-control always amazed Ham, although he had known the bronze man a long time.

"Who took your brother?" Doc asked.

"They will kill him!" she said.

Her voice was charged with horror.

Patiently, Doc inquired, "Who?"

She got hold of herself. "I am . . . my name is Jeanette Bridges. Jen, they call me. You are Doc Savage. You were pointed out to me, once, from a distance. I was told at the time that you follow the rather strange career of righting wrongs and punishing evildoers; that you help people who are in trouble. I need your help."

She did not say this in one breath, but it had that effect.

"Who was the man outside?" Doc Savage asked.

She closed her eyes and shuddered tremendously. "That man—he was the one who warned me. You see, I am an artist. I do fashion layouts for department stores. I take orders in the morning and work in the afternoons. Today I came back to my home a little after one o'clock, and four men were taking my brother away. I realized something was wrong. I confronted them with a demand to know what was going on." She stopped. Her hands trembled. "My brother suddenly burst out in a wild rush of words."

"Your brother's name?"

"David."

"And these wild words were?"

"That the four men were going to kill him—kill my brother!"

"What happened?"

"The four men dragged my brother away. Later that . . . that man out in the hall came back. He said there was something big and terrible involved. He said I should keep my mouth shut about what had happened to my brother. He said I was to forget I ever had a brother. He said it would be too bad for me if I didn't. And after he told me all that, he went away."

"And then you did what?"

"I thought of you," she said. "I came here. That man must have followed me. He set upon me with the knife in the hall."

Doc Savage's eyes became more alive, alert.

"Was an invisible box mentioned?" he inquired.

"A what? What do you mean—invisible box?"

"You do not seem to have read the newspapers."

"Ordinarily, I do. But the last few days I have been too busy."

"You are an artist?"

"Yes."

Doc Savage went away and came back with drawing paper, pencils and erasers.

"Sketch the faces of those four men—or the three who are still alive—as best you can from memory," he said. "Also, sketch their figures and any details about their clothing."

The girl went to work, drawing rapidly.

She was good.

Ham Brooks stared at the line drawing the girl had finished and said, "By Jove! Wait a moment!" Suddenly excited, he sprang to his feet, and went to a filing cabinet. He began hunting frantically.

Doc Savage had been watching the drawing. He glanced at Ham, said, "In the A file, Ham. He is filed under Acquaintances."

Ham found a sheaf of papers. He came back, put a paper under the girl's nose. It had an ordinary newspaper photograph pasted to it.

She stared. "That's him!" she ejaculated. "That's one of the men!"

The cutlines under the picture, the print identifying the subject of the photograph, read:

Elmer I. Ivers, banker, who says the foreign situation will improve.

*   *   *

Jen Bridges jabbed a finger excitedly at the picture. "That was one of the men. How did you happen to have his picture?"

The man in the photograph had wide, thin eyes, a nose that turned up until the nostrils were visible only as two holes, and a thatch of hair that was like the top of an oat shock in general shape. Thick hornrimmed spectacles gave him an additional distinction.

"How do you happen to have this?" the girl asked.

Ham glanced at Doc, and the bronze man shook his head very slightly.

Ham said to the girl, "Oh, we keep a file of such stuff. A kind of rogue's gallery."

Jen Bridges looked around the room at the library and laboratory which showed through open doors. She seemed impressed.

Doc Savage went to a small portable radio, put it in operation. "Monk," he said into the microphone.

Monk, the homely fellow with the pet pig, had a squeaking, ridiculous voice that might have belonged to a small child.

"Yes," he said over the radio.

"Has Uncle Joe Morgan left his office?" Doc inquired.

"No."

"Has he telephoned anyone?"

"Not a soul since you left him, Long Tom says."

"Or received any calls?"

"Not a one," Monk reported.

"Keep a close watch on him and advise me if he makes a move, places a telephone call or receives any, or has visitors, dispatches, messengers—anything he does."

"Right."

The bronze man switched off the radio apparatus. "Miss Bridges," he said, "do you know a Mr. J. P. Morgan?"

"I don't move in those financial circles," Jen said.

"Not that one. This one calls himself Uncle Joe Morgan."

She shook her head immediately. "I do not know him."

"And did, or do you, know Elmer I. Ivers?"

"Who is he?"

"A businessman and banker. He controls the Iverson Chemical Co."

"No, I do not know him," she said. "Except, of course, he was one of the men who seized my brother. I can see that from the picture of him. But that is all I know about him."

"Do you mind staying here with Mr. Brooks?" Doc asked.

"No, I don't mind," she said.

Doc Savage moved into the laboratory and began getting equipment together and stuffing it into his pockets. Ham followed him to the door and watched.

"You are going to investigate Ivers?" Ham asked.

"That is right," Doc said.

Ham glanced back at the girl. He came into the laboratory and closed the door so she could not overhear him.

"Elmer Ivers is one of the men we investigated in connection with the mystery of the invisible boxes," Ham said.

"He happened to know two of the victims," Doc Savage agreed. "But Uncle Joe Morgan is the only man we have been able to locate who knew *all* victims."

Ham started. "Say, doesn't Uncle Joe Morgan know Elmer Ivers, too?"

"He does."

Doc Savage finished collecting gadgets which he might or might not need in the course of the investigation he planned.

As he was leaving, the girl asked, "Are you going to help find my brother?"

"You can be sure of that," Doc told her.

Someone shot at him as he was leaving the building!

The shot came from a distance and evidently from a single-shot silenced rifle, equipped with a telescopic sight. It was probably a rifle with a small bore and fantastic velocity— on the order of a .220 Swift, .219 Zipper, or .22 Hi-Power— judging from the way the bullet hit. The pill of lead, not as large as a bean, was capable of stunning like a stick of dynamite.

Doc was able to judge the type of bullet from what it did to the bulletproof glass of his car window. It practically demolished the outer coat of the glass, which should shatter, and put a big depression in the window.

Doc stopped the car instantly. He did not roll down the window. He waited. No more bullets came. His flake-gold eyes moved unceasingly.

There were at least a thousand windows in the adjacent

batteries of great buildings from which the shot could have come. But nowhere could he detect anything.

Cars blew horns impatiently behind him. He drove on.

Into the radio, he said, "Ham, someone with a good rifle, someone who can shoot well, is watching the building."

Ham said, "I will get hold of Johnny and Pat and have them take a look. It begins to seem that we have stuck our noses into something that is pretty well organized."

"Leave Pat out of it," Doc said.

"All right," Ham agreed.

Pat was Patricia Savage, a young lady who loved excitement. She was Doc Savage's cousin; and, because she was entertaining as well as a handy gadget to have around when there was trouble, the others liked to work with her. Doc also liked to work with Pat. But he considered most of their business too dangerous for a girl.

III

WHAT THE GIRL BROUGHT

Doc Savage did not, ordinarily, go out of his way to hunt trouble, but the present case was an exception.

The big bronze man had been trained from childhood—a weird sort of upbringing, with his being placed in the hands of scientists from childhood onward for development—for the business of righting wrongs and punishing evildoers. The training was the idea of his parents; and the results had been remarkable, as far as making a physical marvel and a mental genius out of Doc.

It was a plan on the part of his parents which could easily have gone wrong and warped the bronze man's character, his disposition, even his soul.

Privately—and the psychologists agreed with him on this point—Doc considered the thing a dangerous experiment which could easily have failed. Or worse, it might have created a kind of human monster.

Fortunately, Doc had inherited a love of excitement and a sense of humor. So the training had been eminently successful.

Many people had come to him for help, and he had aided some; while others, undeserving, or who had sought to use his genius to help line their pockets, had received a painful education.

He had hordes of enemies.

He was proud of them.

He had a great many more friends.

He had gone into the mystery of the invisible boxes because it was intriguing and because the police seemed to be making no headway. He had entered it thoroughly, beginning with a complete investigation of all possibilities, which was how he happened to learn of Elmer Ivers.

Ivers, being a wealthy man, lived in eccentric fashion on board a ferryboat.

Not a ferry which plied across New York harbor. This was out of service, tied up to a dock off fashionable Sutton Place, near the impressive shadow of Queensboro Bridge.

The ferryboat home of Ivers had received a splash of newspaper publicity from time to time, because of its human quality. Ivers, it seemed, had started business life as a huckster of peanuts, popcorn and crackerjack on this identical ferryboat, many years ago. Since, he had grown rich, purchased the old boat and rebuilt it into a bizarre home.

Doc Savage parked his car near the boat. He had driven cautiously and indirectly, keeping a watch on the traffic to make sure he was not being followed.

Afternoon sun was behind the high Manhattan buildings, a few clouds loitered like lambs in the sky, and river traffic moved lazily.

The bronze man used the boldest course. He walked to the dock, strode out on the gangplank and reached the entrance of the ferryboat. He knocked. No answer.

There was a foghorn of the hand-operated type which was obviously intended to double as a doorbell. He gave it a whirl. The thing bellowed like a bull.

Footsteps came to the door, and the door opened.

The man had a burned-up nose, a thatch of hair like the top of an oat shock, thick horn-rimmed spectacles. His clothing was good, expensive. There was a brown stain on the spotless front of his dress shirt, as if a pipe had drooled there.

"I am sorry," he said. "The servants are away for the afternoon."

Doc said, "Ivers?"

The other blinked behind the spectacles. "Yes, I am Elmer Ivers."

"Doc Savage," Doc said.

"I have heard of you."

"May I come in?"

"If you wish."

The man led Doc Savage to a room. It could not be called a cabin, although it was on the ferryboat; it was a room—large, comfortable, a reception office of some kind, evidently, because there were no windows.

There were two doors, one by which they had entered and another, directly opposite.

"Will you wait a moment?" Ivers said. "I left some eggs frying, and I had better—"

He stepped toward the other door as he spoke. Doc knew, then, that plenty was wrong. He jumped for the man. But the other was fast on his feet. He raced through the doorway and slammed the door shut.

Doc Savage hit the door, and it was too solid. He went back and hit the other door, the one by which he had entered. That one was locked, and also solid.

The man began screaming, then. His voice began at a high pitch, and lost tone, then volume. It was like a siren dying down, except that the shrieking was not a continuous sound but a series of rending screeches in descending scale.

The voice silenced.

The whole boat seemed to become full of running feet.

Doc Savage produced an object the size of a cherry from a pocket—it looked a little like a black cherry, of steel—and thrust the tapered stem into the lock of the outer door. Then he got back.

He held his mouth wide open to lessen the concussion when the "cherry" let go. It soon did, with blue flame, awful noise, and violence enough to make the door look as if a dozen axes had worked upon it.

Doc Savage went through the opening.

Men appeared before him.

He looked at them and stopped.

"The fellow went through this other door," he said.

The men were policemen, most of them uniformed. They had guns and tear gas and determined expressions. One of them Doc Savage knew.

"Lieutenant Blosser," Doc said, "the man went through

that door, yonder. As soon as he was on the other side, he began screaming."

Lieutenant Blosser said, "We heard the cries, Mr. Savage." He went to the door.

"It is locked," Doc Savage said.

Lieutenant Blosser took hold of the knob, and the door opened. It was not locked. He glanced at Doc Savage queerly. Then he went into the room.

At once, he reappeared. His face was grim.

He said, "Mr. Savage, you say a man ran in here?"

"Yes."

"A man with a turned-up nose, thick horn-rimmed spectacles, tangled straw-colored hair?"

"Yes."

"He ran into this room and began screaming?"

"Yes."

"Did you follow him into the room?"

"No."

Lieutenant Blosser compressed his lips. "Have you been in this other room?"

"No."

"You are sure of that?"

Doc Savage's metallic features were expressionless, but his flake-gold eyes seemed puzzled. "Why are you skeptical, lieutenant?" he asked.

Lieutenant Blosser stepped back.

"Come in here and see for yourself," he said.

Doc did so. The room had no windows. The only door was the one by which they had entered. There was no means of leaving or entering the room, in fact, except by the door.

A man was dead on the floor. A stubby man with thick spectacles, matted hair, and a nose turned up to show its nostrils.

A cellophane box stood beside the dead man!

Lieutenant Blosser was a young man with clear blue eyes and good shoulders. He also had a jaw suitable for hammering rocks.

He said, "I am sorry, Mr. Savage; I cannot let you examine that box."

Doc Savage glanced at two policemen who had come to stand close beside him.

"Why not?" he asked.

"Fingerprints," Lieutenant Blosser said, and looked at the box.

The box resembled the one which Doc Savage had constructed from cellophane and left on the figurative doorstep of Uncle Joe Morgan. This one, if anything, was a trifle smaller.

"Get a photographer in here," ordered Lieutenant Blosser. "Have him get pictures of that box. Detectives Grant and Mozen, you watch the box. We do not want this one disappearing."

"That is a good idea," Doc said. "And we might take a look at the body."

He started to where the man lay dead on the floor.

Lieutenant Blosser got in his way and said, "I am sorry."

Doc Savage studied him. "What do you mean?"

"You will please stay where you are," the officer said rather stiffly.

The bronze man hesitated. Then he drew out a billfold, opened it and presented a document. "You will find this to be a commission," he explained, "on the New York police force."

Blosser shook his head.

"We are wasting time," Doc said, a trifle impatiently. "There appears to have been a murder here. You will find that this commission bears the rank of inspector, which is above your own, and entitles me to overrule your orders. I regret doing so, but—"

Lieutenant Blosser became pale.

"It is not a license," he said, nodding at the commission. "A license for what?"

"To commit crimes," Blosser said bluntly.

Doc Savage said nothing for a moment. Then he asked, "Have you any objection to my calling Commissioner Strance?"

The white tension on Lieutenant Blosser's face increased.

"It would relieve me greatly if you would," he said. He held his lower lip in his teeth briefly. "As a matter of fact, I was going to do so myself. You see, Mr. Savage, you are in a rather peculiar position in this thing."

Doc looked at him. "Peculiar in what way?"

"We received a telephone tip—anonymous—to the effect that you were behind these invisible-box murders. Also, that Elmer Ivers was to be killed and that you would appear here this afternoon and commit the murder."

Doc Savage made, briefly, the small sound which was

peculiar to him in moments of mental or physical stress, a trilling which seemed to come out of inaudibility and travel musically up and down a scale, then ebb away.

Blosser added, "We came here. Mr. Ivers ridiculed the whole idea. He said he had no enemies; that he did not even know you. But we remained anyway, concealed in the neighborhood. We saw you come; saw Ivers admit you. And then—" He shrugged.

"You say a telephone tip brought you here?" Doc Savage asked.

"Right."

"What time was it received?"

"About an hour ago."

"Was it after one o'clock?"

"Yes, the tip came after one o'clock," Blosser said.

Commissioner Strance, acting head of the police department, was a blunt granite rock of a man who had few words and used them like bullets. He had come up from pounding a beat in Gravesend, and there had never been a question about his honesty. Nor his courage.

He said, "Hello, Savage. Too bad. Don't like it."

A homicide-detail detective came in from the room where the body lay. He had a sheet of paper and an envelope, tinted bronze.

Strance read the paper with hard eyes. He handed it to Doc.

If the police come to you and you tell them anything, even tell them you know me, you will not live long. Savage.

"Found on the body," the homicide man said.

"Yours?" Strance asked.

"Type of paper I use," Doc admitted.

"You write it?"

"No."

Commissioner Strance stared at him strangely but did not comment. Strance was a man of few words, of steel convictions. He was not a man inclined to lean over backward in being fair. He believed, instead, that it was the duty of the courts and juries to decide innocence or guilt.

A detective came in and reported, "We've gone over the boat with a microscope, almost. There's nobody else aboard."

Doc Savage's flake-gold eyes became intent. He did not say anything. He knew by now that he was in a serious predicament.

A fingerprint man came in from headquarters. He had a card on which were Doc Savage's fingerprints.

They compared these prints with a latent print on the crystal of a wrist watch. The crystal was cracked.

"Identical," said the fingerprint man.

Lieutenant Blosser stood in front of Doc Savage. "Watch off the dead man's wrist," he said. "There was evidently a struggle, and the assailant grasped Elmer Ivers' wrist. The assailant left a thumbprint on the watch crystal. The print is yours!"

Doc said, "Mind letting me look at that watch?"

Blosser took a step forward to comply, but Commissioner Strance interrupted with one word.

"No!" Strance said.

In a voice which showed no emotion, Doc Savage asked, "Mind letting me look at the dead man?"

Blosser glanced at Strance.

"No," Strance said. "Clues. He's clever. Might destroy."

Doc Savage showed some of the astonishment he felt. He had been working with the police for a long time; he had done them many favors, and he had, in turn, received favors from them.

Lieutenant Blosser evidently knew what was in the bronze man's mind. He began speaking.

"I fully understand your high position, Mr. Savage," he said. "And believe me, I regret this as much as I possibly can. But you can see the position in which we are placed. We received an anonymous tip that Elmer Ivers was to be murdered by you. To tell the truth, we did not believe it. But we showed up on the scene anyway. And sure enough, you appeared, and Ivers was murdered. All the clues point to you."

Doc made no comment.

Lieutenant Blosser said, "Perhaps you think we are being unduly harsh with you. But let me remind you that several men have died under mysterious circumstances. We have been without clues. The death in each case puzzled our chemists." He swung to a medical examiner. "Saunders," he said, "of what did that man in the other room—Elmer Ivers—die?"

Saunders, a competent-looking man, said, "I cannot tell. I do believe that it is the same thing that killed those other men. A laboratory test will prove the point later."

Blosser looked at Doc Savage. "You see. This is the fifth man to die mysteriously. We cannot overlook this; and, much as we regret it, I am afraid—"

Commissioner Strance interjected a grunt.

"Too many words," he said. He turned to Doc. "You're under arrest. Charge is murder!"

There was just one other development. It happened immediately. Commissioner Strance asked to have a look at the cellophane box which had been found near the murdered man.

Lieutenant Blosser looked satisfied with himself.

"The boxes found on the scene of the other murders have disappeared damned mysteriously," he announced. "So I took good care that this one wouldn't."

"Where is it?" Strance demanded.

"I put it in a pillow case," Blosser said. "And two of my men have been watching it."

He sent for the two men. They came in, carrying the pillow case.

"Open it," Blosser ordered.

One of the men untied a shoestring which he had fastened about the open end of the pillow case, fashioning it into a sack. He stared inside—and became pale. The other detective also looked into the sack. His jaw dropped.

"What the hell's the matter?" Strance barked.

The matter was that there was now no box inside the pillow case!

IV

CONVINCING BLOSSER

Lieutenant Colonel Andrew Blodgett Monk Mayfair and Brigadier General Theodore Marley Ham Brooks were a deceptive pair. Each had, on necessary and urgent occasions in the past, risked his life to save the other. To listen to them associate with each other, no stranger would believe this possible. No one ever recalled Ham's having said a pleasant word to or about Monk. And vice versa. The unpleasantness even extended to their two pets, Monk's pig, Habeas Corpus, and Ham's chimp, named Chemistry. They fought several times a day.

Monk slammed down the telephone in Doc Savage's headquarters.

"They've got Doc in prison!" he said. "We've got to do something."

Perspiration had come out on Monk's homely face.

Ham said, "That is ridiculous."

"It's not so blamed ridiculous but what it has happened," Monk said. "You've been bragging for years around here that you had the brains of this gang, you overdressed shyster. So now you better deliver. Think of something."

Ham stared at pretty Jen Bridges.

Jen's fingers were against her pale cheeks. "This is terrible. I caused it. I asked Mr. Savage to help my brother, and now—"

"We are still helping your brother. Please don't worry," Ham said.

Monk was tempted to walk over and kick Ham in the ribs, and his expression showed how he felt. Monk resented Ham's enjoying the good luck of having been left at headquarters to take care of a girl as attractive as Jen Bridges. Monk could detect signs of Ham's having made the best of the opportunity.

Monk took two angry stamping turns around the room. Then he went to the radio.

"Renny," he said. "You there?"

A voice, a rumbling like something big in a deep hole, admitted that Renny Renwick was present at another radio transmitter.

"We got into the flypaper the first thing," Monk said. "A girl named Jen Bridges showed up here and said her brother, David, had been grabbed and hauled off by some men. Jen is an artist, and Doc had her draw the faces of the men who kidnapped her brother. Doc recognized one of them as Elmer Ivers, a well-known banker and businessman. Doc went to talk to Ivers. Ivers was murdered—one of the invisible-box things. Doc is accused of the crime. Framed!"

"Holy cow!" said big-fisted Renny. It was his favorite

exclamation. He was silent a moment. Then, "You want to know if Uncle Joe Morgan was hooked in it?"

"That's it."

"I don't see how he could be," Renny said.

"He might have called somebody to set this trap for Doc."

Renny rumbled disgustedly. "Wait until I contact Long Tom," he said. "He's riding the telephone line to Uncle Joe Morgan's office."

The consultation with Long Tom, the electrical expert of Doc Savage's group of five assistants, did not take long.

Renny reported, "Long Tom says Uncle Joe Morgan has not used the telephone since Doc left the place. Long Tom also says he has not used any other kind of device, radio or wire, to signal anyone. Long Tom has some kind of a super-sensitive detector rigged up that tells him that."

Monk demanded, "What about you?"

"From where I am posted," said Renny, "I can see right into Uncle Joe Morgan's office. He has not been out of sight. He has hardly been away from his desk. He just sits there and fiddles with his watch."

"How do you mean—fiddles with his watch?"

"Keeps taking it out, holding it in his hands, playing with it, then putting it back in his pocket. And taking it out again. Does that over and over. Acts nervous about the time."

"A man named Ted Parks was to come to see Uncle Joe Morgan at four o'clock."

Renny said, "Ted Parks is the only other man, besides Uncle Joe Morgan, who knows all those men who have died in the invisible-box mystery. That right?"

"That's right," Monk agreed. "That's why Doc wants to talk to Ted Parks. He's mixed up in this mystery some way."

"Just what *is* the mystery?" Renny demanded.

Monk let the radio remain silent for a moment. "You guess," he said finally.

Renny snorted.

"Say, Renny," Monk said, "what about the lip reader you said you could get? Ham was going to hire a lip reader to sit in that office with you and watch Uncle Joe Morgan through a pair of powerful glasses. But you called Ham and said you already had one."

"The lip reader," said Renny, "has been on the job. But she hasn't detected Uncle Joe saying anything. The old duffer doesn't talk to himself, apparently, and he hasn't had any visitors."

Monk looked interested.

"She?" he asked. "you mean your lip reader is a woman?"

"It's Pat," Renny explained. "Pat has taken it up in her spare time. She's pretty good, so I called her in."

Ham Brooks heard that and looked dumfounded. He came over and took the radio microphone away from Monk.

"Look here, Renny," Ham said. "Doc doesn't want Pat mixed up in this. He gave me specific orders to that effect."

Renny did not answer. Instead, Patricia Savage's voice came over the air.

"This is once," she said, "that I get in on one of these things at the beginning."

She sounded triumphant. She liked excitement.

Monk grunted and switched off the radio.

A bit later, William Harper Johnny Littlejohn came in. He was the fifth member of the group of five assistants—six, including the obtrusive Pat. He was a very long, very thin man, a perambulating beanpole who wore a magnifying glass that passed for a monocle in his lapel. He was a famous archaeologist and geologist, and somehow he looked the part.

He used one of his words immediately.

"I'll be superamalgamated," Johnny said. "I do—"

Monk pounced on him immediately. "None of those words of yours," he said. "I'm in no humor for them."

Johnny looked injured.

"No trace," he said, "of the individual or individuals who shot at Doc as he was leaving here to go to see Elmer Ivers."

When they arrived at headquarters, Lieutenant Blosser was not brimming over with accommodation.

"This is a serious case," Blosser said. "However, considering that the prisoner is Doc Savage, I will let you talk to him."

"That's fine of you," Monk said sarcastically. "After all Doc has done for the police."

Ham was also indignant. He popped an afternoon newspaper with his fist.

"Who gave this to the papers?" Ham demanded.

Lieutenant Blosser glanced at the newspaper. He had already read the item, and it had made him feel uneasy. The newspapers, never particularly a booster of Doc Savage, because the bronze man disliked publicity and was not at all co-operative in furnishing the press with sensational news, had not been kind in their stories of the bronze man's arrest in connection with the invisible-box murders.

There were open hints that Doc Savage might not be the benefactor of mankind which he had hitherto appeared to be.

This particular newspaper commended the police on ignoring the bronze man's special privileges.

"I'm not responsible for what the papers print," Blosser snapped.

They interviewed Doc Savage the way a common criminal would be interviewed, through a separating fence of steel mesh. Doc displayed no particular emotion, except that he smiled.

"I would like to know exactly what Uncle Joe Morgan did from the time I left him," he said.

Monk furnished a full report on that. Doc Savage listened without comment.

"Then all Uncle Joe seems to have done is sit at his desk and fiddle with his watch," he said, when the report ended.

Monk nodded. He was concerned and showed it.

"The thing doesn't make heads or tails," he said. "What do you suggest we do next, Doc?"

"Get hold of Ted Parks if you can find him."

"If he doesn't show up to talk to Uncle Joe at four o'clock, that will be a job." Monk glanced at his wrist watch. "It's past four o'clock now, incidentally."

Doc Savage said, "Just keep stirring things up. Later, we may be able to launch a definite campaign."

As they filed out of the interviewing room, Monk muttered disconsolately, "The plain fact is, there's *nothing* we can do, and Doc knows it."

Lieutenant Blosser met them outside. Commissioner Strance was with Blosser.

Strance said, "Blosser is your man. I'm assigning him to you."

Monk frowned. "What do you mean—assigning Blosser to us?"

"Just that."

Monk decided there was an unpleasant implication. He bristled. "You mean," he yelled, "that you suspect *us*!"

When Monk yelled, it was something. Cops dashed out

of doors to see what was wrong. Growing more indignant, Monk took Commissioner Strance by the necktie.

"You knob-headed lug!" Monk said. "If you had any sense, you'd turn Doc loose and let him solve this thing. By locking him up, you're working hand-in-glove with the murderer."

Commissioner Strance had a temper which did not arouse easily. But his neck got red.

"Blosser works with you!" he snapped.

"Watches us, you mean?" Monk bellowed.

"Frankly—yes," Strance said.

Lieutenant Blosser did not seem sensitive about his position in Doc Savage's group of associates. He was not welcome, knew it and didn't mind.

"You guys can outsmart me, I know that," he said. "But I would like to see you let me play along with you. After all, I'm not out to frame Doc Savage. I'm here to see that justice is done."

Ham saw the wisdom of that.

"I think we have the same aims," the dapper lawyer announced. "So there is no objection to your working with us."

Monk—he never agreed with Ham if he could possibly help it—let out a snort that was plainly expressive of *his* opinion.

They went to the vicinity of Uncle Joe Morgan's office. They visited, in fact, the lookout across the street where Renny Renwick and Patricia Savage were keeping an eye on the frightened dealer in small-time stocks.

Colonel John Renny Renwick was a big man who was made very notable by the size of his fists. He had an enviable reputation as an engineer, and a voice which would serve as a foghorn.

Pat Savage was a cousin to the man of bronze. She had Doc's metallic coloring—bronze skin, flake-gold eyes—and was extremely attractive. She seemed to radiate her liking for excitement.

Ham told Pat, "This is Lieutenant Blosser, assigned by the police department to assist us."

"The bloodhounds of the Baskervilles," Monk corrected sourly.

The embarrassed Lieutenant Blosser was much impressed by Pat Savage.

Renny rumbled, "The old geezer hasn't had any visitors yet. He keeps jumping up, sitting down, and fooling with his watch. This Ted Parks was supposed to come at four o'clock, Doc said. It's way past four, now."

Ham took a look across the street at Uncle Joe Morgan's office. He could see the benevolent-looking old gentleman stalking up and down; he seemed to be endeavoring to control himself.

"I think we might as well talk to him," he said. "I tell you what—Blosser, Monk and I will go over and put the conversational bee on him. Jen, you stay here with Pat."

"I'm worried about my brother," Jen Bridges protested. "Can't we do—"

"We're just as worried about Doc as you are about your brother," Pat told her. "This thing seems to be all hooked in together. When we get one straightened out, we'll have them both."

Jen sighed, said, "I guess so," wearily, and sank in a chair.

When Monk, Ham and Lieutenant Blosser got across the street, Uncle Joe Morgan at first would not admit them to his office. Blosser pounded on the door and shouted, "This is the police. Lieutenant Blosser of the homicide squad. Open up!" To which came a quavering demand to know how Uncle Joe could be sure they were police.

"Call headquarters and find out about me," Blosser snapped.

And evidently Uncle Joe did this, because he admitted them.

"Where is this Ted Parks?" Monk demanded, after they had identified themselves.

Uncle Joe became more pale, which didn't seem possible; and flopped into the chair behind his desk like a fish hitting a dry bank.

He didn't know. That was the essence of what he had to say, although he took many words, violent gestures, and tooth-chattering pauses to get the idea across.

"Just why are you so scared?" Monk demanded.

Uncle Joe Morgan blew up.

"I'm convinced I am going to be murdered!" he croaked.

"The victims in the invisible-box things have all been acquaintances of mine."

Then an idea hit Uncle Joe. He looked as if he wanted to get on his knees, but he didn't.

"Could . . . would some of you men, or a policeman, stay with me as a bodyguard?" he asked.

Lieutenant Blosser frowned and demanded, "What makes you so sure that your life is in danger?"

"I just know it," gasped Uncle Joe Morgan. "Only men *I* know are being killed by this thing."

Blosser was far from satisfied. "That note from Ted Parks, saying he would be here to see you at four and that you better be here and not notify the police—did that have anything to do with scaring you?"

Uncle Joe nodded violently. "It certainly did. Believe me, it did."

"Meaning—" Blosser's eyes narrowed—"you think Ted Parks may be one of the instigators of this?"

Uncle Joe seemed to shudder from head to foot.

"Exactly," he said.

Then they drew lots to see who would remain with Uncle Joe. Ham lost, to his disgust, and was stuck with the job—despite the fact that he tried to get out of it by insisting his legal knowledge should be at working freeing, or trying to free, Doc Savage.

Uncle Joe seemed to have no definite reason for suspecting Ted Parks.

"All I can tell you about Parks," he said, "is that he used to live in an apartment on Fifty-fifth Street." He gave them the number.

"Did you tell Doc about that apartment?" Monk demanded.

"I forgot it," said Uncle Joe.

Monk and Lieutenant Blosser collected Long Tom, Renny, Pat and Johnny, as well as Jen Bridges, and lost no time in getting into cars and heading for the Fifty-fifth Street address. All seven of them rode in the same car, a limousine, and it was crowded. Blosser, who was in front, rolled down the window and demanded, "Say, just what do you know about this Ted Parks?"

Pretty Jen Bridges looked puzzled. "Who is Ted Parks? You keep referring to him, but nobody has told me who he is."

"He's the one man besides Uncle Joe Morgan who knows all the man who have died mysteriously," Monk told her. "That's all we have been able to dig up on him."

Big-fisted Renny rumbled, "Well, he's a young doctor. We learned that much. He finished courses in this country and took advanced medicine in Europe before everybody started shooting at everybody else over there. After that, he dropped out of sight, reappeared in New York, was gone again, and then came back. The last time he came back, he had changed. He was thin, looked as if he had been very ill and was deeply sunburned."

"Tanned, you mean," Monk corrected. "Tropical suns, probably. Looked as if he'd had the fever, they said at a club or two to which he had belonged."

Lieutenant Blosser spoke up to then.

Had he not spoken, someone might have noticed that Jen Bridges had settled back in her seat with tight hands and an ebbing of color from her face.

"Say, how—or when—did you learn of all this?" Blosser asked.

Monk snorted. "We started investigating this thing, three days ago. Doc got interested in the murders because they were so weird. We had nothing to go on. So we began checking on acquaintances of the dead men. We found that only two men seemed to know all the victims. The two, as I've told you, were Uncle Joe Morgan and Ted Parks. We were able to dig up quite a bit on Morgan—mostly that the old codger is interested in sailing, and goes away on long ocean cruises on his little boat. But about Ted Parks, we learned less. Parks is a clever fellow, and something of a figure of mystery."

"You mean," demanded Blosser, "that Parks has hidden his actions during the last year or two?"

"I don't know whether he hid them," Monk said, "or was just a modest fellow. Anyway, nobody seems to know much about what Parks has been doing with his time."

Renny said, "Ham learned that at Harvard they considered young Parks a genius."

Monk sniffed.

"They consider *Ham* a genius at Harvard," said the homely chemist disgustedly. "They must be a dime a dozen up there."

*   *   *

The apartment was on the third floor of a walk-up on Fifty-fifth Street, on the wrong side of Broadway. They got the manager to open the door for them. Lieutenant Blosser's badge did that without much argument.

Lieutenant Blosser seemed to be feeling that there was more and more possibility of Doc Savage not being guilty. Monk, Pat and the others felt they were doing well, even if not making much progress.

But what they found in the apartment blew to bits everything they had accomplished.

First, nobody was home. Nobody alive, more exactly.

Secondly, the man dead on the floor had one hand outstretched, with a pencil in the hand, and the flyleaf of a book open under the pencil.

"Parks!" yelled Blosser. "They've killed him!"

Jen Bridges made a sound like the last dying note of a small siren and collapsed on the floor. As she went down, every joint in her body seemed to bend, like the joints in a carpenter's rule.

Monk said, "It isn't Parks. Parks is a younger man. Pat, see if Jen's heart was all right."

Pat bent quickly over Jen Bridges.

The dead man on the floor was a toughened fellow of middle age, not vicious, but with calloused hands, a deeply weathered hide, and snaggled teeth. His clothing was fairly new but looked as if it had come out of a bargain basement. Pants and coat did not quite match, although both were blue.

Lieutenant Blosser stepped close to him, then looked around the room.

"This is another one of those invisible-box killings," he said. "Where's the box?"

There was no box.

Pat straightened from examining Jen Bridges. "She is all right. She just fainted."

Monk swung forward, bent over to look at the pencil in the dead man's hand and at the note on the floor under it.

Monk read—and turned white. Renny Renwick said afterward that Monk lost so much color, and had such a weird expression on his face, that he looked completely like a ghost.

The note:

Savage killed me because—

*　　*　　*

That was all. The man seemed to have died as he finished the word "because."

Lieutenant Blosser read it. He straightened, took a service revolver from a belt holster and held it without pointing at anyone in particular, but so that it menaced everyone.

"This convinces me," he said, "that Savage is as guilty as they come."

V

SLEEPER, MINER AND MONKEY

At ten o'clock that night, it was still warm. The day had been hot, and the heat held on with unabating stuffiness. Heaviness of the warmth penetrated into the district attorney's conference room, which was not air-conditioned. No one in the room was comfortable. The D. A. wiped his face frequently, and Lieutenant Blosser had put a handkerchief inside his collar. Commissioner Strance was red-faced in the heat. Doc Savage was without his necktie, but that was because of the custom of taking neckties off prisoners, so that they will have nothing with which to throttle themselves. There were no strings in his shoes, either. The others—Ham, Johnny, Long Tom, Renny, Pat, Jen Bridges and Uncle Joe Morgan—sat around in discomfort. Of the whole group, Monk was the only one who had removed his coat. Monk did not give a particular hoot about what people thought of his looks; he had long ago realized that nothing he could do would make him much more homely.

Ham Brooks made a statement.

"The whole thing is too pat," said the lawyer. "It's a frame-up. Anybody with eyes can see that."

Commissioner Strance showed his teeth.

"Old stuff," he said; "claiming frame-up."

Ham colored indignantly.

The district attorney—his name was Einsflagen, and he had ambitions in the direction of the governorship—rapped the table sharply.

"I wish you would remember, Strance, that you are not dealing with an ordinary individual," he said. "Mr. Savage is a famous man. He is known all over the world. I can hardly believe this thing about him, and it may not be true. Therefore, he is deserving of every consideration."

Commissioner Strance showed his teeth again, unpleasantly.

"Crook is a crook," he said. "And murder is what electric chairs are for."

No one said anything for a while. Ham breathed heavily. He knew, better than any of the others probably, the gravity of the situation. There was already, Ham stood convinced, enough evidence against Doc Savage for even a mediocre district attorney to get a jury to convict him of murder.

Monk also was silent. He was thinking, remembering the body of the man who had died when the gun exploded in the corridor outside Doc's skyscraper office.

Monk had done something about the body. He hadn't told any of the others. But he wanted Doc Savage to know about it.

The bronze man and his aids, when they wished to communicate without being understood by strangers, ordinarily used an ancient Mayan dialect which they had learned in the course of an earlier adventure. The Mayan tongue, differing from the lingo spoken by the modern Mayans in Central America, could be understood by very few people in the civilized world other than themselves.

Monk began coughing and sputtering, apparently. That was the beauty of the Mayan lingo. You could use it, and still sound as if something was caught in your throat.

Monk said in Mayan, "I concealed the body of the man who was killed when his gun blew up. The others are keeping still about it; so that is one less killing they will try to hang on you."

Doc Savage indicated by a slight gesture that he understood. Monk took out a handkerchief and wiped his lips, then blew his nose.

District Attorney Einsflagen tapped his desk distractedly.

"A most unpleasant affair," he said. "The last victim has not been identified; the man found in this Ted Parks' apartment is the one I am referring to. Neither have we been able to locate Parks."

Ham got to his feet. "Mr. District Attorney, I did not ask for this meeting in order to rehash the case, or discuss the progress being made toward its solution."

Einsflagen eyed him. "Why *did* you ask for the meeting?"

Ham took a deep breath.

"I demand," he said, "that you release Mr. Savage. The evidence against him is planted evidence, a fact that is obvious from the circumstantial nature of it."

District Attorney Einsflagen was in a predicament and knew it. The bluntness of Ham Brooks' demand did not surprise him. He respected the directness more than if Ham had tried to use oratory and persuasion. In Einsflagen's opinion, oratory was only used on fools; and he resented people trying to talk him into things. He supposed Ham knew how he felt, and that was why Ham had been direct.

None of which changed the fact that Einsflagen could not afford to make a mistake. Doc Savage was prominent, influential, not a man to be wronged. Einsflagen felt that, if he made a mistake now, fat chance he stood of ever becoming governor.

He turned slowly to face Doc Savage.

"Mr. Savage, this puts me in a spot," he said frankly. "So I am going to ask you something. I am going to ask you if, were you in my position and had a prisoner against whom there was the circumstantial evidence which is against you, what would you do? Before you answer, I want to point out that the evidence seems to indicate you are certainly guilty of two murders, and possibly four others. Realizing this, what is your answer? If you were in my shoes, what would you do?"

The bronze man's response was prompt.

"The evidence indicates that I am guilty," he said. "That leaves you with no alternative but to hold me."

The color, and relief, slowly came back into Einsflagen's eyes.

Doc Savage began speaking.

"Monk, Ham, and the rest of you—I want you to set your watches exactly with the clock here," he said. "I want all your timepieces to be together. Jen, you and Mr. Morgan please set your watches, also."

Uncle Joe said, "I do not understand this."

"Would you mind complying anyway?" Doc suggested.

The benevolent old gentleman smiled and took out his watch, a large turnip affair of dull-looking metal. He set the hands with the wired time-clock on the wall, as did the others.

Commissioner Strance and Lieutenant Blosser looked on in puzzled astonishment. The district attorney was blank.

Doc said, "Good. Now, here is what I want you to do."

He fixed his gaze on Renny.

"Renny, at exactly midnight, I want you to walk into the advertising office of the *Daily Planet* and insert an advertisement for a man who has slept three weeks at a stretch."

"A what?" demanded the astounded Renny.

"I want a man," said Doc Savage patiently, "who has slept not less than three weeks without waking up, and can prove it. Preferably the proof shall be medical testimony, although that is not absolutely essential."

He pondered a moment.

"We do not need to discriminate in this matter," he added, "so you can advertise for either a man or a woman. But they must have slept three weeks or more."

Renny swallowed.

"Holy cow!" he said.

Doc turned to Monk. "Monk, at exactly one o'clock, in the *Morning World*, I want you to insert an advertisement for a man who is a radium miner."

It was Monk's turn to drop a jaw. "Any particular kind of a radium miner?"

"Just one who has engaged in the business within the last few years for a period of not less than one year," Doc said.

Monk swallowed. "O.K."

Patricia scratched her head and asked, "Don't I get a hand in this?"

"You," Doc told her, "can take charge of the monkey hunt. I want the names and addresses of every person who had bought a monkey, or sold one, during the last six months."

"You mean just here in the city?"

"All over."

"Great grief!" Pat ejaculated.

"That will not be as much a job as you think," Doc said. "Monkeys are very scarce outside of zoos, circus organizations, and a few for organ grinders."

"If you want to know who bought monkeys recently, I'll get the information," Pat said.

"That," Doc Savage told them, "is all."

Lieutenant Blosser started to leave the police station with them. Monk got in front of Blosser, beetled his eyebrows and said, "Don't we ever get a vacation from you?"

"I have orders to continue to string along with you," Blosser said.

"Legally," Ham put in, "you can't do that."

"Keep out of this, shyster," Monk growled at Ham. To Blosser, he said, "Physically, you can't do it either, and I'm the guy who will demonstrate."

Lieutenant Blosser, who had shown few signs of being scared of anything, returned Monk's scowl with enthusiasm. "You lay a hand on me," he told Monk, "and you will learn two or three things in a hurry."

"Come on," Renny rumbled impatiently. "Holy cow! We get tired enough of Monk and Ham squabbling. Do we have to put up with a new addition to it?"

Monk stalked to their car. His feelings were not improved toward Lieutenant Blosser when he discovered that Ham had made use of the diversion to grab the seat next to pretty Jen Bridges, a location Monk had earmarked for himself.

They drove uptown, all of them in one sedan, except Renny, Johnny and Uncle Joe Morgan, who followed in another machine.

Pat was growing more puzzled.

She remarked, "A radium miner, a man who has slept three weeks and people who have bought monkeys."

Jen Bridges wrinkled her forehead. "I do not understand Mr. Savage making such strange requests."

Ham said, "When you're around Doc, you frequently bump into things you don't understand."

Pat was lost in thought for a while longer. Then she did an unexpected thing. She leaned back, a light of relief overspread her attractive face, and she laughed.

When the others stared at her, startled, Pat said, "Brothers, get rid of those long faces. Doc has got the whole thing figured out right now, I'm willing to bet you."

Jen Bridges frowned. "What makes you think that?"

"When Doc starts doing things nobody can understand," Pat assured her, "he is really making progress."

They drove into the garage at headquarters. The garage was situated in the basement of the great building. It was entirely private, its doors actuated by radio control, and was served by a private elevator.

The car containing Uncle Joe Morgan pulled into the garage behind them.

Renny told Monk in an aside, a bit later, "That old Morgan codger worries me. I think he's the most scared man I ever saw. We ought to give him something—a sedative or a hypnotic or something."

"A night's sleep might help him."

Renny shook his head. "The only way he'll get to sleep is for someone to hit him with a sledge hammer."

VI

DANGER FOR DAVID

The sun came up the following morning, throwing its light into the eighty-sixth floor windows of the midtown building. The sunlight splashed over Monk as he read a half-page newspaper advertisement that began:

RADIUM MINER WANTED

"My ad sure got a display," he said. "Renny, how did yours come out?"

Big-fisted Renny Renwick was studying another paper. He rumbled disgustedly.

"Holy cow! They seem to think it's some kind of a gag—our wanting a man who has slept three weeks and can prove it by a doctor's testimony. Here's a story in a box on the front page about it. Couple of other papers are carrying the story, too."

"That's good," Monk said.

"It sounds goofy," Renny complained.

There was an interruption in the shape of an uproar— sound of things upsetting, angry squeals.

"Who's got hold of my hog?" Monk yelled, leaping to his feet.

Habeas Corpus, the pig, shot out of the library, sounding like a small locomotive with exhaust stacks open and whistle going at every other jump. Attached to one of his legs was a string and a particularly hideous photograph of Monk.

Monk captured his pig and untied the photograph.

"Who did that?" he bellowed. "Where's that Ham Brooks?"

"Oh, shut up about Ham!" rumbled big-fisted Renny. "He isn't even here. He is out having breakfast with Jen Bridges."

That didn't improve Monk's temper. He scowled. "The hog didn't just get tangled up in that cord and picture," he said. "There was a knot in the cord."

Renny looked at the photograph of Monk. He chuckled.

"I can understand it's scaring the hog," he said.

Monk subsided into an indignant silence.

It could not have been more than five minutes later when the telephone rang. Monk picked up the receiver. It was a voice he had never heard before.

"Put Doc Savage on here," said the telephone voice.

"Doc," said Monk gloomily, "is in jail. Don't you read the newspapers?"

The voice was silent a few moments.

Then: "Just the advertisements," it said.

"You mean those advertisements in the newspaper?" Monk was interested.

"Yes."

"Which one are you?" Monk demanded. "The radium miner or the man who has slept three weeks or longer?"

"I'm Ted Parks," the voice said.

"Oh, I thought you might be somebody—*who*?" Monk bolted upright. "Ted Parks? Where are you?"

The voice which had identified itself as belonging to Ted Parks was silent a while.

"I'm where I have been hiding out," it said finally. "Listen, since you fellows advertised for a radium miner and a man who has slept three weeks, it's obvious you understand what is behind the murders they are calling the invisible-box killings. You are wise, aren't you?"

"Oh, sure," said Monk, who did not have the slightest idea what connection a radium miner and a sleeper could possibly have with the invisible boxes. "That is, there are some points we don't know. We would like to have them cleared up. Can you do that for us?"

Again the pause.

"Would you care to drop around and talk to me?" asked the voice.

Trying not to seem too eager, Monk said, "I suppose we could. But it might be better if you came here."

"I can't come there."

"Why not?"

"I might not be alive when I get there."

"Well, we can come to see you, then."

"You must promise not to tip off the police."

Monk said, "That won't be so easy. There's a cop named Lieutenant Blosser who has fastened himself on us, and I don't know whether we can give him the slip."

"You've got to."

Monk considered. "All right, we'll do it some way."

"When you slip this cop," said the voice, "come to 346 Westwood Road."

That was all the voice said.

Monk and Renny Renwick wore innocent expressions when Lieutenant Blosser, Pat, Ham and Jen Bridges returned to the reception room.

"We left Long Tom and Johnny finishing their breakfast downstairs," Blosser explained. "There been any developments?"

"All's quiet in the dawn," Monk said. He yawned and patted his stomach. "Renny, what do you say we turn it over to them and go down get a bite to eat?"

Renny tried to look hungry. "Suits me."

They arose, sauntered to the elevator and rode it down to the street level. They headed on a run for the restaurant in the building, flung through the doors, dashed for Johnny and Long Tom.

"Come on!" Monk barked. "We've got a line on this Ted Parks!"

"I'll be superamalgamated!" gasped Johnny.

They dashed outside and scrambled into a taxicab, after Renny warned, "There's a checker-light in the laboratory that lights up when anybody is in the garage. We better not try using one of our own cars."

Renny rumbled at the cab driver, "346 Westwood Road."

"Where'n heck's that?" asked the cabby.

They got out and went hunting a street directory on the newsstand. "I wish I had Doc's memory for streets," Monk complained. They found Westwood Road to be in the Bronx.

The cab ran over to the elevated highway and shot north past the piers that were whiskered with steamship masts and colored funnels. There was very little outbound traffic, and the speedometer wavered around sixty.

Monk chuckled. "We worked that slick. Blosser is sidetracked there at headquarters. And the two girls are safe there, too. Ham can take care of them." He burst out in laughter. "Ham is going to miss this. He won't like that."

They turned off on Westwood Road where it angled down sharply toward the river. It was a decrepit district—old shacks and, close to the river, the remains of an amusement enterprise which had been abandoned.

The place was a cross between an amusement park and a night club, not extensive enough for one and too large for the other. The fence around it had been coated with stucco once, but most of this had scabbed off. The place seemed to be No. 346.

They paid off the cab.

"Go back three blocks and wait for us," Monk told the driver.

That aroused the suspicions of the driver. They watched him drive back the three blocks, hesitate, then go on, increasing his speed. The cab disappeared.

Renny mumbled disgustedly, decided, "Oh, well, we can get another cab."

They decided that a convenient alley was the best approach to the ruin they were to investigate.

Twenty yards inside the alley, a young man stepped out before them. He stood there. He seemed to think they should recognize him.

"Well," he said finally, "haven't you seen my picture, or got my description?"

"Ted Parks?" Monk asked.

"That's right."

The young man was tall, muscular in a slab-sided way. He had dark hair, a somewhat small mouth, eyes which were sunken and hard to read behind large spectacles.

"I figured you would come down this alley," he said. "So I waited here. I had to head you off."

Monk eyed him. "You *had* to head us off?"

"Exactly."

"Why?"

The young man jerked a thumb over his shoulder. "They found me," he said. "That is, they found where I was hiding. But I saw them coming. They're searching the place, now. There are four of them."

"Who are they?"

"Do you know a man named David Bridges?"

"Is that the one," asked Monk, "who has a sister named Jen?"

"That's him."

"We've been hearing of him. We haven't met him. He was supposed to be seized last night by some men and carried off. His sister came to us for help."

The tall, dark, intent-looking young man seemed astonished. Then a grim smile twisted his lips. "That's good," he said. "The sister took you in."

Renny blocked out his big fists. "You mean that girl has been lying to us?"

"That girl is one of the murderers," the young man said. "I don't know whether she has lied to you, because I'm not aware what she has told you."

Renny demanded, "Why should she lie to us?"

The other snorted. "To get next to you, of course! So she could be with you, find out your moves, and tip off her brother so you couldn't catch him."

"Her brother is behind this?"

"Sure!" The young man jerked his head toward the dilapidated ruin near the river. "He's in there, now. He's one of the four men looking for me."

"There's only four men in there, now?"

"Yes."

"Let's take them," Renny rumbled.

The young man seemed apprehensive. "They're tough guys. They may try to use that invisible-box death on you. I don't know what it is, but they may try it."

"Come on!" Monk said.

Johnny Littlejohn held up a hand. "Wait a minute. Parks, suppose you sketch this thing for us? Make it brief. We want to know what is going on."

The young man nodded. "Here it is in a nutshell. Four men have died mysteriously—or rather, six, now. I see by the morning newspaper that an unidentified man was found in my apartment, and my friend Elmer Ivers died yesterday afternoon. I know all those men except the unidentified one. As far as I can learn, I am the only one who has known them all. So I got scared, began investigating, and immediately an attempt was made to kill *me*. So I hid out."

"Why didn't you go to the police?"

"I was afraid they would try to frame something on me."

"That's kind of a thin excuse," Johnny suggested.

"I don't give a damn how thin it is," said the other. "It's the truth."

Johnny was using small words, which indicated that he was excited.

"Uncle Joe Morgan—do you know him?" he asked.

"Sure. A harmless old codger. He knows all of the men who have died, too. But I discounted him. He isn't the kind of an old duffer who would be mixed up in a thing like this."

Johnny was becoming suspicious.

"That isn't telling us much," he said.

"I don't know much."

"Have you told us all you know?"

"Yes."

Johnny took a grim step forward. "When you telephoned Monk, you said you did so because of the advertisements in the newspapers for a radium miner and for a man who had slept three weeks."

The young man backed a pace. His face twisted. Then he lifted his voice.

"Take them, fellows!" he called.

Men began coming out of adjacent doors and windows, men with guns and unpleasant expressions!

"Is there just these four, Nick?" one of the armed men asked.

"That's all," said the young man.

Johnny's expression was assured, calm, as if nothing had happened. It would have done credit to Doc Savage.

"I'll be superamalgamated! You are *not* Ted Parks," he remarked.

"Naturally not," said the young man. "You walked right into it, didn't you?"

Monk said, "And walked right out again!" and kicked the arm which the young man was using to draw a gun. The arm broke in at least two places.

One of the gunmen shot Monk in the chest. Monk walked over to him—rather, he made it in one great jump—and grabbed hold of him. As soon as Monk took hold, the man began screaming.

Monk had a little trick or two which he liked to demonstrate to friends, one of these being to take a silver half dollar between thumb and forefinger and bend it until the edges touched. The man's screaming was more horrible than loud.

Another man bellowed, "A bulletproof vest! They're wearing—" He didn't finish, because Renny got him.

Johnny tangled his long, bony frame around two others.

Long Tom, the electrical wizard, paused to drag out a thing that could have been an iron goose egg, but wasn't. He dropped this; and it popped like a firecracker, throwing out particularly vile, yellow vapor.

"Tear gas!" a voice squalled.

It was a natural, if wrong, conclusion. The stuff was not tear gas. Forms of tear gas could be defeated by a mask. This stuff was more sinister. It worked through the skin pores. Monk was very proud of it. He had worked it out in cooperation with Doc Savage.

Best point of the gas was the method Doc Savage and his aids used in immunizing themselves. They did it by using small quantities of the gas daily on themselves until their systems built up what is sometimes called a tolerance for the stuff. They had done this over a long period of time.

Strong quantities of the gas would make them unconscious. But small amounts, such as exuded from grenades, made them only a little dizzy.

Two minutes later, Long Tom calmly stepped up to the last dazed would-be attacker and knocked him down.

"That," announced the puny-looking electrical wizard, "is that."

It wasn't—quite. Long Tom hadn't taken into account the presence of two other attackers, well clear of the gas. These men were armed with automatic rifles, and they had kept under cover. A kind of reserve troop, as it were.

They showed themselves and their guns.

"Get your hands up!" ordered one man.

Monk and the others stared in astonishment. They had presumed all forces were in the attack. These new entries had caught them by surprise.

"Guess we'll have to blast 'em, Jake," said one rifleman. "They've got bulletproof vests on; so shoot them in their heads."

Monk hastily shot his hands above his shoulders. Renny, Johnny and Long Tom did likewise. They were trapped!

The two automatic-riflemen came close, but not near enough to get into the gas.

"For some reason or other," one of them remarked, "that gas got our boys, but didn't affect these guys."

Monk got an idea. He registered worry.

"Look here, let us step out of this stuff!" he said pleadingly. "If we stand in it, the gas will get us."

The riflemen took the bait.

"Just stand in it, then," one said.

Monk had expected that. He let his jaw sag and his eyes roll, trying to look weak. He sank to his knees. He groaned. He slumped forward on his face.

Renny, Long Tom and Johnny followed the homely chemist's example.

"I'll be danged," said one of the riflemen. "It did get them, at that."

He pulled out a whistle and blew it. It was a police whistle, so it had a natural sound after the shooting.

The police whistle accounted for the misfortune which befell the police patrolman who happened to have the neighborhood beat. The officer arrived in a hurry, gun out, demanding to know what was going on.

"Homicide detail," said one of the riflemen, pointing at his own chest with a thumb. "Look here, will you hold my gun a minute? I want to search those fellows."

He walked toward the patrolman holding out his rifle, butt first, and got close enough to the officer to bump him forcibly between the eyes with the metal-plated walnut. The officer collapsed, not dead, but disinterested.

A truck appeared. It was a large truck with a van body. Obviously, summoning it was the purpose for which the police whistle had been blown.

By that time, the wind had drifted the gas away from the recumbent forms in the alley.

"Load them in the truck," ordered a rifleman. "All of them. We've got to get out of here."

"What about the cop?"

"Oh, let him lay!"

"He saw us," said the other rifleman.

"That's right. Better bring him along, too. We'll get rid of him when we get rid of the rest of them."

* * *

The truck was powerful and noisy. It rumbled northward at a rapid clip, following streets which trucks usually followed. They were not allowed on the boulevards or highways.

One of the riflemen produced a rope from a box and began cutting it into lengths.

"We've got to tie up Savage's men," he said. "Here, help me divide this rope up so it'll go around."

The other rifleman helped him. There were three additional men who had been in the truck when it came. They made, including the unconscious victims and prisoners, a crowd.

The second rifleman said: "Jake."

"Yes," replied his companion.

"When they were talking—did you hear them say something about a man, or somebody, named David Bridges?"

"Yes."

"Who can David Bridges be?"

"He's a brother of a girl named Jen Bridges, didn't they say?"

"Who the hell is Jen Bridges?"

"There you've got me."

They finished cutting the rope.

"What do we do with these guys, now? Knock them off?" asked one of the trio who had been in the truck.

"Not until we catch Ted Parks, or find out where he is," said a rifleman—not the one named Jake. "Them's orders. Find Ted Parks, then croak these fellows and frame it on Parks. Then see that Parks commits suicide before he can spill what he knows to the police." The man chuckled. "Nice, eh?"

They began tying the prisoners. A man took hold of Monk's ankles. Monk became active.

The truck suddenly filled with uproar! But it was a sad kind of an affair, taken generally. Monk and the others had underestimated the effects of the gas, or the good qualities of the tolerance they had developed to the stuff. The gas had not weakened them as much as it had slowed their ability to react.

The upshot of it was that Renny and Johnny were almost immediately knocked senseless with blows from rifle stocks. And Johnny was pinned helplessly under two bodies.

Monk fared better. Monk was a fighter by nature and instinct. It was the thing he liked best to do.

So he got out of the truck. He literally burst down the

tailboard, and piled out to the highway. He did this as a last resort, after he saw what had happened to Renny, Long Tom and Johnny, and understood the same thing would soon occur to him.

The truck was going all of forty miles an hour. Miraculously unkilled, Monk rolled like a ball. He managed somehow to direct his wild tumble so that he ended up near the curbing, on his feet, and running.

He ran somewhat after the fashion of a man with one leg off at the knee. But he made time. And the erratic course he took caused three rifle slugs, and all the bullets from at least one revolver, to miss him.

He got into bushes. He ran.

Ten minutes afterward, Monk stumbled into a small neighborhood grocery. It was a district of small homes and few mercantile establishments.

"Telephone!" Monk gasped.

They stared at Monk, pop-eyed. There was now a little hide left on Monk's hands and features, but not much. His looks were not improved.

He found the telephone for himself and dialed headquarters. Ham answered.

"Ham, please don't give me an argument," Monk said. "Listen to this: Ted Parks is in danger and is to be framed for those invisible-box deaths. Jen Bridges is deceiving us. She may not even have a brother named David Bridges. The girl is a crook."

"You're crazy!" Ham said.

"Listen—Renny, Long Tom and Johnny are in a truck. Prisoners! Headed for I-don't-know-where. They are to be killed. The killing framed on Ted Parks."

Ham was incredulous. "What is this you're telling me? Where the devil are you? You *are* crazy, aren't you?"

"We walked into a trap," Monk said. "Get up here as soon as you can. The truck is headed north. We may be able to spot it. I'll contact the State troopers and have them start watching for it."

"Where are you?" Ham demanded.

Monk turned around, looked at the storekeeper, and asked, "Where am I?"

The man told him, stuttering somewhat.

Monk relayed the information to Ham.

Then the rifleman named Jake and one of the men from the truck came into the store behind guns! They wore masks made out of handkerchiefs. They fired a few bullets into the ceiling.

Monk tried to run, but he was weak, exhausted, his lungs on fire and his legs rubber. They beat him down, hammered him some more, then hauled him outside. Jake paused long enough to pull the telephone loose from its wires, as if it were fruit on a vine, and hurl it at the gape-mouthed storekeeper.

VII

ONE MAN LOOSE

Ham Brooks, in the headquarters reception room downtown, heard some of the uproar in the distant store. He also identified the noise of the telephone being ripped from its wiring. He was not cheered.

He turned a pale color which would have caused Monk to razz him unmercifully, had Monk seen it. Ham thought a lot of Monk, actually.

He upset a chair getting from behind the desk.

"Monk and the others—they got a call from a fake Ted Parks and went to see him. It was a trap." He ran to a corner for his sword cane, an innocent-looking piece of foppery. It was a black cane, the blade of Damascus steel, tipped with chemicals which caused unconsciousness.

Lieutenant Blosser bounded to his feet.

Ham told him, "You stay here. Take care of Miss Bridges and Mr. Morgan."

"I go with you," Blosser said grimly.

Pat had disappeared into the laboratory. She came out with a case of equipment, one of the small bronze metal boxes which they habitually used as containers.

"We'll all go," she said. "What's wrong with that?"

There was plenty wrong with it, but Ham didn't believe there was time to argue. He remembered Monk had said pretty Jen Bridges was a fake. Ham could hardly believe that. He wanted time to think before he committed himself to a decision.

"Come on, then," he said impatiently.

They piled—Ham, Blosser, Pat, Uncle Joe Morgan and Jen Bridges—into the special elevator to the basement garage. They selected a car. Ham did the choosing. He picked the machine they called "the tank."

"Get in!" he barked. "Hurry up!"

Outwardly the car resembled any six- or seven-year-old rich man's limousine. The interior was not much different. But the body was armor plate, the windows the best process bulletproof glass, the body gas-tight. It could knock down a stone wall, or at least come as near doing so as an army tank.

Ham opened the radio-controlled doors while he was starting the engine. The garage doors slid apart as noiselessly as big lips.

They drove out into the street.

What happened then was not excusable because it was unexpected. Ham was looking for trouble. He got it. Violently!

A truck in front of them was big. It had good brakes and it stopped on a dime, almost literally. At least Ham jammed on the hydraulic brakes full force and barely escaped ramming the truck, which had a huge box car of a body.

There were other cars, one on each side. One a coupé, the other a coach, and looking entirely harmless. Too late, Ham realized their looks were deceiving.

He realized this when the truck pulled ahead a few feet, and Ham took his foot off the brake, thinking traffic had cleared and they were going on.

The back end of the truck body dropped down from the top. It formed a kind of ramp.

Ham was astounded.

Another car, a big and heavy one, hit him a hard blow from behind. In the fractions of seconds during which Ham could not get his amazed foot back on the brake, their car was knocked up the ramp and into the truck body.

Like a sheep being shoved into a box.

The thought in Ham's brain was: *"This is crazy! I've seen it in the funny papers! They've done it in movies! And it happened to us once before!"*

But there they were.

Lieutenant Blosser grabbed the door handle.

"Stay in here!" Ham yelled at him.

Blosser was in the back seat. And he did not know that

the car was a fortress, as hard to crack as a good safe. So he paid no attention to Ham's advice. Blosser piled out.

The drop-leaf door of the truck was closing. Evidently, there was an arrangement of pulleys and lines. Blosser took a run, jump, a hard fall, and hit the pavement.

His police revolver was in his hand. One of the cars, the one that had bumped them, was just backing away. Blosser lifted his weapon with the idea of shooting the car full of holes. He did get one bullet into the windshield; then the machine was jumping at him like a great steel animal.

Blosser dodged the car partially, enough so that he was only knocked head over heels instead of being crushed to death. He lost his revolver.

He got the gun again in, it seemed to him, no more than a second. It must have been longer. Because the car was gone, and the truck itself was lumbering around the corner.

Lieutenant Blosser's revolver held five cartridges, and he transferred the lead from these to the back of the big truck. There were no results. Except that the sidewalks cleared magically.

"Police!" Blosser howled. "Police!"

There was a police call box not six feet from him, but he was as excited as a citizen. He never even saw the call box. He tore down the street after the manner of a wild man, loading his gun as he went. All this got him was a briefly tantalizing glimpse of the truck disappearing in the distant traffic.

"*Whew!*" gasped Blosser.

He tried to commandeer a cab, but the first two were strangely empty, and the driver of the third—he looked as American as the Bronx—was strangely unable to understand English. The fourth cab was piloted by a more venturesome character.

But, by then, it was too late. After Lieutenant Blosser had charged the cab around several blocks with the horn blowing steadily, he came to his senses enough to realize that the thing to do was to call the police.

It embarrassed him to remember how often he had given ordinary citizens hell for delaying less time than this in notifying the police when a crime had been committed.

Reaction had gripped Blosser, by now. He was both nervous and enraged.

He found a telephone and shook until he had to brace

his elbows against the wall while he was notifying the radio bureau, then Commissioner Strance, then District Attorney Einsflagen, of developments.

"You had better come down to headquarters after the district men get there," Commissioner Strance told him. "The D. A. and you and I will have another talk about Doc Savage."

VIII

ACTION IN BRONZE

District Attorney Einsflagen wanted very badly to be governor. He'd gotten the ambition when he was a kid who had to deliver papers after school to pay for his own clothes, and it had never left him. Practically everything he did was aimed toward that goal. His speaking, for instance. He had practiced public speaking endlessly, because he figured you had to be good at that to be governor. Whenever the chance presented, he was inclined to launch into elaborate rhetoric.

He was making a speech, now.

It hadn't started out as a speech. The platform delivery had just intruded.

In sum and substance, he was taking fifteen minutes to tell Doc Savage that he was filled with respect for the bronze man's mental equipment and that, therefore, things which Doc Savage did were frequently not what they seemed on the surface.

Take, for instance, said Einsflagen, the matter of the bronze man's interest in contacting a man who had slept three weeks, a radium miner, and people who had dealt in monkeys recently. There was an example, Einsflagen suggested. Three things, all three bizarre, all three bearing no apparent relation to each other. That was an example of how Doc Savage's brain worked. All three things—radium miner, sleeper, monkeys—were doubtless very important, but it befuddled an ordinary brain to try to see what connection they had with the matter in hand.

All of the speech-making led to a point.

This point was that the D. A. did not believe the seizing

of Ham and the others was genuine, or the disappearance of Monk and his party, either.

"In other words," said Einsflagen, "your associates felt the necessity of doing one of two things: Either disappearing, or getting rid of Officer Blosser so they would be unhampered. We do not know which the motive is, I will admit."

For once, Doc Savage's self-control slipped. He stared at them unbelievingly.

"You do not believe my men, and Miss Savage and Miss Bridges, are in danger right now? Perhaps dead?"

Einsflagen showed his teeth in what was no smile.

"We are not completely gullible," he said.

Doc Savage continued to stare at him.

"What are you going to do about this?" he asked tensely.

"We are going to order your men arrested on sight," said Einsflagen. "And we are going to presume that they are *not* in danger, have *not* been kidnapped, and that they *are* in a position to know more about this than they will, or have, admitted."

Doc Savage made his trilling briefly. It had biting, fierce quality.

He said, "I have been a fairly satisfactory prisoner thus far, I hope?"

The district attorney nodded. "I understand you have." He turned to Commissioner Strance. "He has, hasn't he?"

Strance shrugged.

"Smart. Naturally, he's model. Doesn't mean a thing."

Doc Savage came to his feet grimly.

"From now on," he said, "you can expect something else."

They stood a guard outside the door of his cell for that. The guard was a burly cop who didn't like people who enjoyed privileges. They must have picked him for that reason and told him Doc was ex-privileged.

Commissioner Strance did the guard placing. He did it at the urgent request of District Attorney Einsflagen. Strance himself was becoming a little dubious.

"I don't know but what there might be a mistake here," Commissioner Strance told Doc. "But I'm not sure. As soon as I decide you might be innocent, I'll do something about it."

"That," Doc told him grimly, "might be too late."

"Now might be too soon."

Commissioner Strance went away.

The guard looked in through the bars at Doc Savage.

"Let's not have any trouble out of you," he said, not unpleasantly, but firmly.

The cell was one of a battery, a line of them opening on to a second-floor catwalk of steel. Second-tier catwalk would probably be a more apt description. At any rate, the doors all locked from a common bar, controlled by a time clock. The cells opened at a certain hour for breakfast, another for exercise hour, and so on. The rest of the time, it was controlled by a time clock, and nothing but a master key in the hands of the head jailer would open the doors.

It was almost exactly like a penitentiary, except that there was no enforced labor. No labor of any kind. And the prisoners wore their own clothes, minus the usual deletions of neckties, belts and shoestrings.

Word went through the jail that Doc Savage was in the place. It had a rather queer effect. Ordinarily, there could reasonably have been expected a demonstration of some kind. Instead, there was a complete silence. An appallingly complete silence.

It was as if a hawk had appeared over a flock of rather evil birds.

"Cigarette?" Doc asked his guard.

The guard had a red face and little knowledge of Doc Savage, or he would have known the bronze man never smoked.

Doc took the cigarette. He retired to the back of his cell. He did not smoke the cigarette. Instead, he burned a few yarns twisted from his blanket to make the odor and some smoke, but not enough smoke that anyone would notice it was wool burning, not tobacco.

The rest of the time he spent tampering with the cigarette. He crushed one of his shirt pocket buttons and inserted the powder in the cigarette.

The stuff was a chemical intended to be administered through the mouth, but it had the property of also being effective if smoked, like opium.

He let some time pass.

"Cigarette again?" he asked the guard.

The guard grunted and extended the package. Doc had a

little trouble getting a cigarette out. He took the package in his own hands for a moment.

During the instant when he had control of the cigarette package, he was fortunate. He managed to get his doped cigarette into the package, substituting for one he took. He returned the pack to the owner.

He smoked the cigarette he took this time. He sat close to the cell door, smoked it and blew the smoke out through the bars, so that it would tantalize the guard.

It was done subtly and casually, and the guard fell for it. He reached into his pack, pulled out the handiest cigarette, which was the doctored one that had just been planted, and lighted it. He smoked luxuriously.

Doc allowed the proper time to pass. The guard was now glassy-eyed, rather rigid.

Doc said: "Guard."

The man did not answer.

Doc said, "Guard, go to the end of the stairs. Go down the stairs. There is a small automatic fire-alarm thermostat at the foot of the stairs. Strike a match and hold it against the fire alarm. When the bells begin to ring, pull the lever which unlocks all the cell doors."

The bronze man watched the guard walk away. He held his breath. The drug was a result of experiments with hypnotism and artificial aids toward inducing it. It was quite effective, but only briefly, in reducing the victim to a state where he would do anything anybody told him. But he would be in that condition less than five minutes, after which he would drop off in a sound slumber. So the drug, except for such uses as this, was quite useless.*

The guard struck the match. The substance between the electrodes of the alarm points—or a thermostat, if it was that type—did what it was supposed to do.

The fire-alarm bell cut loose.

For the sake of safety for the prisoners, the prison, a modern one, had been designed so that the cells could be

---

*The actual chemical formulae used by Doc are not revealed, for the reason that such information in the wrong hands could do a great deal of harm. Furthermore, many of the chemical concoctions, improperly used, would possibly have fatal results.

quickly unlocked in case of fire without waiting for the master key.

The guard pulled the unlocking lever. There was a rattling. Doc immediately shoved open the door of his cell.

It was a tribute to the criminal world's fear of the bronze man that no one tried to leave any of the other cells.

Doc ran along the catwalk; his feet took the steps in a machine-gun hammering, and he threw the lever back in position to lock the cells again.

The guard was weaving on his feet. "Wake up!" Doc told him. "When the guards come, yell that you are sick! Yell it loud."

The bronze man then went over to the only possible spot of concealment, a point not at all close to the flat steel door that led to freedom.

There was a concerted rush in answer to the fire alarm. Those who came bore fire extinguishers and guns. They shoved the door open, and those with guns came in first.

The guard did his act well.

"I'm sick!" he bellowed. "I'm sick, *sick*!"

And then he fell on his face.

Doc ran for the door when that happened. He had taken off his shoes because the strings were missing and they would have flown off anyway. He went on tiptoes, without much noise, as far as the door, where he was seen.

Men accustomed to routine require a little time to react to something new. A prison guard's job is very dull routine. So Doc got fifty feet of flying start.

He reached another door just as more men came through with fire equipment.

"The fire may be there!" he told them. He pointed to help them out.

Doc was a man who believed in avoiding lies if possible. The fire *might* be in there, of course. Probably it wasn't.

Anyway, it got him through that door, which was the last locked one. He put on speed. He was being fortunate. He had not expected it to click off as it had, like teeth of two matched gears fitting together. Tomorrow there would, he suspected, be a session of carpet-standing for those responsible for his uninterrupted flight.

He knew the layout of the building, now. He broke a window which admitted to an iron fire escape. This, in turn, deposited him in an alley, and it emptied him out on a street.

He kept running. He was barefooted, tieless, hatless. Men do not go around in that condition on New York streets. Not as fast as they could run.

Eventually, he piled into a taxicab which was standing at the curb, motor running, but minus driver. He drove the machine away.

It was car theft, but he was not in the mood to worry about that. For one of the few times in his life, he was angry.

IX

TRAILS

A debonair, if big, old gentleman with a thorn cane walked out of a subdued apartment house on upper Madison Avenue. His hair was white; it looked like a fall of snow on his head. His skin was very light, rather white, in fact. His mustache was the ample type commonly known as a soup strainer, and his Vandyke was clipped like a French poodle.

He twirled his cane, whistled merrily, and asked a policeman where he might find Monsieur Piquen's of Paris, Fifth Avenue Branch. The cop didn't know.

What was more important, the officer didn't know that the old gentleman was Doc Savage in a disguise. This was particularly good, because it happened that the policeman was one who knew Doc quite well by sight.

The exclusive club patronized by Ham Brooks, the lawyer, was in the neighborhood. Doc had visited the place often, which was how he had met the cop.

That test passed, Doc took a cab to the unusual ferryboat home of the late Elmer I. Ivers, banker and financier.

The home was under police guard. Two uniformed patrolmen. Doc walked up boldly and showed them a card which bore the misleading statement that he was Joshua Wheels, a syndicated newspaper columnist. Mr. Wheels was important and carried weight with the police department.

"You say you have permission to examine the boat?" said one of the officers. "I will call headquarters and check on that. Just a moment."

He went away and came back.

"Good, Mr. Wheels," he said. "It is all right. Would you like us to go with you?"

Doc had thoughtfully taken the precaution of telephoning Mr. Wheels, whom he knew very well. He had arranged for Mr. Wheels to get himself permission to make the examination of the ferryboat which Doc intended to make in his place.

"One of you might accompany me, to explain to the servants," Doc said.

He proceeded to give the place a thorough half-hour examination, without making much show of doing so.

"There are several servants aboard, now," he remarked. "I understand that, the night of the murder, there were no servants on the boat."

The policeman, visualizing his name in the widely read Joshua Wheels syndicated column, explained, "Yes, true. They say they were summoned hurriedly to the office of their employer's lawyer. The summoning was done by telephone, and it was the voice of their employer, Mr. Ivers, who talked to them. That is how Mr. Ivers happened to be alone on the boat when Doc Savage came."

"The servants must have been away some time."

"Quite a while," admitted the officer. "You see, the voice on the telephone told them to wait at the lawyer's office until he—the voice that said it was Mr. Ivers—arrived. So they waited around for hours."

"You talk as if the voice did not belong to Mr. Ivers."

"We have no proof, but we think it did not."

"Who do you think it was?"

"I understand the district attorney is working on the theory that it was Doc Savage. It is known that Mr. Savage is an excellent imitator of voices."

"Have *you* any ideas on the point?"

The officer hesitated. "To tell the truth, I think they are making a grisly mistake in trying to saddle this thing onto Mr. Savage." He frowned. "That isn't a popular opinion, right now. But I know criminals have always feared Mr. Savage. To me, that is a good sign."

"But someone," said Doc, "decoyed the servants away so that Mr. Ivers could be murdered?"

"Someone also telephoned the police a tip that Mr. Savage would arrive and murder Mr. Ivers, which was how the police happened to be here. To me, that means Mr.

Savage was framed." The officer put out his jaw. "It sickens me, the way people are turning on Mr. Savage and trying to hang this thing on him just because they can't find anyone else who might be guilty of those invisible-box things."

"Have you any ideas on the invisible boxes?"

"Some kind of a trick, must be," said the officer. "Anyway, they shouldn't turn on Mr. Savage. He has done a lot of good, I understand. And you take a man criminals are afraid of—that man is all right."

"Human nature," Doc suggested.

"Rat nature, seems to me," said the policeman.

Doc Savage turned up next at Fanning's Funeral Home, a subdued and expensive establishment. It was here that the body of Elmer I. Ivers lay.

Doc gained admission, and an inspection of the body, by the same device he had used at the Ivers ferryboat home— pretense of being Joshua Wheels, the columnist.

He saw at once that the body of Ivers was in expensive afternoon attire for interment.

"Where are the clothes he was wearing when he died," Doc inquired.

Astonishingly enough, they had them. "They are here," the attendant said, opening a metal cabinet.

Doc arranged the garments on the table. He inspected them, but did not touch them or turn them after he had spread them out.

They consisted of the pants of a tuxedo, a white shirt of the semi-dress variety with a spotless bosom, a smoking jacket, black leather pumps, and such accessories as black tie and onyx cuff links to go with the outfit. Doc Savage examined the spotless shirt front in particular.

The odd point was that he remembered there had been a brown stain, as if a pipe had drooled, on the shirt front of the man who had said he was Elmer Ivers and admitted him to the ferryboat.

Doc went back and looked at Ivers' body again.

It was not the Ivers who had admitted him to the ferryboat. This was a different man. Not the same man, not the same clothes.

"Quite sure this is Elmer I. Ivers?" Doc asked.

"Oh, quite sure," said the attendant. "The police say so."

Doc Savage took the dead man's fingerprints with an outfit which he had foresightedly brought along.

"Why do that?" asked the astonished attendant.

"Hobby," Doc told him.

On his way downtown, he stopped off at a telephone to get in touch with the writer, Joshua Wheels, and explain, "You have visited the Ivers ferryboat and talked with a policeman named Jones who thinks they are making a mistake trying to hang this on Doc Savage. Next, you visited the Fanning Funeral Home and looked at Elmer Ivers' body twice, and also at the clothing he was wearing when he was killed. You also took Ivers' fingerprints."

"I've been busy, haven't I?" said Joshua Wheels.

"And next you will go downtown to the bank of which Mr. Ivers was president, and you will get Mr. Ivers' fingerprints."

"How do I know they'll have his fingerprints?"

"It is the custom to fingerprint bankers, usually. In case you do not get them, you are going to be disappointed and ask a lot of questions aimed at finding where you can get a set of fingerprints which are surely Mr. Ivers'."

Joshua Wheels chuckled. "Call me up and let me know when I get done doing such strange things," he said. "I wouldn't want to be two places at once, but I do have an appointment with a radio chain for two hours from now."

"You will hear," Doc told him.

The bank had the fingerprints of Elmer I. Ivers, they said. A vice president sent a clerk looking for them. Then, after time had dragged past, the vice president got up to see what was keeping the clerk.

Later the vice president returned, a bit ruffled.

"Very sorry about this," he said. "Seems our file girl has gotten the files mixed up and, unfortunately, we cannot find Mr. Ivers' fingerprints."

Doc Savage's eyes—their flake-gold color was concealed by colored optical caps which fitted directly on the eye pupils—narrowed.

"You mean," he said, "that the fingerprint card has disappeared?"

The vice president took out a handkerchief and wiped the wet beads off his neck.

"Nonsense," he insisted. "We will find it."

Doc Savage made the kind of a remark that Joshua Wheels might have made.

"It will be a very hot day when you do, I imagine," he said.

He left the bank with a conviction.

Elmer I. Ivers had been dead when he came to the ferryboat that afternoon. Already murdered. The fake Ivers had met Doc, planted the scene by summoning the police previously, and everything had clicked to schedule.

There was still the problem of the disappearance of the fake Ivers from the ferryboat.

Doc got the genuine Joshua Wheels on the telephone again.

"You have to pay Ivers' ferryboat another visit," he told Wheels. "Could you cancel that radio appointment?"

"Is it important?"

"Six people, at least, have died. The lives of that many more are in danger."

"Consider the appointment canceled," Wheels said.

Jones, the policeman who did not believe Doc Savage was guilty, was as cordial as he had been before. But he accompanied Doc on this inspection also, which was not to the bronze man's liking. There was no way, however, of getting rid of Jones without arousing a possible suspicion.

"What brought you back, Mr. Wheels?" asked the officer.

"Doc Savage insists that there was a fake Ivers who met him and that the real Ivers was already dead in that room. The fake Ivers ran into the room containing the body, shut the door, then screamed and carried on. Then he escaped, leaving the body of the real Ivers where it had been lying dead."

"I hadn't heard that story," said the astonished Jones.

They went to the murder room.

"Could we get a hammer from the servants?" Doc suggested.

They could. The bronze man went over the walls, tapping, not missing a square foot of space. He got no suspicious sounds. Then he tried the floor. There was a rug, which he rolled back. But no results.

The ceiling was very high; this had originally been one of the upper decks of the ferryboat. It was covered with plywood.

"What is above?" he asked.

Roof, the servants seemed to think. So the bronze man got a stepladder, climbed atop it, tried different parts of the ceiling and found a panel that lifted upward.

Jones, the policeman, gasped in astonishment.

Doc Savage climbed through the aperture. He showed Jones a rope ladder, evidently an ornament from some part of the boat. He dropped it down, and Jones climbed it without trouble to join Doc.

Doc said, "The way the murderer escaped."

Jones was excited. "Then the killer was *not* Mr. Savage. I'm glad to learn that, Mr. Wheels."

The place where they crouched was space between room ceiling and curved roof. It was about three feet high where they were, less elsewhere.

They began crawling and came out on an upper deck. The spot was exposed to the cold sweep of river winds, but it was also in plain view.

"The killer could not have escaped this way," Jones said.

"Why not?"

"I was one of the police party watching this boat that night," Jones explained. "This deck was watched. Men were posted here. In fact, Lieutenant Blosser personally was up here, I think."

"That makes it look bad for Savage again," Doc suggested.

"It sure does," said Officer Jones regretfully.

Doc said, "Will you inform Commissioner Strance of this development?"

"Sure."

The bronze man left the ferryboat and telephoned Joshua Wheels again.

"You have turned up a surprising development in the Savage and invisible-box mystery," Doc told Wheels. "Your findings lead you to feel that a fake Ivers met Doc Savage when he came to the ferryboat that afternoon. The real Ivers was, at the time, dead. The fake Ivers led Doc Savage to the scene, dashed into the room with the body, created an uproar to attract the police, then fled by a more-or-less secret exit leading to an upper deck. Thus, the police were presented with what had to be a murder perpetrated by Doc Savage, or a locked-room mystery."

"I think I had better see that this gets publicity," Wheels remarked.

"Thank you."

"Don't mention it," Wheels said. "I'm happy to step on the toes of District Attorney Einsflagen. The fellow is a trifle ruthless about his ambition."

Doc said, "You have ceased being a dual personality."

"Good. I can just make that radio appointment after all."

Doc Savage went next to the vicinity of the police station to which Lieutenant Blosser was assigned. He entered a telegraph office. He spent some time head-scratching over a pencil and paper and eventually managed to wangle his way into conversation with the manager.

The telegraph office was a small one, with one man serving as manager and operator of the teletype machines over which the messages were sent and received. Doc presented a very credible story about being an ex-operator of "mux," as the teletypes were sometimes called. He called the job by its trade term of "puncher," and began bragging a little.

It was a tribute to the bronze man's personality that he managed to strike up a bosom acquaintance with the operator-manager in not more than fifteen minutes. He told the fellow how fast he could punch out messages. It was a tall story, and the operator professed disbelief. Doc Savage got around behind the counter to demonstrate.

"I will run off a few words first to limber up," he explained.

He wrote:

LIEUTENANT LARRY BLOSSER POLICE DEPARTMENT NEW YORK CITY—WILL BE AT POLICE STATION TO MEET YOU AT FIVE O'CLOCK TODAY WHEN YOU GET OFF WORK— CALL MARY AND TOM FOR ME—AUNT SUSAN— STONEHAM, CONN., 9:45 A.M.

Then he wrote:

THE QUICK BROWN FOX JUMPED OVER THE LAZY DOG. NOW IS THE TIME FOR ALL GOOD MEN TO COME TO THE AID OF THEIR PARTY.

Following that, he said, "Now, here is what I mean."

He proceeded to strike awe into the puncher-manager by showing what speed could be made on the teletype. It was the simplex variety of machine which printed directly on a tape, instead of being a page printer.

Later, he sauntered out of the telegraph office.

He had the tape containing the message he had punched to Lieutenant Blosser in his pocket, as well as a blank and an envelope which he had lifted.

He pasted the tape on the blank in the proper fashion, put it in the envelope, then carried it into the police station.

But, growing suddenly prudent, he left without trying to deliver the message, found a taxi with a large driver, and borrowed the man for the job, at an expense of five dollars.

The taxi driver swallowed the story that it was a gag on one of the policemen—which it was, in a way of speaking.

X

TRAIL TURNS

Lieutenant Blosser took the telegram when he came in to write out a report. He was only idly curious. Then he read it, and his gloves fell from under his arm, where he had been holding them.

His left arm began trembling, the left side of his face twitched. It was a nervous difficulty which manifested itself in moments of extreme stress.

Blosser left the police station as if pursued by an animal, ran around the corner to a parking lot and piled into his car. He drove recklessly.

On Eighty-first Street, west of the Park, he piled out, opened the door of a garage, then drove inside. It was gloomy in the garage, which was a huge place not in use, as far as storing cars for the public.

Inside the garage stood three trucks, one of them the huge machine in which Ham's car had been loaded so unceremoniously a bit earlier. There were four passenger automobiles. None of these were new.

There was a young man leaning against a balcony across the back, a rifle to his shoulder.

Blosser yelled, "Be careful with that thing, Nick!"

The man on the balcony lowered his rifle.

Blosser dashed forward, bounded upstairs to the balcony. "Where is my dad?" he barked.

Nick jerked an indicating thumb; he started to say something. Blosser dashed past him, acting so excited that Nick followed. They passed through a door, close together.

Then Nick remembered something.

"Hey, you didn't close the outside door!" he complained.

"Go close it," Blosser snapped.

Nick swore, returned and descended the stairs, closed the door to the street. He waited there for a while, watching a mirror which had been attached outside a window in the door. The mirror, small and hardly noticeable, afforded a view of the street in one direction; and there was a second mirror for inspection of the other end of the street.

Satisfied that no one was in sight, Nick went back to the balcony. He entered a room in which a man was tied to a chair.

The man tied in the chair looked very much like Blosser. The difference between them was one that could be detected readily enough when they were side by side. But separate them, and it would not be easy to distinguish.

It was a father-and-son resemblance, helped out a little by hair bleach.

Blosser had confronted the older man. Blosser looked ashamed of himself. But he still had his determination.

"Look, dad, I'm in a spot," he said.

The older man said nothing. His face was very sad.

"Look, I got a telegram from Stoneham," said Blosser. "It was from Aunt Susan. She's coming at five o'clock when I get off work."

The older man was still silent.

"She'll recognize me," Blosser said wildly. "She won't be fooled. The cops were taken in, but Aunt Susan won't be."

"What do you want me to do?" asked the older man.

Their voices, like their appearances, were startlingly alike. The same small mannerisms, the same slight touch of south Brooklyn.

"You have to meet Aunt Susan, steer her away from me," said Blosser.

The other shook his head sadly.

"No," he said.

Blosser clenched his fists. "Look here—this is vital. You have to, see. This has gone too far to have it upset, now. I have the cops fooled."

"No!"

"I have the cops fooled," Blosser repeated. "They think I'm you. They have to go on thinking that. I exchanged places with you, and made the police believe I was you, and got away with it. I'm on the inside. I have to stay on the inside. I have to do that because I have to pick up information that he needs."

"Who is he?"

"The guy with the brains." Blosser sneered. "If you think you get told more than that, you're crazy."

"No."

"You won't do it?"

"You know that without asking."

Blosser breathed inward slowly and deeply. "You know me, dad. Nothing stands in my way. I'll kill you if you don't do this for me."

The older man shook his head. There was a kind of complete simplicity in the gesture.

"No!" he said.

Blosser took a gun out of a pocket. Not his service revolver, but a smaller weapon, a single-shot pistol of small caliber and short barrel. A gun which would kill a man as completely as a .45, if aimed carefully, but not make much noise.

Doc Savage came out of the adjacent shadows at that point!

A stool, a three-legged wooden stool, actually preceded him out of the shadows. He threw it with care, accuracy. It turned over twice in the air, struck Blosser's gun hand. Blosser lost the gun.

Doc came not quite, but almost, as fast as the thrown stool. He struck the man with the rifle, Nick, with the edge of his hand at the throat. He grabbed the rifle out of Nick's hands. Nick staggered, sounding like a toy balloon with the air leaving it. Doc hit him. Nick became silent.

Blosser was fumbling for his service revolver with his left

hand. His right-hand thumb was sprained, and one finger was back in a shape it should not have been, out of joint.

Doc came toward him. Blosser stopped fumbling for his gun, tried to square off. Doc stamped on one of his toes. Blosser's guard came down. Doc's knuckles slid just enough after they landed on his jaw to remove some skin. Blosser hit the floor like three or four sticks of loose wood.

The old man sat in the chair, staring at Doc, but not straining against the ropes which held him. He did not say anything.

Doc Savage picked up the rifle and looked through two other rooms opening off the balcony. He went down the stairs and looked in what had once been a room for the garage mechanical department. There was no one.

He examined the trucks, the cars. No one was in them. He looked over the interior of the cars and truck carefully. In one, he found a short rusty-looking hair bristle. It could have come out of a clothes brush; but more likely it was one of the hairs off Monk's pet pig, Habeas Corpus, which had dropped off Monk's clothing.

In the van body, he did an unusual thing. He produced a small gadget, similar to a flashlight, but with an opaque lens. It was a projector of ultraviolet light, and he began going over the truck interior with it.

He found nothing in that truck.

In the other truck, he found his armored limousine. This was apparently the machine in which Ham, Pat, Jen Bridges and Uncle Joe Morgan had been riding with Lieutenant Blosser when another car bumped them from behind and knocked them up into a truck ahead. This, of course, was obviously the truck.

In the sedan, written on the back window, was a message in green fire. Not literally fire, of course. The stuff was a trace of chemical writing left by Ham; he had used a special button off his shirt for the enscribing. Normally, it was unnoticeable. But, under ultraviolet light, it fluoresced brilliantly. So brightly, in fact, that it could almost be read in daylight.

Ham's message:

> They trapped us with the old truck gag. I must
> be slipping! They are going to run their truck and
> our car into the river if we don't come out. They will
> lock the truck on the outside before they do that; so

we will have to give in, I guess. For some reason, they do not want to kill us. I think there is somebody important to their plans who won't continue helping them if we are killed.

Monk, Renny, Johnny, Long Tom have been caught. Pat, Jen, Uncle Joe with me. So they have us all.

I still do not have the slightest idea of how to explain the invisible-box murders, or what is behind it.

Ted Parks, the young doctor, is important. And they are mentioning someone named Rensance.

Ham.

Doc finished the remarkably complete message. Ham must have had plenty of time to write it.

Doc Savage went back to the balcony. The older man tied to the chair stared at him. The fellow still had not said anything.

Doc said, "You are actually Lieutenant Blosser?"

The other nodded.

"If I turned you loose," Doc said, "what would you do? Hope that you would be able to snatch up one of those guns and save the situation?"

The older Blosser gaped in utter astonishment.

Doc Savage went over and examined Nick, who showed signs of returning to his senses. Doc hit Nick again, not hard enough to permanently wreck him, but a clip that would extend unconsciousness.

Young Blosser was stirring, mumbling. Doc shook him, slapped his face lightly. Blosser finally got his eyes to focus, and they fixed on his disjointed finger.

Doc gripped the finger, pulled, set it back in joint. Sudden sweat appeared on Blosser's forehead, but he did not make a sound.

Doc faced the older man in the chair.

He said, "A son kidnapping his father and taking his father's place on the police force—it could not happen." He glanced from one Blosser to another. "It is too fantastic. And you two men are not in character with such a thing. Your son would not do such a thing to his father. There are—I am glad to say they are rare—sons who would do such a thing. But not yours."

The older Blosser twisted his lips.

"I hope they are not as perceiving as you are," he said.

"They?"

"Whoever is behind this."

"You do not know that, of course." Doc said this as a statement, not a question.

The older Blosser eyed him in surprise. "You seem to have come to the truth."

Doc said, "Is it a police trick?"

"You think it is?"

"Yes."

Blosser sighed. "That's right." Then the older man shuddered. "But if those fellows get wise—" He moved his eyes and mouth to imitate a dying man. "What tipped you off?"

"It became obvious that the murderer of Elmer Ivers escaped from the ferryboat past the spot your son was guarding. Only two conclusions could be drawn from that: either you were a crook, or your son had taken your place with your knowledge. There have been cases of a son kidnapping his father, but the people in such cases were not the caliber of you and your son."

"Thank you," the elder Blosser said.

The younger Blosser glanced anxiously at the unconscious Nick. "If this guy wakes up and hears this, the beans will be spilled."

"He will be unconscious some time yet," Doc said. The bronze man swung to the elder Blosser. "Let me have the story."

Blosser hesitated.

His son said, "Go ahead, pop. I think the department has been making a mistake all along about Savage. I don't think he's guilty."

The older Blosser swallowed.

"We are both policemen, my son and I," he told Doc Savage proudly. "Larry, here, is an undercover man. He speaks several languages, and he understands foreign customs. As a matter of fact, he is a member of the section of the police department assigned to ferreting out foreign espionage agents—a section of police activity about which the public knows nothing, incidentally."

The elder Blosser glanced anxiously at Nick.

"Larry first heard of this thing when the rumor came around to him that a mysterious individual was assembling a sinister organization of some sort," Blosser continued. "Dangerous criminals, clever ones, were being employed and paid large sums."

"A foreign agent at work?" Doc suggested, but not as if he believed this was the motive.

Blosser stared at him. "I can tell by your tone that you know it wasn't. No, it is not a spy or sabotage thing. Of course, we thought at first that it was. That is how Larry came to get interested in it. Larry was assigned to sabotage-investigation activities, as I told you."

"What is it, then?"

"Frankly, we don't know."

"Do you know how the invisible-box murders are committed?"

"No."

"Or why they were committed?"

"No."

The bronze man's flake-gold eyes narrowed. "Just what *have* you learned?"

"That the individual behind this has gone to great pains to keep his identity secret, and is succeeding," Blosser said. "Names have been mentioned. A doctor named Ted Parks is involved somehow."

"In what way?"

"Larry here has just heard talk that leads him to believe Parks is the brains behind it."

"Have the police looked for Parks?"

Blosser nodded. "They can't find him."

"Why were the murders committed?"

"We don't know."

Doc Savage paused, went over to Nick, and made sure the man was still senseless. Coming back, he said, "Are you telling me that the police department knows what you are doing and is working with you?"

"Of course. Do you think Larry could have taken my place otherwise? The police department is not that gullible."

Doc pounced on this point. "Just what was the idea of Larry, your son, taking your place?"

"After Larry heard these rumors about a sinister organization being formed, he wangled around until he got himself into it as a member. They investigated him thoroughly, particularly the point about his father being on the police force. Larry has never made a secret of that in his undercover work, or of the fact that he used to be a policeman. You see, that's what he always says: that he was a cop and got bounced. That's his story."

"Larry pretends to be a crooked cop who got fired?"

"Right."

"And so?"

"Out of a clear sky came the order to kidnap me and take my place," said Blosser. "We talked it over and decided to do it. We didn't know what the idea was."

"They gave a reason for your son's taking your place?"

"Oh, of course!"

"What was it?"

"So my son could get inside information for them on the progress the police were making toward solving the invisible-box murders."

Doc Savage was silent a moment; then his trilling seemed to come into existence, a sound so low that it hardly left his throat. He said, "Which does not explain how your son let the murderer escape on the ferryboat."

"Larry didn't know there was to be a killing," said the older Blosser grimly. "He was told to get on the police detail assigned to the ferryboat, if he could. And he did. He was told that a man would leave the boat by the upper deck, sliding down a rope into a rowboat concealed under the dock. This man would move the rowboat along by hand to the mouth of a large drain pipe, which emptied into the river at that point, and hide in the mouth of the pipe until the excitement was over. This was what Larry did and let the man escape. Then he found out there had been a murder, and he went to get the killer. But the fellow hadn't waited in the pipe. He had escaped."

Doc swung to young Blosser. "That right?"

The younger man nodded. "Every word the truth. It sounds wild, but there it is."

"And you do not know the motive for these murders?"

"No."

Doc Savage picked up the rifle which Nick had carried and the two revolvers young Blosser had brought—the service gun and the small single-shot pistol. He tucked the rifle under an arm and dangled the revolvers from a finger.

He went to young Blosser.

"Nick will get back to his senses soon," Doc said. "When he does, tell him he has not been unconscious long. Tell him you drove me off. Tell him I fled. Tell him you have to get out of here in a hurry."

The youthful Blosser eyed him. "Meaning you want to get Nick on the run, so he will maybe lead you to the higher-ups?"

"Right."

"Good!" Blosser got to his feet. He extended a hand. "Give me my service gun."

Doc extended the revolver.

Blosser took the weapon, reversed it, pointed it at Doc Savage's head.

"Get your hands up!" Blosser said.

The bronze man's mouth tightened, but otherwise his expression did not change. "So you have been lying to me?"

Young Blosser was shaking in his excitement. "We haven't told you one damned lie," he said. "There is just one thing we left out."

"You omitted—"

"That we have absolute proof you are the brains behind this infernal thing!" Blosser snarled.

"Proof?" For once, the bronze man's control was shaken.

Blosser pointed at the man called Nick.

"Nick has told me you are behind it!" he said.

Doc Savage reached out, then, and snaked young Blosser's gun. There was dazzling speed in his gesture—and careful calculation, because his thumb dropped on the hammer, holding it back. The gesture was not as reckless as it looked. The gun was pointed at his chest at the moment, and he wore a bulletproof undergarment.

They fought then, briefly, violently! Blosser ended up on the floor, expelling a tooth and profanity. Doc found a rope, a tow rope from one of the trucks, and tied him.

Soon after that, the man called Nick opened his eyes, did some groaning, and got himself organized. He stared at Doc Savage.

Both Blossers seemed to hold their breath as they waited for Nick to speak.

Nick said, "Boss, why did you have to hit me?" He looked straight at Doc Savage, and his voice was sincere as he said it.

Young Blosser expelled his breath, grimly satisfied. The older man dropped his shoulders wearily.

Doc Savage's face suddenly—like an actor going into a part—began to show expression. He frowned. His brows beetled. "Who told you I was head of this thing?" he demanded.

"Why, I got that from—" Nick stopped.

"From whom?"

Nick squirmed. "Listen, I haven't told anybody."

"You told *them!*" Doc indicated the Blossers.

Nick wheeled and cursed young Blosser. "We oughta knowed better than trust an ex-cop!" he snarled.

"Who gave you your information about me, Nick?" Doc Savage persisted.

"I . . . er—" Nick swallowed. "I can't tell you, boss."

"But the man told you I was the leader?"

"Sure! The whole organization knows that. They know you were trying to keep it quiet, but there was a leak somewhere. That was why you had your friends—that Monk Mayfair, and the others—grabbed."

Doc's tone was ominous. "Why did I have them seized?"

"Oh, the organization understands that! They don't know you are the brains in this thing—your friends don't, that is. But they began to get suspicious. So you had to get them out of the way. You ordered them grabbed. They aren't to be killed. They are just to be held until this thing is settled."

"So that is why Monk and the others are not being killed?" Doc said.

"That's the talk."

"And what about Uncle Joe Morgan?"

"Oh, him!" Nick shrugged. "You just had him marked for one of your victims."

"Victims in what?"

Nick looked uncomfortable. "Whatever you're pulling, you know as well as I do that none of us has been told what is behind this."

"And what," asked Doc Savage, "about Ted Parks?"

"He's in with you. He's your partner."

"Parks is my partner, eh?" Doc Savage began to lose expression, to resume his normal composed manner. His voice also lost its emotion. "What do you know of Jen Bridges and her brother, David?" he inquired.

"Them?" Nick shook his head. "Nobody in the organization can figure out who they are, or where they hook into this."

Doc Savage straightened. "But you are positive I am your leader?"

Nick stared at him. "Who you kidding?"

"You think I am deceiving you?"

"If you claim you ain't the boss," Nick said, "you are kidding me. I know you are. I know because I have heard you talk to the organization and issue orders. I recognize your voice. And we found your fingerprints on a telephone you had used. One of the boys used to be a fingerprint man; and, just for fun, he took the prints off the telephone and checked them with your prints, taken off a glass in a restaurant where we watched you eat. They were the same. You're the boss, all right."

Doc struck Nick on the jaw and put him motionless on the floor.

XI

MAN DANGER

Nick escaped ten minutes later. It might have been somewhat less than ten minutes; it was as quickly as Doc Savage could arrange it.

The bronze man first walked over and tested the bindings of the two Blossers. Then, carrying his captured guns, he strolled down the stairs to the cars.

Under the back seat of the least conspicuous car—which was also the slowest—he placed a small fiber case. The case, although not large, was the most bulky thing that had been in his pockets. A little larger than a kitchen match box. He had some trouble getting this up under the cushion springs in such a spot that it would not be noticeable, should anyone sit on the cushion.

He started the car motor and left it running, as if to warm up.

He went up to the balcony, picked up Nick, carried him down and put him in the car.

He had not tied Nick. He made a business of looking around for rope. "Any rope up there?" he called to the Blossers, who naturally did not answer him. Then he went back to the balcony, as if seeking rope.

Reaching the balcony, he dropped to a knee beside the younger Blosser.

"Nick wasn't hit hard enough to make him unconscious," the bronze man said. "He will try to escape. I am going to follow him. You two try to get it through your head that someone is taking infinite pains to get me into trouble. Try to understand that. Notice that Nick did not *know* I was his leader. He had just heard I was. Nick's misinformation was part of—"

The car suddenly meshed gears on the garage floor below. Doc jumped to the railing. To make it good, he yelled. He also fired a pistol, directing the bullet into the floor.

Nick was a scared man. He sent the car headlong at the garage doors, managing to get enough speed so that, when he hit the doors, they burst open with splinters and dust and noise. The car, sadly battered, dived out into the street.

Doc Savage was not pleased. He had not figured the man would be fool enough to drive headlong at the door, batter up the machine so that it might have to be abandoned immediately.

Abandoning the car would, of course, render useless Doc's small radio transmitter which he had planted under the seat with the idea of using a direction finder to keep track of the car.

The bronze man lost no time leaving the garage. He ran until he located a taxi, though Nick and the battered car were gone, by now. Doc told the driver, "Amsterdam Avenue, and fast." Then, on Amsterdam, he said, "Turn right, six blocks." And at the end of the half-dozen blocks, "Stop here!"

The building was as shabby as any on Amsterdam. Doc dropped down a basement stairway, manipulated a lock, at the same time holding a palm against a brick at the side of the door in what could have been an innocent gesture, but wasn't. The hand on the brick operated a capacity-type device which unbolted the door. He went in.

This was the laboratory of Long Tom, the electrical wizard of Doc's organization. Because Long Tom liked seclusion when he worked, few outside the group knew of the place. Doc felt sure the police would not have a guard over it, and he was positive there would be a portable radio direction finder in the place. There was.

Also a great help was the car which Long Tom kept in an adjacent garage. The car was an elderly rattletrap containing a tank-type motor, which meant an airplane motor, liquid-cooled.

The man called Nick left his battered car in the north Bronx, near the Westchester line. He simply parked the car, walked two blocks to a street-car line, got on a car and rode. Later, he transferred from the street car to a bus.

Doc Savage followed him in Long Tom's old automobile. Later he left the car and moved on foot after Nick, as Nick entered a lunchroom.

It was a dining-car-type lunchroom; the clients sat with their backs to the windows, facing the counter and the back bar, which was all shining chromium where it was not steaming coffee urns and polished toasters. Nick ordered coffee.

Soon, a man came and sat on the stool beside Nick. The two seemed to exchange no words. But they left together.

From this, Doc surmised the hideout was near and that the lunchroom was being used as a precautionary contact point, to make sure the coast was clear.

They went, Nick and the man who had met him, to a residential street, where they entered a brick house. It was almost dark by now, and a flash of light showed from the house interior as they opened the door and went in.

Doc Savage moved around to the back. He was carrying Long Tom's radio direction finder, because the device was a gadget of more than one use. The amplifier part of it, for instance, could take a tiny quantity of sound, a fractional decibel of it, and step this up to a blast.

The bronze man attached a sensitive contact microphone to the panel of the rear door, hitched it to the amplifier, then fed the tubes volume.

What he got was disappointing. A refrigerator ran noisily somewhere in the house, its vibration interfering with such noises as were words. One thing he did learn: there was no guard inside the door. So he tried the door. Locked.

He used his belt buckle on the glass in the door. The belt buckle looked cheap. He used the end of the tongue, or, rather, the tiny diamond that was set in the tip of the tongue.

The diamond could groove the hardest alloy steel, so the glass did not give it any trouble. He waited until a car went past, tapped; the glass came out, and he reached in and unfastened the lock.

The place where he stood, now, smelled of food, so it was evidently the kitchen. He went on. He heard feet coming down stairs. Then voices. He got close to the voices and listened.

One voice said, "Hello, Nick. What has happened?"

"I've got up against something I don't understand," Nick said. "Doc Savage has broken out of jail. He talked to me, and he acted as if he ain't the boss. In fact, when I told him he was, he bopped me on the jaw. He started to load me in a car, I don't know what he planned. I got away."

"How come you made the break?"

"I got the idea he was mad because I let the cat out of the bag about everybody knowing he was boss. So I tried to cover up by skipping."

"You think he was actually mad?"

"If he wasn't, he was acting darn funny."

Doc Savage's metallic face was grim. *They actually thought he was their employer.* The situation had not seemed believable, but now he was convinced.

It was, on the whole, clever, and diabolically so. It indicated an agile brain as well as a tenacious and fiendish one. What better basis for starting a criminal enterprise than to build up an identity as another man, particularly one notable enough that there could be no doubt about what individual you were pretending to be?

Nick's words stabbed into Doc's summary.

"What about the Rensance thing, Joe?"

"That goes through tonight," Joe said. "This Rensance is being blockheaded about it, so that's too bad for him."

"Are all the prisoners here?" Nick inquired.

"No. Orders came through to only keep the ones we got with the Ted Parks trick up at that old amusement park."

"That Monk, Long Tom, Johnny and Renny?"

"Right. They're here."

Doc Savage tucked his apparatus under his arm and walked into the room where the two men were talking.

"Take it easy, fellows," Doc said in a calm tone.

They gaped at him.

To Nick, Doc said, "Sorry about the tap on the jaw I gave

you. It was a little distressing to find out that my identity was not the secret it was supposed to be."

Nick exhaled relief explosively. "So you *are* the chief!"

Doc made no comment on that. Because he was a man who always went to great pains to do exactly whatever he said he would do, and to be whatever he said he was, he did not commit the trivial deceit of telling Nick he *was* his leader. He was, however, letting Nick draw that conclusion.

The distinction between deceiving a man, and not actually lying to him, was one which Doc Savage was careful about. Monk and the others were moved gleefully to declare that Doc Savage had never actually told a lie.

Nick was deceived. The other man, likewise.

Doc asked, "How many of the boys are here, Joe?"

"Why, just Jig, upstairs watching the prisoners," said Nick's companion. He was a round blond man with flashing white teeth and only a certain scraped-bone grayness in his eyes to indicate his vicious character.

"Sit down," Doc said, "and tell me how things are going."

Joe licked his lips. He was extremely interested in Doc Savage.

"You mean about Rensance?" he inquired.

"Right," Doc said calmly.

Joe was evidently an ambitious boot-licker. He expanded, began to fawn. He fell over himself to offer a full explanation.

"It's all set," he said. "Rensance has balked. So the word is to knock him off. But *you* would know what the word is." Joe grinned at Doc Savage. "It's all set."

"Do you know the exact details?"

"I . . . er . . . sure." Joe was somewhat uneasy, for he might have felt that he shouldn't know the details.

"Repeat them," Doc ordered. "Let us see if anything has been balled up."

"The gang is to close in on Rensance at nine thirty," Joe said. "They are to meet at the abandoned gatehouse on the estate. At thirty-five past nine, the man will show up with the—whatever it is."

Doc took no chance. "The whatever-it-is?" he repeated and waited.

"The invisible-box business."

"You do not know what the murder method is?"

"Not me." Joe sighed. "That's one thing I don't know."

"How long," asked Doc, "would it take to get to Rensance's place?"

"Not long," Joe said. "Half an hour, maybe."

Doc Savage made elaborate show out of looking at his watch. "Care to go there with me, Joe?" he asked. "I need a driver to the spot."

Joe sprang to his feet. He was eager to get in solid with the big boss.

"Sure, sure!" he said. "You should see me drive. I used to tool a car for Legs Diamond in the old days."

They left the building, walked down the street, reached the car in which Doc Savage had arrived. They climbed in the machine.

Doc went through the motions of a man who had forgotten something—exclaiming, snapping fingers.

He said, "Wait here. I want to tell Nick something." To make Joe less suspicious, he added, "To tell the truth, I do not trust Nick too far."

Jig, the man watching the prisoners upstairs, had no eyebrows. There was nothing else peculiar about him. He was a long, lean man of nondescript feature and average clothing. But he had no eyebrows.

Nick said, "This is the chief."

Jig said, "Pleased to meet you, Mr. Savage." He extended a hand.

Doc took the hand and put on pressure. The pain doubled Jig forward for a moment. Doc slapped him on the back while he was doubled over. It was a robust, friendly slap.

"Great fellows, all of you," Doc announced.

He gave Nick a hand-shaking and a slap on the shoulder for good measure, which somewhat astonished Nick.

Both Nick and Jig looked at their aching knuckles and, still looking at them, sank down to the floor. The sinking was not immediate, but it was complete.

Doc removed the hypodermic ring which had been on his finger when he did the back-slapping; it would repeat and inject half a dozen doses, if necessary, of unconsciousness-producing drug. He placed the ring in the metal case where he ordinarily carried it.

Monk, Renny, Long Tom and Johnny were sitting in

large overstuffed chairs, hands tied, faces taped. Doc removed the tape. They began coughing up sponges.

"I'll be superamalgamated," said Johnny, spitting sponge. "Pyrotically invidious phylum porifera."

Long Tom stared at him. "Says which?"

"I was eating that damned sponge so I could yell for help," said Johnny in small words. "I had it half eaten." He looked displeased.

Doc untied Monk and indicated he was to free the others.

"Listen," Doc said.

They gave him attention.

"It stands this way," Doc said. "Mysterious murders. Invisible boxes. No reason. Uncle Joe knows the victims. So does Ted Parks. Parks has vanished mysteriously. We begin investigating. So they start framing the killings on me. Jen Bridges comes to us with a story of a brother who has been kidnapped, but the story has not been substantiated. I was put in jail. You were grabbed in a body and held here. Ham, Jen Bridges, Pat and Uncle Joe Morgan have been grabbed, also, and are being held elsewhere."

The bronze man broke his summary off for a moment. Then he said, "That is all repetition. But I want you to get it straight."

Monk said, "About the radium miner, the man who slept three weeks, and the people who've bought monkeys—where do they come in?"

Doc seemed not to hear that.

He said, "The latest victim intended seems to be named Rensance. I have tricked the thug named Joe into taking me there. You fellows follow. Be ready for action."

Long Tom said, "We have no weapons."

Renny blocked out his big fists, rumbled, "These are all the weapons I need." He was angry.

"Me, too," Monk said hopefully.

Joe was a talker. He did not bother opening the conversation with the weather; he got right to the subject in which he was most interested. Himself. He was a great guy, Joe was—to hear him tell it.

He was not a bad driver. He admired the car, particularly the power of the great motor which Long Tom had put inside the hood.

"You want the police to bother us for speeding?" Doc asked once.

That slowed Joe. Because there was plenty of time, they stopped at a roadhouse and had coffee. The route was taking them north into the section of large estates.

At twenty-five past nine, Joe pulled the car into the brush beside a lane. He got out. Doc followed him. They came to a great stone wall and an iron gate, with a keeper's lodge of stone close by. The gate stood ajar. They passed through.

It was then nine thirty.

The gate-keeper's lodge was in darkness. But a door opened, disclosing that there was dimmed light inside.

A voice from the door said, "Get in here before somebody sees you."

They entered the lodge. The man who had called to them threw the door shut, then tripped a switch which made the lights bright. He showed them the business end of a pump-action repeating shotgun, ten-gauge, at least, from the size of its barrel.

"Kindly join my collection," he said.

He was, Doc Savage realized, Ted Parks.

Arranged along one wall were four men. Their hands and feet were tied.

XII

THE VAGUE MR. RENSANCE

Doc Savage and Ted Parks looked at each other. There was no doubt in Doc's mind that this young man—large, brawny, shoulders stooped slightly, eyes strained behind thick spectacles—was Ted Parks. In their preliminary investigation of Uncle Joe Morgan and Ted Parks, Doc and his aids had dug up an old picture of Parks.

Parks' lips parted. He lost color.

"I'll be damned!" he said hoarsely.

He started to lower his gun, then lifted it again.

Doc Savage paid no attention to his indecision. He turned, tapped the astounded Joe on the jaw with a fist and stretched him out on the floor beside the other prisoners. There was a hank of rope handy. He tied Joe.

"Any more coming?" he asked Parks.

"I—" Parks swallowed. "I don't know."

Doc said, "There seems to be one special man who does the so-called invisible-box murdering. Has he shown up, yet?"

Parks shook his head. He was bewildered. "I . . . I don't get this. How did you show up here?"

"A long story," Doc told him. "Let me have *your* story."

"You are supposed to be in jail," Parks said. "I . . . I've been trying to figure how to get in touch with you, since I saw those advertisements for a radium miner and a man who had slept three weeks."

"Those advertisements meant something to you?" Doc asked.

"I'll say they did!" Parks exclaimed.

Interruption, a voice, came from outside the stone keeper's lodge. It was Monk. He called, "Doc, everything all right?"

The bronze man held out a hand. "Your gun, Parks." After hesitating, Parks handed over his shotgun.

Doc went to the door.

He told Monk, "The murderer is not here. He was to be five minutes late, I think. Scatter. Watch for him."

"We'll grab him," Monk declared grimly.

"Do that without warning him," Doc said. "Give him absolutely no warning. *And do not go hear him.*" The bronze man passed several gas grenades out to Monk. "Use these. And whatever you do, don't go near him."

"That won't be much fun," Monk said.

Monk liked a physical fight.

"Get close to that fellow," Doc said, "and there is probably nothing that will save your life."

Impressed, Monk moved back in the darkness. With Renny, Long Tom and Johnny, they scattered to keep a watch, dividing up the supply of gas grenades among themselves.

Doc closed the lodge door and swung to face Ted Parks.

"We have time to hear your end of this," he said.

Parks nodded. He looked miserable. His eyes fixed on the floor. "My end of it isn't very sweet."

"Tell it."

"I guess it wouldn't have happened to me if I had been a different kind of a guy," Parks muttered. "But I've always been as poor as that church mouse you hear about. I've had to make my own way. I've had one goal all my life—to be a great doctor. Not a surgeon. A specialist in research. Finding cures for cancer, sleeping sickness, treatments for chagres fever, dengue disease, tularemia, and things like that. I've worked hard—"

Doc said, "We checked on your past life. It is very commendable."

Parks straightened. "All right, you know my career means everything to me. That is why, when this thing the police call the invisible-box death began striking, I was afraid to go to the police. I was a coward. All I could see was that the thing would result in the Medical Association expelling me, barring me from the profession I've spent my life learning."

The grinding agony in his voice showed how he feared being thrown out of the profession.

Doc asked, "The murders were framed on you?"

"The first ones, yes." Parks nodded. "The police do not know it, yet, but they were."

"How?"

"Those so-called invisible boxes were made in my laboratory! I discovered the process."

Doc Savage said quietly, "You discovered the whole murder method, did you not?"

Parks stared at him. "How did you know?"

"A guess. It would take a highly scientific mind, such as you have developed, to do the job."

Parks groaned. "I didn't discover it with the idea of using it to murder anybody."

Here, one of the bound men made a noise, got their attention. The fellow said with terror in his voice, "What will they do with us for our part in it?"

Parks' answer was a snarl. "Electrocute you, no doubt!"

The scared prisoner licked his lips. "I ain't directly guilty. I didn't know—"

"The hell you didn't, you yellow rat!" said one of his companions.

The frightened man burst out with what he wanted to tell them, wailing, "The plans were changed tonight! The guy with the—the murderer was to go direct to get Rensance. He wasn't to come here, until he finished the job. We were to watch the gate. That was all."

Doc Savage took a step forward. "You mean—"

"Rensance may be gettin' killed right now!" the man wailed. "And remember, I'm tellin' this to prove I'm innocent of any intent—"

Doc yanked the door open.

"Monk, Ham, the rest of you—watch this place!" he called. "Watch these prisoners!"

He ran toward the distant mansion.

The house was not actually visible, except as a lump of shadow, a presence in the night rather than a reality. No windows were lighted.

The path had a covering of blacktop composition. Doc's feet made some noise on it, as little as he could manage. Nearing the house, he paused briefly, stripped off his shoes, carried them.

He pounded hard on the first door he reached. Then he went on. Shrubbery around the house was high, tangled. He waded in it, found there were no doors until he reached the back. Here there was a wide veranda, a door opening from that.

He waited. He heard the door at the front of the house open. No one came to the rear door. No one left by any of the windows. He knocked on the rear door.

The man who opened the door was no servant. Yet, a house this size would have three or four servants, at least.

"Yes?" said the man.

He was an old gentleman, with white hair, clear eyes, ruddy skin. Blue-gray smoke curled from a cigarette in a long holder.

"Mr. Rensance?" Doc asked.

"I—yes."

"Where are the servants?"

Rensance lifted the long holder to his lips, drew in cigarette smoke. "I beg your pardon?" Blue smoke dribbled off his lips.

Doc Savage studied the man. He noticed the fellow's left hand was a tight fist.

"Has he come yet?" Doc asked.

"Who?"

"The man who was going to kill you."

Rensance did not show by word or expression that the statement meant anything to him. His eyes did not widen; his mouth did not move in the slightest. He lifted the cigarette holder to his lips slowly and drew in long and deep. And the holder snapped in two pieces in his fingers; the cigarette flew upward, a skyrocket of sparks in the night.

Doc put a hand against Rensance's chest, pushed him back into the house and came in after him. He shoved Rensance down in a chair. He yanked down an elaborate cord attached to a servant bell and tied the man with it. The cord was deep-blue velvet and made a very tight knot.

There was no one in the house when Doc searched it. The only light was burning in a photographic darkroom on the second floor. Evidently, Rensance was an amateur photographer. The darkroom had finer equipment and more of it than many a commercial shop.

Some of the paper on the darkroom floor was crumpled black lightproof sheets from packages of printing paper, some was ruined prints, and some of it was paper bindings off packages of currency.

$1,000.00
$5,000.00
$10,000.00

That was the way the printed figures on the bindings ran. None was smaller than a thousand, none more than ten thousand dollars. Doc gathered them up. There was a good handful. He might have missed some.

He took them down and showed them to Rensance.

"I presume you paid off after all," he said. "How long has he been gone?"

Rensance closed his hands slowly and with force, as if he was molding hard snowballs.

"Half an hour," he said.

"Is there a telephone to the gate lodge?"

"Yes."

Doc Savage located the telephone. At the other end, Monk finally answered.

"Look sharply, Monk," Doc said. "There was a hitch. Our man came here early. There was no murder. Rensance paid off. But the killer may show up there at the lodge."

"So money is behind this, the root of evil," Monk said amiably. "O. K. We'll peel our eyes for the guy."

Doc Savage swung back to Rensance.

"How did the man happen to come early?" he asked.

"I got in touch with them."

"How?"

"Carrier pigeon."

"Carrier pigeons," Doc Savage said, "roost at night."

"It was before dark. About four o'clock, in fact."

"Have you any more pigeons?"

"One. They just sent me the two." Rensance shuddered. "I know who you are, so I imagine you have escaped from jail and are trying to clear yourself. I did not imagine you were guilty. Yes, they sent me only the two pigeons. I was to use one if I decided to pay. I have one pigeon left."

"How much did you pay?"

"Two hundred thousand dollars," Rensance said.

Involuntarily, Doc made the trilling sound which was his peculiar expression of intense excitement. The sum was enormous. Fantastic!

"Plain extortion?" he asked.

"Nothing else."

"If you had not paid—"

Rensance was getting more ruddy. His skin seemed to have the peculiarity of getting red instead of white when he was intensely disturbed.

He said, "Death, they told me. I was approached a few days ago, after the first three of those mysterious murders the police and newspapers refer to as the invisible-box murders. I was told those men had been killed because they would not pay sums demanded of them. I was informed my contribution was two hundred thousand dollars."

Doc Savage said, "You should have gone to the police and the newspapers immediately with that."

Rensance breathed in and out deeply, the air whistling slightly in his nostrils.

"Newspapers," he said, "are what they kindly sent me, with the suggestion that I read them. I did so. I saw plainly that the police were hopelessly at sea to explain the deaths."

"So you decided to pay."

"No, I went to the police. I told them the whole story."

Doc Savage was taken by surprise. He had not known

that. The police, who usually worked with him—they were hardly doing that on this case, however, which was understandable—had in the past kept him informed on such points. He had presumed that the police were in the dark as to the motives.

The authorities were not, it seemed, in the dark. They simply had not turned the information over to the newspapers.

"Your first reaction was not to pay, then," he said.

"Right."

"What changed your mind?"

"You remember the death of Elmer I. Ivers?"

Doc looked at Rensance to see if the remark was some kind of grisly gag. Apparently it wasn't.

"Slightly," Doc admitted.

The death of Elmer Ivers was only the incident which had led to his being arrested by the police and charged with murder, so he had some cause to recollect it.

"The police knew Ivers was in danger, and they were guarding his boat," Rensance said grimly. "But he died anyway. When that happened, my courage broke."

"The police should be guarding you," Doc said. "Why aren't they?"

Rensance shrugged. "They are watching my city apartment. They think I am there. The place has a back door, which I used. I came here to make my payment. I was ordered to do that."

"Do you know who is behind this?"

"A man named Ted Parks," Rensance said.

Like a bullet following an explosion, there was an echo to Rensance's statement. A yell. Not Ted Parks' voice. Not the voices of any of Doc's aids.

It said, "Pat and Jen are here! Help me quick!"

It came from the vicinity of the gate lodge.

Doc Savage was watching Rensance as the cry came. There was expression on the man's face suddenly, the kind of an expression that would follow the jab of a needle.

Doc swung to Rensance, fastened a hand on the man's arm. "You know that voice. Who is it?"

Rensance whitened rapidly, but said nothing.

"Who is it?" Doc demanded.

"The man I paid the money to—I think," Rensance said.

There had been delay, a moment or two. It angered the

bronze man. He seized Rensance, propelled the man to the nearest window.

Doc put crashing volume in his voice. "Monk, the rest of you! Be careful! That was a trick!"

He got an answer, a quick whistle from someone. A dash-dot-dash in code. The letter "K." Short for okay. They had heard his shout.

Gripping Rensance's arm, he hauled the man out of the house almost bodily. He left by a window because he was not sure now but that the doors might be watched. He began running.

Rensance stumbled frequently; he had trouble with his going. The man was out of shape, his arm soft enough under Doc's fingers to be filled with water.

But they met no one until they neared the gate lodge, where Doc stopped.

The bronze man called, in Mayan so no one but his aids would understand, "You fellows identify yourselves. Do not use English."

Monk's squeaky voice came from the left. "Long Tom is with me," the homely chemist said. Johnny was to the right, Renny to the left. Ted Parks was with Renny.

"Have you found anyone?" Doc called in Mayan.

They had not.

"Monk, come here," Doc said. "Do not move. Do not make a sound."

Monk approached. The bronze man turned Rensance over to the chemist, saying, "Watch him."

Moving away, the bronze man found a spot to listen. There was no sound but the night insects, distant traffic, a train very far away. Then, off to the right, he heard what the ears of the others had not caught: A man going away.

Doc called in Mayan, "Get away from the lodge. Get at least a hundred yards away. Come here first, though."

They joined him—Renny, Monk, Long Tom and Johnny. He gave them a flask. Ted Parks also joined them.

"Rub this liquid over your faces and hands," he said. "Sprinkle it on your clothing."

Renny unscrewed the flask cap. He smelled the contents. He gagged. "Holy cow!" he gasped. "Worse than a skunk."

"Rub it on yourselves," Doc said. "Rub it on Rensance, too."

He poured some of the stuff in his own palm, smeared it over his exposed skin, letting drops spill on his clothing, as he ran in the direction of the footsteps he had heard.

The stuff stung his skin. It smelled. The odor was nothing like the one Renny had attributed to it—skunk—but it was as distinctive in its way. He was careful to keep it out of his eyes. Once he heard Monk bleat out in involuntary agony behind him and decided the homely chemist had not been as careful about his eyes. Doc had forgotten to warn them.

He heard, shortly, a motorcycle engine start up, then roar away. He got one glimpse of the machine, its headlight, a spike of white which it pursued. It was far away. He fired once, using one of the guns he had captured. It was too dark to see gun sights. He missed it. It was one of the few times in his career that he had used a gun on a person and—he thought of this grimly—the first time he had ever missed with a shot when it was vitally important that he should not miss.

He went back to the others, and Monk said, "I'm blind! I'm as blind as a bat."

"He means in one eye," Renny amended.

"It will not last," Doc said.

"It won't, huh?" Monk was relieved. "It's sure hell while it does last."

Long Tom said, "Doc, that fellow yelled out that he had Jen and Pat. Why did he do that?"

"Possibly to decoy you away from the lodge," the bronze man said grimly.

Monk began, "Say, what was that stuff we rubbed—" He stopped. "To get us away from the lodge? *Say*—" He whirled and headed for the gate lodge.

"Easy!" Doc warned.

They went to the lodge. The bronze man used a flashlight, first on the lodge exterior. All windows, both doors, were closed.

Astounded, they watched Doc's actions. Watched him go to first one window, then another, and explore inside the rooms with the flashlight beam. They saw his face go grim, and they came to his side when he gestured.

They looked through the window at the men motionless on the floor. The prisoners they had left there. All four of them, still tied.

And now quite dead!

They stared at the semi-transparent box, which might have been made of cellophane, which stood on the floor inside the window. Stared until their eyeballs seemed to grow cold.

Doc made a slight, but grim, noise and went to the door.

Ted Parks gripped his arm.

"Wait," Parks said hoarsely. "I'll go in."

"This is not necessary," Doc told him. "This liquid smeared on our faces and clothing will protect us."

Parks was trembling. "We can't be sure. I'll go in. I am responsible for the existence of this horrible thing. If it kills me—"

He opened the door, entered, then closed the door behind him.

"I'll be superamalgamated," Renny said thoughtfully. "I believe that took nerve."

Parks struck a match. He found a newspaper, set fire to it. They watched him, growing more puzzled. Parks walked around the room several times, holding the newspaper like a torch. The paper burned. He fired another.

With this blazing torch, he got down on the floor, crawled around. He poked his torch under the tables, the chairs. He got up and poked it up against the windows. All the time, his eyes seemed to be straining, seeking something that he was not finding.

Once he dodged back wildly, and they saw that his face was like greased ivory under the smeared liquid. But he got control of himself. He went on sticking his torch into various places.

"Holy cow!" Renny said.

Later, Parks opened the door.

"Everything is all right," he said.

Then he quietly fainted.

XIII

THE PIGEON

Long Tom Roberts, the electrical expert, finished examining the dead men.

"It's another case of the invisible-box death," he said. "But farther than that, you can't prove a thing by me."

The tension, the horror, made him speak barely above a whisper.

Monk Mayfair took off his coat and put it on the floor. He placed the semi-transparent box on the coat, after thumping and examining the box and saying, "If this isn't cellophane, I'll eat it." He then tied the various extremities of the coat together to make a package. Then he searched through the lodge and came back with an old gunny sack. He put coat and box in the sack and tied the sack mouth.

"This is one box that won't get away from anybody," he declared.

Ted Parks stared at Doc Savage. "We cannot report these deaths. The police will insist you are responsible."

The bronze man nodded. "Do you know where the murderers' headquarters is?" he asked.

"I know one place," Parks said. He gave an address.

"No good," Doc told him.

"Why not?"

"That is where Monk, Renny, Long Tom and Johnny were being held," Doc explained. "It was a hide-out for a part of the gang. We want their real headquarters, assuming that there is where Ham, Pat, Jen and Uncle Joe Morgan will be held."

Parks said miserably, "I cannot give you any idea where the rest of your associates are."

Rensance said in a terrorized voice, "Perhaps they are dead."

"Shut up!" Monk snarled at him. "I don't like that kind of talk."

Renny blocked out his big fists and loomed over Rensance. "You might know more than you've told us, fellow. I've got a notion to work you over to see what comes out." Emotion made the huge engineer's deep voice have the sound of a truck on a bridge of loose boards.

Rensance trembled helplessly. "I've told you all I know."

"Yeah?" Renny grabbed him. "You *sure*?"

Doc said, "He seems to be telling the truth."

"We have to find Pat and Ham and the Bridges girl," Renny rumbled. "That old Morgan fellow, too."

Renny's voice was not stable. He was, if they stood there much longer, going to fly to pieces.

"Come up to Rensance's house," Doc said quietly.

Walking back to the mansion eased the tension somewhat. Ted Parks had difficult going. He had recovered quickly from his faint. But he was weak, and several times both knees buckled simultaneously, although he did not fall.

Parks was evidently thinking, too. When they were in the big house, he faced them.

"This Bridges girl," Parks said. "What does she look like?"

Monk described her. Monk's memory for feminine pulchritude was dependable. The description of pretty Jen Bridges was almost photographic.

Ted Parks heard the description to its end.

"That is my sister," he said.

And he quietly fainted again.

Doc Savage examined Parks, and his nod to the others indicated that this faint was no more serious than the other one.

"Rensance," Doc said, "where is that pigeon?"

"I'll get it," said Rensance nervously.

"Yeah, and I'll go with you," Renny told him, making no secret of his distrust.

The two of them went away, brought back the pigeon. It was an ordinary carrier pigeon in a not-too-clean cage of wire. A parrot cage. As they carried the cage, the pigeon flapped its wings a little to balance itself. When the cage stood quiet on the table, the bird eyed them placidly, then closed its eyes and seemed to sleep.

"Tame cuss," Long Tom commented.

Doc indicated the bird. "Long Tom, Renny, Monk and Johnny—all of you stay here the rest of the night and *guard that bird.*"

"Guard it?" Long Tom said, surprised.

"Do not let it get away," Doc told him. "If it does, it will mean losing the only chance I can see of locating Pat and Ham and the others."

They were impressed.

"Rensance will stay with you," Doc added.

"And I'll guard *him,*" Renny declared.

Doc turned to Rensance. "Have you a car?"

"My limousine," the wealthy extortion victim replied. "You may use it."

Doc picked up the unconscious form of Ted Parks. "Show me the car," he directed.

. They walked through the house to a connecting garage. Monk trailed. He was in the throes of puzzled surprise. "So Jen Bridges is really Parks' sister," he said. "Now, I wonder why she told us her name was Bridges. I guess Parks is the brother she was so worried about. But why'd she tell us he had been seized? Wonder if he was seized?"

Doc made no comment.

The night was darker when Doc drove out of the estate with Ted Parks limp on the seat of the limousine beside him. Lightning that was not heat lightning promised rain in the south. He drove rapidly.

He had noticed a fountain pen in Parks' pocket. He used the ink from this to cover his face as best he could, darkening it. There had been a chauffeur's topcoat and uniform cap hanging on a nail in the garage. Both articles were very old, but he had brought them. He put them on. The cap was too small; he had to rip it up the back to give it a resemblance of a fit.

By that time, Parks had regained consciousness.

"Feel better?" Doc asked.

"Jen," Parks said hoarsely. "So she got mixed up in this. I was afraid she would."

The bronze man drove at a sedate speed, joining traffic on a boulevard."

He said, "She came to us, gave the false name and said you had been seized."

"Trying to help me," Ted Parks muttered. "I might have known she would do something like that after she found out I had taken the fake name of Bridges."

"You went under an assumed name?"

"After the murders began, yes. Jen found it out. Her name is not Jen, incidentally. That is, her first name isn't Jen. She is Susan Eugenica Parks. I guess the Eugenica gave her the nickname of Jen." Parks considered for a moment. "I telephoned her to bring me some clothing, and she telephoned back to the number and found out I was using the name of Bridges. She demanded to know why. I wouldn't tell her, naturally. She got the idea I was in trouble. Which I was."

"And she ended up by coming to me for help," Doc said.

Parks nodded. "She evidently did that when she found I had disappeared from the place I was staying under the name of Bridges. That must have made her distraught."

Doc asked, "Where were you staying as Bridges?"

Parks told him, naming street and number. A walk-up on Fifty-fifth Street, on the wrong side of Broadway. The place where one of the invisible-box victims had been found.

Parks must have read Doc Savage's thoughts.

"I know a dead man was found there," Parks said. "That was their first direct effort to frame you. Before that, it had been indirect."

"What did you do after you left there?"

Parks became eager to explain. "A man was watching the place, so I trailed him. I was trying to find out who was behind the sinister thing. I trailed this fellow here and there. As a matter of fact, that was all I did. I didn't learn anything. I finally became desperate, decided to grab a bunch of them and scare them into telling me what they knew."

"You think those men back in the gatekeeper's lodge knew the identity of the man behind what is happening?"

"I'm sure of it."

"Most of them seemed to think it is me," Doc said.

"They were deceived."

"These men did not think it was me?"

"No, they knew who it actually is," Parks insisted. "Else, why do you think they were killed?"

Andrew Blodgett Monk Mayfair was a peculiar fellow. As ugly as a nightmare in a thunderstorm, he actually loved beauty, but was ashamed to indulge publicly. He had a penthouse-laboratory in the Wall Street district—where no one lived, except a few eccentric captains of finance—where he had turned himself loose. Ham Brooks called the place a "plush-lined monkey's nest," which was not an inept descriptive.

Doc Savage went to this laboratory. At the hour of night, the building was deserted. To get to Monk's perch in the clouds above the money mart, you opened what looked like a rusty freight door and found a fine gilt elevator, all private. So it was not hard to arrive unnoticed.

Doc removed his coat, drew on a set of rubber gloves, an all-enveloping jacket, and prepared to don a germproof mask. "You will help," he told Parks.

"What are you going to do?"

"Prepare cultures of some germ which will affect a man quickly, but which can be cured by use of the proper serum," Doc explained. "The disease also needs to be contagious."

"I still don't get it?" Parks was frowning.

Doc arranged microscope slides before a case in which Monk kept germ cultures. "We want to give someone a quick, violent, perhaps fatal, disease," he said.

"How will it be carried?"

"On that pigeon," Doc told him. "Or in a container attached to the pigeon, which will be so arranged that it will scatter the germs over the victim when the container is opened. A small container, necessarily."

Parks began to get the idea. "How about a toxic poison? I think I remember a place where we could get some bushmaster venom. There's few things more fatal."

"Where did you learn about bushmaster venom being available in New York?"

"Fellow in South America told me about shipping it to a firm up here."

"You were in South America long?"

"Four years."

Doc said, "We do not want venom. We want germs! Let us see what Monk has available."

Parks joined the bronze man. He was startled by the completeness of Monk's laboratory.

"Why, this is amazing!" he exploded. "I never had anything in his section as complete as he has right here devoted to research in bacteriology and toxicology."

Doc made no comment. His own laboratory was many times more complete than this. He watched Parks work and knew that he had been guessing correctly about the young man. Parks had great skill.

The sun came up with a shower of gold on the hills of Westchester and was cast back in jeweled reflections from the windows of the Rensance home.

Doc sat in the library and wrote with a pen:

When you opened this message, you released enough germs—tularemia, dengue fever, sleeping sickness—to kill you and everyone you come in

contact with. So consider yourself paid off for trying
to frame me.   Ted Parks.

"Parks, you think that looks enough like your printing?
Or do you want to copy it off yourself?" Doc asked.

"I print about like that," Parks said.

Doc placed the message in the trick container they had
rigged. It would release a shower of germs, and the germs
were genuine. He attached the container to the pigeon.

He freed the pigeon. It flapped away in the morning
sun, climbing, setting out to the east.

"Holy cow!" Renny rumbled. "The pigeon will give these
guys something they'll have to get a serum to combat. That
the idea?"

Doc nodded. "And the serums for those diseases cannot
be had everywhere. We will watch the places where they are
distributed, or have them watched, and will check everyone
who needs serums for treating those diseases."

Long Tom came in. "Three telephone lines are all that
come into the house," he said. "I have them rigged up on
separate instruments."

"That is good," Doc said. "You and Johnny and Renny
get on the telephones. Start calling chemists and pharmaceu-
tical concerns dealing in remedies for tularemia, dengue
fever, and sleeping sickness."

Long Tom nodded. "You want particularly to be notified
of anybody who wants treatment for all three."

"They might get one serum at one place and go to
another for the other," Doc said. "So do not depend too much
on their asking for all three serums at the same spot."

The electrical expert nodded. He and Renny and Johnny
became busy on the telephones.

After that, there was no sound but the quietly efficient
murmur of their voices and the clicking of receiver hooks as
they recalled operators to the lines.

Monk had no telephone. He paced nervously, uneasy
because he had nothing to do; he felt he was not accomplishing
anything.

"Doc, where's my pig, Habeas Corpus?" he demanded.

"At headquarters. Do not dare go get the animal. Police
will be watching the place."

"Yeah, I guess they will at that. What about Chemistry—
poor Ham's pet?"

"Chemistry," Doc said, "seems to have been with Ham when he was grabbed. No one has seen anything of the chimp since."

XIV

THE SKEPTIC

The hands on a bank clock stood at the hour of four in the afternoon when Doc Savage walked into a telephone booth in a drugstore and called New York police headquarters. He got Lieutenant Blosser.

"Yes," said Blosser.

It was the father.

Doc said, "Savage speaking. Do you still feel I am guilty of these invisible-box murders?"

The elder Blosser hesitated. "I'm afraid so," he said.

"Would you care to be shown differently?"

"I sure would," Blosser said instantly.

Doc told him. "Bring your son. Come to Westchester county. He gave an address. "Enter the place. I will contact you there. But you must come alone."

"Why alone?"

"We are about to try to clear all this up," Doc Savage informed him. "It may be dangerous, and certainly it is no job for a bulky force of men. Four of my associates are free and will help me. Also Ted Parks. So come alone. Two more men will not make our group too bulky."

"My son and I will be there alone."

"You promise that you will bring no outsiders?"

"No outsiders." Blosser then repeated the address for certainty.

"That is right," Doc told him.

That ended the telephone conversation.

Doc had a bite to eat, then approached the address he had given Blosser as a meeting place. The spot was another store. This one sold cigars. A small candy shop was located diagonally across the street; and, from this, a view could be had of the cigar store's interior. Doc took a booth, ordered a soda and waited.

He saw both Blossers arrive and enter the cigar store. Doc went to a telephone, called the cigar store.

"Will you page Lieutenant Blosser?" he said.

To the elder Blosser, who came to the telephone, he said, "I wonder if you would drop down the street five blocks turn to the right one block and wait on the corner?"

"What's the idea?" Blosser demanded.

"I will meet you there," Doc said. He hung up.

Then he watched the Blossers leave the cigar store. He stepped out on the sidewalk and watched them enter their car. He saw no visible evidence that they had given a signal, or that other police were with them.

So he met them on the corner he had indicated.

Both Blossers seemed a little suspicious.

Doc told them about the pigeon, about the germs, about the serums and antidotes for the germs which must be obtained in a hurry and could only be obtained at a few spots.

"Why, that's a slick one!" Blosser exclaimed. "Did it get results?"

"Come on," Doc Savage said, "and we will see."

Haze of twilight was gathering like fog among the trees as they drove their cars into roadside brush and unloaded. The spot was a remote one as far as human habitation was concerned. It was not far, though, in miles from the city.

Long Tom and Johnny were with the Blossers and Doc Savage. They had driven in a second car. The Blossers and Doc had ridden alone in the police machine, which was a big sedan of the type used by the detective bureau. It had no identification on the outside to show it was an official car, other than license plates, but it was equipped with radio and weapons.

"Need guns?" young Blosser asked.

"Probably," Long Tom told him.

They moved a few yards into intense undergrowth. Monk Mayfair appeared alongside them with the startling abruptness of a jungle denizen.

"Hello, there," Blosser said.

Monk frowned at him. He had not liked Lieutenant Blosser in the beginning, and he did not like him now. "It was Doc's idea to ring you in, you pest," Monk told him.

Lieutenant Blosser looked startled. He was not accustomed to such blunt talk.

Doc asked, "What is the situation, Monk?"

"Seems all right," Monk told him. "As you know, two guys showed up and bought some of the necessary serum, and we trailed them."

Lieutenant Blosser said, "Just because a man bought serum, I don't see how you could be sure—"

"They bought treatment for tularemia, dengue fever and sleeping sickness—*all three*. It's not likely anybody but these rats would need all three at the same time. Those three diseases don't commonly run together."

Blosser was impressed. "I see."

Monk turned back to Doc. "The chemical house managed to hold these guys by telling them they had to get the serum and it would take half an hour, then the firm got in touch with us. We trailed the men to"—he gestured into the woods—"that house in there. They're all there. It's their headquarters."

Doc addressed Blosser. "We are going to close in on the place. Are you with us?"

"Absolutely!" Blosser declared.

The bronze man produced a case closed with a zipper, opened it and handed out bottles containing liquid.

"Smear this stuff on your faces," he said. "Never mind the smell."

"It goes good in the eyes, too," Monk said dryly.

Lieutenant Blosser stared at the bottle, puzzled. "What does this do?"

"Keeps the invisible-box death away from you," Monk informed him.

Blosser gaped. "I don't believe that!"

Monk snorted.

"How does it keep it away?" Blosser demanded.

Monk ignored him.

Blosser took a step forward, grabbed Monk's arm, and rasped, "Look here! If you fellows know—"

Monk brought his arm slowly down and around and twisted out of Blosser's fingers. "You put your hands on me again," Monk told him, "and I'll pull them off and stuff them in your ears."

Blosser retreated hastily. In Blosser's private opinion, Monk Mayfair was about as safe as a can of nitro-glycerin. Which was what Monk wanted him to think.

Meekly, Blosser smeared the stuff over his face and hands. He sprinkled it on his clothing. His father did likewise.

Doc Savage led the way, and they worked through the trees and brush.

Blosser touched Doc's arm, asked, "You think your friends—Ham, the two girls and Morgan—are alive?"

"Probably."

"What makes you think that?"

"The man behind this has gone to elaborate pains to build up the impression that I am masterminding the thing," Doc explained patiently. "He has given the impression that my aids are not to be killed for that reason. That was part of the build-up. He cannot murder them now, without destroying the impression he has so painstakingly created."

"That's logical," Blosser admitted.

The house was large and ancient, partly of stone, the rest of wood. It was not a mansion; it might have seen the days when it was one, but that had been at least fifty years ago. The north wing needed a new roof.

Long Tom and Johnny and Monk were joined by big-fisted Renny, who had been watching the place at close range with young Ted Parks.

The Blossers eyed Parks intently. The younger Blosser gripped Parks' arm.

"You are under arrest," Blosser said, "for suspicion of complicity with Doc Savage in these murders. There is a great deal of evidence pointing at you as one of the killers, as well as at Doc Savage."

Doc was displeased. "I thought you two officers came here to learn the truth."

"And make arrests," Blosser told him coldly. "I have just made one of them."

Without a word, Monk belted young Blosser on the jaw with his fist. Blosser was out for a moment, then sat up groggily, gasping. "What . . . what—"

"That," Monk told him, "was the cancellation of your arrest. You came along to observe, not start asserting authority."

Blosser subsided, concerned with the ache in his jaw, with the grim air of Doc and the others. The darkness was getting more intense. And Doc and the rest seemed to be doing nothing but waiting.

Finally, "Use that chemical on your skins again," Doc

said. "Then spread out. We will approach the house from four directions. No one make any noise. Start getting inside, and try to find the prisoners. That is the first job."

The Blossers watched the others fade away into the darkness.

"You stay with me," Doc told them.

"What about this Parks?" demanded the younger Blosser. "You trust him?"

"Completely," Doc said. "He risked his life last night to make sure we were safe."

"Where does he hook into this?"

"Parks developed this thing you have been calling the invisible death," Doc told him.

Young Blosser literally lifted off the ground. "*What?* Great grief! And you let him run around loose?"

"Quiet!" Doc said. "Here is the house."

The Blossers became reluctantly silent.

Doc added, "My men are completely armed and protected. We will go ahead. You follow."

Doc went forward quietly, drawing a species of hood over his face, a thing that was something like the chain mesh hoods worn by medieval knights. This one was lighter, and the face-piece was of transparent plastic which would arrest any slug carrying less than a thousand foot-pounds of energy. That included most revolver bullets.

He reached a side door, waited. They had outlined a plan of action earlier.

Rensance was to knock on the front door. Rensance had been concealed in the darkness nearby, had not come out while the Blossers were being introduced to the situation. Rensance was embarrassed about having paid extortion; he was anxious to redeem himself. His courage had returned.

Knuckles thundered on the front door. The sound was so loud that the Blossers jumped.

Rensance bellowed, "Quick! Let me in! Open up! I've had to kill one of Doc Savage's men!"

Doc shot out a hand and grabbed young Blosser just as the officer was bent on charging around to the front.

"Trick," Doc whispered. "Quiet!"

Rensance was a good actor. He squalled, "Please let me in! I've got one of Savage's men here! He's dead!"

Doc knew the situation: Rensance at the front door. Monk sprawled out on the walk. Monk with red ink wet on his face. With more red ink in his mouth, so that he could gurgle realistically at the psychological moment. With a knife haft appearing to protrude from his chest. A piece of fakery.

When enough commotion was going on in front to have distracted attention, Doc reached for the doorknob.

The door was not locked, and he went in, cautiously, on toes. The Blossers followed him. No one seemed to be in front of them.

Doc whispered, "Careful about rubbing off that liquid you smeared on yourselves. That is all that stands between you and death!"

The elder Blosser halted abruptly. "You mean if men come here who haven't that stuff on them, they will be in danger?"

Doc said, "They will be facing fairly certain death."

Blosser made a sound that was horror. He wheeled and, before Doc could stop him, leaped back to the rear door.

"Stay back, men!" Blosser bellowed into the night. "There's danger here! Stay back! Don't raid the place!"

The trees tossed echoes of his yell back in the darkness.

Then silence for a moment.

"Who were you yelling to?" Doc asked.

There was something bitter, condemning, in the bronze man's tone which shocked Blosser.

"My men," he said. "Policemen."

"I thought you said you were not bringing officers," Doc said.

"I know." Blosser was miserable. "I was not taking any chances, that's all."

"That precaution," Doc told him, "quite possibly may result in all of us losing our lives."

The bronze man was as near as he ever came to being violently enraged. He seized young Blosser and slammed him across the room. The officer ended up sprawling in a corner. Doc shoved the older Blosser toward the same spot.

He said, "Stay there!" and there was no doubt but that he meant it.

He lunged across the room, tried a door. It was locked. He retreated, brought an arm back, flung an explosive grenade. It exploded against the door like a Fourth-of-July torpedo. The door, through some freak of concussion-tortured air, jumped outward instead of inward. It floated around like a big leaf in the flame and smoke and splinters.

Doc walked through the wreckage.

Monk yelled, "Come on, boys! Joe, Jerry, Fred—you take the left. Half a dozen of you head for the upstairs. The rest of you come with me! Don't crowd!"

Which was typical of Monk in a fight. Sounding like an army. Actually, he was alone.

No Joe, Jerry and Fred. No half dozen to go upstairs. Only Monk. Roaring and bellowing and having the time of his life.

The fight was on, now. And no one had been taken very much by surprise, thanks to the warning Blosser had been forced to shout to the police.

Doc realized both Blossers were following him. Father and son, close together. He whirled on them. And the father snapped, "All right, we made a mistake. So we'll do our part of this fighting."

Monk was yelling to more imaginary men.

At the other end of the house, Renny had started doing the same thing. He was telling his hypothetical army to take the basement.

Some one of the defenders, impressed, bellowed, "Get rid of the prisoners down there!"

That meant the captives were in the basement. Doc headed for the stairs going down. No great ingenuity was exercised in houses of this size, fifty years ago; so he knew about where the basement steps should be. They were there.

He went down. Lieutenant Blosser and his father trailed close on his heels. Their feet was a hard drumming on the steps.

They were shot at, once at the foot of the stairs. The bullet made the side of Doc's left hip ache with a glancing blow, went on, and chipped the bone in young Blosser's left leg. Blosser fell silently, trying to save himself, and upset Doc. They sprawled on the basement floor.

The man with the gun fired again. That one was a complete miss. Doc reached him, chopped down on the gun arm with a fist. Blosser pounced on the gun when it fell.

"Ham!" Doc called.

Ham's voice answered immediately, "Watch out, Doc! They're turning, loose those infernal mosquitoes!"

Ham called from the coal bin, it developed. Doc went

into the place with a flashlight. Three very black, indignant figures proved to be Ham, Pat and Jen Bridges.

"Where are the mosquitoes?" Doc demanded.

"Next door—their workshop," Ham yelled.

Doc told the Blossers, "Untie these people!" and went next door.

He found a room crowded with makeshift chemical apparatus and numerous cases of fine bronze mesh wire. The cases contained mosquitoes of rather unusual species, large and colored, rather like hornets. Large mosquitoes, but not giants. New Jersey has them as big. These were a tropical variety, however.

A man was opening a window. Obviously, his idea was to escape by that route.

Half a dozen of the cages were open, with mosquitoes escaping!

The man did not see Doc until the bronze man reached him. Then he half turned. Doc slugged him! Then Doc picked the fellow up, pitched him out through the basement window.

Chemicals were plainly marked. He picked up three jugs that were inflammable in content, smashed them on the walls. Then he touched a match, and flames crawled like red animals.

He went back and got the prisoners, who were now loose.

"Climb out through the window," he said, "and run for it."

The window was actually a coal chute. They clambered atop the coal, worked out through the chute. Doc came last. It was a tight fit.

There was fighting in the house. Not much. One gun crashing.

Doc lifted his voice.

"Run for it," he shouted. "That 'invisible-box' death is loose!"

He bellowed in Mayan, so that his men would understand and not be likely to mistake his voice for another.

Monk, Renny and the others piled out through windows.

Inside, a voice began bleating in terror.

"Help me!" it screamed.

Monk said, "That's old Uncle Joe Morgan! I'm going in after him."

The homely chemist dived back inside the house. He was not gone long. He had Uncle Joe Morgan over his shoulder when he reappeared. Uncle Joe was tied hand and foot.

Doc said, "You fellows have flares. Light them and scatter them. Blosser, bring in your policemen. As that house burns, those fellows will have to come out. They may have to come out sooner to escape the mosquitoes. Apparently, we have them cornered."

XV

WATCH

Lieutenant Blosser, the father—both father and son were lieutenants, which made it confusing—looked tired when he walked into Doc Savage's office at ten o'clock the following morning.

He carried Ham's pet chimp, Chemistry. He deposited the animal on a table.

"A policeman found him hiding out in the woods," he said.

Monk scowled at the chimp. "Now I *don't* like policemen," he said. "Why'd you have to find that blasted critter?"

Ham snorted.

Pat Savage, Jen Bridges, Uncle Joe Morgan, Long Tom, Renny and Johnny were in the library. All of them looked very tired, but much relieved.

"Where is Mr. Savage?" asked the elder Blosser.

"He and Ted Parks will be here soon," Monk explained. "For some reason, Doc wanted us all together."

Blosser nodded. "The police department owes you an explanation." He fumbled in a pocket, and produced a packet—an article inclosed in waxed paper. He unrolled this. It was a glovelike gadget with thick fingertips. It was made of some kind of composition similar to rubber, but more sticky.

"This," said Blosser, "explains how Doc Savage's fingerprints got in the wrong places."

Monk came over and eyed the glove affair.

"Doc's fingerprints on that?" he demanded.

"Worked into the plastic with a system of photo-engraving," Blosser said. "At least, that's what the police expert tells me. Says he just got copies of Doc's fingerprints and made up these things. The plastic is impregnated with an oil similar to the oil on human skin. It wasn't exact, of course. But it had us fooled."

Monk said, "He was a scientific cuss, the guy behind this."

Blosser nodded. "The fellow must have been."

"Take those death-dealing mosquitoes," Monk grunted.

Blosser hesitated. "You know, the department is a little dubious about those mosquitoes being able to kill a man instantly."

Monk shook his head. "They didn't kill him instantly. It took a few minutes, maybe more than an hour."

"But those men murdered in the gatekeepers' lodge at the Rensance estate—"

"Were murdered with big injections of the poison," Monk said. "Later examination of the bodies will show that."

"But there were mosquitoes loose in the lodge."

"Sure, on the chance we would barge in and get bit."

Blosser was still doubtful. "The department experts," he said, "do not entirely believe the mosquito story."

"Oh, it's simple enough," Monk told him. "Parks was working on the problem of disease-carrying mosquitoes. He was tackling it from the angle of determining just what poisons or germs mosquitoes could carry in their systems without themselves dying. He found out mosquitoes *could* carry a poison that would kill a man, and not leave much trace."

Blosser strode to the window. He glanced at Jen, hesitated.

"I don't mind saying Parks isn't clear yet!" he finally said.

Jen became pale.

"Nonsense!" Ham snapped, and got a grateful look from Jen which Monk immediately wished he had received.

"The murderer simply got a lot of mosquitoes and doped them up with poison," Ham said. "Then he put them in a cellophane box, sent them to the men he wanted to kill—the men who wouldn't pay the sums he asked. That was all there was to it."

"Yes, but the boxes disappeared," Blosser said.

"They couldn't have."

"One of our policemen had one of them which vanished."

"He lost it."

Blosser became indignant. "He did not!"

"All right, I'll prove that the boxes are ordinary cellophane," Ham snapped. "Monk had one of them wrapped up in his coat and shoved in a gunny sack. He turned it over to me to take care of. I've got it right there in the corner. I looked at it not thirty minutes ago, and the box was still there."

"Show me," Blosser challenged.

Ham got the gunny sack, emptied it and became gap-jawed when there was no box.

Monk Mayfair burst into a howl of laughter. "You should see that face of yours!" he told Ham. "It's even dumber than usual."

"What became of it?" Ham asked vacantly.

"Those boxes were made of stuff that just evaporated," Monk said. "In other words, it wasn't cellophane. It was a colorless semi-transparent composition which was volatile at room temperatures. Or you might call it soluble in air. You know these capsules you take medicine in—you know how they dissolve in water? Well, this stuff dissolved in air."

Lieutenant Blosser interrupted. "If I hadn't seen some of the things Doc Savage has developed in the line of scientific gadgets, I wouldn't believe that."

Monk chuckled. "I think the smartest thing Doc did was advertise for a man who had slept three weeks, a radium miner, and the addresses of monkey purchasers."

Blosser was startled. "I still don't understand that."

"Why, Doc did that to tip off the gang that he knew what was going on, but at the same time not give them the idea he knew too much," Monk explained. "This poison is a development of the stuff—germs or whatever they are—that causes sleeping sickness. Any man who had slept three weeks would have to have sleeping sickness of some kind. As soon as Doc advertised for a man who had slept that long, the villains knew he was on the sleeping-sickness trail."

"And the monkeys?"

"Monkeys are used by scientists in experiments with the effects of sleeping sickness and other similar diseases," Monk told the officer. "That was simply another tip-off for the villains."

"Savage wanted them to get scared?"

"Sure. So they'd do something desperate enough to give him a line on them. They did. They began grabbing us, so we couldn't help Doc investigate."

"I see."

Jen Bridges spoke up. "The radium miner—what was he for?"

"That," Monk confessed, "is one I haven't figured out."

A few minutes later, when Doc Savage arrived, Monk put the query to the bronze man.

"Hey, Doc, we can't figure out why the radium miner."

Doc Savage moved to the middle of the room. Parks took a position near the door.

Doc said, "The radium miner? Why, that was a warning to the man behind the extortion murders that we had a clue to his identity. It was intended to excite the fellow."

"How?"

"Because of the method he was using occasionally to signal his men."

Blosser shook his head. "I don't get it."

Doc nodded to Parks. Parks stepped outside, and came back bearing a long box of an affair which had at one end a hood that fitted over a man's head, after the fashion of the light-cloth on a photographer's studio camera.

Long Tom recognized the gadget instantly.

"A homemade fluoroscopic scanner," he declared.

Blosser stared. "A what?"

"It is used to locate objects giving off radioactive emanations, such as X rays."

"Or like radium?"

"Or like radium," Long Tom agreed.

Blosser lost his control and sprang to his feet. "Look here, I'm getting tired of all this talk about scientific gadgets!" he howled. "We want results. Commissioner Strance and District Attorney Einsflagen want to know who the man behind this was. None of our prisoners will admit knowing. Who was he?"

"The man behind it," Doc Savage said, "was the one who used his watch to signal his men."

"Huh?"

Doc said patiently, "In the very beginning of this thing, the brains of the organization had to signal his men to make an attempt on my life, and prepare a trap for me. We were watching him; so he was not able to talk to anyone, write a message, use a radio, or speak over a telephone. He had surmised such a situation might develop, and he was prepared for it. This fellow liked gadgets. So he had rigged up the device for spotting radioactive emanations. He had put a bit of radioactive mineral inside his watchcase. The watchcase was lead-covered. Lead will stop radium emanations of small power, such as these were."

Blosser understood that. "You mean he just opened and shut his watchcase to make dots and dashes, and somebody across the street, or somewhere nearby, watched through that fluoroscopic scanner and read it."

"A trifle fantastic," Doc admitted, "but true. As I reminded you, this mastermind is rather silly on the subject of chemical and mechanical gadgets."

"Who is he?"

Doc turned to Ted Parks. "Parks, who is one of the cleverest men you know along that line? Who was your assistant for some time in your experiments?"

"Why, Uncle Joe Morgan, there," Parks said. "I went to South America on Uncle Joe's small boat, and he helped me with the work on mosquitoes—"

Doc said, "Morgan, let us see your watch."

Uncle Joe Morgan cursed terribly, sprang to his feet. They did not, however, find out what wild thing he contemplated doing because one of his ankles was tied to his chair, and he fell flat on his face.

It was a simple matter for Monk to stroll over and sit on the back of Uncle Joe's neck.

Monk looked at the chimp, Chemistry, with an expression that was almost approving.

"Now I know what has been tying tin cans and ugly pictures to my hog," he said. "Ham, you've taught that danged what-is-it of yours to tie knots."

Doc removed the watch from Uncle Joe Morgan's pocket and tossed it to Blosser without a word. Blosser examined the watch. He held it in front of the contrivance for making radioactive emanations visible to the unaided eye.

"Uncle Joe it is, all right," he said. He sure set a trail to you, Doc, and to Ted Parks when Parks threatened his chance to get all that money."

After that, he went to the door and yelled at a policeman posted in the hall.

"Fetch a pair of handcuffs in here, Andy," he said.

BIRDS OF DEATH

Contents

I

TO CATCH A CANARY

The afternoon sun sprayed gay cream-colored light on the tall buildings which surrounded the park in the center of the city. But shadows lay across most of the park itself, taking the glare off the sidewalks and darkening the trees.

The darkest shadows in the park were probably those in the low bushes beyond the lagoon.

In one of these bushes was the canary. It was a genuine, if ordinary, canary, as yellow as any canary. It flew around a little.

Two men had watched the canary fly down from a window of one of the apartment houses. The two men were now trying to catch the canary.

They were rather serious about it, because on catching the canary depended whether or not they would kill a man.

One pointed. "There is goes, Abner. Right there," he said.

He was the small man, the well-dressed one, the important one. He had the suit by the Fifty-seventh Street tailor, the custom-made shirt, the five-dollar cravat. He was the short man, the thin one.

Abner—the other man—said, "I'll get around the other side of the bush, Mr. Manley. You wanna give me the end of the net, huh? Maybe we can pen the dang thing up."

He was the big man, the one who was crudely dressed. Not cheaply attired. Crudely. The crudeness was in the size of the checks in his suit, the raw, ungentle color of his shirt. No one would ever call his necktie a cravat. It was common necktie, forty-nine cents on Broadway.

The dang thing referred to was the canary. They went about the business of catching it.

There was one other mistake no one would ever make about them, and that was: They were not friends, they couldn't be. And neither could they be business associates. The only possible status between them was that of the man who gave orders, and the one who executed them. One was

Brains, and the other was Muscle. More nearly exact, one was Thug Muscle.

The net was half a dozen yards of the stuff called "mosquito bar" in the South, or mosquito netting. Mr. Manley had thoughtfully provided himself with this. It was still in the paper sack, the way it had been handed to him in the store where he bought it. He took the net out of the sack.

"Take the end, Abner," he commanded.

At the edge of the park, the towering apartment house showed a window-freckled wall.

From the apartment-house window out of which the canary had flown in escape a few minutes ago, a man leaned. He waved his arms. He put his hands on edge against his mouth and shouted. What he yelled was not understandable.

"Mr. Manley," said Abner.

"Yes?"

"A man is yelling out of the window."

"Who is it?" demanded Mr. Manley.

"I think it's that servant, Julian."

"You sure it's not Benjamin Boot, himself? Be sure about that. If it's Boot looking out of that window now, I want to know it."

"It's the servant."

"Good. The servant is shouting to attract Benjamin Boot's attention. Boot is probably in another room of the apartment," said Mr. Manley. "Abner, let's catch that canary."

They stretched out the mosquito netting. The afternoon breeze caught it and wafted it like a plume of smoke. Six yards was eighteen feet of netting, and it was hard to manage.

The canary sat in the bush and twittered derisively at them.

High up in the apartment-house window, there was a change in figures leaning out. The servant, Julian, withdrew. Another man appeared. He wore a dressing gown that was very yellow indeed, about the color of the canary.

Abner said, "Benjamin Boot has come to the window, Mr. Manley."

"Good," said Mr. Manley. "Punch me, and draw my attention to him. Let's make this a well-rounded job of acting."

Abner punched Mr. Manley, pointed at the window. Mr. Manley looked up. The man in yellow robe waved his arms like an airplane propeller. Mr. Manley pointed at the bush where the canary sat, and waved back. The man in the yellow robe disappeared from the window.

"He's coming down here," said Mr. Manley. "Hurry up and catch that damned canary. And Abner—remember this is part of a murder, and the police do not think murders are funny."

Benjamin Boot sprinted through the park with yellow robe flying. Under the robe he wore buff-colored pajamas, and bedroom slippers of matching color clung to his pounding feet.

He arrived all out of breath at the scene of the canary catching.

"For gosh sakes, don't hurt Elmo!" he exclaimed apprehensively.

Benjamin Boot was a tall young man with an excellent pair of legs, superb shoulders—in fact, a body that was so perfectly fashioned that it was beautiful. His hands, however, were very large and knobby, and his face extremely homely.

Elmo was the canary.

"Come, Elmo, come, come," said Benjamin Boot anxiously. "Say, I'm sure glad you fellows caught Elmo."

Concern and delight mingled on Benjamin Boot's homely face, and the result made the face something with which to haunt a house. Young Boot's face was not exactly ugly. Stupid was more the word. The face was a dumb, illiterate, foolish, simple, shallow, dense, donkeylike, wooden one.

Mr. Manley smiled.

"Glad to be of service," he said heartily. "I just happened to notice the bird as I was passing by, and this stranger"—he glanced at Abner—"was kind enough to assist me, weren't you, Mr.—"

"Mr. Jones is the name," lied Abner.

"I am Mr. Manley," said Mr. Manley.

The owner of the canary extended a toadlike hand.

"I am Benjamin Boot," he said. "This is my canary, Elmo, and I sure love him. I wouldn't part with Elmo for anything. I couldn't get along without him. That jackass of a manservant of mine, Julian, accidentally let Elmo out of his cage. I'm everlastingly grateful to you fellows."

"It's nothing," said Manley. "I'm glad to be of service. It was fortunate I had this mosquito netting along. I was taking it home to my wife, who was going to make some butterfly nets. She collects butterflies."

Benjamin Boot eyed the netting.

"The net is all messed up," he said. "I'll buy you some more."

"You needn't mind."

Benjamin Boot thrust a hand in his robe pocket, then looked crestfallen. "Gosh, I haven't any money with me. I was going to offer you a reward."

"Oh, no, no, we couldn't think of that," said Mr. Manley.

"Nah, we couldn't," echoed Abner, rather reluctantly.

Benjamin Boot showed a great deal of concern.

"Mercy me, you gentlemen just have to let me do something for you to show my gratitude," he said.

"You don't owe us a thing," insisted Manley.

"Oh, but I insist, I really do. Would you—ah—accept a drink and some cigars in my apartment?"

Mr. Manley melted somewhat. "Well, now," he said, hesitating, "I might do that. How about you, Mr.—"

"Jones," said Abner. "Yeah, I might stand a snifter of whiskey."

"Oh, my, I'm afraid I don't have anything that strong," said Benjamin Boot, abashed.

"O. K., I'll go along and take the cigars, then," said Abner hastily.

They moved toward the apartment house.

Benjamin Boot, showing exquisite delight over the recovery of Elmo, walked ahead, cooing to the canary and petting the bird.

Mr. Manley and Abner dropped behind.

Abner whispered from the side of his mouth, "This guy is a pantywaist. Hell, he's silly over the damned bird!"

Mr. Manley nodded. "Fine, fine. Our plan of bribing Julian to release the canary was excellent. It is getting us invited into Boot's apartment."

Abner asked, "When we get this milk-toast in his apartment, what do we do?"

Mr. Manley eyed Abner appraisingly.

"You have your knife, Abner?"

"Yeah."

"Do you think you can get it in Benjamin Boot's back without too much fuss?"

"Just watch me!" Abner's face became uneasy. "What about the servant, Julian?"

"I have a knife of my own for Julian," said Mr. Manley.

"It's gonna be a pipe," said Abner. "Like takin' two babies."

A Mr. Manley and an Abner who were highly satisfied with themselves got into an elevator in the apartment building and were carried to the twenty-third floor, where they stepped out into a cream hall that had only one door, the single door indicating that Benjamin Boot's apartment was a large one. Apartments occupying entire floors in this neighborhood cost around twelve thousand dollars a year.

Benjamin Boot unlocked the door, and stepped back for Mr. Manley to enter. They went inside. Benjamin Boot stepped in after them. He hit Mr. Manley a blow on the jaw. He turned and hit Abner's jaw a blow. Neither punch seemed hard, but the recipients flew backward and actually bounced off the walls.

Benjamin Boot examined Mr. Manley and Abner for signs of consciousness. He distinguished none.

"Julian!" he called.

The manservant appeared. He was a skinny man who perpetually looked as if he had an apple about half swallowed.

"Julian," said Benjamin Boot, "here they are."

"Yes, sir," replied Julian.

"Now what do we do with them?"

"I don't know, sir."

"Are they the pair who bribed you?"

"Yes, they are, sir."

"Which one," asked Benjamin Boot, "actually paid you the money?"

"This gentleman," said Julian, indicating Mr. Manley.

"I suggest you return the sum you accepted, Julian. Since you did not fulfill your contracted duty, you did not earn the bribe. I shall myself reimburse you handsomely for doing the proper thing. Honesty always pays, Julian."

"Yes, sir," said Julian. "Shall I tie them up?"

"Yes, tie them by all means. But first, let me examine the contents of their pockets."

Their pockets proved to have no contents except a little silver and paper money which in grand total was not twenty dollars. A pair of knife scabbards, one on each man, was a different matter. Benjamin Boot withdrew the long steel blades which these held and tested their edges admiringly with his thumb. He flipped the blades away and they stuck in the hard oak paneling. It was rather expert flipping.

"Nothing to identify them," he remarked. "What an excellent pair of unidentified corpses they would make!"

Julian, the manservant, looked frightened. "The police, sir, have so many ways of doing things," he said. "It might be of danger to—ah—"

"I contemplate no violence, Julian."

"I am glad, sir." The servant was relieved.

They tied Mr. Manley and Abner. The manservant did the preliminary placing of the ropes, but Benjamin Boot tied the actual knots. He did an excellent job.

Benjamin Boot walked to a window, stood there rubbing his jaw and contemplating the park. Behind him, Elmo the canary twittered in his cage, to which he had been returned. Suddenly Benjamin Boot whirled.

He said, "Julian, are you sure you don't know why these men approached you with their silly scheme for getting into my apartment?"

"I have no idea," insisted Julian.

"It's a confounded mystery, then!" snapped Boot.

"Yes, sir."

"The dangerous part of it is," said Boot, "that the mystery involves Miss Moldenhaeur and her father, it would seem."

"Yes, sir."

"I've got to get at the bottom of the thing, Julian. I didn't sleep at all last night, wondering about it. I can't have that. I've got to have my sleep. To say nothing of the fact that I'm in love with Miss Moldenhaeur."

Julian ventured, "Begging your pardon, sir, but I do not think Miss Moldenhaeur is aware of your deep affection. Perhaps if you made some slight move toward letting her know—"

Benjamin Boot shook his head vehemently. "Nothing doing. I told a young woman I loved her once. She looked at my face, and didn't stop laughing for a week."

"I'm sorry, sir," said Julian.

"I was sorry, too,'" said Boot. "I also ruined the laughter-filled young lady's father in a business deal, and the laughing damsel had to become a waitress in a greasy-spoon restaurant. I was sorry I did that, too. I was sorry all around. I'm always the one who is sorry. I was a baby lying in my cradle when I started being sorry about being born so homely."

"Yes, sir."

"Lay out my gray business suit, Julian. And see that I get dressed in a hurry."

Benjamin Boot walked through a living room with heliotrope wallpaper in delicate design and dainty furniture, into a bedroom with tender pink-coral walls, a white wall, and a lovely old bedroom suite in ancient ivory. There were flowers growing everywhere, several more canaries, and exquisite pictures on the walls. The apartment was a thing of loveliness, arranged with a touch somehow more dainty than a woman could have managed.

"Julian," said Boot, "did you ever hear of man named Doc Savage?"

"Yes, sir," replied the servant.

"What have you heard about him?"

"Mr. Savage composed a series of selections particularly adapted to the violin," Julian replied. "There is a touch of genius to the work. They are going to become famous in future centuries."

Benjamin Boot was surprised.

"Oh, so he composes music, too! I had heard of him as a scientist. One of my mining companies is using an invention of his for using very short ultraviolet rays to locate deposits of fluorescent minerals at night. Such minerals as scheelite, which is seventy percent tungsten."

Julian hesitated. "I . . . ah . . . have heard of Doc Savage as a man of violence, too."

Benjamin Boot laughed.

"That," he said, "is why I am going to see Doc Savage about this confounded mystery. I think this affair needs his peculiar brand of violence. And, take it from me, Julian, the violence of Doc Savage is in a class by itself."

"Yes, sir."

"Also take good care of the two prisoners, Julian. In case they should escape, I feel almost sure I would separate you from your ears."

"Yes, sir."

II

MYSTERY AT MOLDENHAEUR

Benjamin Boot entered a skyscraper in the center of the city. He was exceedingly well dressed, twirled a cane, and hummed thoughtfully. Seen from the rear, he gave the impression of a male movie star, but viewed from the front his homely, stupid, asinine face so dominated his appearance that he looked like a harmless half-wit out for the afternoon.

The skyscraper was the tallest in that part of the city. He went to the elevator starter.

"Doc Savage?" said the starter. "Go around that corner there, and take the private elevator."

"I have heard his headquarters are on the eighty-sixth floor?" said Boot. "Is that correct?"

"Take the elevator around the corner," said the starter.

Benjamin Boot took an elevator operated by push buttons. On the control there was only one button, and that one was labeled, *Doc Savage*. He punched the button. The cage rose only a few floors—no more than five—and stopped, the door opening.

Boot found himself in a brightly lighted room, undergoing an inspection from two men.

Boot took a look at the two men, and wondered if he could have accidentally gotten into an office which booked animal acts for side shows.

One of the men examining him had a pet pig with enormous ears and long legs. The other man had a pet baboon—some kind of an outside member of the monkey family, at least—which had a marked resemblance to the fellow who owned the pig.

Boot warmed toward the homely man. The latter was one of the few individuals Boot had ever met who was as homely as himself.

"Ah, good afternoon," said Boot.

The homely man stood up. "I'm Monk Mayfair." He nodded at his companion, who was already in evening dress, tails. "This fashion plate is Ham Brooks. What can we do for you?"

"My name is Benjamin Boot," said Boot.

"The owner of the Boot Mines?" asked Ham Brooks, the dapper man.

Benjamin Boot nodded. "And some railroads, ships and ranches and things," he said. "I came here in the hopes of seeing Doc Savage."

"You're in the right place," Monk informed him. "This is the going-over station. We look you over, and find out if your business is important enough to interrupt some experiments in electrochemistry that Doc is conducting."

Boot frowned. "Just what position do you gentlemen occupy in relation to Mr. Savage?"

"We're his right and left hands," Monk said.

Ham Brooks said, "That's exaggerating, Mr. Boot. Mr. Savage has five assistants, of whom we happen to be two."

"Brooks . . . Brooks," said Boot thoughtfully. "I have heard of a noted lawyer by that name. A Harvard man. Quite famous. Any relation?"

"No relation," Ham said, smiling, "but I happened to be the lawyer of whom you are thinking, I imagine."

Benjamin Boot was impressed. If Doc Savage had an assistant the caliber of Ham Brooks—Brigadier General Theodore Marley Brooks, his full title—the man himself must be extraordinary.

He said, "I want to see Mr. Savage about a mysterious thing that has happened. A business associate has disappeared, and a young lady of whom I am . . . er . . . fond, who is also the associate's daughter, has become strangely terrified. On top of that, two men have just sought to kill me."

Ham examined Boot's face thoughtfully.

"That sounds urgent enough," he said.

Doc Savage exceeded any of Benjamin Boot's expectations. The name of Clark Savage, Jr., had come vaguely to Boot's attention several times in the past, but his actual knowledge of Doc Savage was not extensive. He had heard that the man was a scientist, student, something of a mental wizard—and had a unique hobby of righting wrongs and punishing evildoers in the far ends of the earth. Savage had a name of being the man to go to when in trouble of such a nature that the police might be helpless for one reason or another.

"Goodness!" said Benjamin Boot. "I didn't expect a

giant . . . er . . . I mean, how do you do, Mr. Savage. My name is Boot—Benjamin Boot."

Doc Savage's unusual features included remarkable flake-gold eyes that were like tiny pools of the metal always stirred by tiny winds. His size was huge, yet proportioned so that is was not apparent until one came close. His skin was deeply bronzed, and his hair was straight, a bronze hue a little darker than his skin. The total effect was almost that of a man made out of metal.

"Please be seated, Mr. Boot," he said.

Boot sat down. He held his hat in his hands. He said, rather embarrassed, "I—ah—your associates passed me. I had heard of Mr. Brooks, the attorney. The other man—Mr. Monk Mayfair, I believe he said his name was—was a stranger."

Doc Savage said, "Monk Mayfair is probably the most skilled industrial chemist in the world."

Two things about the remark astonished Benjamin Boot. First, the idea of a fellow as dumb-looking as Monk being a famous chemist. And secondly, the rather amazing quality of control and vitality in the bronze man's voice.

"I'll try not to waste your time," said Boot. "Is it all right if I start my story?"

"Proceed."

"I am Benjamin Boot, and I am a rather wealthy man, owning a number of enterprises. I am not saying I am wealthy because I am proud of it. In fact, the contrary. I happen to be wealthy because I was born into this world such a homely, stupid-looking fellow that there was nothing for me to do but devote my time to making money. Girls would never have anything to do with me, and I have few men friends, because they invariably make cracks about my looks, and I do not like that. So I'm a lonely man, and a rich one. I love beautiful things. I spend much time in my greenhouses with my flowers, or in my aviaries with my birds, or listening to fine music and admiring fine paintings."

Doc Savage nodded. His flake-gold eyes had traveled over Benjamin Boot completely, from head to foot, with such a thorough intentness that Boot felt as if his mind had been read.

Boot said, "I have a business associate named Winton Moldenhaeur."

"The industrialist?"

"Yes."

"Head of the Moldenhaeur Chemical Enterprises?"

"Yes."

"Proceed," Doc Savage said.

"He has disappeared—or something has happened to him," said Boot. "We had a deal on. I was to meet him four days ago. He didn't keep the appointment. I couldn't locate him. No one connected with him seemed to know what had become of him."

"What about his family?"

"I went to see his daughter, Liona," explained Boot. "I saw at once that the young woman was terrified. I asked her where her father was. She said she didn't know. I saw all during her conversation that she was beside herself with fear, or some such emotion."

"Did she explain why she was frightened, or did you ask?"

"I asked. She said she wasn't. That was not the truth."

"Then what?"

"I suggested that we notify the Missing Persons bureau of the police department that her father was gone. She burst into tears. All her terror seemed to be brought out by my suggestion that we call the police. She practically ran me off the place."

Benjamin Boot was silent for a moment, frowning.

"I love Liona Moldenhaeur," he said. "I have never told her so. I probably never shall. I would not want her to laugh at me. It would hurt me deeply. But I left there—left her home—wanting to help her more than I ever wanted to help anyone else."

"And then?"

"And then two men tried to bribe my servant, get into my apartment, and kill me," said Boot. "I have the two men prisoners. My servant is watching them."

Doc Savage asked, "Did you tell Miss Moldenhaeur anything else?"

Boot shook his head.

Then, "Oh, yes, I did," he said. "I told her I was going to help her whether she wanted it or not. I remember that now."

"That might have a bearing on what happened to you," the bronze man said. "By the way, Mr. Boot, just what do you want me to do?"

"Investigate this. If Miss Moldenhaeur is in trouble, help her. Help her father."

"That sounds like the job of a private detective."

"That's why I came to you."

"You seem to misunderstand," Doc Savage said patiently. "I am not a private detective, nor are my associates. We are simply a group banded together by love of excitement, more than anything else, to do things which we think need doing."

"I'll pay—"

"We do not accept pay."

"I'll pay any reasonable sum to any reasonable charity you suggest," said Benjamin Boot.

"I am sorry."

Benjamin Boot started up. "You mean you won't help me?"

"I am sorry, no."

Boot purpled. "But why?" he yelled.

"I see no necessity of explaining motives. Good evening, Mr. Boot."

Benjamin Boot yelled, "This is a hell of a note!" and stamped out.

Doc Savage swung to the box-shaped office intercommunicator on the inlaid table in the reception room where he had been talking to Benjamin Boot. He flipped the switch on the box, said, "Monk."

"Yeah?" said Monk Mayfair's small, rather squeaky voice.

"That fellow Boot," Doc said.

"Yes?"

"He is on his way out of the building. You and Ham follow him. Check on everything he does. If he goes to his apartment, pay him a visit, make use of your special police commissions, and take charge of the two men he says tried to kill him."

Monk asked, "Are we stepping into this trouble Boot seems to have found?"

Doc said, "We are going to learn more about Mr. Boot before we commit ourselves. Better get going, you two."

"Right," Monk said.

Doc switched off the intercommunicator. Adjacent to the reception room was a larger room containing a scientific library. Beyond that—and covering the remainder of the eighty-sixth floor of the skyscraper—was the scientific laboratory.

The bronze man used a short-wave radio transmitter in the laboratory, called into the microphone, "Johnny, Long Tom, Renny."

Almost instantly, a voice answered, "Long Tom."

Then, in a few moments, "Renny speaking," rumbled a deep voice that could have come from a sleepy bull. "I don't think Johnny is on deck. He went up to Westchester, where some explorer from South America has a pre-Inca tablet of some kind that he wants Johnny to translate."

Doc said, "Renny, Long Tom, meet me in forty-five minutes at a spot half a mile south of the Winton Moldenhaeur mansion in Bayside."

"Right," Long Tom said.

"Holy cow, so something has started!" Renny rumbled. "I'll be there."

The bronze man got a few things from the laboratory, small articles which he placed in the pockets in the fabric of a bulletproof vest which he donned. The vest was not of steel plates, the usual construction, but was made of a chain alloy mail which was lighter, more flexible, and fully as good.

He took a car from a private garage in the basement. A garage, its driveway on a side street, which passers-by no doubt mistook for a delivery entrance, if they gave it any thought at all. He used a sedan, an ordinary-looking machine, and drove fast.

Because he did drive fast, he was able to spot the man who was following him. The man drove a coupé, small and fast. But his frantic dodging in an effort to keep the bronze man in sight made his presence obvious in the rear-view mirror.

Doc drove more slowly. He changed his direction, so that he was not heading toward Bayside, although still going in the general direction.

He kept in the traffic of a parkway, got into the region of truck farms, and turned off on a narrow road, paved with blacktop.

It was getting dark now, being the time of the evening when the sun does not seem to furnish sufficient light for driving, and yet automobile headlights also seemed inadequate.

The road was quite deserted.

Doc Savage reached under the dash and twisted a small valve in a copper pipe line of small diameter. The engine then made a faint frying noise as the chemicals from a tank poured through the line into the hot exhaust line, were turned to vapor by the heat, and came out of the exhaust pipe a grayish fog, as if the motor was burning a little cylinder oil.

Doc drove on three quarters of a mile, turned into a crossroad, backed, and retraced the route he had just come.

He stopped his machine near the coupé which had been following him. The coupé now lay on its side in the ditch.

The bronze man put on a gas mask, got out, went to the coupé.

A young, square-bodied man with a freckled face and red hair was asleep from the gas in the car. Doc Savage pulled him out. Doc looked in the glove compartment, and then in the baggage compartment at the rear of the coupé, but found nothing except some rusty tools.

Doc put the young man beside him, and drove toward the Moldenhaeur place in Bayside.

III

THE HORRIBLE THING

The Winton Moldenhaeur mansion sat in nearly a hundred acres of carefully-kept grounds. From the mansion itself—there were several buildings perched on a bulking knoll overlooking Long Island Sound—a paved road led curvingly through the trees and beyond a stone-arched gate, where it joined a highway. Some distance south on this highway, a lane turned off through some scraggled trees.

Doc Savage pulled into this lane, stopped under the trees. Two cars, two men, were already there. The men—Renny and Long Tom, the pair he had radioed—approached.

Colonel John Renny Renwick, was almost as big a man as Doc Savage, and notable for the overgrown size of his fists and his perpetually sad expression. He had considerable reputation as an engineer.

Major Thomas J. Long Tom Roberts looked as if he had matured in a cellar. He had no color, no appearance of health. The impression of feebleness was deceptive, as many a robust fellow had discovered. His specialty was electricity.

These two members of Doc Savage's group of five associates stared at the burly red-headed stranger in the bronze man's car.

"Holy cow!" Renny exclaimed. "Who's the sleeping beauty, here?"

"I do not know"—it was a peculiarity of the bronze man's

that his voice rarely showed any emotion—"but he was following me. I released some of that gas Monk is trying to develop for use by military airplanes in battle, and he has not yet recovered from the effects."

Renny and Long Tom showed no surprise at the bronze man's matter-of-fact casualties. They had heard him sound as unconcerned with violent death crashing toward him, and knew it was a sign of his amazing mental control. A stranger would have been astounded.

Doc added, "We might go through his pockets."

O'Brien O'Callaghan was the unconscious red-headed man's name. They found that on his driver's license. The license was New York State.

"Name sure fits him," Renny said, chuckling. "He's sure a bit of the ould sod. Faith, and that he is."

Long Tom fanned through the contents of Mr. O'Callaghan's billfold. "Six hundred and ten dollars," he said. "He goes well heeled."

Doc Savage went through some papers from the young man's pocket.

O'Brien O'Callaghan was associated with someone named Sam John Thomas, Inc., in the capacity of general research engineer.

There was also a newspaper clipping. It said:

> Aboard the *Yankee Clipper* when it arrived from Portugal today was Sean Larkin, Irish politician, Maurice Revel, French minister, and O'Brien O'Callaghan, of South Africa.

The clipping was dated two weeks previously.

"He isn't a small-timer, whoever he is," Long Tom remarked. "Flying the Atlantic by plane these days costs money."

Doc Savage turned a flashlight on O'Brien O'Callaghan's skin. It was deeply tanned. In fact, it was like leather. He opened the young man's shirt. The skin there was also tanned.

Doc took off O'Callaghan's shoes and socks.

Renny stared and said, "He's been going barefoot."

Long Tom Roberts got down and poked the soles of O'Brien O'Callaghan's feet with a thumb. "Regular hoofs," he said. "The skin on the bottom of his feet is half an inch thick. He's gone barefoot for years."

Doc Savage made no comment, except to ask, "Which one of you prefers to stay here with him?"

Neither Renny nor Long Tom preferred it. Finally, "Oh, well, I'll match you to see who stays," Long Tom said. And then, when he had lost, he grumbled, "The lug probably won't want to talk to me when he wakes up."

Doc Savage and Renny climbed in one of the cars and drove toward the Winton Moldenhaeur estate.

The gate was big, but it was closed with steel. The stone walls were at least a yard thick, and to the left and right there were small pillboxes of stone, perforated with windows high up.

A man put his head and a rifle out of the right-hand pillbox, asked, "Who're you guys and whatcha want?"

Big-fisted Renny Renwick turned the beam of a flashlight upward. It illuminated the rifleman, disclosed that he had a round, determined face, red nose, large ears, and the general air of a rock.

"Holy cow!" Renny exclaimed. "It's Ollie Saff. Imagine finding you here!"

A flashlight beam jumped down upon them, and Ollie Saff said, "For the love o' little fish! My old boss, Renny Renwick!"

"How are you, Ollie?" Renny said. "I haven't see you since that dam job on the Nile River, years ago. What on earth are you doing here?"

"I'm a night watchman," said Ollie Saff. "And danged if I don't like it better than contracting!" He shifted his flash beam to Doc. "Is that Doc Savage? I've heard a lot about him."

Renny said, "Yes, it's Doc Savage. Come on down, Ollie. We want to talk to Moldenhaeur."

Ollie came down, threw the gate open. "You won't talk to Moldenhaeur," he said. "Anyhow, nobody has seen him for several days."

"Miss Moldenhaeur will have to do then, Ollie," Renny said.

"Well, she's here." Ollie Saff eyed them, rubbed his jaw uneasily. "You know, I'm glad to see you fellows. Something is wrong here."

"What?" Doc Savage asked.

"I don't know. All I know is that Liona Moldenhaeur is

scared stiff for some reason, afraid to leave the house, and afraid to have anybody come. That's why all the servants have been laid off, and only I'm here. And I'm not allowed near the house. My orders are to stay down here with a rifle, and not let anybody in."

"That sounds rather unusual," Doc told him. "Are you going to let us in?"

Ollie Saff chuckled.

"Officially, no," he said. "The stone wall around the estate is wired with a burglar alarm. One of those capacity things which goes off if any prowler comes near the top of the wall, or tries to tunnel through." He peered at them foxily. "I guess the thing didn't work. Anyhow, I haven't seen you."

"Thank you," Doc Savage said.

"You're welcome. When you leave, I wish you'd satisfy my curiosity about what is wrong up there."

Doc nodded. "You knew Mr. Renwick in Africa?"

"Renny? sure. On the Nile job. British government project."

"It is a small world, after all," Doc remarked conversationally. "How long since you left Africa, Mr. Saff?"

There was an abrupt silence.

"Four years," Ollie Saff said.

Renny said, "It was only three years ago when you worked with me on the Nile job."

"Uh—I left right after that," said Ollie Saff.

Doc said, "Well, thank you very much for letting us in."

Ollie Saff made no comment. He seemed rather subdued.

Doc Savage and Renny left their car parked near the gate, on the outside of the estate, and walked along a winding path bordered with tropical pines, overhung with weeping willow.

"He seemed a little uncertain when he left Africa," Doc remarked.

"Yes, didn't he?" Renny muttered. "That guy you caught following you, O'Brien O'Callaghan, was from Africa, too."

Doc offered no comment but he turned abruptly off the path, and started to circle back to the gate, keeping in the cover of the shrubbery.

"Where you goin'?" whispered Renny.

"Did you notice Mr. Saff's shoes? Very large. They seemed uncomfortable on him."

"Holy cow!" Renny said.

Early in his strange career of righting wrongs and punishing evildoers, the bronze man had developed a gas. The gas was an anaesthetic, quick-acting, odorless, colorless, and produced a harmless unconsciousness. Ordinarily the bronze man carried it in thin-walled gas containers, liquefied, which would burst and disperse the stuff without too much commotion.

From concealment in the darkened shrubbery, Doc Savage broke an anaesthetic gas container near Ollie Saff. The man shortly collapsed.

Renny removed Ollie Saff's shoes.

"Yeah," he said. "Been going barefooted a long time. Sole hide like leather."

"Is his skin tanned?" Doc asked.

Renny looked. "Like an Indian."

Doc Savage remarked thoughtfully, "It does not take long for a man to lose a tan in civilization."

Renny grunted. "I'll see if he's got anything else interesting on him."

Saff didn't have. They left him there. Renny said, "He'll wake up in twenty minutes or so and wonder like the dickens what made him faint, but otherwise he'll be all right."

Doc Savage was already walking toward the Moldenhaeur house.

Liona Moldenhaeur was a frightened girl in a gray slack suit. Her face was not beautiful in a spectacular sense, but she was attractive. She looked kind. Her face was pale. Her eyes were dark. Her hair was still darker, although not as dark as the barrel of the automatic shotgun she held when she opened the door.

"Miss Moldenhaeur?" Doc Savage asked.

She had her mouth open, obviously to order them away in words they would not fail to understand. But the bronze man's voice, the power and friendship in it, stayed her, caused her to look at him. She had switched on the portico light. Looking at Doc Savage impressed her even more.

"I . . . yes," she said, hesitating. "I am Miss Moldenhaeur."

"This is Mr. Renwick," Doc said. "I am Clark Savage. Could we speak with you?"

"I . . . I'm afraid not," she said. "I'm very—well, I'm not feeling well. If it's business, you can take it up with my father's general manager."

"It is not business."

She frowned. "It couldn't be anything else. I have never seen you before."

"Do you know Benjamin Boot?"

Her eyes flew wide, exposing the utter fear in their depths. "Yes . . . yes, I do."

"He suggested we come."

Liona Moldenhaeur's lips compressed. "Ben Boot is a fool. I told him I don't want help. You go back to him and tell him to mind his own business."

Doc said, "Two men tried to kill Mr. Boot this afternoon, another man tried to trail me here. The name of the latter man is O'Brien O'Callaghan. Do you know him?"

Her eyes went even wider. Then they narrowed.

"O'Callaghan—" she said. "No . . . no, I do not know him."

Doc watched her. "Where is your father?" he asked.

Color left her face. "He . . . isn't here?"

"Where is he?"

"He went away. A business trip."

"Why are you becoming pale?" the bronze man asked.

Her answer was motion. She jumped back, tried to slam the door. The bronze man, moving with what looked deceptively like idle unhaste, was inside before she got that done. And with a continuation of the same unexcited movement, he took the shotgun out of her hands.

Renny followed them inside and closed the door.

The girl sank down on a thronelike hall chair, covered her face with her hands.

Doc Savage said, "We are sorry, naturally, Miss Moldenhaeur. But something is wrong. We have decided to investigate it. There is nothing—we hope—that you can do to prevent that. Why don't you take a sensible attitude?"

She began to tremble, then to sob. She was, the bronze man saw, in no condition to talk.

"You stay with her," he told Renny.

He left the big-fisted engineer with Miss Moldenhaeur, and began searching the house. He took the ground floor first. The place was as magnificent as it had seemed from the outside. The rug in the west-wing parlor was an Oriental piece worth fully twenty thousand dollars, and the other furnishings were in keeping. The bronze man searched systematically, unawed by the magnificence.

The only thing he found on the ground floor was evidence—

in the shape of undusted furniture, mostly—that servants had not been in the house for several days. In the kitchen, only one person, apparently, had been preparing meals.

Upstairs, it was different.

There was a locked room. The bronze man examined the door. It was heavy. The lock was a modern one; the keyhole did not go entirely through. He rapped, received no answer, and went to work on the door lock with a thin metal probe, one of the gadgets which he had brought along. He worked three or four minutes, during which there was no sound from the room, and got the door open.

It was a bedroom, a huge thing, fitted with a desk and office equipment as well as sleeping accommodations.

He went to the man on the bed. The man looked as if he might be asleep.

The man was tall, a well-preserved, fifty perhaps, and there was a feeling of competence about him. He looked so natural, so certainly asleep, that Doc spoke.

"Wake up!" the bronze man said.

The man did not move. He had the features of the girl downstairs. Doc had never met him. But the man was so famous that his picture had often been in the newspapers. He was the industrialist, Winton Moldenhaeur.

Doc took his wrist. There was no pulse. Winton Moldenhaeur was not breathing.

And yet there was the conviction, absurd though it might seem, that the man was not dead.

Too, his feet were extremely calloused.

As Doc Savage came down the stairs, Liona Moldenhaeur looked at him. She had stopped sobbing. "You . . . you found him?" she asked.

The bronze man nodded. "How long has he been that way?"

"Since a week from last Monday," she said.

"That would be ten days."

"Yes."

For the first time the bronze man's face showed a ripple of astonishment.

He said, "The man is your father, of course?"

She nodded.

"All right, give us the story," he said. "First, tell us why you were trying to keep his condition secret?"

Liona Moldenhaeur shuddered. "Two weeks ago, he told me he was afraid something horrible would happen to him. He made a peculiar request. He said that if he should die, he would not be dead. He said that if he did die, or appear to do so, I was not to call a doctor, or let anyone see him. He told me a doctor would not be able to help, and that he would be pronounced dead by the doctor, and buried, or turned over to an undertaker and embalmed. I think that is what horrified him the most—the fear of being embalmed."

Doc Savage's flake-gold eyes fixed on the girl. "Your father knew something was going to happen to him?"

"Yes."

"How did he know that?"

She said, "I am not sure, but I think he had been threatened."

"Threatened by whom?"

"He gave me no details."

"None whatever?"

She shook her head. "Absolutely none. He refused. I . . . I thought his mind might be affected from overwork, and I think he realized what I thought, and it irritated him."

"Had he been overworking? Or showing previous signs of worry, or excitement?"

"It began the day before he had that talk with me about not calling a doctor in case something weird happened to him—and above all not allowing him to be embalmed. Prior to that, I had noticed no difference in him."

Doc Savage asked, "And this thing that has happened to him—when did it occur?"

"In the afternoon. I . . . I just found him like . . . the way he is. On the bed. I thought . . . I would have sworn, he was dead. But I know"—her eyes got round with horror—"he isn't really dead."

"Has there been any change in him?"

"None whatever. He has been exactly like that."

"Have you cleaned the room, altered it in any way?"

"No."

Doc Savage was silent a moment, as if assembling details, considering them.

He inquired, "Has anyone besides Benjamin Boot showed an interest in your father?"

"Oh, yes, naturally. His business associates, of course. I told them he had—gone on a trip. I got rid of the servants by giving them all vacations. And then—there was the white-haired man."

"The white-haired man? Who was *he*?"

She shook her head again. "I don't know. but he came here twice, demanding to see father. He seemed to know that father was in the . . . condition . . . he is in. I got the idea he had been sent here to . . . or told to come here, rather . . . to learn for *sure* that father was in the condition he is in."

"What did you do?"

"I . . . I was horrified. I refused to let the man in, and threatened him with the shotgun. He went away."

Doc Savage asked, "Did this white-haired stranger give you a name?"

"Sam John Thomas," she said.

Renny jumped, said, "Holy cow!"

The girl whirled and demanded, "Does that name mean something to you?"

Renny looked at Doc Savage, who was inscrutable. The big-fisted engineer swallowed, straightened out his face.

"Nope," he said. "I don't know any Sam John Thomas."

Which was, technically, the truth. But according to the documents in the pockets of O'Brien O'Callaghan, O'Callaghan was associated with a concern named Sam John Thomas, Inc.

Doc Savage asked, "Miss Moldenhaeur, is that all you can tell us? Think hard, please. There must be some detail, something you think might have a bearing on this thing." She shuddered. "Nothing," she said. "I . . . I've racked my brains for days. I haven't the least idea what it is about."

"What were you going to do about your father?"

She sank down on a chair, put her face in her hands, and said through her fingers, tremulously, "I didn't know. It has been driving me mad."

Doc moved toward the stairs, obviously intending to go back to Winton Moldenhaeur.

He paused, asked, "By the way, you said you got rid of the servants. But there is a watchman at the gate."

"Yes," said Liona Moldenhaeur. "Ollie Saff. He has been a great help. He has kept everyone away."

"Except Sam John Thomas," Doc suggested.

"Yes, except Thomas."

"Has Ollie Saff been in your employ long?"

"In father's, yes," the girl replied. "Father brought him

here two weeks ago, just before this... happened. He said Mr. Saff had been working for him for years, and was a thoroughly trusted man. He also said that, in case anything *did* happen to him, I was to keep Saff here and accept his aid."

Doc Savage made no comment on that.

But big-fisted Renny rumbled, "What kind of a job would your father give Ollie Saff where he would go barefooted and almost naked in a hot tropical sun for two or three years?"

The girl showed her surprise.

"My father said Mr. Saff had been working in his office," she said, "for several years."

Doc Savage went up the stairs, out of sight.

Renny eyed the girl. Renny's face was even more woeful than usual, which, contrarily enough, meant Renny was pleased with the situation. Not that he was elated over the misfortune of the Moldenhaeurs, or anyone else who was in trouble. The satisfaction was personal. Renny liked trouble. The kind of trouble he liked most of all was the mystifying kind.

This was satisfactorily mysterious. A man named Benjamin Boot had become alarmed when two men tried to kill him, and had appealed to Doc Savage for aid. Benjamin Boot had felt the only explanation of the attack attempt lay in something mysterious at the Moldenhaeurs. And he was right. There seemed to be ample mystery at the Moldenhaeurs.

If Renny would have been any sadder, he could not have helped bursting out laughing.

He hoped there would be some action connected with it.

He was thinking about the action when there was a rap on the door, and he opened the door immediately, to face Ollie Saff. Ollie Saff was excited.

"Listen," gasped Ollie Saff. "I just fainted, or something, down at the gate, and when I woke up, *this* was in my hand."

Renny stared at an object indistinct in the darkness.

"What is it?" he asked.

"Something from Africa," said Ollie Saff.

Renny was so astonished that he neglected his normal amount of caution to bend forward and peer at what was in Ollie Saff's left palm, thereby completely forgetting to pay attention to Saff's right hand, which contained a blackjack that promptly whipped around and made a perfect connection with Renny's head behind the ear, where it would do the most damage. Renny was conscious of an explosion, then conscious of nothing.

IV

DANGER FROM AFRICA

Mr. Saff swatted Mr. Renwick again, just to make sure. "All right, take him away," Saff said.

The order brought half a dozen men out of the shadows. They were not masked, except that tension was holding their faces tight. Tension and, in a case or two, open fear.

Liona Moldenhaeur stared in wordless terror.

She heard a man say, after staring at the recumbent hulk of Renny Renwick, "Hey, this is a Doc Savage man!"

"Sure," said Saff. "So what? Take him away."

The man said, "Listen, I don't want no part of Savage." He started to back off.

Ollie Saff drew a revolver and cocked it. "We can't have that," he said, in a voice completely cold and determined.

The man who wanted no part of Doc Savage changed his mind. He seemed to decide that he wanted a lot to do with Doc Savage, as long as it would permit him to go on living.

Liona Moldenhaeur came out of her horrified trance then. She began screaming. Her shrieks set the farm dogs barking and the chickens cackling in alarm on farms nearly a mile away. It was the first indication of a thing which they later found out about her, that she had once studied to be an opera singer.

Ollie Saff said something—it was not in English—that must have been profanity. He leaped for the girl, seized her. There was no sense in trying to silence her after that bugling shriek, and he did not seek to do so.

She hit him.

"Cut that out, you!" he said.

She kicked his shin, stuck a thumb in his eye, and pulled his hair.

"Help me!" he snarled at his companions. "Gimme a hand. Doc Savage is somewhere around the place."

Two men helped him with the girl. They ran, the whole

group of them, taking along Liona Moldenhaeur and Renny Renwick, down the winding road toward the gate.

Ollie Saff stopped long enough to plant a flashlight—switched on so the beam blazed—in the grass where it illuminated the door of the house.

"Keep a watch," he ordered. "If Savage comes out, we may be able to pot him."

Liona Moldenhaeur resumed her screaming.

"Beller," Saff told her. "See what good it does you."

They approached the gate to the estate.

There, to Liona's astonishment, Saff said, "Hell, we don't need the girl. Throw her away."

The two men carrying Liona must have been expecting the order. They promptly pitched her into a bush. The bush was a rose clump, plentiful with thorns, and it was not pleasant.

Clawing out of the shrub, Liona ran in pursuit of the men.

"Mr. Savage!" she screamed. "They're going this way!"

The men had a car parked close to the gate, a driver in it, the motor running. They piled into the machine. The car stood there a moment, while one of the men aimed deliberately at the girl. She knew, even before he shot, that the man could have hit her, because she stood full in the glare of the automobile spotlight. But the bullet missed her. It missed her at least twenty feet, which was too much of a miss to have been an accident.

Another strange thing—Ollie Saff laughed. He laughed heartily, as if something had gone very much to please him.

Then the car containing Saff, his half dozen men, and Renny Renwick, went away at high speed.

And Doc Savage appeared beside Liona Moldenhaeur.

The bronze man asked a question which surprised the girl. "Did one of those men laugh?" he demanded.

"I . . . yes," she said.

"They probably decoyed me away from the house so they could get your father," he said.

He wheeled, ran back in the direction of the house. Liona Moldenhaeur followed him, but he far out-distanced her. He was in the house, upstairs, and back outside when she arrived.

"They got your father, all right," he said.

"But—"

"Listen!" he said sharply.

She strained her ears. There was nothing, she thought, other than the night sounds, the barking of a dog in the distance, cars on a faraway highway.

He said, "Is there a road north?"

"An old one, between the estate and the Sound," she said.

The giant bronze man left her then, abruptly, silently. His going was fabulously ghostlike, and she stared in amazement at the surrounding darkness.

Then, two or three minutes later, she heard a car motor. It was on the north road, the old one, and it departed in a great hurry. She realized that the bronze man's hearing must be extraordinary, so that he had heard sounds from that direction.

Shortly afterward, he returned.

"They had another car waiting," he said. "Ollie Saff moved in on us from the front, got Renny and you and used him as a decoy to pull me away from the house. The other gang was waiting in the back. They simply crept in, got your father, and left."

He took out of a coat pocket an object that might have been a kitchen match box, except that it was black, had two dials and a tiny grilled opening. He held the box close to his lips and told it essentially what he had just told the girl. He added, "Get in the car and get here as soon as you can. Bring O'Brien O'Callaghan with you."

"All right," the box said, and Liona realized it was an extremely compact radio outfit.

Doc Savage entered the house, ran upstairs to the room in which her father had been lying. Liona followed him, and watched him search.

She had heard of this unusual bronze man before—she was recalling that now. A friend, a young man who was interested in science, had talked about Savage at a party; she was recalling things the friend had said, not the exact details, because the subject had held no interest for her at the time and, because she was not awed or even mildly intrigued by celebrities, she had not paid much attention. But she remembered the tone of the friend's remarks. Savage, the friend had seemed fully convinced, was a phenomenal individual with capacities and abilities amazingly developed.

Liona got a sample of the bronze man's uncanny ability as she watched.

She saw him go to the one thing which was out of place in the room. And yet she, who knew the place thoroughly, had not noticed it before.

He examined a canary cage which hung on an ornate gilt stand.

"Where is the canary?" he asked.

Liona stared. "Why . . . I . . . I don't know," she said.

"It was not in the cage when I entered the room the first time." The bronze man examined the cage. "Apparently there has been no bird in it in some time. Should there have been?"

Liona nodded. "Why, yes. Yes, my father had a canary. He has had it for more than a year."

"Where did he get it?"

"Mr. Boot gave it to him. It was a birthday gift."

"Did you notice when the canary disappeared?"

She tried to remember. "No, I don't recall."

"Have you see it since your father became the way he was?"

She paled. "No, I haven't."

An automobile horn hooted in front of the building. Doc Savage slipped the canary cage from its hook, took it along down to the car.

Long Tom Roberts complained, "Blast it! I missed the excitement. You say they got Renny?"

Doc Savage nodded. He took Liona Moldenhaeur's elbow. "You had better come with us," he said. "There is no point in your staying here alone."

"You are going to look for my father?" she asked anxiously.

"Naturally. For Renny, too. And for the reason behind your father's condition."

Long Tom said, "This O'Brien O'Callaghan is beginning to come out of it."

Doc Savage examined O'Callaghan. When he pinched O'Callaghan, the latter stirred dazedly. Doc calmly clipped O'Callaghan on the jaw with a fist, prolonging his period of senselessness.

"Drive to Pat's place," Doc told Long Tom.

Patricia Savage was an extremely attractive young woman who had the bronzed hair and golden eyes of the Savage family. She met them in her private office in the beauty establishment which she operated for the benefit of a Park Avenue clientele, charging unearthly prices.

Her eyes lighted, "Trouble?"

Doc Savage said, "Pat, we have a young lady here, Miss Liona Moldenhaeur. Something we do not yet understand has happened to her father. She may be in danger herself. While we are trying to get at the bottom of the thing, I wonder if you would look after her."

Pat eyed him narrowly. "Is *that* all that is wrong?"

"Renny has been seized by some fellows," Doc admitted.

Pat made an exaggerated gesture of pretending to faint. "Now the earth can come to an end, because there's nothing more startling left to happen!"

This remark, meaningless to Liona Moldenhaeur, was perfectly understandable to Doc Savage and Long Tom Roberts. In the past, they usually had a great deal of difficulty with Pat Savage, trying to keep her from getting mixed up in their troubles. Pat liked excitement.

Doc Savage said, "You understand, Pat, that you are to take no part in this thing."

Pat's face fell. "Now you sound more like yourself. I suppose there is no danger whatever connected with looking out for Miss Moldenhaeur."

"None, I hope," Doc admitted.

"Dang!" Pat said. She took Liona's arm. "Come on, darling. Don't misunderstand me and think you are not welcome, because you *are*."

Doc Savage drove back to his headquarters building. He drove fast. There were many special gadgets—the gas equipment, for example—on the machine, and these included a police siren. He used the siren to clear traffic, supplemented with two lights which ordinarily appeared to be fog lights, but glowed redly upon operation of the proper switch.

They entered the private elevator carrying the O'Callaghan.

Long Tom said, "There's someone upstairs," after a glance at an indicator button inside the cage.

Doc touched what seemed to be an ornamental rivet high up on the cage side. The rivet was a push button, and a moment later an answer came from a concealed loud-speaker.

"Inquietude is a supererogation of turgescence," the loud-speaker remarked.

"Johnny," said Long Tom.

Johnny was William Harper Littlejohn, notable archaeologist and geologist, eminent user of big words, and a man who was taller and thinner than it seemed any man could be.

There was one favorable thing about Johnny's big words. He never used them on Doc Savage. No one knew exactly why.

Johnny said, "I just got back from Westchester County. That pre-Inca tablet the fellow had was no more pre-Inca than I am. In fact, it was not as much. Some fellow had faked it within the last year and palmed it off on him. Say, what is going on here? I dropped in at headquarters to find out what is going on, and nobody is here."

Doc Savage told him. He used remarkably few words to do it, and said, "Moldenhaeur is not dead, and yet he was not alive. I have never seen anything like it. It was rather incredible, whatever was wrong with him."

Johnny was impressed.

"Ollie Saff and his men have Renny," Doc continued, "and Monk and Ham are trailing Benjamin Boot. And we have a man named O'Brien O'Callaghan, who should be able to give us some information."

"What do we do about Renny?" asked Johnny uneasily.

Doc said, "Johnny, you take one of our cars. Long Tom, you take another. As soon as I can get hold of Monk and Ham, I will have them take cars and help you. Use the cars which have powerful short-wave ultraviolet light projectors equipped for mounting. Drive over those Long Island roads, and keep your eyes open."

"That's a long chance," Johnny said thoughtfully.

"Yes, it is," the bronze man agreed. "But Renny was wearing the same type of clothing as the rest of us, garments treated with metallic salts which are highly fluorescent under ultraviolet light. He may regain his senses, tear off bits of clothing or any personal object and drop it in the road. It is a slim possibility, but the only one we have at the moment. I will keep in touch with you by radio."

"Any idea where they might have been taking Renny?"

"None at all," Doc said. "But it is fairly safe to assume that they would remain on Long Island. Bridges and ferries are their only method of leaving Long Island, and they would suppose that we immediately notified the police to watch those. We did not, but they would not know that. So confine your hunting to Long Island."

"Right. We'll do our best with the ultraviolet lights."*

"And the airports," Doc added. "They might have used a plane."

Long Tom and Johnny departed.

Doc Savage switched on a recording device which was connected up with both the telephone and radio receiver. This somewhat complicated gimmick would record any call made to the headquarters in his absence.

Monk and Ham had not called in, he found

He put O'Brien O'Callaghan in a chair, and used restoratives.

When the O'Callaghan got around to opening his eyes, and his predicament seeped into his mind, he took it calmly. He rubbed his jaw.

Doc Savage said, "The soreness is not serious. We found it necessary, or at least convenient, to clip you several times on the jaw."

O'Callaghan grimaced.

"It feels like you had run a locomotive back and forth over it," he said.

"Have you any idea where you are?" Doc inquired.

O'Brien O'Callaghan looked around. He nodded.

"I have heard of this place," he said, "so I can guess."

Doc told him, "You realize you are in difficulties, of course. We prefer to work with as little turmoil as possible, and without force. So I will ask you if you have any intention of talking to me."

"I don't mind talking to you."

"Of telling me the truth, I should have put it," Doc said.

_B_

---

*The ultraviolet wave lengths of light utilized by Doc Savage in this instance have been developed beyond the experimental stage by science. The light, being of a wave length invisible to the eye, is called "black." It is being used more and more in prospecting for ores. For example, more than a hundred varieties of ores which fluoresce under "black" light are found in one California county alone. These include the tungsten-bearing scheelite, halite, calcite, hydrozincite, types of borax, colemanite and many others. Uranium-bearing minerals fluoresce vividly. The apparatus used by the ore prospector is usually a portable 6-volt outfit. The method of prospecting can only be used at night, because the presence of daylight glare so much stronger than the fluorescence blots out the fluorescent phenomena entirely. Among the animals which fluoresce under "black" light are horned toads, lizards and snakes of many varieties.

O'Callaghan considered that. "I guess I had better."

"You were watching this building?" Doc asked.

"Yes."

"And followed me when I left?"

"Yes."

"Why?"

"I was trying to find out," said O'Brien O'Callaghan, "what in the dickens is wrong with my boss."

"Who is your boss?"

"Sam John Thomas, of the company by the same name. I am employed by the company. I am called a general research engineer."

Doc said, "All of which we learned by examining the contents of your pockets."

"I'm telling you the truth. That's what you want, isn't it?"

"What is wrong with your boss?"

"He's scared. He isn't himself." O'Brien O'Callaghan stared at the floor. "I don't know what is wrong. A week ago, about, is when it happened. He wouldn't tell me what is wrong. I got the idea, though, that he feared some kind of terrible danger."

Doc Savage asked, "And how did you happen to be trailing me?"

O'Callaghan lifted his head.

"That's easy. It was because of something I overheard the boss say over the telephone. It was just part of a sentence. '—*know damned well Doc Savage could stop it!*' That was all I heard. Sam John Thomas wouldn't talk to me when I asked him about it. He became violent. I could see he was in a state of terror. I think a lot of my boss, so I started looking into it on my own hook. I was investigating you. That's how I happened to be watching you."

"Where is your boss now?" Doc asked.

"At his country home, I imagine."

"Where is that?"

"On Long Island."

"Near the Winton Moldenhaeur estate, by any chance?"

O'Brien O'Callaghan's forehead puckered. "I never heard of anyone named Moldenhaeur," he said.

"Your boss, Sam John Thomas, paid the Moldenhaeur estate a visit recently," Doc said.

"I can't help that. I don't know any Moldenhaeurs. Never heard of them."

Doc Savage was silent a moment.

"Do you own a canary?" he asked.

O'Callaghan stared in astonishment. "That's a funny one!"

"What is funny about it?"

"Somebody sent me a canary day before yesterday," said O'Brien O'Callaghan. "I don't know who. It just came by messenger. The messenger said a woman hired him to bring it to me. Why do you ask?"

Doc Savage was silent.

"So—a woman sent the canary," he remarked finally.

V

FROM A DRUGSTORE

The telephone had, instead of a bell, a buzzer which gave forth a high-pitched and not unmusical note. When it sounded, Doc Savage picked up the instrument.

It was Monk. "Well, people have started dying," Monk said. "Two of them so far."

"Who?" Doc asked.

"Those guys who tried to get Benjamin Boot. Their names seemed to have been Mr. Manley and Abner. They're plenty dead. It happened this way: We trailed Benjamin Boot, like you said to, and he went different places and fooled around as if he was mad and trying to take time to think. Then he went to the apartment where he lives, and then was when we walked up to him. We told him we wanted the two prisoners, and he surprised us by not objecting."

"When did Mr. Manley and Abner die?"

"Right after we got up to Ben Boot's apartment with him. We went in the apartment, and Boot told his servant, named Julian, to bring the prisoners. The servant went in another room. He came rushing right back yelling that they were dead. Sure enough, they were."

"Where are you now?"

"Boot's apartment."

Doc Savage said, "I will be up there immediately."

He hung up the receiver, and turned to O'Brien O'Callaghan.

In a voice which held no particular emotion, the bronze man remarked, "Naturally, your misfortune befell you because you happened to be trailing us, and that made us suspicious. But your story explains several things. By the way, how long have you been with Sam John Thomas, Inc.?"

"Oh, several years," said O'Brien O'Callaghan.

"For the last several months, have you been situated so that you would have noticed any gradual change in your boss, any slow build-up of overwork which might result in a collapse, and nervous breakdown, of which this imaginary terror, in case it is imaginary, might be a symptom?"

O'Brien O'Callaghan shook his head vehemently.

"I've been sitting right here in the New York office for several months," he said.

"At a desk?"

"Yes."

"Then," said Doc Savage, "I am to presume you got those callouses on your feet sitting at your desk. And the sunburn, the deep leathery tan of tropical sun, all over you body—also at your desk?"

O'Callaghan swallowed. All his muscles seemed to slacken.

"My lying didn't go very far, did it?" he muttered.

"Not very. Are you going to come across with the truth?"

O'Callaghan shook his head again.

"No," he said. "We might as well get that understood."

"Truth serum," Doc Savage said, "is not very pleasant to take. It depends for its operation upon so addling the conscious nervous system that the victim is unable to distinguish between truth and falsehood, and cannot think clearly enough to concoct lies."

O'Brien O'Callaghan leaned back. He was determined.

"Bring on your truth serum," he said. "I don't believe the damned stuff will work."

Doc Savage went to a cabinet, got out a hypo needle, and filled this with a villainous-looking chemical concoction. He approached O'Brien O'Callaghan. The red-headed freckled-faced young man came up out of his chair. He brought the chair cushion with him, tried to hurl it in the bronze man's face. Doc moved enough to make it miss.

Callaghan came in with his left out, chin buried in his

shoulder, carrying himself like a man who knew how to fight. He feinted a few times with his left, saw what he thought was an opening for a right uppercut, shot it in—and found himself sitting on the floor. He groaned, took hold of his jaw.

"You oughta been decent enough to hit me somewhere else," he said thickly.

Doc kneed him down on the floor, held him there, and used the hypo.

"Unfortunately, there is no time to use the truth serum on you just now," the bronze man explained. "This stuff will keep you quiet for a while. Incidentally, it is harmless."

A few minutes later, O'Brien O'Callaghan was a slumbering hulk of a young man sitting in a closetlike aperture in one wall of the laboratory. The niche had a comfortable chair. Doc closed the door, which became an indistinguishable part of the laboratory wall, with a seemingly very heavy piece of apparatus in front of it. The niche was ventilated.

The bronze man rode uptown.

Monk Mayfair let him into the Benjamin Boot apartment. Monk had a worried look, and his pet pig, Habeas Corpus.

"They're in the library," Monk explained.

A twittering sound filled the air, and the bronze man listened to this for a moment.

"Canaries?" he asked.

"A load of 'em," Monk said. "Flowers, and paintings, and all kinds of fragile gimcracks. This Boot has the tastes of a woman. But he's got the nerves of an alligator, too."

Doc Savage asked, "Did Boot seem to meet anyone when you were following him?"

"No."

"Where are the bodies?"

They were in the room adjoining the library, and the strange look on Monk's face was a slight forewarning of what to expect.

Doc made a brief inspection, then turned to Monk.

Monk squirmed. "Well, are they dead?" he asked nervously.

"What do you think?" Doc asked.

Monk stared at the bronze man, apparently wondering if he was being ribbed. Then the homely chemist wiped perspiration off his face.

"No pulse, no heartbeat, no breathing, no nerve reaction," he muttered. "They say you stick a pin in a dead man and the hole don't close up if he's dead. Well, I tried pins on both of them, and the holes didn't close." He waved his arms. "And yet I get the feeling they are *not* dead!"

Doc Savage asked, "When you followed Benjamin Boot, you are sure he met no one?"

"He didn't meet anybody."

"Did he buy anything?"

Monk stared. "He went in a drugstore. He could have bought something."

"What drugstore?"

"The corner drugstore, three blocks south of here."

Doc Savage nodded. He went into the other room and summoned Ham Brooks. So that only Ham and Monk could overhear, he spoke rapidly. He told them what had happened, and about Johnny and Long Tom being engaged in combing Long Island roads with the ultraviolet light.

Doc said, "I want you two to join Johnny and Long Tom at that job. Get cars at headquarters, and mount projectors on them. Fortunately, we have enough powerful long-range projectors to equip the cars."

Ham nodded. "We will get in touch with Johnny and Long Tom by radio and find out what roads they have covered, so we don't duplicate each other's work."

"Good."

Taking their pet pig and pet chimp along, Monk and Ham left the beautifully furnished apartment of Benjamin Boot.

Benjamin Boot confronted Doc Savage. He said, "I don't understand this. You said you wouldn't help me, and then you turned up, or your men did. What were you doing—checking up on me?"

"Yes."

"Well, you didn't find out anything against me," said Benjamin Boot, "because there isn't anything."

Doc Savage said, "You entered a drugstore down the street?"

Boot hesitated. "Yes."

"What did you buy?"

"I . . . some cigarettes."

Doc Savage went to the telephone, called the drugstore, three blocks to the south, and said, "This is a police matter," and described Ben Boot, asked if he had been in the store recently, and what he had bought.

Having received an answer, Doc hung up and faced Boot.

"You bought perfume," he said.

Boot reddened. "All right, all right, it was perfume and not cigarettes," he said. "So what?"

"Why didn't you tell the truth?"

Boot's color deepened. "I'm sensitive about buying perfume," he said. "I like it, but I do not like being jibed at when I buy it."

Doc Savage said, "It might be better if you did not let your sensitivity interfere with your veracity."

"What do you want to know?" Boot muttered.

"Would you care to hear what happened at the Moldenhaeur estate?" Doc countered.

Boot sprang to his feet. His face was anxious. "Yes, what goes on there?" he demanded.

Doc Savage told him the story—with reservations. The reserved items included all reference to canaries, to calloused feet, to tanned skins, and Africa. But the bronze man was very detailed about the strange living-dead condition of Winton Moldenhaeur. Another point which the bronze mad did not mention was the present whereabouts of Liona Moldenhaeur. Boot pounced on that point at once.

"Where is Liona now?" he demanded.

"In a safe spot," Doc said. "Have you noticed that I mention Moldenhaeur's weird condition as being the same, apparently, as the condition of the two men in your apartment?"

Ben Boot's face went blank. "What do you mean?"

"The two men, Mr. Manley and Abner, if that was their names, seem to be in a condition which might be described as completely suspended animation. Notice that I say *completely* suspended. In a normal case, immediately following death, certain chemical and physiological changes begin occurring in the body, these resulting in rigor mortis, among other things. The presence of chemicals in the shape of medicines may in a case of normal death arrest certain otherwise natural processes, just as embalming arrests normal putrefaction. But in the present case—Mr. Moldenhaeur and these two men—none of the normal after-processes of death are proceeding. Normal death might be called a suspension of the processes which supply life and animation and consciousness, but *not* a suspension of all activity in the body, chemical for the most part. The present thing consists of both—both a suspension of life and animation, *and* a suspension of all natural chemical activity as well. Does that make sense to you?"

"What you are saying is that they are dead, and yet they aren't dead?" Boot inquired.

"Something like that," Doc replied. "By the way, when you returned to your apartment with my two men, and they asked for the prisoners, did *you* go to get the prisoners?"

"No."

"Then you had not seen the two men since you left to come to my headquarters?"

"That is right."

"Who did go to get the prisoners?"

"My man here, Julian."

Julian immediately began having trouble with the half-swallowed apple in his throat. It went up and down.

"I . . . I didn't do anything to 'em," he mumbled.

Doc Savage's voice was quiet, the kind of a tone that would be very reassuring to an innocent man, but equally alarming to one who was not innocent.

The bronze man said, "You need not be excited, Julian. We merely wish to ask some questions. How long did it take you to ascertain the men were dead?"

"Not . . . not more than a minute," Julian replied.

"Mr. Boot sent you for the two men, and you were not gone more than a minute. At the end of that minute, what did you do?"

"I rushed back in here shouting that they were dead," said Julian.

"That's right," said Benjamin Boot. "Julian was in a dither."

Doc Savage did not take his flake-gold eyes from Julian. "In that minute, you learned both men were dead?"

"Yes," said Julian.

"That was fast work," Doc said. "I would say the finest of doctors would have difficulty telling for sure that two men were dead, and do it in a minute."

Julian paled. "I wasn't sure. I just—it just came over me that they were dead, so I rushed in here."

"Then what?"

"We all went to look at the two men as soon as we could get the door unlocked," Julian said.

"Oh, the door was locked now?"

Julian said, "In my excitement, I slammed the connecting door, and it has a spring lock. I was so wrought up I could not find the key immediately."

"How much delay was there?"

"Not over two or three minutes. Maybe five."

"Would you swear it was no more than five?"

"I don't know," Julian said.

Benjamin Boot said, "Let's say that no more than ten minutes elapsed. I'm sure that will cover it."

"Thank you," Doc Savage told him. The bronze man leaned back and looked around the room. "You have a number of canaries, haven't you?"

"Yes, I like canaries," replied Boot.

"I see you have some large Belgians," Doc remarked. "And I noticed you go in for variety. There are hooped, bowed, feather-footed, topknots and various hybrids, among other types of canary. I believe that bird yonder is a hybrid of canary and siskin, that one there a citril hybrid."

Benjamin Boot smiled. "You seem to know a bit about canaries."

Doc Savage did not go farther into the subject of canaries. He glanced at Julian.

"Julian," he said, "will you do one more thing for us?"

"Yes, sir," said Julian. "Of course, sir."

"Take off your shoes and socks."

"Eh?"

"Take off your shoes, Julian. Then your socks."

Julian thought that over. Then he decided that, instead of removing his shoes and socks, he would remove a flat automatic from its hiding place under his left arm, and see what luck that would bring him.

VI

CALLOUSED FEET

Doc Savage seemed hardly to be watching Julian at the moment the servant decided to turn Wild West. But the bronze man lifted out of his chair, and had hold of Julian's wrist about the time the gun came into view.

Julian was fast, had nerve, knew how to use a gun. On top of which he was desperate. He began shooting. His haste was such that he even grooved his own shoulder with a bullet. He fired three more times, and the lead knocked grooves in one wall, broke a light fixture.

Doc held him. Julian kicked with both feet, flogged with the one arm which did not hold the gun. He said things, loud angry and violent things, most of which were in English, but some in dialect. The dialect was definitely foreign, and undoubtedly primitive.

A fist on the jaw finally silenced Julian.

Benjamin Boot had been dancing around with a chair. He looked disappointed. "I was going to brain him," he said, glaring at Julian. "The cheek of the devil. He's one of my enemies, of course. He's mixed up in it."

Doc Savage asked, "How long has the servant been in your employ?"

"He worked for me three years about five years ago," said Benjamin Boot. "Then he quit. About a month ago, he turned up and wanted a job, so I hired him back."

"Then Julian has only been with you a month?"

"Well, slightly less, I would say. Three weeks might come closer."

Doc Savage stripped open Julian's shirt. Julian's skin was very deeply tanned. Next, the bronze man removed the servant's shoes and socks.

Benjamin Boot had been looking on in astonishment.

"Gracious!" he said.

The callouses on the bottoms of Julian's feet were thicker than any callouses yet seen.

"My!" said Benjamin Boot. "What on earth made his feet like that?"

Doc Savage said, "It looks as if he might have gone barefoot in a hot sun for a long time, not so many weeks ago."

"Why, that's very strange!" said Boot. "Julian told me he had been clerking in a store in Hartford, Connecticut, for a long time just prior to his coming with me."

The bronze man made no comment. He walked into the room where the two "dead" men lay, and began another examination. This one was thorough. It included blood samples, spinal fluid samples—every known preparation for a scientific search and analysis.

He spent more than an hour at that task. Finally, after he

had stowed samples in a case for later analysis in the laboratory, he straightened.

"Mr. Boot," he said.

"Yes."

"Will you look over your canaries?" Doc Savage suggested. "Examine them closely, and see if you notice anything unusual or unnatural."

Puzzled, Benjamin Boot made a thorough inspection of his canary flock. He called the birds by names, whistled at them to get them to singing to him, and was otherwise thorough. He nodded his head in satisfaction.

"Nothing whatever is wrong with my canaries," he said.

Doc asked, "Are they all here?"

"Yes."

The elevator attendant at the Benjamin Boot apartment house was somewhat puzzled when they carried the two "dead" men out of the building. Doc Savage had sprinkled some rubbing alcohol—Ben Boot had nothing so base as whiskey in his apartment, he explained—on the two men to give the impression they were inebriates. Julian looked more alive, although still limp.

The elevator attendant seemed more astounded by the fact that drunks were being taken out of the Boot apartment, than by the fact that the three men were completely out.

Doc put them in the back seat of his car.

"You had better go with me," he told Benjamin Boot.

"Thank you very much," said Boot heartily. "I do want to be with you. That may enable me to help Miss Moldenhaeur."

Doc Savage headed south on Central Park West, then took the west side to avoid the theatrical district which, although the night was getting on, was still brilliantly lighted and crowded. He reached back and rapped Julian again on the jaw.

Benjamin Boot continued, asking, "Do you think we will be able to help Miss Moldenhaeur?"

"Miss Moldenhaeur is perfectly safe," Doc said.

"I mean her father, of course."

Doc asked, "What was the nature of this business transaction you had scheduled with Mr. Moldenhaeur when he met with this misfortune?"

"Oh, that." Boot shrugged. "We were going to combine

one of his smelting companies and two of my copper mines and make an efficient unit out of them."

"Could that have had any bearing on this matter?"

Boot shook his head violently. "There is absolutely no possibility that it could have."

Doc Savage asked, "Do you know a man named Sam John Thomas?"

Boot nodded. "Slightly, that is all," he said. "I believe he is on the directorate of a concern of which I am also a member of the board."

"What company is that?"

"The Century Projects Corp."

The name told little enough about the company, so Doc asked, "What is the concern's business?"

"It has various manufacturing holdings," Boot replied. "Say, what are you going to do next?"

Doc said, "Question O'Brien O'Callaghan, and investigate Sam John Thomas."

The bronze man drove into his private garage in the basement of the midtown building which housed his quarters. He shifted the two "dead" men to the elevator, carried them up to the eighty-sixth floor, and unloaded them, along with Julian.

He spent the next two hours making a scientific examination of the two, and running tests in the laboratory. He drugged Julian.

One interruption occurred when Monk Mayfair called in, his small squeaky voice sounding irritated over the radio. Monk reported, "Nothing yet. No sign of Renny."

"Keep looking," Doc directed. He got O'Brien O'Callaghan out of the concealed niche in the laboratory wall.

Benjamin Boot looked at O'Brien O'Callaghan and said, "I never saw this fellow before."

The O'Callaghan rolled his eyes. He tasted his lips, as if they were bitter. "What day of the month is it?" he muttered.

"It is still the same night," Doc told him. "Are you ready to have that truth serum tried on you? Incidentally, I can assure you that it will not be pleasant. You will probably live through it, although there are cases of men who have not, and you will not feel the same for several days. The latest scientific opinion, in fact, is that truth serum does an injury to your mind that may be more or less permanent."

O'Callaghan licked his lips again.

"I don't suppose," he said, "it would make any difference if I told you why I'm *not* telling you the facts in this."

"It probably would not," Doc told him. "You can try, if you wish."

O'Callaghan was lost in contemplation for a moment.

"It's because there's too much at stake," he said. "I can't make myself think the situation is so serious that we have to ring in any outsiders."

Doc asked, "Are you at all familiar with my organization and its methods?"

"I've heard of you," O'Callaghan said. "I've heard you were honest."

"You do not believe it?"

"One of the first things I learned on this earth was that it was always safest to go on the assumption that there wasn't such a thing as an honest man," said O'Callaghan.

Doc Savage turned away. "We are wasting breath, I see. There seems to be nothing to do but try the truth serum on you."

"Wait a minute," called O'Callaghan. "How about a compromise? How about you taking me out to talk to Sam John Thomas, my boss? What he says to do, I'll do."

Benjamin Boot exclaimed, "Ah, no doubt this is a trick!"

Staring at Boot, O'Brien O'Callaghan demanded, "Who is this homely goon who doubts my word?"

Boot registered indignation. "I am Benjamin Boot," he snapped.

The O'Callaghan showed sudden interest. "Say, I've heard of you, goldilocks. You're director in a company in which my boss, Sam John Thomas, is also director."

Doc Savage showed a great deal of interest.

"What concern is that, O'Callaghan?" the bronze man demanded.

"Century Projects Corp."

Boot snapped, "I am a director in dozens of corporations."

Doc Savage said, "Come on, O'Callaghan. We will talk to Sam John Thomas. Boot, do you want to go along?"

Benjamin Boot hesitated. "I—yes, I will," he said. "But I think it is a trick. I don't trust this man O'Callaghan. I seem to read menace in his face."

The O'Callaghan told Boot, "I'd hate to say what I read in your face. It would make the devil blush."

They went downstairs—after Doc drugged Julian, placed him and the "dead" men in the same niche which O'Brien O'Callaghan had lately occupied—in the elevator, riding directly to the garage. Boot and O'Callaghan were not even looking at each other.

They stepped out into the garage, and Pat Savage said, "Well, good evening. Or, rather, good morning, it being well past the hour of midnight, when evil is supposed to stalk."

Pat sounded brightly alert.

Doc Savage frowned at her. "What are you doing here?"

"Why, Miss Moldenhaeur and I couldn't sleep," Pat explained, "and we decided to spend the rest of the night helping hunt Renny."

"How did you know about the hunt for Renny?" Doc demanded.

"I have a radio. I overheard Monk and the others reporting to you and talking to each other."

Doc said, "You will have to go back to your place."

"Nothing doing," Pat announced. "You let me in on this, and when I'm let in, I don't stop with my foot in the door. It's whole hog or nothing for me."

From past experience, the bronze man knew the futility of arguing. He had tried it before, and gotten nothing for his pains. His five associates respected his judgment took his orders without question. Pat Savage respected his judgment, also, but only took such orders as appealed to her.

In an alarmed voice, Benjamin Boot said, "If this girl heard your men reporting by radio, what is to keep anybody who has a radio receiver from hearing them?"

Patricia answered that.

"Nothing," she said, "except an unscrambler gadget that is about three vacuum tubes and a cogwheel more complicated than a television receiver. You see, Doc's outfits are equipped with them, and so are mine. I don't think anybody else overheard."

Doc frowned. "Where did you get your scrambler, Pat?"

"Stole it out of here one day," Pat replied calmly.

Benjamin Boot was examining Liona Moldenhaeur rather self-consciously. "Good morning, Liona," he said. "I . . . I'm sorry I stirred up this mess, but it seemed the thing to do."

Liona Moldenhaeur nodded. "You were right, Ben," she said. "I realize that now. I'm the one who should be sorry— sorry I did not tell you all about it when you first wanted to help me. I . . . I understand I was the cause of two men trying to kill you."

Ben Boot beamed. "I think that's what the two men were going to do, but they didn't make the grade. And it wasn't your fault. Probably they were tackling me because I was showing an interest in the mystery."

O'Brien O'Callaghan was also examining Liona Moldenhaeur. The O'Callaghan seemed greatly impressed by Liona's qualities.

"Come on," Doc Savage said briefly. "We will all visit Sam John Thomas."

Sam John Thomas lived as befitted his wealth, and as became a modest man. His estate was large, but it was not devoted to fancy shrubbery, as was the Moldenhaeur place, but to farmland which was in production. The place looked profitable.

The house itself was not much more than a stone cottage, crowning without spectacle a low hill which dropped down sharply to the waters of a cove. There was a boat in the cove, a large deep-water cruising yacht, possibly eighty feet in length.

The night was dark around them as they pulled up to the house. The car's headlights seemed unnaturally bright.

Doc Savage got out of the big sedan. He said, "Pat, you stay here with Miss Moldenhaeur, Mr. Boot and Mr. O'Callaghan."

"Right," Pat said.

"I'm going with you," Boot snapped.

He tried vainly to get the door of the car to open. He wrenched at the handle, pounded at the glass.

Pat said, "You might as well compose yourself. This car locks up tight, and I'm the only one who can open it. You stay here, as Doc suggested."

Boot subsided, scowling, and watched Doc Savage vanish into the darkness.

The bronze man moved cautiously to the house, carrying a listening device which he had taken from a compartment in the car. The listener gadget was simple—a ribbon microphone of the contact type, feeding into an amplifier which threw its output into a headset. He used the listener on various windows in the house.

There was no living thing in the house, he decided.

Death there might be; he had no way of knowing. But no living thing.

He approached the boat. With caution and with silence, keeping in the shadows, he drew near a small dock to which the yacht was tied. All portholes were dark, and there was no sound from the boat. But he detected, very faintly, the odor of pipe smoke. Not odor of a pipe, but of smoke, carried ashore by a breeze which blew across the boat.

He tied a string to a bush, then moved away, took concealment behind a tree.

"Mr. Thomas," he called.

There was no answer. Water insects had been making small noises around about, and they went silent. The stillness was of infinite tension.

Doc Savage made his voice take on a ventriloquial quality, so that its source was doubtful.

"Thomas," he said, "we want to talk to you. It's about Moldenhaeur."

No answer.

He pulled the string to the bush and the bush shook.

Flame spouted from the fore deck of the boat, and a bullet clouted the bush which was moving. The shot echoes whooped off the hills, and a long time afterward came gobbling back from across the water.

Doc Savage threw a glass-ball anaesthetic grenade, lobbing it at the gun flash. He heard it break softly. He threw two more. A man made the sound a man would make collapsing on a boat deck.

The bronze man recovered his string. It was a silken cord, long and very stout, equipped with a grappling hook on one end, and it had many uses. He rolled it carefully, then went aboard the boat.

The white-haired man lay on the boat deck. There were documents—membership cards in exclusive yacht clubs, mostly, and a driver's license—which indicated he was Sam John Thomas. He seemed to be sleeping. At least his breathing was regular and deep. Doc pinched him, and he did not move.

The bronze man searched the rest of the yacht. There was no one else aboard. He noted that all portholes were fastened, all hatches battened, all companions secured firmly except one, that exception being the companionway nearest where Thomas lay.

It appeared that Sam John Thomas had been barricaded on the yacht.

Doc went back to his car, said, "All right, open up, Pat."

Benjamin Boot piled out of the machine and yelled, "What happened? We heard a shot?"

"Thomas was on his yacht, behaving like a cornered man," Doc said quietly. "We will question him."

Pat, who had worked with the bronze man before, was a little surprised. Doc was talking more than usual. Normally, neither persuasion nor dynamite would move him beyond a cryptic remark now and then. It had been Pat's experience that the less the bronze man said, the more progress he was making. She was wondering why he was talking so much, explaining his moves before he made them. She suspected he had some object in doing that.

Doc walked back to the yacht, following the others, telling them where to go.

Pat, noticing that he *did* walk behind them, got a cold sensation on the back of her neck.

They had Sam John Thomas in the salon of his yacht when he came out of the gas stupor. He blinked at them.

Pat stood against a wall. The feeling she was having was stronger now, the impression of danger, of tension. She could tell from the bronze man's extremely calm manner, from the continual motion of his flake-gold eyes, that she was not wrong.

Doc said, "You are Mr. Thomas?" to Sam John Thomas.

The man nodded. "Who the devil are you?"

Doc indicated O'Brien O'Callaghan. "This young fellow work for you?"

The man's eyes flicked at the O'Callaghan. "Hell, O'Brien," he said. "What on earth does this mean?"

O'Brien O'Callaghan shrugged. "This is Doc Savage. I don't know whether you have heard of him. He follows a rather unusual career—righting wrongs and punishing evildoers, he calls it. I call it sticking his beak into other people's business where he's not wanted."

Thomas looked at Doc Savage. "I've heard a great deal about you," he said.

He seemed impressed.

O'Brien O'Callaghan said sharply, "Don't tell them anything, boss!"

Benjamin Boot grunted angrily, stepped forward and acted as if he was going to do nothing but tap the O'Callaghan on the chest. He did tap O'Callaghan's chest with his left hand, but after the second or third tap his right fist came whistling up and around to O'Callaghan's jaw. O'Callaghan's teeth came together with a loud noise, as of two rocks meeting hard, and he would have fallen backward stiffly as a stick of lumber would fall, had Pat not caught him and lowered him to the floor.

Pat stared at Boot. "Some wallop," she said. "I saw sparks fly when his teeth came together."

Boot smiled at Pat. He leveled an arm at Thomas. "The thing for you to do," he said, "is tell the exact truth about this affair."

Sam John Thomas scowled.

"I don't think I have anything to say," he said.

Doc Savage suggested, "You might explain why you were so anxious to see Winton Moldenhaeur a few days ago. You recall you visited the Moldenhaeur home and Miss Moldenhaeur would not let you in. Did you know that something—peculiar—had happened to Mr. Moldenhaeur?"

"I have nothing to say," said Thomas.

"That blasted O'Callaghan!" Boot said angrily. "He persuaded him not to talk."

"Will you take off your shoes, Mr. Thomas?" Doc said.

Sam John Thomas was obviously startled, and he did what seemed natural under the circumstances. He shook his head. Then, after looking at Doc Savage and realizing the futility of argument or resistance, he shrugged and began unlacing his black Oxfords.

He wore a neat business suit, a shirt which was well-cut and evidently custom made, an expensive wrist watch, a lodge ring on one finger, a lodge emblem in his lapel. His face was innocent for a man of nearly fifty, and a rich man. His eyes were clear blue, and now that the effects of the gas were wearing off, he was beginning to focus them without trouble. He was in all a fine, gentlemanly figure of a man, but scared. Scared! There was no doubt of that. It showed in his eyes.

He kicked off his shoes.

"Now your socks," Doc said.

Thomas removed his socks.

His feet were extremely calloused.

Doc Savage asked, "Do you have a canary, Mr. Thomas?"

The man was startled. "Why. . . how did you know that?" he asked.

"Most everyone seems to have canaries in this affair," Doc Savage said. "Where did you get yours, and how?"

Thomas frowned. "It was sent to me. Three days ago. It bore the card of a friend of mine, Adam Latimer. But I telephoned Mr. Latimer, and he insisted he did not send it. I was rather puzzled. I detest birds."

"You do not know who sent you the bird?"

"No."

"What did you do with it?"

"I still have it. I detest birds, but I did not know what to do with this one except keep it. Eventually, I intended giving it to someone. When I had time to do it, that is."

"You have been rather busy?"

"Yes."

"How did your feet become so hardened?"

Sam John Thomas compressed his lips. He fell into a silence that was obviously going to be as permanent as he could make it.

Doc Savage tried one more question.

"What are you afraid of, Mr. Thomas?"

He got silence for an answer.

The bronze man turned to Liona Moldenhaeur. "Miss Moldenhaeur," he said.

"Yes?" She was surprised.

"Will you show us your feet?"

"My feet!" She stiffened. "What an insane suggestion!"

"Will you?"

"Why—" She began losing color. Her face turned pale so swiftly that they could see the change. "No!" she exploded. "Of course I won't!"

The bronze man said patiently, "We are involved in something very serious and very horrible. We are trying to get at the bottom of it. You must help us."

Quite white now, she snapped, "Don't you dare touch me!"

Pat Savage looked extremely cheerful. Pat was a slender girl, but her slimness was deceptive. "Doc, you're wasting time," Pat said. "Let me do it. I've been taking jujitsu lessons and I'd like to try them out."

Doc said, "Go ahead."

Pat advanced on Miss Moldenhaeur, a hand extended, saying, "Come on darling, don't be nasty about this." Liona Moldenhaeur tried to slap Pat, which must have been what Pat expected, because there was some motion, violent and intricate movement, hard for the eye to follow, and when the swirl of skirts subsided, which it suddenly did, Liona was flattened out helpless and Pat already had one of her slippers off. Pat stripped at a silk stocking.

"Calloused," Pat announced. "As horny as a hoof."

They could all see the hardened sole of Liona Moldenhaeur's small foot, so the remark was hardly necessary.

Benjamin Boot had been stunned with the abruptness of Pat's move, apparently. But now he got his wits together. And his rage went climbing.

"What do you mean—manhandling Miss Moldenhaeur that way?" he shouted.

He rushed forward, obviously to drag Pat off Liona.

What then happened to Mr. Boot would have been highly entertaining had anybody been in the mood for humor. Pat used a grip on his necktie for initial leverage. During the first part of what she did to Benjamin Boot, she inserted an extended pair of forefingers into his eyes, temporarily disrupting his vision. Boot left the floor and turned over in the air at least twice. He hit the floor. Dust flew up from the carpet.

Doc Savage shook his head, said, "Pat, you are too rough with that. You'll injure somebody."

"I need more practice," Pat said gleefully. She sat on Boot's back, held him flat and gasping with a variation of a wrestling toe hold. She looked at the shoe she was holding. "I wonder about *his* feet," she said.

Doc said, "The same thought has occurred to me."

"Shall I look?"

"Do."

Boot's immaculate patent-leather Oxfords came off easily. He wore them rather large. His socks were anklets, and as easy.

"Oh, oh!" Pat said.

Doc Savage examined briefly.

"Boot's feet are as calloused as any of them," he remarked.

VII

MELEE IN A MARSH

Doc Savage loaded Benjamin Boot, Sam John Thomas, O'Brien O'Callaghan, and Liona Moldenhaeur, into the back of the sedan, where they made a tight-fitting, disgruntled group.

Pat looked them over. She gave an opinion.

"A fine bunch of liars, all of you," she said.

The sedan was equipped like a limousine—there was a panel of glass, inch-thick bulletproof glass in this case, which rolled up out of the back of the front seat to make a partition. Doc raised this. Then he made a small speech in an unconcerned voice.

He said, "As Pat says, some or all of you are lying. All of you have calloused feet, and no one of you cares to explain why. All of you have canaries, or some connection with canaries. So I am afraid you must regard yourselves as prisoners."

He closed the door to the rear compartment of the car.

Pat put her lips close to the window, and said, "To save you some possible headaches, be advised that you couldn't break out of the back of that car with less than dynamite. And in case you start acting funny, all we have to do is pull a lever up here, and you'll get a dose of that anaesthetic gas."

Doc got behind the wheel. Pat slid in beside him.

"Where do we go now?" Pat asked.

"Back to the laboratory," Doc Savage said. "I want to make some more experiments with those two men who made the attempt on Boot's life."

Pat nodded. Then she frowned. "This stuff about their feet," she said. "I don't get it."

The bronze man suggested, "There seems to be a great deal at stake."

"Why won't they talk?"

"Some of them are confused, perhaps," Doc said. "Others are full of greed and schemes. Maybe one or two do not fully trust us. Mixed motives, as a whole."

Pat settled back and the car began moving. She said,

"You knew when we went to the boat that the girl's feet and Boot's were calloused. I could tell there was something wrong, the way you walked behind and watched everyone."

Doc made no comment.

He was listening to the radio receiver. It had been turned on throughout, but there had been nothing from it but the frying of static, occasionally the vague interference of some station not on the wave band. Because the speech went through a scrambler, the interference was quite unintelligible.

But now a background noise of a microphone had cut into the carrier.

Ham Brooks' very Harvard accent said, "Do you happen to be listening, Doc?"

The bronze man said, "Yes, Ham," into a microphone.

Ham said, "Finally I think we have something. A bit of a job it was, too. But Long Tom located Renny's handkerchief with the ultraviolet light. It was on a road, a rather deserted part of countryside. The road leads to a mud flat where a bunch of old barges are drawn up. We think Renny is being held there. And possibly Moldenhaeur, too."

Ham gave the location of the road. "This is flat country," he warned, "so be careful about using headlights. It should be near enough daylight that you won't need them, anyway."

Flat was a mild descriptive for the country around the road where Ham Brooks and Monk Mayfair met Doc Savage's car. It was marsh; with more vegetation, it would have been an impassable swamp. Grass of a type which thrived in salt water grew high and rank.

Ham glanced into the car, exclaimed, "By Jove! Who are these people?"

Pat told him, "They all have calloused feet, and some of them have canaries, and they're all full of lies. That's about all I can tell you. Oh, yes, they're all connected in one way or another with a company named Century Projects Corp."

Monk examined Liona Moldenhaeur. He was favorably impressed.

"I think somebody should stay here and watch the prisoners," he declared. "I'll do that. Me and my hog."

Ham looked indignant.

Doc said, "Ham, both you and Monk and Pat had better stay here and keep an eye on the guests."

Ham nodded. "Come over here," he said. "I'll show you

why we think both Renny and Moldenhaeur may be on the barges."

A hundred yards down the road, he turned off on a patch of firm ground, and approached two parked cars. Both machines were empty. Ham used a flashlight cautiously.

Pointing at the car nearest the road—the machine had obviously been the last one to arrive at the spot—Ham said, "In the back of that one, we found a couple of buttons off Renny's coat. It was the one Renny was in, all right."

Then Ham went to the second car. He dragged out a blanket that was soft and expensive, and monogrammed "WM" elaborately in one corner. "Recognize this, by any chance?" Ham asked.

"On the bed on which Moldenhaeur was lying when I saw him," Doc said.

"Then they brought Moldenhaeur here, too."

Doc Savage examined the prints made by the car tires, sinking to a knee several times for a closer inspection of details. More water had seeped into one set of tracks than into another; grass seemed a little more recently mashed by one set of tires.

He said, "The cars came here about an hour apart. First, Moldenhaeur was brought. Then the machine carrying Renny arrived." He extinguished the flashlight he had been using.

Ham was surprised. "We supposed Renny and Moldenhaeur were brought at the same time." He pointed, finger following the road. "About half a mile down that way is the water. The barges are scattered around. Johnny and Long Tom are down there. They are expecting you. Monk slipped down and told them you were coming."

"All right," Doc said.

"Imitate a farm dog barking in the distance," Ham said. "They will know it's you."

Doc directed, "Keep a close watch on Thomas, O'Callaghan, Boot, and Miss Moldenhaeur."

From the swampy nature of the flats around about, the marsh might have been expected to run into sea gradually. But it did not. The line of demarcation was sharp. There was even a sand-mud beach, deep water fairly close to it, and marsh grass leading up to the beach. Out to sea, or in the direction of the sea, rather, for the sea did not properly touch the spot, was a long and low neck of land that was not much more than a sandbar.

There were seven barges. Two of these did not count, for they were submerged until only odd parts of them stuck out of the water. One other barge lay on its side, more or less. The other four were drawn up on the mud where they had been floated at some high spring tide and left. They were worn beyond usefulness, and discarded here to rot in peace.

Doc Savage imitated a dog barking in the distance. It was not a difficult trick—the hard part of learning the deep-in-the-throat art of ventriloquism; once that was mastered, it was fairly easy to do tricks with various sounds.

He heard an answer. It was not a good one. So bad, in fact that he hoped it would not be repeated. He made for the sound.

It was Johnny, the long, lean archaeologist of big words. He was proud of his effort. "I should have been an animal imitator," he declared.

Long Tom joined them a moment later.

"The middle barge," Long Tom said. "They're on that, near as I can tell."

Doc said, "Wait, you two."

The bronze man then went forward. He was distrustful of the beach, of the tall grass near it, and he made a wide circle. Up the shore a short distance, he removed much of his clothing. He took to the water. Enough of a breeze was blowing to ripple the surface, and the sun was not yet up, or even near enough the horizon to lighten the night. He approached the barge cautiously.

His distrust included the wood of the barge. He explored carefully with his hands, located an iron fitting that would certainly support him.

There were at least two fast speedboats tied to the east side of the barge, he noted.

But the talking was going on near the bow, in the long box of a deckhouse. Ollie Saff's voice. Doc Savage moved close, got against the deckhouse, an eye to a crack.

Saff had his legs wide apart, fists on his hips. He spoke to Winton Moldenhaeur.

He said, "Last chance, Moldenhaeur."

Winton Moldenhaeur was now a man very much alive, but extremely ill. Ill to the point of caring for nothing. He slumped in his green sickness, on his haunches on the floor, arms out on either side, palms on the floor, propping himself erect.

There were seven men, not counting Moldenhaeur. Seven visible ones. And others, no doubt, who were out of sight. The crack did not give a view of the whole room.

Saff bristled rage. "Come, come!" he snapped. "I didn't follow you out here for nothing! You are the only one holding out. Thomas has come around to my way of thinking. So has Boot."

Winton Moldenhaeur said, "Damn you, no!"

Saff said, "This thing is in two parts. I have one part. You, Thomas and Boot have the other part. Together we can get rich."

Moldenhaeur glared sickly at him.

"You stole your part."

Saff shrugged. "Sure. I got it. But then, I was along with the rest of you when you got hold of the thing. I'm as much entitled to it as you are."

"You were working on a salary and we were risking the money we invested in the expedition," Moldenhaeur countered.

"This is just an argument."

Moldenhaeur said nothing.

Saff tried again. "Look, now. You better use your head. I have the antidote, or whatever you want to call the stuff, that will bring you out of it. I've demonstrated that. Didn't I just bring you out of it?"

Moldenhaeur scowled. "You gave the infernal stuff to me in the first place!"

"Sure, sure—but we've got only the supply of it we stole from you. When that's gone, we're licked, I admit. But before it's gone, you'll be a dead man. So what is holding out going to get you?"

Glaring at Saff, Moldenhaeur demanded, "Who is in this with you?"

"Nobody," Saff said. He laughed. "What gave you such an idea?"

"You haven't the brain to tackle it alone."

Saff sneered.

"Who," asked Moldenhaeur, "got Doc Savage mixed up in this affair?"

"It was Boot, damn him!" Ollie Saff cursed Benjamin Boot at some length.

The two fell silent, both angry.

* * *

Doc Savage considered what he had heard. An expedition to somewhere—a tropical jungle—would account for the tanned skins and calloused feet; an expedition to some spot where they had been forced to go primitive.

And they had found something that caused the "death" effect. And an antidote.

They were all in it—Moldenhaeur, his daughter, Thomas, O'Callaghan, Boot, Saff, Mr. Manley, Abner, these other men.

Now they were fighting over the spoils. Ollie Saff's group had terrorized—the way Saff told it—Boot, Thomas and the Moldenhaeurs, and Boot and Thomas had given in. That, then, explained why Ben Boot and Sam John Thomas had not wanted to talk. The girl had been silent because of her father. And O'Brien O'Callaghan, of course, worked for Thomas, so he was being silent because of orders.

That all held together—except for one thing.

If Benjamin Boot had called Doc Savage into the case—which he had—why had he then refused to tell the truth? Why had he painted it a mystery when he visited the headquarters with the story of the attempt on his life, and his worry about the girl he admired, Liona Moldenhaeur? That part needed some explaining.

The shot came rapping out of the distance.

Pat's scream followed. It was not a shriek of terror—it was made up of words, a warning. But the words were not distinguishable, and more shots interrupted them.

Men came diving out of the barge deckhouse. Two of them were just inside the door. They appeared with flashlights, and the beams landed upon Doc Savage.

The bronze man pitched forward. There was time only for his fists. He landed one blow, dropped a man. The flashlight climbed up in the air, scattering light over water, barge and beach as it whirled, and fell overboard.

Doc was not as fortunate with the second man. The fellow was going backward, trying to get away. He went in through the door, tripped, hit the sill and stretched out flat on the floor. Going in, Doc walked over him.

There was a gasoline lamp and an astounding number of men in the room. Doc made for the lamp. His eyes searched, tried to locate Renny. But Renny was not in sight.

Doc got the lamp, threw it at Saff. There was a pistol in

Saff's hand, and he held up gun and hand to ward off the lamp. It hit him. The brass chamber of the lamp hit the gun hard enough to split. The gasoline in the chamber was under pressure. It spouted out, sheeting into flame.

Saff, suddenly a pillar of fire, screeched. He went back, had luck, and found the door. He went over the side into the shallow water and mud.

Streams of burning gasoline ran over the floor like red snakes.

To the right, there was a rectangular opening, a ladder standing in it.

Doc carried his anaesthetic grenades in a small metal case. He got this out, opened it, and dashed the case on the floor, very hard.

Then he jumped for the opening in the floor, went down it.

A man howled, "Gas! Gas! Get outa here, you guys!"

Doc knew then that it would be too much to hope that anyone would be overcome by the anaesthetic. He held his breath, used his flashlight.

The mud was about knee-deep, about as thick as automobile grease, and part of a coat, the tail, protruded from it. Doc grasped the tail and pulled. A form came up. A body that had been immersed completely in the mud came into view.

The size of the fists, more than anything else, showed that it was Renny Renwick.

The bronze man lost no time, but shouldered Renny's huge form, climbed back up the ladder. The fire was spreading in the deckhouse. The rectangular opening, fortunately, was out of view of the door.

Doc had breathed down below. But now he held his breath. The gas was effective only when inhaled.

He popped a pair of smoke bombs down on the floor, one near the door, one just outside it. They turned into fat clouds of intense black smoke.

The bronze man dropped Renny beside the ladder. He went back down again. He needed more air.

While he was in the hold of the barge, where the gas had not penetrated, he threw his flashlight beam around. In the extreme bow, there were large shelves, and these were laden with packing cases.

Outdoors, there was an abrupt moan. A huge sound, as if

a great bullfrog had turned loose. It was a machine pistol, a compact weapon of the type carried by Johnny and Long Tom. A burst of rifle and pistol fire replied.

Then someone put a pistol muzzle through a crack in the barge hull and shot the bronze man in the back.

The bulletproof vest stopped the slug, but the blow knocked Doc sprawling. His flashlight landed somewhere in the mud and sank. For moments, he wallowed desperately, trying to get to his feet again. The chain-mesh armor of the vest, while infinitely lighter than the plate type, had the disadvantage of not scattering shock as much. It was like being kicked by a well-fed mule.

Several bullets hunted unsuccessfully for him, splattering mud and clouting the barge hull.

Coming to his feet, the bronze man found the ladder, held his breath—no small job, with the agony in his back— and climbed. The smoke made it intensely black in the deckhouse. He found Renny.

He could not see the fire. Flames burned his legs. He made the door, got outside, jumped overboard and landed in the waist-deep mud and water.

"Here!" someone bellowed at him from the stern. "We're getting in the boats!"

The voice belonged to Ollie Saff, and it meant they were using the speedboat to escape.

Doc changed his voice, shouted, "Wait for me!"

He shoved Renny's form a few yards, left Renny on a hummock of mud, safely away from the fire, face out of water.

Then the bronze man went wallowing boldly for the speedboat. He reached the bow of the boat. A man was there, trying to turn the bow out to sea. Doc helped him. Then he climbed on to the coaming deck of the boat, hauled the other man up.

The big motor of the craft let out a shuddering moan, and they gathered speed. Doc Savage and his companion lay on the coaming, braced against the windshield.

From shore, a machine pistol gobbled suddenly. In the boat, there was profanity, and a man collapsed. Doc kept down, behind the glass windshield. He could tell, from the sound of the striking machine pistol bullets, that they were mercy slugs, merely shells charged with chemicals which produced temporary helplessness. It was the type of bullet Johnny, Long Tom and the others usually employed in the machine pistols.

Saff cursed steadily for a few minutes.

"Where's Moldenhaeur?" he snarled.

"I got him here," a man said.

"Good!" Saff snapped. "Hey, you, turn this boat around."

The man running the speedboat did not like that idea. He started to object.

"Turn it around!" Saff screamed.

The man obeyed. Doc Savage and the other man lying on the rounded bow portion of the speedboat clutched each other to keep from rolling overboard.

The boat roared back toward the burning barge for a while.

"That's far enough," Saff said disgustedly. "Hell, the barge is going to burn to the water's edge!"

A man groaned. "That means all the stuff and the antidote will be destroyed."

"It'll be worth it if Savage burns in the barge," Saff growled.

"He will," a man declared. "I tell you, I shot Savage right square in the back."

Ollie Saff turned to the speedboat operator again. "Head for LaGuardia Airport," he ordered. "You know where that is, don't you?"

"You mean the big—"

"Yeah, I mean the big New York airport. Only we're interested in the transatlantic seaplanes."

"That's a long way—"

"Can you make it by ten o'clock?" Saff demanded.

"Sure," said the man at the wheel.

"All right, do it," Saff ordered. "We're going to grab one of those big planes, the one that leaves at ten o'clock."

"Hell, we've got nobody capable of flying a job like that," a man interrupted. "I'm a navigator, and I could tell where we were going. But as for flying it—"

"We'll make the crew fly it for us," Saff snapped.

Doc Savage grasped the shoulder of the man lying with him on the coaming. He squeezed the shoulder until the man gasped. Doc Savage moaned loudly. He croaked: "They... shot... me!" Then he made a blubbering noise, a few gasps, and had a convulsion.

Eventually he rolled off the coaming into the water, giving his body a shove which sent it clear of the propellers.

The boat passed him with a roar; its wash ran over his head. The noise of the speedboat exhausts immediately slackened.

He heard Saff bellow. "What the hell happened to *him*?"

And the man on the coaming answered: "He was shot!"

"Turn around," Saff ordered. "Pick him up."

Doc swam furiously, and when the speedboat got close, dived. He kept under the surface. Ghosts of light traveled over the water, indicating they were using the boat spot and flashlights. When he had to have air, he took it with only his nose above the surface, then sank again. And finally the speedboat departed.

VIII

THE PILOT

A flushed sun, harrassed by storm clouds, was dispelling the night when Doc Savage crawled out of the water and walked along the mud-and-sand beach, the inlet on one side, the vast marsh expanse on the other. Gulls moved fretfully overhead.

Pat Savage met him. Pat looked too angry, too horrified, for tears.

"Renny," she said chokingly. "He . . . Monk and Ham say he is like . . . like . . . he isn't alive, and he isn't dead."

"Like Mr. Manley and Abner?" the bronze man asked quietly.

Pat nodded. "And like Mr. Moldenhaeur."

Doc said, "There is an antidote. They brought Moldenhaeur out of it."

Seizing the bronze man's arm. "Oh, Doc!" Pat gasped. "You mean . . . he can be cured? Renny can?"

Doc said, "He *can* be."

She stared at him. "Can we?"

"We do not have the antidote," he said.

"Is there a chance to get it?" Her voice was stark.

"That remains to be seen," he said.

Johnny, Long Tom, Ham and Monk were working over

Renny. Or were standing around him, rather, looking helpless. They had carefully removed the mud, and one of them
had driven their car to the spot.

What remained of the barge was pouring a cloud of
smoke into the air.

Long Tom pointed at the front of the barge.

"It burned like a furnace," he said. "There must have
been something inflammable, chemicals or something, stored
in the front. You never saw such a fire for a while."

Doc Savage said nothing. His metallic features were
inscrutable, his manner composed.

Monk stepped forward, "Doc, we lost all the prisoners.
Miss Moldenhaeur, Boot, Thomas, O'Callaghan—everybody
we had in that car."

The bronze man did not comment.

Monk added, "They came down the road. They had a
new car, and they didn't use their headlights. They must have
sent a man or two ahead to scout, and they located us. They
set a trap, and we fell for it."

Ham entered the conversation. The usually dapper lawyer was mud-smeared, and his voice was full of self-disgust.

"A nice bunch of saps we were!" Ham said. "I heard a
man moan in the marsh nearby. I . . . I thought it was one of
you and you might have got hurt. I got out to look—"

Monk said, "I told him not to do that, but he—"

Ham's fists knotted. He strode over in front of Monk,
snarled, "This is one mistake you better not ride me about,
you homely goat!"

Monk subsided. Ordinarily, he took a great deal of
pleasure in ribbing Ham unmercifully. Their existence, in
fact, was a perpetual quarrel. But Ham was in a bad mood.

Ham faced Doc. "They jumped me. Pat and Monk got
out to help. They were all around us, loaded for bear. They
chased us into the marsh. Then they grabbed all the prisoners and got away with them."

Doc Savage walked over to the remains of the barge. He
got a long plank, and began to splash water on the flames
with it, extinguishing them slowly.

"Monk," he said.

"Yeah, Doc."

"I want every burned fragment, every bit of ash, metal,
or any particle of anything, no matter what it is, that remains
of the front of this barge. Load it in the car—not our car, but

one of their two machines. Their two cars are still back there in the marsh, are they not?"

"Yes—the cars they brought Renny and Moldenhaer here in. Both machines are still there."

"Use those," the bronze man directed. "Take the stuff you gather to our water-front hangar, and load it in the biggest plane. Put Renny aboard the plane. Go to headquarters and get that butler of Boot's, Julian, and load him in the plane. Keep him drugged. Load Mr. Manley and Abner in the plane also. You will find those three in the hiding place in the laboratory where we usually keep prisoners."

Monk nodded. "Then what?"

"Load plenty of gasoline on the plane, and stand by the radio for orders."

"Right."

The bronze man's flake-gold eyes drifted to Renny, then back to the smoldering barge. "When you collect the remains of the front of that barge, you can leave the timbers, all but a few scrapings from the outer surface. That will cut down the bulk of the load."

Monk nodded. "You want all of us to be ready to take off on a long trip in the plane?"

"Yes," the bronze man said.

Monk watched him walk to the car, slide behind the wheel, and drive away.

The transatlantic passenger plane—Bermuda, the Azores and Portugal—was afloat at the passenger loading dock. The ground crew were putting last touches on the craft before its take-off.

A car came across the field, drew up at the dock. The machine bore the markings of the airline, and the executive head of the line alighted. He was followed by a burly, swarthy, black-haired man in a pilot's uniform.

The pilot of the transatlantic plane saluted the executive, said, "Good morning, Mr. Lane."

"Good morning, Hal," said Lane. "Will you get your crew together at once inside the plane? I have something to say to them."

The pilot was puzzled, but he assembled his navigator, radioman, mechanic, co-pilot and steward.

Lane, the chief executive of the line, talked for some

minutes to the crew. Then he reappeared and addressed the black-haired man who had come in the car with him.

"They are willing to go through with it," he said. "The pilot insists on going along. The navigator is the only one who seems dubious, and he is the only married man aboard. I took the liberty of ordering him to remain behind. The pilot will serve as navigator, ostensibly."

"Good."

"You will take over as pilot."

The black-haired man nodded.

"However," said the airways executive, "I am not going to let this thing happen to our regular passengers. I will put aboard enough of our employees, whom I shall ask to volunteer, to make up a pretended passenger list. I will insist on that requirement. Is that satisfactory?"

Again the dark man nodded.

"All right, take over," said Lane. "And good luck, Mr. Savage. The thing seems wildly fantastic to me, but, if I may speak frankly, you own enough of this airline that your requests must necessarily be granted, regardless of what I personally think of their sanity."

The manager apparently realized he had expressed himself with more bluntness than tact, because he looked nervous. But Doc Savage said, "Your position is well taken. If you had expressed any other opinion, I would doubt *your* sanity."

Lane smiled faintly. "I'll go get volunteer passengers together," he said. "The plane will take off at ten, as scheduled."

The airport attendants, unaware of any change in routine, finished servicing the big ship. A few minutes before ten, trucks arrived, and mail sacks and air express was placed aboard.

Later, half a dozen passengers filed into the plane.

Doc Savage took the pilot's compartment. In the polished window, he gave his reflection a last inspection, checking on his disguise. He had changed the contour of his face—not by using such conventional methods as paraffin fills—with the use of chemicals which caused swellings, harmless and not particularly unpleasant, of face tissue. The effects would last several days. He had altered the color of hair and skin with dye, and his flake-gold eyes with optical caps of tinted nonshatter glass, unlikely to be noticed even on close inspection.

The regular pilot, Hal Stevens, shook hands with him.

The co-pilot, Tom Vanstein, did likewise. And the radioman, mechanic and steward exchanged brief greetings and wishes for good luck. They seemed a competent group, unafraid, rather eager for the excitement.

"Believe it or not," said Odets, the radioman, "this transatlantic run is about the most monotonous job there is. I'm going to relish the trouble, if any."

Doc said, "Can you change your radio transmitter so that, when the switch shows off, it will actually be on?"

"Yes, I could."

"Do so."

The bronze man's eyes moved over the expanse of water in the direction of Flushing. A motorboat was moving idly in the distance, following the far shore. Doc used field glasses briefly, then replaced them in their case. Unless he was much mistaken, the boat carried Ollie Saff and a number of others.

It was ten o'clock.

The wind was coming from the west, which made it necessary to taxi downwind, then turn and come back into the breeze in order to make a take-off into the wind.

The bronze man drove the four big motors idly, and the plane crawled across the surface. It drew near the Flushing shore.

The loitering motorboat turned, lifted up its nose, took a white bone of foam in its teeth and came scudding toward the plane.

The bronze man turned the great plane expertly, but not too hurriedly.

The motorboat got directly in the path of the ship. Doc throttled the motors, and the plane drifted idly. A man—Saff— stood up in the speedboat, waved his arms.

The steward opened the plane window and shouted, "Hey, you! You're blocking our course!"

"Hold it!" Saff bellowed. "I've got a message for you. We're government agents."

The speedboat approached the plane, drew alongside. The steward held open a door.

Saff climbed into the big transatlantic seaplane and took a gun out of his pocket. Other men followed him and showed more guns.

"Radio operator, get away from that set!" Saff snarled.

Ollie Saff was well acquainted with the arrangement of

the plane, and he had instructed his men with care. They spread rapidly, covering the—they supposed—passengers.

Saff said, "Nobody who does what he's told is gonna get hurt."

Doc Savage put his hands up meekly. Sitting where he was at the controls, he could see the speedboat below. There were bound figures in the craft—five of them. Liona Moldenhaeur, her father, Sam John Thomas, O'Brien O'Callaghan, Benjamin Boot, all of them were captives and being taken along forcibly.

A man stood at the door of the pilot's compartment. He held an automatic as black as evil, asked, "You the pilot?"

Doc Savage nodded.

"Sure, and what yez think you be pullin'?" he asked with a brogue.

"Black Irish, eh?" The man with the gun showed his teeth unpleasantly. "You sound too much like a cop for me to like you. Hey, you there—you the co-pilot?"

The co-pilot said, "Yes."

Turning his head, the man called, "Pilot and co-pilot are up here, boss."

"All right," Saff said. "Pilot and co-pilot stay aboard. All the rest of you unload. Passengers and everybody."

The co-pilot looked at Doc Savage. He moistened his lips, then tried to twist the fear off them with a grin, but did not quite succeed. The thing had become something besides a promise of interesting excitement; it was trouble now. Serious. Deadly, too. Men who stole several hundred thousand dollars' worth of transatlantic seaplane were not likely to take chances.

Doc Savage watched the personnel and passengers of the plane being loaded into the speedboat. Moldenhaeur, Boot, O'Callaghan and Thomas have been loaded on the plane.

Saff came forward. He looked at Doc.

"You the pilot?" he asked.

The bronze man gave him a stare under dark, beetling brows. "What about it?" he asked.

"Get hold of the airport dispatcher and tell him nothing has happened," Saff ordered. "Then take this thing off and head it for the open sea."

Doc scowled. "And if I don't?"

Saff cocked a pistol he was carrying. "We'll try getting along without you, then," he said.

Doc went through the motion of weakening. "The radio is in back," he said. "You got rid of the operator."

"Can you operate the outfit?"

"Yes."

"Do it," Saff said. "And I'll be right there listening."

Doc Savage said something unintelligible, but which had the ring of a "damn" and a "hell" and similar comment. But it was not English.

"Come on, come on, get moving," Saff ordered.

Doc obeyed. But he kept mumbling in the strange tongue while he went back to the radio cabin, closely trailed by Saff. He kept muttering while he fiddled with transmitter and held the microphone close to his lips, but scowled at Saff while he did so. With his free hand, he held a headset to an ear.

He said, "Hello, flight seven reporting. That delay down here was just some sightseers in a motorboat. We got rid of them. Taking off now." He seemed to listen for a moment. "O. K."

He threw switches, put the headset down and stood up.

"They don't suspect anything," he told Saff angrily.

Saff grinned. "Get back and take off. This will give us ten minutes or so leeway." He pointed into the east. "You see those clouds? Head for them."

When the plane had moaned across the comparatively smooth water, climbed above the Triborough Bridge and banked around, heading out to sea, Saff heaved a grunt of satisfaction. He tapped Doc on the shoulder.

"You're doing fine, Black Irish," Saff said. "Just keep it up. We'll give you the course. We've got a navigator aboard, so don't try any navigation of your own."

Saff went back into the cabin for a moment.

The co-pilot threw Doc an anxious glance.

"Everything is going all right," Doc told him.

"What language were you swearing in?" asked the co-pilot, trying to make conversation. "I don't believe I have heard it before."

The bronze man made a quick negative gesture, indicating silence.

He did not want to discuss the matter. The language had been Mayan, and it was not profanity; the emphasis on the words had simply made it sound like swearing. He had started it back in the pilot's compartment in order to make it appear that he was indulging in disgruntled muttering—but the muttering into microphone had been specific instructions to Monk and the others to take the air and follow, by radio compass, the carrier wave of the transatlantic plane radio transmitter. The radio transmitter had not been set on the airport dispatcher's frequency, but on the wave length used by the bronze man's associates.

The Mayan tongue was almost unknown in the civilized world. The bronze man and his aids had learned it in the course of an adventure in a remote Central American valley. They had used it since to communicate with each other when they did not wish to be understood by listeners.*

IX

ATLANTIC CHASE

That was on Saturday.

It was late Sunday when Ollie Saff showed Doc Savage the muzzle of his gun, and pointed downward. "Land," he ordered. "That inlet."

The bronze man brought the plane down on smooth, stagnant water, the mouth of a river. Following Saff's instructions, he swung the ship into the wind and waited.

A boat put in an appearance, circled them cautiously, a man standing up and staring at them.

Saff threw open a window, bellowed, "Get the gasoline, you fool!"

---

*The use Doc Savage makes here of primitive Indian dialects for secretiveness in communication is not new. It was used by American troops in the World War, when American Indian telephone operators were employed to thwart enemy wiretappers. In the recent training of American troops, the same subject has received public attention, use being made of Indians who speak unwritten dialects. Because the dialects are primitive, as well as not being written, there are no words for such modern war gadgets as tanks, so that the Indians using the lingo to convey information by telephone or radio find it necessary to improvise descriptive groups of words, calling a tank, for instance, something like a "big turtle moves fast, spits fire."

The man in the boat yelled back, "*Si, si, señor*. I make me sure he ees you. Keep your shirt on me."

"Get the gasoline!" Saff squalled.

The motorboat went away. It came back towing two flat-bottomed craft loaded with five-gallon gasoline tins. They began loading the fuel.

Doc Savage moved back to the door, said, "Be sure that is high-test stuff. Ordinary gasoline isn't so good in these motors."

Saff snapped, "Get back in there. It's the right kind of gasoline."

The bronze man went to the radio cubicle, looked inside. A man was sitting there with an automatic. He sneered. Doc shrugged.

He went back to the pilot's compartment.

The co-pilot stared at him anxiously. "There's palm trees on shore. Where do you think we are?"

"Somewhere on the eastern coast of Brazil, probably."

"Did you get in contact with your men by radio?"

"They had a man watching the radio outfit."

The co-pilot shuddered. "I wonder what this will turn into? They're loading the tanks plumb full of gasoline."

Doc Savage did not seem concerned.

It was dark before they took off. Dark on Sunday evening.

Tuesday afternoon.

There had been jungle below for a long time. Now there were mountains, almost entirely of stone, nakedly ominous.

Twisting a white, tired, frightened face, the co-pilot asked. "How do you suppose they had that gasoline waiting? The first time in Brazil, the second time on the African coast?"

"Cabled ahead before they ever stole the plane in New York," the bronze man said.

He was watching the instruments, compass and altimeter; from time to time he watched an object below, checking drift as best he could.

Without instruments, he was having trouble keeping an exact track of their whereabouts. The crossing of the South Atlantic had been particularly confusing. They had seen no ships during most of the trip.

Instruments took care of everything except the measurement of wind drift. To check that, Ollie Saff's navigator had used the method employed by the regular navigators on the transatlantic routes. He had dropped overboard a thin-walled glass container filled with powdered aluminum. This hit the surface of the sea, burst, and the powdered aluminum made a shiny slick which the navigator could watch through his instruments. A man had stood over Doc Savage with a gun whenever this was done, to prevent him getting even a naked-eye check on the drift. Charts had been kept from him.

"Africa?" the co-pilot asked questioningly.

Doc nodded. "Interior somewhere."

"There hasn't been a sign of civilization," said the co-pilot, "for several hundred miles."

A man put his head in the compartment. "Pipe down," he ordered. Then he pointed. "You see that mountain range yonder? The peak with the snow on it?"

The peak was not much different from others they had passed. A little higher, possibly. More naked. There had been snow on some of the others.

"Go south of it," the man ordered. "Then turn east and fly straight east by southeast."

The bronze man followed instructions. The mountain range pushed upward, and he could distinguish the terrain in more detail. Africa, beyond a doubt. And a very remote section. An area that was probably fenced off from penetration by deserts to the north and east, impassable jungles to the south and west.

The peak swung slowly under the left-hand wingtip, its snow-helmeted crest above them.

"All right, all right," said the man. "East by southeast now."

The earth dropped away sharply; they had been but a few hundred feet above the rocky terrain, and now within minutes the ground was thousands of feet below.

"Go down," the man said.

Ollie Saff elbowed the man aside, growled, "I'll take over now." To Doc Savage, he said, "Keep losing altitude. Not too fast. And watch out for currents. They are like cyclones in here."

Doc said, "You have flown in here before?"

"Sure," Saff said. Then he scowled. "Don't let a long nose get you into trouble, buddy."

There was jungle beneath. Incredible jungle and incredible stone, as if great hands had taken the jungle and the mountains and mashed them together.

A ridge of verdant green wheeled back and disclosed a lake the color of indigo.

"Land on the lake," Saff said.

The lake was extremely deep. The intense blue of the water, like a polished gun barrel, came from the depth. Doc Savage watched their wake spread out slowly until it reached the shores of the V-shaped inlet into which the plane moved.

Ollie Saff stood beside Doc Savage in the pilot's compartment, staring down at the water, then at the shores, searching for landmarks.

"There!" he exploded, pointing. "There it is."

A spire of stone came up from the depths, its top forming a submerged island perhaps a dozen feet in each dimension, and no more than four feet beneath the surface.

Looking down in the utterly clear water, they could see a steel chain lying on the top of the islet. One end of the chain seemed to be secured to a kind of bridle of three hawsers which were secured to irregularities in the stone itself.

Saff punched the co-pilot.

"Jump in and pick up that mooring line," he ordered.

Saff was grinning when he gave the command. The reason for his mirth was immediately apparent when the co-pilot jumped into the lake. Because the co-pilot shrieked, grabbed up the chain, and snatched the rope ladder with wild haste. His teeth were rattling by the time he had made the chain fast to a mooring ring and climbed into the cabin.

"That water's cold as ice!" he gasped.

Saff said, "Lay down on the floor, you two!"

Doc Savage and the co-pilot obeyed. Their hands were lashed, and their ankles. They were dumped into a compartment.

"There'll be a man on watch," Saff warned. "So don't try any tricks."

The compartment door was not closed immediately. Watching developments through it, Doc saw that Winton Moldenhaeur, his daughter, O'Callaghan, Ben Boot, Sam John Thomas—all the prisoners—were being unloaded, put aboard an inflated rubber life raft.

The raft was the usual type, one that could be inflated in a few seconds by the compressed carbon dioxide gas in a small cylinder. They made two trips with it, ferrying everyone ashore. On the last trip, only one man returned with the raft.

This one man was evidently to be their guard. After he had looked in on them, he walked back in the cabin, settled himself in another compartment, and made himself comfortable— judging by the sounds.

"How long have we gotta stay tied?" the co-pilot shouted at him.

"Shut up," the man called.

"These ropes are too tight," complained the co-pilot.

The guard asked, "You want me to kick your teeth in? Or you want to keep your blabber shut?"

The co-pilot subsided, rolled over to face Doc Savage— and his eyes protruded. For the bronze man was sitting up, and the ropes were no longer on his wrists and ankles.

Doc shook his head for silence, indicated a thin blade of steel that was like a flat wire. He had carried that in a tubing sheath in his jacket collar, where it was no more noticeable than one of the horsehairs used to stiffen the collar foundations of cheap suits. Its serrated, tempered edge had cut through the ropes readily—would saw through fairly hard iron, if necessary.

He leaned close to the co-pilot, said, "Call the fellow. Raise a rumpus," in a whisper.

The co-pilot nodded, began to kick the wall with his bound feet and howl in anger, demanding that his ropes be loosened, that he be told what would happen to him, that it be explained what this was all about—anything he could complain about. Doc Savage sat back, draped the cut ropes innocently over his ankles and wrists so that they seemed to be tied, and waited. But the guard only laughed noisily at them.

Five minutes of steady noise from the co-pilot, however, got results.

The guard wrenched the door open, launched a kick, and Doc Savage got his foot like a bear trap. The commotion inside the compartment was violent for twenty seconds or so. A fist on the guard's jaw, squarely against the end of it, made him sleep.

Doc cut the co-pilot free.

"Watch this fellow," the bronze man ordered.

He went back to the radio cubby, entered, examined the

apparatus. Power during flight was furnished by a wind-driven generator; the landing of the plane had silenced this. Doc examined the apparatus, then switched over to battery operation.

"Monk," he called. "If you hear this, answer in Mayan," he added, using the Mayan tongue himself.

Johnny Littlejohn, not Monk, replied almost at once. "I'll be superamalgamated!" Johnny exploded. "Say, that radio carrier wave we've been trailing for days went off the air a while ago, and were we worried!" He forgot to use Mayan.

Doc asked, "Is everything all right aboard?"

"Yes," Johnny said, remembering and using Mayan.

"You have Julian, Mr. Manley, Abner, aboard?"

"Right."

"Has Julian talked?"

"No, we can't get anything out of him," Johnny admitted. "We came off in a rush without any truth serum, or we would have tried that on him. Say, how much longer is this chase going to last? All the way across Africa?"

Doc asked, "What kind of country are you flying over?"

"Mountains. The dangedest mountains you ever saw."

"Take a radio bearing on my transmitter," Doc directed.

"Long Tom already has it."

Doc said, "All right. Fly at right angles to your present course for five minutes, keep track of your ground speed, and take another bearing on me. I'll come back on the air."

Doc Savage closed down the transmitter, sat watching the chronometer, waiting for the five minutes to elapse. He heard a commotion which was evidently the revival of their guard, and, to judge from the sound, the fist of the co-pilot putting the man back to sleep.

After the five minutes had nearly passed, Doc went on the air again, and Long Tom took another radio bearing.

"All right, you have your fix," the bronze man said. "Where the two bearing lines cross, you'll find a lake in the mountains. It is a very blue lake, and our plane is sitting on it. Fly very high, spot the lake, and immediately head north."

Doc glanced out of the windows of the plane.

"There is a cloud bank in the north," he added. "Hang around in that for about two hours, which should be just a little before sunset. Come in high, cut your motors, and land on the far end of the lake. That would be the east end."

"Is it big enough—the lake—that no one can see us from where you are?"

Doc said, "No, but the water is very cold, and the air warm. As the sun goes down and the air cools off, the cold water will condense the moisture in it and cause a fog, probably."

"Right. We'll spot the place. Have you any idea why they made this wild dash for Africa?"

The bronze man seemed not to hear the question. He said, "If I am not here, the co-pilot will be in the plane." Then he switched off the radio.

He began removing his clothing. He stripped down to shorts, then found a sheet, removed the airline emblem on it, and fashioned himself a breechcloth.

Next he found a can of dark graphite grease, and began smearing his skin with the stuff. By judicious husbanding, he got the grease to spread from head to foot, turning him quite black.

He told the pilot, "Watch for my men. If Saff and the others return, cast off the mooring, start the plane motors and taxi down the lake away from them."

The pilot gaped at him. "Great snakes, you're not going to *swim* to shore! You'll freeze! I tell you that water is colder than ice!"

The bronze man opened a door in the hull of the plane, a door away from the direction which Saff had taken, and slid into the water.

X

THE STRANGE CANARY

The grease helped some. But the water was still cold. Doc Savage was in excellent physical condition—he made a practice of taking an average of two hours' intensive exercise daily—but the ice chill of the water clutched at his muscles with invisible force.

He gulped in several deep breaths of air, then put a metal clip over his nostrils, and placed between his lips a chemical "lung" gadget which resembled nothing so much as a toy balloon complete with metal mouthpiece for inflating.

The thing would filter breath and add depleted oxygen. Its effectiveness was limited to considerably less than half an hour.

But, using the gadget, the bronze man was able to sink beneath the surface and swim for shore. He used a very simple method of keeping his bearings—because to swim a straight line under water, with no visible object for a guide, is almost impossible. The sloping sun formed a patch of brightness down in the depths, but its light was confusingly diffused by the water. Its shadow, however, was noticeable. He kept his directions by the shadow, after a fashion.

The coldness of the water was not as bad after he got in motion. But the chill was bitter. In fact, the stone bottom of the lake, when he finally touched its upward slant, felt as if it was covered with ice.

He came out of the water beneath overhanging jungle bushes. The air was hot, as if a furnace door had been opened.

The bronze man found sand and dust, worked his hands in it, getting rid of the grease on his palms. He treated the bare soles of his feet likewise.

The graphite grease making him as black as any aboriginal inhabitant of these jungles, he moved along the shore. He found that the rubber boat had been lifted out of the water, carried along a path.

The path was a wide, cleared one. Feet had used it enough to keep down the vegetation. Doc glanced at the jungle above the path, then grasped a limb, swung up. An instant later, he was standing on the limb. He went up a vine, hand over hand, more than twenty feet. He walked out a long limb, dropped off it feetfirst into space, landed on another limb, kept his balance, and went on.

He came to a clearing. In the center stood a circular hut made of stones and mud. The hut was obviously a white man's method of construction, built for the purposes of defense.

There were portholes. There were holes in the roof for watching the treetops, and these were covered with windshield glass from a plane, as defense against poison blowgun arrows. In addition, the hut was situated so that it commanded the path all the way to the lake. A stream of water trickled out of one side of the hut continually, indicating the structure had been erected over a spring.

Ollie Saff stood in the center of the clearing. Several of his men were with him, and more were coming out of the stone citadel.

All of them were stark naked except for breechcloths.

Saff was lecturing one of his men in emphatic terms.

"I don't give a damn if your feet *are* tender," he was saying. "You go barefooted and like it. It ain't safe to wear shoes, or clothes, neither."

The breechcloths they were wearing were all a brilliant yellow color. From their looks, they had been fashioned hastily out of a bolt of yellow cloth.

"Hurry up," Saff yelled at the hut.

Liona Moldenhaeur appeared, wearing a length of yellow cloth wrapped in sarong fashion. Her father followed. The other prisoners also appeared—Boot, Thomas and O'Callaghan.

Saff put his gun inside his breechcloth, took care that its presence was not noticeable. "You guys be sure your guns are out of sight," he warned his men. "And come on."

They filed away into the jungle, following another path that led upward.

Doc Savage dropped silently from leafy heights where he had been crouching, watching. He landed a few feet from the crude stone blockhouse.

For moments he crouched there, listening, every sense acute. His manner had changed to the tense, alert caution of an animal. Finally, he moved to the door of the hut, went in, after closing his eyes long enough for them to become accustomed to the gloom that would be inside.

Just inside, he stopped, his eyes on the floor. There was a design in yellow on the floor, a likeness of a bird, a canary. It was nearly a yard in its longest dimension. Doc sank to a knee to look closer. Made of hundreds of yellow pegs, colored yellow and thrust into the hard earth. The heads of the pegs were tapered, sharp as needles, and coated with something sticky and dark. Possibly poisoned.

There was evidence that everyone using the hut had carefully stepped clear of the strange, poisonous yellow picture on the floor.

In the hut there were bunks, shelves, pegs. The pegs supported clothing. The place was divided into two rooms. A glance showed the bronze man that the second room was exactly like the first, except that only Liona Moldenhaeur's clothing was there.

The remains of the bolt of yellow cloth from which the breechcloths had been fashioned lay on one shelf.

Doc examined empty packing cases. These had contained supplies. They were marked:

MOLDENHAEUR-THOMAS
AFRICAN EXPEDITION

The hut obviously had been constructed months ago. The bronze man noted also that the empty packing cases were old. Certainly they had not been brought by Saff.

This spot, apparently, had been the headquarters of the original expedition to this part of Africa. He searched for some time, hoping to locate something that would indicate just who had made up the original expedition personnel. But he found nothing to give that information.

He stepped outside, careful to keep clear of the yellow bird picture of sharpened pegs on the floor.

Outside, he picked up a rock, carefully scraped a series of pictures on stone near the hut entrance. Picture writing. The Mayan symbols for danger and death. He drew them prominently, so that they would warn his aids, should they reach here before he returned.

The warning was against the sharpened yellow pegs which composed the bird picture. He was convinced they were poisoned.

Once again he took to the tree lanes. He went forward rapidly. Monkeys chattered shrilly at him, and once an ape showed him an ugly, astonished face, then made a sound like a large insect and bounded away through the intertwining limbs.

The sun was behind the western mountains now. Shadows were crawling into the valleys, darkening the incredible tangle that floored the jungle. Up high, where the bronze man moved, there was more light, space for movement.

And abruptly, in front of him, lunging upward, there was a cliff. Of dark stone, coffee-colored, the sheer surface was not smooth, but serrated with numerous cracks and water-worn channels.

Doc Savage dropped lower, kept closer above the path, so as not to lose it. He was, he knew, going slower than Ollie

Saff's group, but there was no helping that. He distrusted the path, preferred the way he was traveling.

Then, suddenly he was a motionless image, staring.

They were sitting still. All of them. They were on low stones. The stones were arranged in a circle. And in the center of the circle, on a stone block, stood the yellow bird. The bird was as high as a man. Its brilliance, the startling contrast of its lemon-yellow against the dark cliff and the surrounding jungle, made it seem larger.

They sat perfectly still.

Doc Savage watched them. Not until one of the men made an angry swat at a fly was he sure they were alive, and not stricken rigid by some mysterious power.

Saff cursed the man who had belted the fly.

"Cut that out!" he snarled. "Sit still, you fool! You make a couple of moves like that, and you'll be a dead duck. And so will the rest of us."

"But these danged bugs! They bite like lions—"

"Shut up!" snapped Saff. "Sit still!"

They sat still after that. Waiting.

Beyond the circular ring of stones with the statue in the center, there seemed to be a path that led upward. But there was no one on the path, no stir of movement in the numerous niches in the steep face of stone.

The sun sank lower. In the distance, very faintly, Doc Savage heard a plane motor. He heard it shut off.

The group sitting with such agonizing rigidity did not hear the plane, apparently.

Then, high on the face of the cliff, there was a whistling call, the cry of the strange yellow birds. It rose sharply, whipped to peak, sank away in a musical tone that faded.

Then, so unexpectedly that Doc Savage jumped, two dark-skinned men stepped out of niches in the cliff, where they had been concealed. They were natives, as dark as blacks, but without the thick lips of the Senegambian. Nor did they have the overlong arms, the flat noses depressed at the base common to the Gabun, Congo, or Mozambique types.

These could have been Arabs, although they were darker. They were well-built men, muscular, with the completely erect carriage of peoples whose women carry burdens on their heads from childhood.

They stood perfectly still after they appeared. But they held, poised at their lips, long reeds. The reeds were blowguns.

The whistle came again from the cliff..

Doc lifted his eyes.

In the setting sun, which reddened the face of the cliff, a column of men had appeared. They came down what was obviously a well-worn trail on the cliff. They marched with stately precision.

Slight sounds drew Doc's eyes downward. It was, he saw, as well that he had not come on foot. There were natives in the brush below, well-hidden and motionless watching the group around the yellow bird. They were armed with blowguns, some of them with short throwing spears.

The cavalcade came down the cliff, surrounded the yellow bird, and stood perfectly still in their tracks for a while. This formality over with, they walked over and looked at the white men. They gave particular attention to Liona Moldenhaeur.

"*Ya inta*," one of the natives said. "*Da min deh?*"

Doc was startled. The language was Egyptian. A greeting. Ollie Saff looked helpless.

"Talk to him, Moldenhaeur," he ordered. "And don't try any funny stuff, either."

Moldenhaeur returned the greeting of the native in halting Egyptian.

He added, "We have returned because we wish to again enjoy the peace of your land. We have brought with us friends, whom we hope you will like and befriend, as you befriended us before."

The leader of the natives said something Doc did not catch.

Saff turned to the others after Moldenhaeur whispered to him.

"Come on, everybody," Saff said. "It's O. K. They're taking us to where they live."

Doc Savage watched them go upward and eventually disappear. He remained where he was, keeping an intent eye on the natives in the jungle, the ones Saff had not seen.

The bronze man was puzzled. The Egyptian language was good, and in some respects these natives resembled Egyptians. But this country could be nowhere near Egypt. Even the headwaters of the Nile must be hundreds of miles away.

Finally the watchers in the jungle walked over and began conversing with the two hidden guards.

Doc lifted his eyes. The reason for the relaxed vigilance was apparent. The column composed of natives and whites had gone out of sight.

Then, unexpectedly, a whistle came from the direction of the lake. It was very faint, but it started a commotion. The armed natives jumped to the alert. Then, as one man, they dived through the jungle in the direction of the lake.

From the lake were coming fight sounds. Yells, a shot or two. Other noises of fight.

The bronze man made for the lake.

XI

DANGER AT DUSK

The lake was blanketed in a low fog. In this gray abyss, there was excitement, violent movement. Doc heard the sounds long before he reached the lake.

Then, close to the shore, he heard a man swimming furiously. Other noises of a canoe being paddled. Then the canoe seemed to overtake the swimmer. There was a commotion, howling and splashing. The swimmer seemed to have upset the canoe.

Doc identified the howling.

"Monk!" he called.

Monk liked noise with his fights.

"Where's the shore of this danged puddle?" Monk roared.

"This way," Doc said.

He ran to the water's edge, listened. Monk was swimming with about as much stealth as a paddle-wheel steamer. There were more canoes after him. At least four of them.

Monk came floundering out of the water. He was exhausted, and fell almost at once.

"The whole . . . African army . . . is after me!" he panted, lurching to his feet.

There was no doubt about that. A short spear made a whispering sound, then a skating noise as it glanced off rock and stopped almost at their feet. The tip seemed to be coated with a chemical.

"Come on," Doc said.

He seized Monk, helped him to the jungle. A sharp pain hit the bronze man's shoulder; the missile went on, whistling. It was a *runga*, the throwing stick with a knobbed end much used by natives over central Africa.

Monk stumbled again, gasped, "I . . . I'm tuckered out."

Doc Savage said, "Hang on my back."

Monk obeyed. The bronze man, seemingly not greatly hampered by the homely chemist's considerable weight, leaped, grasped a limb, went up. He followed a dangling vine through space for fully eighty vertical feet, then the vine began to break loose from his leafy anchorage above, and let them down. Monk squawked in horror, but the bronze man, seemingly unconcerned, fastened to a passing limb, and a moment later was walking through space on a narrow, swaying limb.

He made a leaping drop of more than a score of feet, caught another limb, shot through space again, and after that took shelter in a great leafy forest giant.

Monk croaked twice, managed to whisper, "Jug-just let me go. This is worse'n being chased by them natives."

Doc found a substantial tree crotch.

He whispered, "They seem to have lost our trail."

Monk grabbed the limb, held to it for dear life. He was something he seldom became. Pale.

Doc asked, "What happened? Is there a chance of helping the others?"

"N-not now," Monk said. "They got us in that fog. We landed on the lake, all right, and the co-pilot of your ship used the radio so that we could spot him with a finder. I guess maybe we made a little noise. Anyway, we tied the two planes one behind the other, and all got into one plane to talk it over. Then was when it happened."

"What happened?"

"Dugout canoes, about fifteen of them. And some rafts made of reeds. They paddled out, got all around us in the fog, and piled aboard like nobody's business."

Doc remembered the spear and the *runga*. He asked, "Did they kill anyone?"

"That's the funny part," Monk said. "They seemed bent on taking everybody alive. Ham and I got in the water, but they caught Ham. I got away. They chased me with canoes. That's all I know."

"The others were overpowered?"

"Sure," Monk said. "There must have been a hundred natives. And those cusses are as strong as wild cats."

Some time later—a quarter of an hour, possibly—there was a mass movement of canoes out of the fog. It was so dark now that torches were necessary. These consisted of long sticks with bundles of greasy bark and vines fastened to the ends. They gave off as much smoke as light.

Monk watched them unload. Monk had recovered his breath, his strength, and his desire for a fight.

"Look at them," he said. "They got my hog."

This was true. The pig, Habeas Corpus, was tied to the end of a pole so that he could be managed without danger to the life and limb of his captors.

Doc Savage watched closely. Long Tom Roberts was battered considerably, and the co-pilot had a skinned nose, but the other prisoners did not seem to be in any worse condition than could have been expected if they had merely walked ashore without the attendant trouble of being captured.

Pat was along, as was Johnny. Renny was being carried, as were Mr. Manley and the man called Abner.

The entire group moved away from the beach, leaving the canoes. They were trailed by Ham's pet chimp, Chemistry. The animal appeared to have reached shore by swimming. They could hear Chemistry's angry squawking, and once a native threw a clod at him.

Doc said, "We will trail them."

Monk's arm tightened around the limb. He had decided it was a hundred feet to the earth, and en route downward there was various interference in the form of limbs and, for a landing pad, a thorn tree growing out of some jagged rocks.

"Hang on to me again," Doc said.

Monk was not enthusiastic about it, but he did so. He was less enthusiastic as the bronze man calmly stepped off into space, hit a limb with a breath-taking jar, went off it as if it was a spring board. Monk closed his eyes. He did not open them until they were on the ground.

"Whew!" he said. "I think I'll get me a nice quiet job making dynamite."

Doc said, "They may have a guard over the plane. We will see."

The bronze man approached the beach. He left Monk concealed behind a bush, moved through the darkness, and shortly located a group of four guards watching the flotilla of dugout canoes.

The bronze man had a few anaesthetic grenades inside his breechcloth, and he used these, getting quite close. The dark graphite grease, much of which still remained on his boyd, helped him blend with the darkness.

Shortly the four watchmen slept.

"The planes," Doc said. "We can work fast, get back before they wake up."

They paddled out on to the lake. The air, now that the sun was gone, was bitterly cold. The bronze man used his ears often in the fog. There were tiny waves on the lake, and he located the planes by the lapping of these waves against the hulls.

"*Min henak,*" the bronze man called softly in Egyptian.

"Hey," Monk whispered. "What's that? Arabic, ain't it?"

"Egyptian," the bronze man said. "I'm trying to find out who is on the planes."

There was no answer to his hail, however.

He moved forward with the canoe, came alongside the planes, and swung aboard one of them, moving cautiously. Convinced that the craft was empty, he went to the other ship.

"*Oa!*" a voice snarled. "*Da min deh?*"

There was a guard at the plane, after all.

To the snarled demand of who was there. Doc replied, "You fool! Why are you not in the rear plane as you were told to be?" He used Egyptian, but slurred and muffled it by holding his head down and his hand in front of his mouth, so that his accent would be disguised.

Simultaneously, he used a gas grenade—the only one remaining—to overcome the watchman. The wind was blowing from his back; he simply held his breath and crushed the grenade in his hand. The anaesthetic gas was bitingly cold, almost freezing, on his hand for a moment as liquid turned to vapor. Then there was a loud splash as one of the guards fell into the lake.

Doc said, "Find the fellow, Monk."

"I got him," Monk said.

They hoisted the dripping watchman into the plane. In the craft they found five others, all dark natives, heavily armed. They had piled down wherever they were standing when the gas hit them.

* * *

Monk announced, "Well, we got us a collection of spears, anyway. Hey, look. Poisoned arrows, too."

Doc said, "Let's have some of those arrows."

Monk passed him some of the missiles. They were not actually arrows, but darts. They were smaller than the conventional hand darts used in dart games, although made somewhat after the same plan. The tip was a large thorn which had been grooved and roughened to hold the gummy substance which Monk had called poison.

Monk watched the bronze man get out a portable microscope, the compact chemical laboratory which was part of their equipment when they had plenty of space for it, and go to work.

"Look," Monk said uneasily, "ain't we gonna do somethin' about Ham and Pat and Johnny and Long Tom and Renny? What about them?"

Doc said, "There were a hundred natives in the party which captured them. Two of us could not do anything with a crowd that large without gas. And we do not have enough gas to make the attempt worth while."

But we oughta be trailin' them. How we gonna find 'em?"

"Every indication is that their village must be close," the bronze man said patiently.

He continued to work with the magnifier, and with various chemicals which he was applying to the gummy stuff on the end of the dart.

"Monk," he said.

"Yeah?"

"I want you to mix some chemicals," Doc said. "Make a thick liquid of them."

"What chemicals?" Monk asked.

Doc Savage told him, naming the ingredients in the order in which he wished them mixed.*

---

*It has been the practice of the publisher of Doc Savage to eliminate the exact chemical formulae of gases, poisons, and other mixtures which Doc employs from time to time. This is not done because the chemicals which the bronze man employs are fantastic, impossible, or non-existent. Rather, it is not the wish of the author to furnish aid to criminals or others not entitled to it. Knowledge of many of these chemical formulae, in the wrong hands, would be dangerous. Hence the exact ingredients of a gas or a chemical concoction employed by Doc are seldom published. We hope that this lack of exact information, in the few cases in which it is eliminated, does not detract from the interest of the Doc Savage adventures.

Monk was puzzled. "What the dickens good is that stuff?" he inquired. "It's not a gas, not a poison. It ain't food, drink, nor nothing that I can make any sense out of."

The bronze man did not answer; in fact, he apparently did not hear the inquiry. Monk glanced at him—they were using a flashlight with the lens wrapped in a handkerchief, for light—and grinned.

Experience had told Monk that when Doc started not hearing questions, things were picking up. Progress was being made. The homely chemist snorted, began mixing the stuff as directed.

"All right," he said finally.

Doc was still analyzing the substance on the points of the darts.

He said, "Monk, take an essential part off each of the motors. Nothing heavy. Something we can load in the canoe, wrap in a piece of canvas, and bury on the beach."

"Right," Monk agreed.

A quarter of an hour later, the homely chemist climbed back into the plane carrying a necklace of motor parts. He had carefully strung the parts, as he removed them from the engines, on a line, so they would not get lost, then slung the line about his shoulders.

"Doc, you find out what the stuff on them arrows is?" he asked.

"It is no ordinary type of plant or serpent venom," the bronze man said.

Monk stared at him. "Say, do you suppose—"

"Possible," Doc said.

Pointing at the arrows, Monk demanded, "You mean that goo can cause—well, like Renny is. It ain't death, and it ain't ordinary unconsciousness."

"The condition," Doc said, "is best described as suspended animation, or a complete suspension of all ordinary processes."

"That's what I mean. You think the stuff on that arrow does it?"

"It is very possible," the bronze man admitted.

Monk frowned at the arrow.

"Brother, I'm going to steer clear of them things," he said.

* * *

Twenty minutes later, they were ashore.

"Monk, you stay here and have things ready to go from this end," Doc Savage suggested.

Monk finished burying the airplane parts. He had waded out into the shallow water of the lake's edge to bury the gadgets he had removed from the motors. The waves would cover traces of the burial. The parts of metal would not be harmed by submersion.

He straightened. "Doc, I hate to miss a fight," he said. "And I can't see where I'd do a bit of good here."

"We'll have to travel in the treetops some of the time," Doc said.

Monk was distressed. "O. K.," he said. "I'm not hot about that flying trapeze stuff, but I'll go through with it."

They moved through the jungle, traveling slowly, and climbing most of the time. The fog which had been so thick close to the lake water abruptly dispersed. They saw that it was moonlight.

They stepped out into a clearing. Something made a loud whistling noise close at hand, and ran away. Monk took to a tree in double-quick time.

"A reed buck," Doc said. "They are comparatively harmless."

Monk muttered, "I don't care for these jungles after night," and climbed down again.

With the closing in of complete night, the jungle had burst into noisy and hideous life. There was a moist sneeze close by, causing Monk to reach for another tree. All around them were low sighs and leafy stirrings, vague sounds that were unintelligible and ominous. With a violence fit to stand the hair on end, a jackal let go with a volley of barks, then was suddenly silent, and some other animal emitted a long gurgling noise that was as final as death. They could smell a rather unpleasant odor which Monk thought was probably a hyena.

Doc said, "This must be the only lake for miles. All the wild life comes to it for water."

"They can have it entirely to themselves," Monk declared.

Doc Savage was carrying a heavy pack wrapped in canvas. Now he vanished up a tree, and when he rejoined Monk, he was without the pack.

"We are getting near the cliff," he said. "You wait here."

*   *   *

The bronze man went away again. Monk walked over with the intention of sitting down on a small boulder. The boulder, however, emitted several bloodthirsty grunts and took after him, moonlight glinting on yellow tusks. It was an excellent display of agility that put Monk up a small tree ahead of an irritated wart hog. He sat there, thinking unpleasant things about Africa, the universe in general, and Ollie Saff in particular.

When Doc Savage came back, he was without the heavy pack. He carried, instead, a bundle of yellow cloth and a jar containing the brew of chemicals which Monk had mixed in the plane.

"There seems to be only one path up the cliff," Doc said. "And that is guarded." The bronze man tossed Monk half of the yellow cloth. "Take off your clothes," he said, "and make a breechcloth out of this."

Monk listened to the prowling night insects. Some of them sounded like airplanes. He shrugged and began undressing.

Doc Savage used the breechcloth he had been wearing to rub the dark grease off himself. The task took some time, although he enlisted the help of some fruit juices.

He picked up the jar of chemicals.

"Rub this on your skin," he said. "Cover every square inch of your body, and put it on thinly, rubbing it in until the skin absorbs it, the way you use cold cream."

Monk complied. By the time he finished, he had a sensation of rebellion in his stomach, and his head felt as if it had been rotating.

"It's makin' me sick," he muttered.

"The effects will wear off," Doc said.

They set out through the jungle as soon as the bodily coating had been applied. Monk was racking his brain, trying to figure out what earthly good such a mixture of chemicals would do. He could think of none. None whatever.

Smooth going suddenly came underfoot. A path. And ahead, towering dark in the moonlight, was the cliff.

Doc Savage spoke. His voice was loud, charged with power and volume.

"*Salamat!*" he said. "*Salamat, salamat.*"

He kept repeating that. Monk remembered enough

Egyptian to remember that this was a rather common greeting, the equivalent of "How do you do."

Then his hair threatened to stand on end. For the bronze man, hitherto almost completely invisible in the darkness, had turned to a man of gold.

Now walking forward, Doc was a giant figure of luminescent ocher, a living statue that might have been made of glowing gold.

It startled Monk only slightly less to look down and find the same thing had happened to himself.

Then he understood it. In the pack which Doc Savage had brought from the plane had been an ultraviolet light projector. And the chemicals which the bronze man had ordered mixed would fluoresce with a yellow-green luminescence under ultraviolet light.

The unusual statue of the golden bird appeared. Doc led the way to it. They walked very close to the thing, and stood there, perfectly still.

Monk was a little disappointed. It has first hit him that the yellow bird might be made out of solid gold. The moonlight was bright enough to disillusion him, however. Made of wood, and painted. Not a particularly artistic job of wood carving, either.

He fell to examining the surroundings, trying to spot the projector of ultraviolet light. The ultraviolet rays, of course, were invisible to the unaided eye, and the type of filters which Doc Savage used shut off visible light wave lengths completely, so the projector was not visible. He decided, however, it had to be near the cliff face.

Then the natives appeared. They came slowly, stopped just outside the ring of stones that were like benches. One of the little dark fellows put back his head, and a whistle came from his lips, shrill and piping, rising high, then falling, trailing away.

The whistle was echoed from the cliff top, then again, at a greater distance.

No one spoke aloud.

Out of the side of his mouth, not moving his lips, Doc warned, "Say nothing. Do nothing."

There were about twenty men in the column which came down the cliff face, following the path which was indistinguishable from a distance. They filed to a stop outside the circle of stones.

"*Auz eyh?*" one of them said gruffly.

Monk recognized that as a demand of what they wanted. But Doc's answer was too fast for him to follow. He watched with interest. Then the native spoke again, more violently.

Doc told Monk, in English. "We are not welcome. No one they do not know seems to be wanted."

The bronze man burst into fluent Egyptian. It seemed to Monk that he was using more care with his diction, so there would be no misunderstanding about his meaning.

The native's answer was more mollified. Deferential, in fact.

Doc advised Monk, "I have explained that we have influence with the yellow birds. Presumably these yellow birds are their deity, or the symbol of it."

The native spoke again, gruffly again, then waited for a reply.

In Egyptian, Doc said, "Our patience grows short. We do not expect an argument. We come bringing nothing but wisdom and friendship. You are our friends. It is time you began acting like it."

His tone more than the words got action.

The leader of the natives gestured briefly. Doc Savage and Monk stepped forward. As soon as they were out of the invisible ultraviolet rays, their bodies naturally stopped fluorescing.

Doc remarked idly. "You see, we have but to step near the golden one to glow warm in its favor."

That was apparently the first reference to their golden color which the bronze man had made. His silence on the point had evidently been more effective than a long speech on the subject. The natives were awed. None of them got overly close. Which was just as well with Monk.

They worked up the face of the cliff. Their guides had lighted torches, and these gave some illumination, also making dancing shadows that were treacherous.

Halfway up the cliff, they abruptly entered a cleft, followed this for a quarter of a mile, and came into a valley. The valley was wide, floored with rich land—as nearly as they could tell in the moonlight—and tilled fields.

Cultivation of the fields was apparently of a primitive sort. The fields were not noticeably larger than backyard gardens. A small herd of zebra were grazing in one of the patches, and an angry native rushed them, hurling his *runga* at them. He lost the *runga*, the zebra strolled off leisurely, and the column went on.

Monk asked, "Where is this going to wind up?"

"The substance they used to induce that state of suspended animation evidently came from here," Doc said. "Ollie Saff and the others made a rush back here to get a new supply, after what they had on hand was destroyed when the barge burned."

"I don't see—"

He didn't finish. A village had appeared in the moonlight. If anything was needed to prove that these natives were not Negroids, the structure of the village did it.

The houses were of stone. Not impressive compared to modern city buildings; but here in the jungle, they were noteworthy. The structures were square. Some of the doorways were arched; most of them had a flat slab over the openings to hold up the remaining wall.

They came to a large building, by far the largest in the village. There were no doors in this. Access to the top of the wall was by a long flight of steps made of stones piled without mortar.

Doc Savage and Monk were led to the top of this.

Without warning, they were shoved off.

Their treatment up to that point had been so polite, the manner of their captors so deferential, that they were caught napping. Even Doc was surprised, found himself sprawling into space.

They fell about a dozen feet.

The bronze man landed prepared for anything. But nothing happened—except that Monk came down with a loud and distressed grunt beside him.

Above them, the spokesman of the natives made a short speech.

"We have decided to do with outsiders as our ancestors have always done," he said.

XII

THE LIVING DEAD

The silence was very deep for a while. It lasted until the natives on the wall went away.

Monk groaned. "I fell right square on my whatchacallit," he complained.

A voice in the nearby darkness made a remark.

"It's too bad it wasn't your head," it said. "Then you wouldn't have been hurt."

"Ham!" Monk howled.

The two congenial enemies found each other and did some delighted back-pounding. "I thought you had drowned," Ham confessed, "and I was worried sick." Monk said, "I was sure worried about you, too."

Then they recovered themselves. They began insulting each other.

"You missing link!" Ham accused Monk. "What kind of stupidity got you caught?"

Doc Savage said, "We—or I did—underestimated the brains of these natives. We tried to work on their superstition, get them to thinking we were superior deities, and join them."

"Oh, you're here, Doc," Ham said in the darkness. His voice became worried. "That's what Ollie Saff and the others tried to do. They walked right into a trap."

Doc asked, "Have you found out the situation—the details?"

"Most of them," Ham said. He lifted his voice. "Miss Moldenhaeur, will you come here, please?"

Doc was silent. Then he asked, "Are you *all* in here together?"

"Sure." Ham chuckled grimly. "Ollie Saff and his crowd are over on the other side. We had a knock-down-drag-out fight, bare fists only. Everybody had been disarmed. And we licked them."

Liona Moldenhaeur arrived. Pat Savage was with her.

Pat said breathlessly, "I'm sure glad you got here, Doc. We've got to figure out something. These natives aren't fooling."

Doc said, "Miss Moldenhaeur?"

"Yes."

"Your father and Mr. Thomas led an expedition here previously, did they not?"

"Eleven months ago," Liona Moldenhaeur admitted. "It was in the beginning an expedition for the Eastern-Metropolitan Museum. It started out as—well, one of those hunting trips which rich people take and call expeditions."

"Was your finding of this valley the result of a plan, or an accident?"

"Accident, mostly. He sighed it from the plane. We were using a seaplane for scouting. We landed on the lake, and built a headquarters near the shore. It was really a fort. We spent several weeks getting acquainted with the natives, winning their confidence slowly."

There was a stirring on the other side of the compound. Ollie Saff and his associates, probably. The prison seemed to be a simple walled inclosure.

Doc Savage asked, "Did you find out about this drug—we will call it a drug—immediately?"

Liona Moldenhaeur swallowed audibly. "Almost. Within a few days."

"Do they tip their arrows with the stuff?"

"Yes. But it takes a much larger dose than a mere arrow wound to cause the . . . the effect you saw in my father."

"How do they administer this larger dose?"

"Internally. They make their victims swallow the stuff. They put it in crude capsules made out of intestinal—you know, the same thing we used to make sausage skins out of. These are forced down the victim's throat."

She was silent a moment, then continued, "The arrow wound induces a slight effect, a kind of paralysis. When they shoot game, a zebra, for instance, they nick it with the arrow. The animal becomes paralyzed. They then approach the animal, and force it to swallow a capsule or two. In the case of a large animal, several capsules. The circulatory system then carries the drug throughout the body. Or usually it does. As a result, the effect of—everything suspended—is throughout the body. Sometimes, though, an extremity, such as a foot or a leg, is not affected and that, in time, will—rot. In the case of a man, that would be horrible. That possibility is what terrified me so when they did it to my father."

Doc Savage asked, "Who gave the stuff to your father?"

"Why—Ollie Saff, of course."

"What was his object?"

"To get control of the drug."

"Has Saff admitted that?"

"Of course."

"When?"

"Why—well, it was today."

"He didn't admit it before today?"

"No."

Doc Savage turned and strode across the compound, halting in the moonlight not far from a group of figures huddled against the wall. After a while, one of the figures swore at him. It was Saff.

"You got us into this!" Saff snarled. "You burned the stock of the stuff we had on that barge."

Monk, across the inclosure, heard this. He guffawed as if he thought it was very funny. He did not manage to get much humor in his voice.

Doc Savage glanced up at the compound wall. There were no guards in sight. He could tell, from the flickering red light and columns of dark smoke, that fires had been built around the place.

He peered at Saff and the others, stepping closer to identify them.

"Saff," he said, "why did you go to so much trouble over that drug?"

Saff swore, said, "It's worth a fortune, damn you!"

"For what purpose?"

"Preserving meat," Saff snapped. "That's what these natives use it for. Hell, it'll put the whole packing industry out of business!"

"How do you arrive at that conclusion?"

"Hell, anything that's dosed with that drug—the meat won't spoil. You won't need railroad refrigerator cars, refrigeration on ships to keep fresh meat—nothing. It'll put those big packing plants out of business. Anybody likes fresh meat better than preserved stuff. That's what this will give the public—fresh meat, not refrigerated meat, because this thing works entirely different than just freezing it; it just stops all changes in it without freezing."

"The idea seems fantastic," Doc said.

"It seems like a cold billion dollars or two to me," Saff growled. "You just ain't got the imagination to grasp it."

Doc asked, "What do you think the natives are going to do with us?"

Saff's answer was a stream of spoken violence, senseless threats against the natives, and about what would happen to them if they didn't let him go.

Doc walked away in the middle of it, went to his men. "Ham," he said, "just who is here with you?"

"Sam John Thomas, O'Brien O'Callaghan, Benjamin Boot, Liona Moldenhaeur, and her father," Ham replied.

"Is Mr. Moldenhaeur able to talk?"

The pleasant, if strained, voice of Moldenhaeur answered this inquiry with, "If there is anything I can tell you, I will be glad to do so."

"Where is Renny?"

"Over here," replied Renny's deep rumble.

"You are all right?" Doc demanded.

"I'm sick as a curly-haired dog," Renny complained. "But they brought me out from under the effects of the stuff, if that is what you mean."

"Where did they do that?"

"Took me out some place—a kind of a hut they've got rigged up to treat you with the stuff that brings you out of it. Take it from me, it's not any fun, either."

Winton Moldenhaeur interrupted, "You see, Mr. Savage, this drug is behind all this trouble. We realized, all of us, what a boon it could become to the food industry. Strangely enough, it will preserve fruits and vegetables as well as meats. A second treatment makes the preserved substance fit for consumption. In the case of a living animal or person, animation returns without the subject seeming to feel much harm, other than a violent illness which wears off."

Doc asked, "How many of you came here on the original expedition?"

"All of us. That is, all except those thugs Ollie Saff has hired."

"Mr. Manley and Abner?"

"Yes." Winton Moldenhaeur nodded grimly. "The way I understand it, Mr. Manley and Abner started out to double-cross everyone and grab the secret for themselves. They were going to murder Mr. Boot, Mr. Thomas and myself. Fortunately, they did not get away with the first crime, the murder of Mr. Boot."

Doc Savage was thoughtful for a while.

He said, "This drug—the rights to it—how did you all intend to share in it?"

"It was assigned to a holding company," Moldenhaeur said, "of which Mr. Boot, Mr. Thomas and myself were stockholders. The sole holders, in fact."

"The Century Projects Corp.?"

"Yes, that is the one."

Doc Savage walked over to Monk, asked, "How do you feel?"

Monk looked at the stone walls, bathed in the moonlight. Pale-red light from the fires outside the compound colored the trace of night fog that was beginning to wrap the village. The smoke crawled up like dark worms.

"I'd feel a lot better out of here," Monk admitted.

Doc said, "We can reach the top of the wall without much trouble. Form a pyramid."

Pat darted forward.

"No, Doc!" she gasped. "You can't. The sides and top of that wall are covered with thorns. When they laid the mortar, they laid small branches of thorn trees in it, the thorns projecting. And the thorns are coated with that drug."

Doc asked Monk, "Think you can stand the pain?"

"Sure," Monk said. "I can. But what about the drug?"

Ham stepped up anxiously. "Listen, Monk did most of the fighting back at the planes, and he's tired. Why not let me help on this?"

Big-worded Johnny said, "I'll be superamalgamated! Count me in on that, too."

Doc Savage said, "You will get your chance, if this works out."

The bronze man moved over and spoke in a whisper to Monk. Monk emitted an astonished grunt, said, "I'll be danged!"

"Monk will help me," Doc said. "Make a stand, you fellows."

The "stand" consisted of a pyramid, Long Tom and Ham for a base, Johnny for an elongated peak. Up this climbed Doc Savage, then Monk.

Pat had been right about the thorns. They pricked the bronze man's hands, his elbows and shins. He avoided them as best he could, gritted his teeth against those it was impossible to avoid, and got on the crest of the wall.

He reached down and hauled Monk up beside him.

The natives around the fire below saw them then. One squalled an alarm.

"*Oa!*" the man bellowed. "*Oa, oa!*"

Doc said, "Come on, Monk!"

They leaped off the wall, landed sprawling beside the fires, and began fighting. Monk emitted a howl that outdid the best native effort, and suddenly was the center of a pile of human figures.

Doc Savage dropped two men quickly. Then a third man rushed in, and Doc seemed stupidly slow in dodging a fist blow. The impact sent him to his knees. The man struck him again. Doc swung back, but erratically.

"*Akhiran!*" the man yelled in Egyptian. "At last! It takes effect on him."

A moment later, Doc Savage and Monk were both stretched out, arms and legs pinned by excitedly triumphant natives.

"*Bass!*" an authoritative voice ordered. "That is enough."

The speaker, the native who had been in charge of the group which had brought Doc Savage and Monk to the village, walked around the two prisoners thoughtfully.

"The big one is clever," he said. "But he did not think of the thorns on the wall. He will know better next time. Take them away, both. Take them to the hut, and revive them. Then thrown them back in the compound with the others."

Inside the prison wall, Winton Moldenhaeur translated the orders for the benefit of Pat and Ham and the others.

"They are going to cure them of the effects of the drug, and bring them back," he said.

XIII

ALIVE AND NOT DEAD

Five minutes later, Doc Savage went into action. He sat up, took a native by the neck. He got another native by the straight black hair. He slammed their heads together.

Simultaneously, Monk came up suddenly with his legs and got the head of a native between his knees. He lay very still for a few moments, making a face and straining. Then he released his native. The fellow was too dazed to dodge the homely chemist's fist.

Monk said, "There was only the three of them, wasn't there?"

They were in a low-ceilinged stone room that smelled violently. Sole light was supplied by a primitive stone lamp in which floated a burning wick. A more modern lamp probably graced the boudoir of Cleopatra.

"Only three," Doc said.

The bronze man swung off the stone slab on which he had been placed.

Immediately he was interested in a long vat arrangement, a stone tank, at his side. The natives had been pouring liquid from large jars into this. There had already been liquid in the stone tub, but they had been increasing the quantity.

Monk came over and smelled of the stuff.

"Say!" he exploded. "That stuff is a little like that junk we smeared on our bodies. I mean—I smell some of the chemical in this that was in that."

Doc said, "There is some similarity."

"Hey! Then you didn't mix that stuff up just so it would fluoresce yellow?"

"Not entirely. It was also an antidote—or I hoped it was an antidote, and it turned out I was right—against the drug they were using to induce that condition of suspended life."

Monk was incredulous. "When did you figure out the stuff?"

Doc said, "You remember I got in several hours' laboratory work on the thing in New York? I had Mr. Manley and Abner in the laboratory at the time, so that the reaction of chemicals on them could be observed. Following that, I had several days—or the time of the flight from New York here—to consider the results."

Monk shivered. "Is there likely to be any bad effects from this stuff?"

"It is doubtful if we will feel entirely normal for a number of weeks. Such a shock to the human system could not pass without effects."

Monk grunted.

"What now?" he asked.

"The planes," Doc said. "We will have to get some weapons."

"Well, what're we waitin' on? We know the trail."

They reached the lake, but not without difficulty. The two guards at the foot of the cliff path were taken by surprise, but they put up a sizable bout. Monk slugged his opponent five times squarely on the jaw before he induced a state of unconsciousness that was satisfactory. Monk was unpleasantly amazed.

"I'm sure losin' my wallop," he declared.

Doc explained the weakness was probably due to the drug which they had rubbed on their skins, and which their systems had absorbed.

They reached the lake, climbed in a canoe, took their bearings carefully, and paddled out to the plane.

The matter of guards in the plane was bothering them. But it solved itself. There were no guards.

Monk chuckled. "When we used that anaesthetic gas on 'em, it scared 'em. They got the idea the planes were hoodooed, so they went ashore, probably."

They loaded the canoe with machine pistols and what ammunition they could carry.

Doc said, "We will take only mercy bullets, and a few drums of explosives."

"Right," Monk said. "I hope we can get back to the village before they find out we got loose."

Doc said, "They had no suspicion that we had immunized ourselves to the effect of their drug. They will not be particularly concerned about us."

They paddled ashore, beaching the canoe well down the beach from the point where there was likelihood of guards being posted. Shouldering the ammunition packs, their breech-cloths thrust full of machine pistols, they worked through the noisy tropical jungle.

The two guards at the base of the cliff were still unconscious. Doc lead the way upward. Monk climbed behind him.

They passed into the cultivated valley. Life in the place evidently was not all roses, for they could hear an uproar off to the north, and see torches; a dozen or more natives seemed to be trying to herd some large animal, apparently a belligerent rhino, out of a field. The animal set out in industrious pursuit of part of the group, and they saw that it was not a rhino, but some kind of buffalo that was as black as a polecat.

Doc stopped some distance from the prison compound, lifted his head, put his hands to his mouth, and shouted in Mayan.

He told those in the compound to get ready for a break. He said that he would shortly drop a rope over the wall, and that they were to be prepared to leave in a hurry. He told them to acknowledge hearing him by staging, in five minutes, a noisy dispute.

"Come," he told Monk, "before someone investigates the queer language."

There were dogs in the village, and they were doing so much howling and fighting that an outburst of strange words was hardly anything to be noticed. But they changed their position hastily. Two of the dogs barked at them industriously, became tired, and left.

In the compound, Pat Savage and Liona Moldenhaeur had a loud quarrel. It was brief.

Doc said, "They heard our signal. From now on, we work fast."

They separated. Monk headed straight for the prison. Doc circled to come in from the other side.

They both charged the rapid-firing pistols with drums of mercy bullets as they ran. The slugs were even more effective than solid lead, because any kind of a hit by one of them would produce rather abrupt unconsciousness. The period of senselessness was short, however. Not more than fifteen minutes at the outside. Doc recently having made a change in the slugs to get quick results, so that he had found it necessary to sacrifice their period of effectiveness. Quick results were usually the most important.

Doc began firing first. He put the initial burst into the legs of standing men. The deafening roar brought the other natives around the fires to their feet. After that, he shot low, quick bursts, switching the machine-pistol muzzle.

He ran forward. Some of the natives were going down; others were still on their feet.

He reached the slanting stairway of loose stones, bounded up it. A crude ladder made of twisted fiber and sticks dangled on the outside of the wall. He hauled it up, tossed it over on the inside.

"Come on out," he said sharply. "Hurry!"

Ollie Saff, in a horror-stricken voice, yelled, "What about us? You ain't gonna leave us here!"

They should, Monk thought grimly.

He heard Doc ask Winton Moldenhaeur, "What will they do to Saff and his men if we do leave them here?"

"Kill them," Moldenhaeur said. "But that's what they have coming to them."

Doc called, "After the others, Saff. Climb up. But do not try anything."

Saff blubbered something thankful.

Uproar had overspread the village by now. The natives seemed to find it necessary to indulge in some preliminary howling before they got into action. Women shrieked. Babies cried. Dogs barked. Warriors popped out of the windows of stone huts. They bellowed at other warriors.

All the prisoners were out of the compound by now. Nobody was letting any grass grow under his or her feet.

Doc ordered, "This way!"

He was distributing the machine pistols—five of them—to Pat and his aids, together with ammo drums.

He set out for the cliff path. The streets were as narrow as any in Cairo, little more than hallways between stone walls. They ran down and through these, following the bronze man, making enough noise that they would not lose each other.

Suddenly there was a commotion at the rear of the column. Pat shrilled out angrily. And Monk emitted a howl that ended in mid-bellow. Doc wheeled, raced back to them.

Pat was beside herself. Also without her machine pistol.

"That Saff!" she shouted. "He grabbed my machine pistol. Monk's, too!"

From down the street, back in the direction they were leaving, Saff shouted at them.

"If you think I'm going to leave here without a new supply of that drug and the antidote, you're crazy!" Saff snarled. "I'm going back after it."

Pat said, "His men are going with him, too."

Doc shouted, "Come back, you fools!"

Saff swore at him.

They listened to the foot-pounding of Saff and his men going back toward the compound.

"Pat, how many bullets were in your pistol?" Doc asked.

"The drum was about half full."

Monk said, "Mine was nearly empty."

Doc Savage made a grim sound.

"Saff is walking into plenty of trouble," he said. "He evidently doesn't know we were using mercy bullets. Those natives around the compound aren't dead. They will be waking up in a few minutes."

Monk chuckled cold-bloodedly.

"We should worry about Saff," he said.

Doc Savage wheeled. "One thing sure, we can not stay here."

He led the way on toward the edge of the village. A few times, they encountered dark figures, but these sprang out of sight in a hurry. They were women and children mostly. Now and then an old man.

Winton Moldenhaeur dropped back to join Doc Savage. Benjamin Boot was with him.

Moldenhaeur said, "I think we are lucky. I believe the men of the village were having a meeting about us. They seem to be gathered at the other end of town, most of them."

Benjamin Boot said, "Listen!"

In the distance, one of the machine pistols let out a prolonged hoot. Whoever was firing the weapon simply came back on the firing lever and did not let up.

Monk, thinking of the fire mechanism of the machine pistol, groaned, "He'll jam that gun! He'll burn it all—"

The machine pistol stopped suddenly.

It did not resume.

"What'd I tell you!" Monk said. "He jammed it."

They listened. Ben Boot said, "But they had another of those guns to—"

"I had the safety on mine," Pat declared, sounding satisfied. "I'll bet he can't find it. Those dinguses are complicated."

A tide of battle noise rolled to their ears. It was not pleasant, for there was death in the voices, terror in the screaming for help, for deliverance. They could hear and identify the shouting of the native warriors who poured in from the far side of the village, converging on the region of the prison inclosure. They could, at long intervals, distinguish Ollie Saff's voice in the uproar. It was even possible to gauge the direction of the battle tide from Saff's tone—confident in the beginning, startled, horrified, desperate, and at last in death, shrieking out terribly in a long sound that somehow ended with complete finality.

Monk said, "I guess Saff found it too complicated, all right. He sure sounded complicated."

They were now outside the village, and they went on to

the cliff path and down that and out in the canoes to the planes.

<h1 style="text-align:center">XIV</h1>

THE LOVER OF GOLDEN BIRDS

Dawn did not come up like thunder out of the east. Quite the contrary, it arrived with a breath of silence. The jungle noises suddenly stilled, as if everything had stopped, and it was daylight. The fog disappeared from the surface of the lake as if through the operation of magic.

The two planes drifted on the calm surface of the lake.

Doc Savage sat on the wing of one of them, and watched the yellow birds. They were tiny canarylike things, and they came up out of the jungle in thousands, in great flocks.

He watched the yellow birds. At times they were so numerous that it was as if someone had suddenly spread a great yellow blanket against the green of the forest.

Winton Moldenhaeur came and sat beside him.

"A strange place," Moldenhaeur said. "They are Egyptians, you know."

"You have their history?" Doc Savage asked.

Moldenhaeur nodded. "They came from Egypt a long time ago. Centuries ago. They brought those birds, which are canaries, or were canaries originally. They settled here, and for some reason, the birds flourished. The yellow birds are their symbols of religion. But of course you noticed that."

"Yes," Doc said. "You fellows took some of the yellow birds back with you, on your first trip?"

"Yes. That's how we all happened to have canaries. We—ah, I understand Mr. Boot and Mr. Thomas and my daughter lied to you about the golden birds. They didn't want the secret of the drug to get out. My daughter even released my golden bird for fear it would draw suspicion."

Doc said, "It was a great ado about nothing."

"Nothing! Good God! That drug will—"

"Is worthless."

"*What?*"

Doc Savage was silent a moment.

"Not entirely worthless, perhaps," he said. "But quite no

account for what you were using, or intended to use it for, which was the preservation of foods."

"But that's impossible!" Moldenhaeur exploded.

"Did you have chemists work on it?"

"Well—Mr. Boot is a chemist. He experimented with it. He said he thought the taste could be eliminated."

"He was mistaken," Doc said. "When you expose meat to that stuff, there is a slight taste remaining. You know the taste, and you know it is not pleasant. These natives do not mind it, because—well, they eat ants, and such morsels. But the civilized palate would not accustom itself to that taste. And there is no way of eliminating it."

Benjamin Boot had been listening. He came and sat down beside them.

"I am sorry to hear that," he said gloomily.

The bronze man studied Boot's homely face. Boot was watching the golden birds.

Boot said, "They are beautiful." He was still staring at the birds.

Doc Savage remarked, "You like beautiful things, do you not?"

Boot nodded solemnly. "More than anything," he murmured.

Monk let out a shout.

"Hey, Doc," Monk called, "there's that chief of them natives waving at you from shore. He must want to have a powwow."

Doc Savage took one of the canoes. The occupants of the planes watched him paddle to a point on the beach. The native leader came forward alone.

The two men talked alone for some time.

Then Doc Savage paddled back to the planes at a leisurely pace. He had in the Canoe Monk's pig, Habeas Corpus, who had disappeared in the excitement. Ham's pet chimp, Chemistry, had already been located earlier.

Monk greeted his hog with suspicion. "I bet he's been associatin' with them dang wart hogs. I saw one of them things last night. It tried to eat me."

Ham said, "For years, I've wondered what breed of hog that Habeas is. Now I know he *is* a wart hog."

Renny, looking much better this morning, asked, "What did the head guy want, Doc?"

"Just an offer to drop matters," Doc said. "It seems that they are satisfied. Ollie Saff's men are dead. That seems to have been enough to quiet them down. In fact, they are scared. They want to give us all we want of the drug and the antidote, in return for our going away and leaving them alone."

"What did you decide?" Renny asked.

"To take enough of the stuff for experimental purposes," the bronze man said. "As a matter of fact, if I am not wrong, this drug might explain something that science has never been able to fathom about the ancient Egyptian method of embalming. They were far better at the art than modern embalmers, it is generally admitted. There may be a connection between their skill and this drug."

Doc Savage turned slowly to face Benjamin Boot.

"Incidentally," he added, "I have a message to you from Ollie Saff."

Benjamin Boot stiffened, turned white. "Uh . . . me—" He wet his lips.

"Mr. Moldenhaeur," Doc said. "This drug secret was turned over to a holding concern named the Century Projects Corp. Is that right?"

"Yes, it is," Moldenhaeur told him, puzzled.

"Who held the stock?"

"Mr. Boot, Mr. Thomas, and myself."

Doc Savage nodded. "And tell me, did the Century Projects concern hold any other property?"

"Oh, yes," Moldenhaeur said hastily. "It controls several factories. A number of industries, in fact."

"Then," Doc Savage said, "if a man should try to force you and Mr. Thomas to sign control of the corporation over to him, he would own it. Provided, of course, the man—in this case Ollie Saff—was only a figurehead working for Mr. Boot here, and Mr. Boot went through the motions of giving him his interest in the concern, too?"

Benjamin Boot shot to his feet. Terror had lighted his face. An unthinking kind of fear, a desperation that left room for nothing but flight.

He dived into the lake.

He never came up.

It was that simple. And more correctly, he never came up alive. The bitterly cold water must have stopped his heart, and he was—they found this later, when they located the body with grapples—carrying a heavy pistol in his hip pocket, which pulled him into the depths.

Liona Moldenhaeur stared at Doc Savage. "Is Ollie Saff alive?"

"No."

"But you said—"

"That I had a message for Boot from Saff? Merely a figure of speech for the thought I was about to express."

Monk was peering down into the indescribably blue depths of the lake.

"Boot liked pretty things," remarked the homely chemist. "He sure picked some purty blue water to fall into." He shivered.

THE WEE ONES

I

Johnny began barking a few minutes after ten o'clock. It had gotten dark at eight.

Johnny was John Fain's Great Dane, and under normal conditions the only thing to do when he started an uproar was to look into the matter and then scratch his chest for him the way he liked, or fan his stern with a folded newspaper, depending on what he had on his mind.

Tonight it was different. The dog's barking started John Fain to trembling violently. Fain was already pale, and almost ill with incredulous disbelief, so stricken in fact that he would not have been surprised at himself for fainting.

But the trembling took him by surprise.

He eyed his hands foolishly, like a man who had discovered a hole in his new fifty-cent socks. John Fain was a hard-muscled man of forty who had never before seen his hands shake of their own accord. His physical fitness was one of his prides. He took setting-up exercises daily, even had a gymnasium in the basement of his home, although his wife, Grace, had laughed at him for that. Grace didn't believe in exercise for exercise's sake, because her metallic nerves obviously didn't need it.

Then there was the bluish haze overhead.

This haze, a slightly darker azure hue than tobacco smoke, made a layer about two feet thick against the ceiling. It was semi-transparent; at least it was possible to discern the rough texture of the plaster ceiling. It smelled of ozone. Ozone. The stuff you smell after a lightning bolt hits close.

And there was the female clothing on the floor.

This clothing, a young woman's garments, lay in a rather shapeless pile and consisted of one complete outfit for one woman. A young woman. Slippers, hose, panties, garter belt, brassiére, and a beige dress in a sculptured model. All just piled there. But not arranged as if they had been casually dropped there. Not quite.

The scarf, John Fain thought . . .

The scarf was missing.

At the south end of the room, the window was down

from the top, and the haze was gradually drifting outdoors.
The stuff was clearing out of the laboratory. The apparatus
was making noise. The generators, two of them, were whin-
ing, and a condenser was leaking now and then with a
popping sound, and tubes were humming.

Fain shook his head violently.

"Nuts," he said.

It didn't do much good. He didn't fool himself.

The dog was still barking. He sounded excited, but
puzzled, too.

Fain discovered the hole in the window screen.

Slashing hadn't made the hole in the screen. Actually,
there was not a hole in the screen; the screen wire had been
loosened by prying away the moulding, or forcing it outward
by a blow, then bending up the loosened corner of the screen
wire. The opening thus made was about large enough to pass
a man's two fists held close together.

Fain put his hands in his coat pockets. He could feel
them shaking there, actually knocking against his ribs.

"Lys!" he called.

The name burst out of his throat, jumped past the
constriction there, loud enough to be a shout. But it got no
answer.

"Miss Smith!" he tried again.

He did better, a little, that time, but it drew no response.

Fain shut down the apparatus, threw switches and pulled
plugs. He did this more from habit than from conscious
thought, because he had spent most of his life working in a
laboratory, It was the same sort of a gesture a motorist makes
in switching off his engine after he has had an accident.

"What the hell kind of a gag is this?" he demanded
loudly.

The silence, for that was all there was now, made the nape
of his neck creep.

Gag. Sure, a gag. He began telling himself that was what
it was, because he wanted to believe that was it. A gag.
Couldn't be anything else.

He went over to look at the hole in the window screen.
He had to make himself go, and he didn't like that. He
examined the window sill, and there was a little dust there,
he saw. The laboratory didn't get a cleaning as often as it

should, because he didn't like to have his tools and books disturbed.

After he had looked at the dust film a while, he knew his face must be quite white, or maybe it was blue, as if it were cyanosed. It felt that way.

He began repeating to himself that it was a gag, and he was in earnest now, for he really needed to think that. *Gag, gag, gag. It's gotta be a gag. Hell, am I going nuts?*

The footprint on the sill was clearly defined in the dust, slender and feminine. The trouble with it was that it was about two inches long.

There was a peach tree outside, one branch of which had grown close to the window sill.

He went to the door, stepped out into the night.

His home was in the country, on a hill. Below and about half a mile away he could see the plant. Electrar Corporation. His plant. Not large as some industrial plants go these days, but it was all paid for and it was his and it was making good money now and had a sure future. Worth about five millions, probably.

He had built his home on the hill because he liked to look at the plant whenever he wished. Not bad for a man of forty, Fain liked to think. Worth the unrelenting work and attention to business which the plant had cost him. The plant was his life. That, and his research work. But of course they were the same thing, since the results of his research had built the plant.

Beyond was the town, Hammond City. Not quite a city, for the population, last census, had been 14,575, although it was slightly larger now. The streetlights made even patterns; lighted window were plentiful, and the business district was a distinct glow. An average, prosperous, midwestern town.

John Fain drew in a deep breath.

"Johnny!" he shouted. "Get him! Johnny, get him, boy!"

This was harmless. Johnny was a city-apartment-raised dog; there wasn't a bite in a carload of him. He was really Mrs. Fain's dog; she'd had him before she and Fain were married, two years ago.

But Johnny had one hair-lifting vice. He liked to dash right up to people, barking like hell. When he did this he was like a lion twenty feet tall, strangers said. John Fain felt the same way, because the dog had surprised him with that trick a time or two. Johnny weighted about a hundred and forty pounds; he was the size of a calf. He would frighten the pants off any practical jokers hanging around tonight.

"Take him, Johnny!" Fain yelled. "Get him!"

But the big dog behaved strangely, bouncing around the yard, saying, "Woof! Woof!"

"Damn!" said John Fain, although he didn't feel like saying damn. He felt more like having a good shake, from head to foot.

He said, "Johnny! Lie down!"

The dog now came to the porch, as big as thunder, and as noisy.

"Lie down, Johnny. Down."

The dog did not lie down, which was strange, because lying down was probably the thing he did most enthusiastically, next to bolting his dinner.

The telephone began ringing. It rang two longs, which was the laboratory ring.

John Fain actually ran back into the lab, to the telephone. He was that glad to get hold of something tangible, something believable.

The fluorescent lights in the laboratory took a moment to come on after he threw the switch, and he had the telephone in his hands before the bluish light spilled into the room.

"John? Golly, I hope I didn't bother you," a voice said.

"Gard!" Fain exclaimed.

"That's right. Look, John, I hope I didn't interrupt you in the middle of anything."

Gard's in trouble, Fain thought. Gard McKim was never conscientious about other people, particularly about such small things as bothering someone at work, unless he was in something sticky and wanted you to put a jack under him.

"What is it, Gard?" Fain asked.

"Look, John, my car is out of gasoline and Ikey, darn him, won't give me a drop."

Outdoors the dog, Johnny, suddenly barked. He barked loudly for a moment, stopped, whined.

Fain said, "Gard, where are you?"

"At Ikey's filling station."

"Oh."

"What the hell?" Gard said. "You sound funny, John."

Fain thought: Shall I tell Gard about this? Gard McKim had come in as manager of the plant about a year and a half ago. Fain hadn't liked him at first. Gard McKim was all business, and cold-blooded business, too. After he got hold of Electrar Corporation as general manager, the plant began to grow like the devil. He was directly the opposite of John Fain. Fain was a dreamer, a creator. McKim was aggressive, a go-getter. Now, a year and a half later, John Fain felt that McKim was exactly what the plant needed. He didn't particularly like McKim even yet, any more than he would have developed a fondness for a shark, but he considered the man invaluable.

He decided he wouldn't tell Gard McKim what had happened.

He asked, "Gard, whose car have you got?"

"Yours."

"Okay. In the baggage compartment, behind the spare tire, there is a five-gallon can of gasoline."

"Oh, thanks." Gard McKim was silent a moment. "John, I found that gas can last night and emptied it. And I've no B coupons and Ikey won't give me any gas without coupons."

John Fain said, "I know, Gard. But I filled the can this afternoon again."

Gard McKim swore with pleasure.

"John, you're sure God's gift to improvident lugs like me," he said.

He hung up.

John Fain hung up himself. He put a hand to his forehead and found wetness under it. There was wetness on his cheeks, on the backs of his hands. He was in a nervous perspiration from head to foot.

"Miss Smith!" he called. "Miss Lys Smith!"

There was no answer.

Sick with terror now, he went to the house.

His wife was on the terrace with another woman, long gin drinks before them. The way to the garage led past the terrace, and John Fain stopped for a moment, said, "I'm going to drive downtown a moment, dear."

He saw then that the other woman was Faye Linsky, and at another time, when his mind was not in such a grisly turmoil, he probably would have been surprised. He barely knew Faye Linsky. The girl was in some department or other at the plant and he had met her only once or twice. She seemed a quiet, gentle sort. Not exactly Mrs. Fain's type.

"Good evening, Miss Linsky," he said.

She said, "Hello, Mr. Fain." She could have been a little tight. Maybe not. It might have been excitement, restrained, and perhaps it was the last thought which motivated his next question.

"Have you seen Lys Smith around?" he asked.

Faye Linsky looked puzzled.

Grace Fain explained, "Lys Smith is John's laboratory assistant." She turned to Fain. "No, I haven't seen Lys recently, darling. Not for an hour or two, when she came to work."

Faye Linsky asked, "Why?"

The question shocked him; he didn't know why she should ask it. Or maybe his wonder was just the product of his upset condition.

"If you see her, tell her to wait in the laboratory until I get back," he said, not answering the Linsky girl's question directly.

"Of course, darling," Mrs. Fain said.

He went to get his car.

The garage was on the west side of the house, and it was an ample sort of a place with room for a station wagon and three other cars, and electrically opened doors and a little workshop in the back where the chauffeur could keep things in order. Of course there wasn't any chauffeur now because of the war. There wasn't a station wagon, nor three cars either. There was only one car; Fain had two really, but Gard McKim was driving the second.

He was behind the wheel when he heard Mrs. Fain scream.

The shriek did a great deal to his already strumming nerves. It nearly pulled the cork out for him; for a moment he thought he was going to have one of those things the doctors called a nervous collapse. Then he was out of the car and running.

His wife's scream had been terrible, and its echoes, glancing back from the valley to the east of the house, had the same guttering quality of horror.

"Grace!" he shouted. "What happened?"

His wife was standing with an arm upraised, her hand clutching the cut-glass bowl which had contained ice cubes for their drinks. She was all ready to throw the bowl. She was peering into dark corners of the terrace, under the bushes; she wasn't moving about, just standing still and peering.

Faye Linsky came out of the house. She had a quart bottle of ginger ale.

"What happened?" Fain asked the Linsky girl.

She shook her head. "I was in the house."

Suddenly Mrs. Fain screamed again. She hurled the glass bowl. She hurled it at a darkened spot under some bushes near the corner of the terrace. The bowl broke with a jittering crash.

The Linsky girl said, "For God's sake, Mrs. Fain, what's the matter?"

They saw then that Mrs. Fain was hurt. Her leg, the right one, was welling crimson from a point below the knee.

Fain's wife seemed to snap out of her horrified preoccupation with something near the terrace. She screamed again, this time with words. She shrieked, "John! Oh, John! Something horrible attacked me!" And she threw herself in her husband's arms.

John Fain had thought nothing could shock him much worse, but this did. He looked over his wife's head with glazed eyes, and he saw that the servants had appeared.

There were two servants, the maid and the cook. Annie Rice was the maid, and Mrs. Giggins the cook. Fain did not have a very high opinion of them, particularly of the morals of the maid, Annie Rice. And Mrs. Giggins, a respectable old lady, was a terrific gossip. For that matter, they were both gossips, which was another reason Fain didn't like them to tidy up his laboratory.

"John!" Mrs. Fain gasped. "John, you'd better call Doctor Willimetz."

Fain took her to a chair, or started to; when she hung back and wailed. "Please! Take me away from this terrace!" he changed his mind and took her in the house.

He examined the wound on her leg.

"This is only a cut," he said.

"Get Doctor Willimetz!"

"First aid will do the job, Grace," he explained patiently. "Times like these, the doctors are busy and—"

She looked at him with glazed fright.

"Don't you understand—I want to know whether I've gone insane!" she said, and there was nothing rational about the tone of her voice.

"What cut you?" he asked.

She looked at him wordlessly. He had the feeling she wasn't going to answer, but he tried again.

"Grace, what was it?" he asked.

"I won't tell you," she said.

He turned to the cook, Mrs. Giggins. "Will you telephone Doctor Willimetz." His voice was hoarse.

Mrs. Giggins said she would. Her eyes were as large as saucers.

"John!" his wife gasped.

"Yes?"

"Will you—look—on the terrace." Her words were separated by intervals of strain.

"Look for what?"

She didn't answer. She wasn't going to answer. He went out on the terrace, very carefully, and looked. He turned on all the lights, the floodlights that illuminated the yard and which they didn't use because it was patriotic to conserve lights. He hunted for a while, and he didn't find anything. There was nothing where the glass bowl had broken. There was no dust that would have retained fingerprints.

He went back into the house.

Mrs. Giggins was saying, "I got Doctor Willimetz. He will come right out."

John Fain cleared his throat. His voice wasn't normal, but it was as normal as he could make it.

He said, "Keep all the lights on. Miss Linsky, will you stay with Grace? You too, Mrs. Giggins?"

They said they would.

"I've got to go to town," John Fain said. "I'll be back as soon as I can."

He went to the garage and got in his car, drove toward town.

II

The telegraph office for Hammond City was located in the business district adjacent to the Merchant's Hotel. It was not a large place, and the manager, Mr. Bartlett, had been the manager for nearly twenty years. Of late, because of the scarcity of help, he had been coming down himself one night a week to let the regular evening operator have a day off. The office remained open until midnight because of the Electrar plant business.

"Why, hello Mr. Fain," said Mr. Bartlett. "I haven't seen you in a long time."

John Fain tried to make his voice natural. He said, "No, Mr. Bartlett, I don't get downtown much any more."

"Things keeping you busy at the plant, eh?"

"Rather."

"These times are keeping us all busy."

John Fain drew out a telegraph blank, picked up a pencil. On the address line, he wrote: DOC SAVAGE, NEW YORK CITY. . . .

The text of his message proved more difficult. He wrote the address with considerable vigor, because it represented— the name did—a life preserver for his sanity. He had a great deal of confidence in Doc Savage, although he knew the man but slightly—had met him only once, in fact, more than a year ago. For a moment he was distracted by his own inability with words so suddenly after he had written Doc Savage's name, as if by merely writing the name he'd settled things. There was going to be a lot more to it than that.

Finally he got enough words together to make:

WISH YOUR AID ON MATTER BORDERING COMPLETE FANTASY STOP VITAL IMPORTANCE STOP WILL YOU COME AT ONCE.

That was what he wrote, but it struck him as inane, silly. Unable to improve on it, though, he signed his name and shoved it across the counter. As an afterthought, he withdrew the message, added: PRESIDENT, ELECTRAR CORPORATION after his name. That was in case Doc Savage should think the message came from a nut.

Mr. Bartlett said, "New York City. . . that's a right fair-sized town. Shouldn't there be a street address?"

"I imagine he's well enough known," Fain said. "Anyway, I don't know his street address. They'll find him, I'm sure."

"I'll send it this way if you wish."

"Do."

"You want me to charge it to the plant account?"

"No, I'll pay for it personally."

John Fain paid for the telegram and left.

* * *

It happened that John Fain's message was one of the last taken by Mr. Bartlett for transmission before he closed up and went home. He handed it to the operator, began checking up the day's receipts and entering them in the forms, and had not finished when the operator got his hat and coat and paused at the door to say, "Good night, Mr. Bartlett."

"Good night, Fred."

Mr. Bartlett locked the cash and the money-order code in the safe, tidied up his personal desk, and lit a cigar. He locked the front door, and followed his usual routine, which was to go to the south one block, then half a block west to a parking lot where he kept his car.

However he followed this routine only as far as the alley halfway between McPherson and Broad Streets, where he was hit over the head with a hard object and knocked senseless.

The striking was down by a man who stepped up behind old Bartlett. A second skulker had waited in the alleyway.

"He out?" the latter demanded.

The one who had struck the blow did some wrist-holding. "Yeah, out." He was relieved that he had found a pulse.

"Get his keys."

"Okay."

Mr. Bartlett's keys were not hard to find, and the two men cooperated in dragging the old man into the alley.

"Reckon you'd better bop him again?"

"Nah, I don't think so."

"He got any dough on him?"

"Didn't find any."

"Okay. Let's go."

They walked to the telegraph office. They did not skulk, but neither did they make themselves conspicuous. The night was not particularly warm for the season, a circumstance which enabled them legitimately to turn up their coat collars and yank their hats down. The shadows hid their faces.

One said, when they reached the telegraph office, "You unlock the door. I'll keep look-out."

"No, you fool, act as if we were on legitimate business," the other ordered.

They tried several keys without attracting any unwelcome attention; finally the door swung inward. They entered.

"Turn on the lights," one ordered.

"But hell—"

"Turn on the lights!" the first man growled. "You want a night cop to notice us prowling around in here without any lights and figure something has gone wrong? Where's your head."

"What if some guy wants to send a telegram?"

"Just accept it."

But no one came in, and they found what they had come after.

They found the telegram John Fain had filed.

"Oh, my God!" The searcher said when he read the message.

The other one read it, and he said, "Let's get out of here with that. No, better take a copy of it. We might as well not advertise this any more than we have to."

They left, after copying the message, and locked the door behind them. They walked three blocks rapidly, got into a car, and drove to an apartment house in what was known as the Country Club Addition, one the swankier parts of town. Sportier was probably a better word. Sporty, and not always on the up-and-up.

Their apartment was on the second floor rear, and they did not turn on the lights for a while, not until they had pulled the shades.

"I always hate living on the second floor," the shorter of the two men complained. "The damned neighbors always looking in your windows."

The other said, "It's always easier to slide out of a second-story window in case of a raid." There was nothing in his manner to show whether or not he was in earnest.

They searched their apartment thoroughly.

"I don't know why we're doing this," the tall man complained.

He got on the telephone. Hammond City had the dial system, so there was no worry about operators listening in. But the man spoke enigmatically, anyway. He said: "The shipment contained the merchandise you believed it contained. . . . Yes, that's right. No, no details, just the bare merchandise. . . . Who? Well, hold your hat. It went to Doc Savage, in New York City. . . . Yes, it sort of got me, too. Okay, hang on."

236 / A Doc Savage Adventure

There was a wait now, and the man put his hand over the mouthpiece and told his companion, "Thinking what to do."

"Scared?"

"You bet. That's the reason for the thinking."

"I was scared, too."

"You weren't by yourself." He took his hand off the mouthpiece to say, "Yes... Yes, I guess that's the thing to do... Okay. Sure. We'll meet you." He hung up.

The other man was leaning forward from the hips, lips parted. "Well?" he demanded.

"We get the hell to New York," he said, "and try to take care of this Savage at that end."

III

Clark Savage had a sensible arrangement. He was unmarried, had no close family ties, did no entertaining at all in a social sense; so he did his living at his laboratory-office. This included his sleeping. He had a folding bed arrangement in a cubicle off the laboratory, and there was also a bath and a clothes locker and a kitchenette. The latter was a joke to his five close friends who frequently worked with him. Doc was an awful cook. His friends considered this remarkable for the reason that Doc had so many other abilities that it didn't seem possible he could be such a Ptomaine Pete when he got hold of a skillet. His friends didn't even consider his jungle cooking safe. So the kitchenette was purely atmosphere. The headquarters' layout of laboratory, library and reception-room-office was located on the eighty-sixth floor of a midtown building, had a wonderful view and was about as unnoticeable as a sore thumb. Anyone who wished could visit the place, and get shunted into the screening room on the twelfth floor where the cranks were sorted from those who had legitimate business. But the twelfth-floor sieve didn't function at night, and it was Doc's custom to switch off the doorbell and the telephones when he wanted to get some sleep. By closing the reception room and library doors, he wouldn't hear knocking on the hall door, hence slept in peace.

It was hammering on the door however, which awakened him. He turned over, focused one eye on his wrist watch and saw that it was the ungodly hour of 5 A.M. He waited for the pounding to stop and the visitor to go away.

Neither happened.

The pounding got louder. It had a frantic, determined violence.

Doc Savage got up and put on a dressing robe and stepped into his shoes, resisting a normal impulse to carry one of the shoes to the door with him and use it to swat the pest over the head.

Habitual caution asserted itself when he reached the door.

"Who is it?" he asked.

"My name's Chesler," said a hoarse and frantic voice.

"Chesler who?"

"François Chesler," the voice said. "My God, I've got to talk to you!"

Doc did not open the door immediately. He knew no one named François Chesler. He also had quite a few enemies collected over a period of time, and some of these were possessed of an abnormal amount of ingenuity.

The man outside cried, "I think they poisoned me."

He sounded so earnest about this that Doc overcame his inclination to take his time and find out what this was all about. He opened the door.

François Chesler seemed to be alone in the hall. He spoke in terror. He said:

"They made me swallow something. I think it was poison." He peered at Doc Savage. "You're a doctor, aren't you? Can't you do something?"

Doc examined the man's face intently. He decided that Chesler was poisoned, all right.

He hauled the man inside and closed the door. He asked, "What kind of poison?"

"I don't know," Chesler said. "It was in capsules."

Doc took him into the laboratory. The thing to do was get it out of the man, whatever it was.

In the next ten minutes, he learned quite a lot about Chesler without asking the man any questions and without a word from Chesler.

Chesler worked with his brains, and evidently made good money at it. At least he had soft hands and a two-hundred-dollar suit, a fifteen-dollar shirt and a twelve-dollar cravat. Any necktie that cost twelve dollars, and anything of that quality from Kiel's on Madison Avenue cost that much at least, was not to be called a necktie. It was a cravat. Chesler was about five feet six, weight about a hundred and sixty. He was nearsighted, and wore glasses, and he had an arrested case of pyorrhea.

The poison was nicotine.

"Nicotine," Doc told him. "But it's out of you now, and I don't think it got enough of a hold to hurt you."

"Nicotine?" the man said. "You mean like in tobacco?"

"Yes. But this was nicotine, the alkaloid of tobacco, which is almost as deadly a poison as prussic acid. It's an oily liquid, volatile, acrid, pale amber in color, and smells strongly of tobacco when the air gets to it. The salts are dextrorotatory although the free base is levorotatory."

"That sounds bad."

"It could have been."

"I don't smoke."

"That might make it a little worse. You wouldn't have a partial tolerance for it. But it obviously hadn't been in you long."

"Only a few minutes."

"Who gave it to you?"

"There were four of them."

Doc Savage put the instruments he had used in the sterilizer. He said, "Maybe you'd better tell a complete story."

François Chesler wiped sweat off his forehead. "That's exactly what I want to do."

He was, he explained, French. Apparently wishing to prove this, he changed into French, which he spoke excellently and with a patois which only a real Frenchman would be likely to use.

"I'm a French private detective, you might call me," he said. "And I've got hold of something too big for me to handle, and I thought of you."

He paused and examined Doc Savage as if seeing him for the first time.

"Lord, you're big," he added.

"What about your story?" Doc asked.

Chesler licked his lips. "I've heard a lot about you, even in France and England. You have a terrific reputation."

"You don't need to do a buttering-up job," Doc said.

Chesler jumped. He looked frightened. "I didn't mean it as flattery. I'm not trying to sell you anything."

"Let's hear your story."

Chesler nodded, said, "Your business, or perhaps I should say your hobby, is helping people out of trouble and righting wrongs and punishing evildoers who are outside the law, isn't it?"

"Business," Doc said, correcting him. "Not a hobby. And it isn't quite that Galahadian or melodramatic."

"Well, that's why I was coming to you." Chesler wiped perspiration off his face again. The ordeal he had undergone had brought on a nervous sweat. "I am employed by Conciero Et Cie, a Paris private banking concern, in an effort to trace down certain movable assets which the Nazis appropriated— stolen is the word—during their occupancy of France. These particular assets consist of some three million dollars worth of paintings, a Raphael and two Fra Angelicos among them."

He paused to make a soothing gesture.

"I know you're not a ferret for any company which lost property during the mess in Europe," he continued. "But it so happens that these particular paintings represent the trust funds of Le Matin Safran, a home for the blind. Without this fund, God knows what will happen to the blind inmates of the place. It was for this reason I thought of you."

Doc removed his dressing robe and began getting dressed. He was a bronzed giant of a man, remarkably muscled, in fact almost unnaturally muscled. His hair was a bronze only slightly darker than his skin, and his eyes were a very light brown, a flake gold color.

Chesler continued: "I'll make a long story short. I traced the gang with the paintings here. I found out they are going back to Europe with them. They have managed passage on a ship, have the paintings aboard. They learned I was on their trail, tried to kill me. I got away."

Doc was knotting a solid-color tie. He said, "You want me to board this ship with you and get the paintings?"

Chesler nodded.

"It won't be entirely simple," he said. "I'm afraid we'll have to sail on the ship and do our job enroute. It will be hard finding the paintings."

"When does this ship sail?"

"In about an hour."

"Have you made arrangements to get aboard?"

"None whatever. We will have to do that with ingenuity."

*   *   *

They met Monk Mayfair and Ham Brooks in the lobby. Monk Mayfair was Lieutenant Colonel Andrew Blodgett Mayfair, and there was not much mystery about his nickname of Monk. He looked like a slightly advanced form of ape, a physical appearance that did not fit with the fact that he was one of the world's leading industrial chemists—whenever he took time off from chasing excitement to work at it. He had been kept on the Army's inactive list throughout the war because his activities as a Doc Savage aide were considered more important. He'd raised plenty of hell about this, but with no luck.

Ham Brooks was a lawyer. He outranked Monk, his full title being Brigadier General Theodore Marley Brooks, but it made no difference because he was on the inactive list also for the same reason. He was a slender man with the large flexible mouth of an orator and a mania for fancy clothes, always in the best taste.

He and Monk Mayfair liked to work together, and they quarreled continuously.

Doc met them coming into the lobby as he and Chesler were leaving, and they were fussing about who had gotten whom out of bed at this ungodly hour.

Monk was saying, "There was no need of you waking me up, you overdressed shyster. I was sleeping like a top . . ."

"Which probably explains why you're so dizzy," Ham said. "Hello, Doc."

Doc Savage examined them suspiciously. "It must have taken an earthquake to get you two up this early."

"I wouldn't call Ham an earthquake," Monk said.

"The telegraph company routed me out, Doc," Ham explained. "They said they had a wire for you that looked important, and they couldn't raise you at the office."

"Oh."

Monk was eyeing Chesler. "Who's your friend?"

Chesler was smiling. His smile said: "I'm happy to meet you, gentlemen."

Doc said, "He claims his name is François Chesler, but he's probably lying."

Chesler lost the smile.

"Who is he?" Monk asked.

"A fellow who turned up a while ago, beat on my door,

and when he heard my voice, took a couple of capsules of nicotine."

"Blazes!" Monk was astonished.

François Chesler was astonished too, but more unpleasantly. "You're being ridiculous!" he exclaimed.

Doc shook his head. "How long do you think it takes a capsule to dissolve? One of them hadn't yet when the stomach pump brought it up. Your international story was good, but . . ."

"Watch him!" Monk yelled.

Chesler had taken off. His feet made some cuffing noises on the floor as they tried to get traction, then he was under way.

If it had not been for the man behind the cigar counter, Chesler would not have gotten far, probably.

Doc was carrying a small handbag into which he'd thrust what clothes he thought he might absolutely have to have; he watched Chesler, calculated the man's speed and direction, then took a forward step and down like a bowler. The handbag skidded across the smooth parquet flooring, engaged Chesler's ankles, brought him down. Chesler landed spread out, slid several feet on his stomach, turning slowly so that when he got up he would be facing them.

The man who'd been behind the cigar counter by now had lifted into view.

He roared, "Let 'im go!"

He had a voice like a railroad engine in a tunnel, and also something which was wrapped in a newspaper. He was trying to get his hands on this object in just the correct places. When he succeeded, fire and noise came out of the end of the parcel. It was a gun disguised to look like something else.

He shot from the hip, he was behind the counter, and he didn't do an accurate job. The first shot broke a display case containing advertisements from the observation roof of the building.

Ham Brooks and Monk Mayfair were making for François Chesler or whatever his name.

They didn't stop for Chesler. They kept going. There was a recess ahead, a passage between the central shafts which contained the batteries of elevators. They got to it.

Doc Savage was moving also. He went down low, to get

the cigar counter between himself and the man's gun, and headed for another recess.

Chesler was on his feet. He ran.

The gun made two more loud reports, and the man holding it yelled at Chesler, "Wait, you dope! I gotta car."

The two of them dashed outdoors, and a car engine and gears began making a racket.

Ham Brooks looked at Monk Mayfair and began laughing. He said, "Junior, that woke you up, didn't it?"

"That guy was trying to kill us." Monk was alarmed. "What's so funny about it?"

Doc Savage was standing in the street, staring after the departing car. Suddenly he made a dash for the sidewalk and a sheltering doorway. A shot noise came bumping along the street, following the violin-string snap of a bullet.

"They're a little reckless," Doc remarked.

"Did you get the license number?"

"I think so, but it probably won't help much, if the car is stolen."

Monk had lost his hat during the recent maneuvers. "I'm a little confused," he confessed. "Just who were those guys?

"The second one was a complete stranger," Doc admitted. "And a more complete surprise," he added.

"What about the first one? What's his name—Chesler— what about him?"

Doc explained the circumstances of François Chesler's visit, and repeated the story Chesler had told about the valuable paintings.

Monk ran a hand through the rusty bristles which served him as hair. "He told a wild one, didn't he."

Doc nodded. "He probably hoped it was wild enough that I would forget to ask him for his credentials as a French private sleuth."

"He was a phony?"

"Probably."

"What about his picture story?"

"We can check on that," Doc said. "What was that you fellows were saying about a telegram that brought you here?"

"Ham's got it," Monk said.

Doc Savage read John Fain's telegram from Hammond City. When he looked up, Monk and Ham were eyeing him questioningly.

Monk asked, "Think there's any connection?"

"It shouldn't take long to find out."

IV

Sunlight, slanting down through a thin stratus cloud layer, took on a gentle silver quality. Penetrating the eighty-sixth floor windows, it spilled across the reception room rug, slightly brightened the big inlaid table that was the largest piece of furniture, and fell across Doc Savage's shoulders as he leaned over the telephone. But the light was not quite bright enough to make a shadow, Doc noticed. He proved this by trying to make different shaped shadows with his free hand while he was waiting. Finally a voice croaked at him in the receiver.

Doc said, "Yes. . . . I see. Well, that was quick work." He thanked the croaking voice and hung up.

Ham Brooks made a pair of quizzical bows out of his eyebrows, demanded, "Don't tell me that they caught the two guys already?"

"Only identified the car," Doc explained.

"Whose was it?"

"Belongs to a man named Gilliam who lives in a Lexington Avenue apartment. He reported it stolen about an hour ago."

"Oh."

Doc added, "The license plates hadn't been changed."

"That supposed to mean anything?" Ham was puzzled.

"It means they were in a hurry. They didn't feel they had time to bother about changing license plates."

"Let me see that telegram," Ham said. He studied the message, added, "This was sent from Hammond City at 11:45 last night and received here at 12:10 this morning. Let's see . . . five hours ago . . . a hundred and ten miles to Hammond City about . . . an hour in a private airplane, say, plus another half hour to get in town from the nearest flying field . . . that adds up to them being pretty busy."

"If they came from Hammond City," Doc said.

"Yes. If."

Monk Mayfair was busy on a second telephone. He was having trouble with somebody, and having it in French, which he didn't speak too well. What French Monk did speak, however, was well fitted for a row. He had learned it long ago from a French chemistry student who, as a gag, had taught Monk a vocabulary consisting almost exclusively of French cusswords.

Doc Savage was disturbed. "They'll arrest you for talking like that over the telephone."

Presently Monk hung up. "That button-head!" he said, eyeing the instrument unpleasantly.

Ham asked, "Who were you talking to?"

"That French outfit that's got a place in Radio City, the one with the fancy show windows."

"Who did you have, the janitor?"

Monk was doubtful. "I guess so. Some guy said he was *un gêrant*. Is that janitor?"

"My God, you were talking to the manager himself! The biggest French firm in the city. What'd he do, spit in the telephone?"

"Nah, he parleyvooed my fransay all right. They got a French dictionary up there, a kind of who's who of the business firms in France. He says there's a banking company named Conciero Et Cie, and there's a home for the blind named Le Matin Safran."

Ham Brooks was astonished.

"Then François Chesler was telling the truth!" he exclaimed.

Doc said, "Or he was smart."

He was not convinced. He picked up the telephone, asked for the long-distance operator, and placed a person-to-person call for John Fain, Hammond City. Waiting for the call to go through, he contemplated the ceiling thoughtfully.

"Nicotine is not a poison you pick up just anywhere," he remarked.

A deeply pleasant and puzzled voice said, "Hello. This is John Fain speaking."

Doc asked, "Are you in a position to talk without being overheard?"

"Why, of course." The man sounded surprised.

Doc identified himself, added, "I called about that telegram."

"What telegram?" Astonishment succeeded surprise in the man's voice.

"The telegram you sent me last night from Hammond City," Doc said.

"A telegram which I addressed to Doc Savage?"

"Yes."

"I sent no such message, Mr. Savage," the voice said. "I assure you that I hardly know you, and that I certainly did not impose on you. No, I sent no message."

"This is Mr. John Fain?"

"Yes."

"What is your occupation, Mr. Fain?"

"I am president and sole owner of the Electrar Corporation of Hammond City."

"I see." Doc contemplated the ceiling wonderingly. He added, "Very well, Mr. Fain, and thank you. Sorry to have bothered you."

Monk Mayfair had been on the telephone again during the long-distance conversation. There were two outside lines into the office, and he had been using the second to call the harbor master's office.

Monk said, "Doc, there was a ship sailed about when Chesler said it was going to sail. The *Confiteurs*. It sailed for France."

Doc Savage was eying the telephone doubtfully. "That fellow knew the telegram was an imposition on us," he said. "He knew that much about it."

"You mean the message from Hammond City is genuine, the guy said?" Ham asked.

"The man said exactly the opposite," Doc admitted.

Ham made a statement. He made it sound as if he had solved everything.

"The telegram from Hammond City was a red herring," he stated. "Somebody hoped we would dash off to Hammond City on a wild goose chase and not go to France on that boat." He became a man of action, added, "The thing for us to do is grab a plane and fly out to that steamer and board it."

"That sounds logical," Doc admitted.

"Sure it does."

"Except for one thing," Doc added. "I think the French angle was the red herring."

Ham was startled. "How do you figure that?"

"A hunch."

"Based on what?" Ham asked skeptically.

"The feeling that I know when a man is lying," Doc said. "Chesler was."

Ham opened his mouth, closed it while he thought for a while, then said, "I've seen you wrong a few times, but not very often. I think you're wrong now."

Monk Mayfair grinned. He liked to oppose Ham's ideas. He said, "I favor looking into the Hammond City angle."

Doc asked, "What is the harbor master's number?" Monk gave him the number, and Doc asked the speed of the French ship *Confiteurs,* and its course. The harbor master refused to divulge this; he would give it personally, he explained, but not over the telephone. There was still a war going on, and the information came under the heading of strictly secret. He knew Monk personally, he added, or he would not have revealed that the ship had sailed.

"Give me an idea of its speed, then," Doc suggested.

"Sure. That's no secret," the harbor master said readily. "Anybody could dig that up by looking in the pre-war ship registry. It's nine knots cruising, not over twelve top. She's slow."

Doc thanked him and hung up. He told Monk and Ham, "The boat is slow. We can waste as much as a couple of days investigating Hammond City, and still have time to overhaul the ship by plane."

Ham was relieved. "Good idea. That won't put me out on a limb."

Doc asked, "How soon can you and Monk be headed for Hammond City by plane?"

"In practically no time."

"Hey!" Monk was confused. "What do we do after we get there?"

"Find out if a telegram was sent, and let me know as soon as you can. I'll be on the first train leaving for Hammond City after twelve o'clock. Send me a wire on the train if you find out that soon, and you should."

"Want us to check on this John Fain?"

Doc nodded. "And another thing—find out who could have taken my telephone call a minute ago and pretended to be John Fain."

Ham blinked, startled. "You think it wasn't Fain on the phone?"

"I'm sure it wasn't."

"How the . . ."

Doc lifted a hand. "I'm afraid I forgot to mention that I remember what John Fain's voice is like. It wasn't Fain on the telephone."

Ham registered such a look of surprise that Monk burst into laughter.

V

The Municipal Airport at Hammond City was located five miles east of town on the river flats and had a paved north-south runway, brick hangar, brick line shack, and not much activity. The gas pumps, one for seventy-two octane and the other for eighty octane, were in front of the line shack. A middle-aged man stood in front of the hose pit and made listless come-hither gestures with his hands, guiding the plane carrying Monk Mayfair and Ham Brooks to the gas pit. The man's overalls looked as if he had used them to wipe off a motor. When he thought they were within hose reach, he made a dragging motion with one finger across his throat, signifying they should cut the motor.

Monk told the man, "We'll want ninety octane."

"Ain't got it."

"Well, eighty, then. And hangarage."

"No hangar room," the man said. "Have to stake her out."

Monk didn't like the idea, because it was the season of the year when hail storms were occasional. He shrugged. There was nothing else to do. "Where do we sign in?" he asked.

"Book in the line shack."

There was enough cigarette smoke in the line shack to make Monk sneeze. Ham was leaning over the registration book, pencil in hand. But he was listening to the conversation of three men who were in the line shack. Catching Monk's glance, he indicated, by moving his eyes, that Monk should listen also.

A fat man with crossed eyes was saying, "That's wrong. My wife talked to a neighbor woman who got it straight from the Giggins woman who cooks for the Fains. Mrs. Fain didn't go to the hospital. She was too bad to be taken."

"I heard she was."

"Mrs. Giggins says it was the same thing this guy Blake got away from."

"You say Blake's in the hospital?"

"Yeah, in the part where they put boobies. The doctor thought he was nuts."

The third man spoke. "I think somebody's nuts," he said. He was a solid looking man in a blue suit and a cap that said TAXI. "I don't believe none of this stuff," he added.

The fat man sneered at him. "The way science is goin' ahead, who can say what is possible and what ain't. When them scientists are experimentin', half the time they don't know what they're doin'."

The other man, who was nondescript, said, "I saw a movie once—"

"I don't believe a damned word of the goofy thing," the taxi driver said.

The nondescript man was offended. The fat one was contemptuous. He said. "You're so smart, Alvy, how come you're driving a hack for a living at your age?"

This made Alvy mad. "You're a bunch of idiots!" he yelled. "By God, any time I get scared over such a thing, I'll be ready for a strait-jacket."

Apprehensive lest there be a fight, Monk said, "How about a cab into town."

"Okay," Alvy said. He examined the pair with whom he had been conversing. He spit on the floor.

The road to town was a straight mouse-colored slab of concrete between tall, gaunt poplar trees. Alvy, still angry, said, "Them guys is goofs."

"What was the fuss about?" Monk asked.

"Aw-w-w-w," Alvy said. "There's a story going around that somethin' terrible got away from John Fain in his laboratory last night, and is attackin' people. It probably didn't happen." Alvy sounded as if he wanted them to be sure that he himself didn't take any stock in the story.

Monk asked, "What was it that got away?"

"I dunno," Alvy said. "Somethin' about two feet high."

"That's not very big," Monk said.

Alvy grunted. He said, "They're sayin' this thing got hold of Mrs. Fain and crippled her up, though."

"Who is Mrs. Fain?"

"John Fain's wife."

"Oh. Is he the Fain who owns the Electrar Corporation?"

"Yeah."

Monk pushed the conversation, suggesting, "Got away from him in his laboratory, eh?"

"So the story goes."

"Didn't Mrs. Fain see it?"

"She ain't talking, supposedly." Alvy scratched his head. "Fain ain't got anything to say, either. And Fain didn't go to the plant this morning."

"Sounds queer," Monk said.

Alvy admitted it did, added, "A guy named Blake, a bird who works in a filling station, kind of got the story going hot. He says some kind of a damned thing got after him on his way to work this morning, and he barely got away." Alvy sighed, settled back. "Nuts to it."

Ham Brooks contemplated the back of the driver's head. He asked, "You know the Fains?"

"Just by sight."

"Oh." Ham was surprised. "You knowing so much about it, I thought maybe you were close to the family."

"Me? A taxi pusher!" Alvy snorted. "Hell, the story's all over town."

Ham looked out of the cab windows at Hammond City. "It's a pretty good-sized town," he remarked.

"Yeah," Alvy said. He had missed the point.

"What have you got here?" Ham asked. "A bunch of gossips?"

"Oh." Alvy turned his head. "You mean how did the story get all over town so quick? Damned if I know. Just got, I guess."

"Somebody spreading it?"

"Hell, it don't need no spreading. Half a dozen guys have told me about it already. Whenever it goes back, it goes to them two Fain servants, Annie Rice and Mrs. Giggins."

Monk Mayfair cleared his throat. "You know this filling station fellow, this Blake?" he asked. Monk had a freak voice; any perceptible amount of excitement made it rise in scale, so that he sounded about thirteen years old.

Alvy shook his head. "But I know where he works."

"This story fascinates me," Monk said. "What do you say we drive past and have a word with Blake about it?"

Alvy was not averse to this. "I'd like to hear it straight from the horse's mouth myself," he said.

* * *

Their arrival in the Gray Cross Filling Station created quite a stir. Two men dashed for the cab, one an attendant and the other, it seemed, the owner himself. The pair fell over each other polishing the windshield and checking the tires. Alvy said out of the corner of his mouth. "Boy, look at 'em shake the lead out of their pants. They think I'm maybe gonna give 'em all my business."

Monk and Ham strolled into the station and got a coke from the red dispensing machine.

"You Blake?" Monk asked.

"Yes."

"We heard about your experience this morning," Monk said invitingly. "What's the straight on that?"

Blake said, "Be with you in a minute." He went into the station. He was a thin, stooped man with very black eyes and a mouth with downturned corners.

Alvy said, "You guys know your meter's running."

"We know it," Ham said.

They could not see what Blake was doing inside the station. The morning was pleasantly warm. It was fifteen minutes past eleven o'clock, Monk saw when he consulted his wrist. Alvy pondered, then shut off the engine of his cab.

Presently Blake came out. "Had to call my wife," he said. His brown tie was crooked. "What'd you wanta know?"

"We heard about your experience this morning," Monk told him.

"Oh, that." Blake licked his lips, leaving them moist and shiny. "Well, it beat any damned thing you ever saw."

"What happened?"

"Something got after me."

"That's what we heard." Monk was encouraging the fellow by showing great interest. "What was it?"

Blake said, "It happened out on Euclid Avenue, before daylight, on my way to work. Euclid leads on out to Euclid Road, where the Fain house is situated. But this happened about a mile from the Fain place."

"What was it?" Monk asked.

"It sure scared me, I can tell you," Blake said. A car had driven into the filling station. "It was dark, but there was light enough for me to see it." Three men got out of the car which had just arrived. It was a touring car, black, 1939 model. Blake licked his lips again, added, "I ran like hell, I can tell you." The three men wore masks made of white handkerchiefs.

Monk frowned at Blake.

"What's the matter? Ain't you gonna tell us what it was?" he demanded.

One of the three men who had arrived in the touring car said loudly, "You looking for information, bub?"

Monk wheeled. He saw the masks. "Hey!" he exclaimed. "Put that gun away!" The man didn't put his gun away, however, and his two companions also produced guns.

"Get in our car, both you guys," the man said.

Blake and the owner of the Gray Cross Service Station both had their hands in the air the last Monk and Ham saw of them. They looked very scared. Too frightened, Monk suspected, to call the police immediately.

"Point that thing the other way," Monk urged. "It might go off."

The man gave Monk a harder gouge in the ribs with the revolver. "Hey Charlie, guess what," he said.

"What?" asked Charlie.

"The missing link's afraid of getting shot."

Charlie looked at the man in the front seat with him and said, "The missing link's afraid of getting shot."

"The hell you say," said the other man.

This comprised the conversation for several blocks. The car moved at about twenty-five miles an hour, turned various corners, and finally lined out on a street that rapidly took it out of town. The road grew bumpy.

Ham Brooks' hat was dislodged in passing over one of the bumps, and he raised his hands cautiously to fix it more firmly on his head.

"You wanta get shot?" the spokesman of their captors asked.

"No."

The man relayed this information to Charlie. "He don't wanta get shot."

"He don't wanta get shot," Charlie told the driver.

"That's too bad," the driver said.

Monk, who was enraged and frightened, demanded, "What is this, a clown act?"

"What's your name?" Charlie countered.

"Nuts," Monk said.

"Maybe you ain't the guy we want, then," Charlie said. "The guy we want is named Monk Mayfair." Charlie hung the muzzle of his gun over the back of the seat menacingly. "Sit still. Bill, frisk 'em."

Bill went through their pockets, first by slapping, then by emptying the pockets. finally he became interested in what was inside their shirts, and unbuttoned their shirts to look. "By God, iron underwear!" he exclaimed.

"What's that?" Charlie demanded.

"They got bulletproof vests on," Bill said. He became doubtful. "Or I guess that's what they've got on." He wrenched open Ham's shirt, tearing off two buttons. "Look. Ain't that what it is?"

Ham was angered. "This shirt cost twenty dollars!" he yelled. "Be careful with it!"

Charlie was peering at the vests. "That's what it is, a bulletproof vest," he said. "Say, you better shoot 'em in the head when you shoot." He pointed his gun at Monk's left eye. "Bill, look in their billfolds and see it they're the guys."

Presently Bill announced, "That's right. Brigadier General Theodore Marley Brooks and Lieutenant Colonel Andrew Blodgett Mayfair."

Charlie was pleased.

"We hit the jackpot," he said.

The car drove more slowly now, and the road was worse. They were in a woods and the road was no longer paved. It did not look as if it was used much.

Ham Brooks, having done some thinking, told Monk, "These guys must have been watching the airport."

Monk had been thinking himself. "Either that," he said, "or that guy Blake called them when he was using the telephone."

Charlie grinned at them. "Which do you think it was?" he wanted to know.

Monk didn't like Charlie's gin. He didn't like the way Bill was taking the money out of their billfolds, either. "You going to rob us?" he demanded.

"You won't mind," Bill said.

"The hell I won't! I'll make you wish—"

"Not unless you become a ghost, you won't," Bill said. "You're going to be dead."

The driver said, "Don't get them excited."

"Let 'em get excited," Charlie said. "I'd rather shoot a bird on the wing than a sitting one; any time."

Bill eyed Monk and Ham. "Go ahead, start something," he invited.

"No, thanks," Monk said.

He was sure they were going to be killed. He was surprised at the assortment of sensations this knowledge produced in him. He decided he didn't care for any of the feelings, though. It was unreal. He knew the men intended to kill him, but it didn't produce any of the feelings he supposed a man had before he died. Maybe the thing had come too suddenly.

Shortly the car turned off on a course where there was no road, only weeds and low brush which scraped and whacked against fenders, running-boards, chassis. This did not last long. The car stopped.

"Whoe-e-e-e!" Charlie gasped, giving the driver a frightened look. "You didn't need to drive so damn close to the edge!"

"This heap's got good brakes," the driver said. "Whatcha worried about?"

With horror, Monk stared at an expanse of green water in front of them and some thirty feet below. The water looked filthy and deep. It covered about an acre, and was the lake in an old quarry pit.

Bill said, "We ain't very original. Lots of bodies have been put in quarry pits." He leered, demanded, "Maybe you'd like a more original death?"

"Cut out the funny stuff," Charlie said. "Go see if anybody's around the place."

Bill went away, pushing through the brush, stopping to look all directions.

Monk told Ham, "These guys are funny as skeletons."

Ham looked at Monk in horror and said, "What are you trying to do, make a joke of it? Don't you see they intend to kill us?" His face was the color of an aluminum utensil which had been out in the weather a considerable time.

"Shut up!" Charlie ordered.

The driver got out of the car. He stumbled over a rock, which he kicked in a rage; then he picked up the rock and threw it in the water. He watched the green ripples, like the crawling movement of a grass snake, with satisfaction.

"I damned near got drowned right there when I was a kid," he announced. "Twenty-five feet deep, if she's an inch."

He went around behind the car, put his shoulder to the machine and shoved. It moved several inches, enough to put Monk's hair on end.

"We can push her right over," the driver added.

A crashing in the brush caused them all to hold their breath. But it was Bill coming back.

"Didn't see nobody," Bill said.

"You look good?"

"What do you think I am, a fool?"

Charlie eyed Bill with sudden suspicion. "Let's see that dough you took off them," he said.

Bill produced some greenbacks. "They only had about a hundred," he said. He tossed the money on the grass. "Good thing we are on a salary," he added.

Wrath suffused Charlie's face.

"There was more dough than that!" he said.

"Dammit, you think I'm holding out?" Bill was injured. "Search me, if you want to."

"Sure, after you went off in the brush and hid it!" Charlie yelled.

The driver was holding an automatic pistol. He was aiming it carefully at Monk.

The driver said, "First things come first, don't they?"

He pulled the trigger.

VI

The 1:15 train out of Grand Central was made up of day coaches, but it was a streamliner and went express as far as Hartford, after which Hammond City was the next stop. Thinking Monk and Ham might have wired him care of the train, or that a message might come aboard at Hartford, Doc Savage found the conductor, in whose care any such telegram would be given, and identified himself. The conductor, having heard of Doc Savage, was impressed, and said that if anything came in, he would see that it didn't lie around.

Doc had dropped his suitcase in the last seat in a coach, so that no one was facing him, in order not to be conspicuous. Not that he had a bobby sox public. But he was often recognized, and it was embarrassing to be pointed at. If he were in show business, he imagined he would learn not to mind, and probably to like it. Exhibitionism was the life blood of show business.

Approaching his seat, he noticed a woman had occupied the other half, automatically noted also that she wasn't hard to look at.

"Pardon me," he said. She stood up to let him to the window seat, where he'd dropped his suitcase. She was possibly twenty. He asked, "Care to sit by the window?"

Her response was in a pleasant voice. But it wasn't what he expected her to say.

"Did you know you're being followed?" she asked.

Alarmed, he examined her. Blue eyes, nice lips, a nose that wasn't as straight as it could be, but nice anyway.

"By male or female?" he asked.

"Female," she said. "And I don't mean myself."

"Oh," he said. He thought he sounded foolish, but not as foolish as he felt. Enroute to the station and all day in fact, he had taken the utmost precautions to learn if he were being trailed. Not to shake the trailers, if any, but to learn if he were being followed. And he suddenly remembered that he had been looking only for men shadows. A dozen women could have trailed him, he suspected.

"This must be my dumb day," he said.

"I followed you from your office," the girl said. "Didn't you see me?"

"That's what I mean," he said. "Dumb. No, I didn't. But you might have done such a good job that I wouldn't have noticed."

She shook her head. "I'm not an expert. I never did it before."

"What does this woman look like?"

"Tall. Dark hair. Cruise-tan frock with notched collar and box pleats in the skirt. Brown accessories."

He said, "I wouldn't know anything about notched collars and box pleats." He pondered. He did not recall any particular dark-haired tall woman. He said, "I didn't notice her."

She nodded.

"I'm Faye Linsky," she said. "However, I don't think you're supposed to know me. I'm a friend of the Fain family."

*　　*　　*

He studied her for some time, at least a minute. She *was* nice looking. And he decided she was frightened. She had very good control of herself, but she was frightened. Actually, he reflected, she might be as scared as the devil. He put no trust at all in his judgment of what a woman was feeling or thinking.

He played dumb, said, "Fain? Do I know a Fain?"

"So you didn't get the telegram." She sounded surprised.

"What telegram?"

"Mr. Fain said he sent you one last night."

"Oh." He pondered some more. "Who do you think I am?"

"I know who you are. You're Doc Savage. Mr. Fain has a snapshot of you."

This was true, Doc recalled. He had met John Fain about a year ago when he had visited the Electrar Corporation plant for the War Department to organize a department to produce an advanced type of radar. At the time Fain's laboratory assistant, a Miss Lys Smith, if he recalled her name rightly, had taken a snapshot of a group which included Doc. That must be the picture.

He asked, "Fain send you?"

"Yes."

"Why?"

"Mr. Fain has gone into seclusion. He wishes me to conduct you to him."

"Seclusion?" Doc said. That could have different meanings. "Hiding, you mean?"

Faye Linsky hesitated. Her face, for the first time, changed from composure to troubled concern. "Mr. Savage, something quite horrible has happened, I am afraid," she said. "You are going to Hammond City, aren't you?"

"There doesn't seem much point in denying it," he admitted. "Yes, I'm going to Hammond City."

"Good." She put a hand on his arm. "You do not need to trust me if you don't wish."

She let the hand remain on his arm. The fingernails were done in a shade he believed was called gingerbread. He asked, "What happened?"

"You're going to be disappointed in this," she said. "I was visiting the Fains last night. Mrs. Fain and I were on the terrace, playing gin rummy. It was a little after ten o'clock when the Fain's Great Dane, Johnny, began barking. The dog barked strangely, so strangely that both Mrs. Fain and I noticed the difference. The dog was at the laboratory, which is about a hundred and fifty feet from the house. We heard Mr. Fain calling for Miss Smith—"

"Lys Smith, his laboratory assistant?" Doc asked.

"Yes. He called her two or three times. His voice wasn't natural. Then Mr. Fain came past the terrace, on his way to the garage. He stopped to ask if we had seen Lys Smith, and his voice really was strange. Mrs. Fain told him we hadn't seen Lys, and he went on. I went into the house to get some ginger ale for our drinks."

She paused, took the hand off his arm, made the hand into a tightly clenched fist. She looked as if what she was thinking was about to lift her out of the seat.

"Mrs. Fain screamed," she said. "It was—well—it was an utterly frightening way for a woman to scream. I ran to the terrace. Something had wounded Mrs. Fain in the leg. Suddenly she threw the glass bowl which had contained cracked ice, threw it at something under a bush."

"At what?" Doc asked.

"I don't know. She wouldn't say, except that she acted like it was a *thing*." She looked up at him from wide, scared eyes. "This sounds as if some child was telling a horror story, doesn't it?"

Doc thought: Or a pack of lies. But he said, "It sounds very unusual."

She gathered together gloves and purse, said, "I missed my lunch. What do you say we finish this in the diner. Or have you eaten?"

"Good idea," Doc agreed.

The diner was surprisingly uncrowded, and they were able to get a table for two. When the head-waiter had placed the menus and pencils and pads in front of them and gone away, Faye Linsky said, "To return to the story: Mr. Fain instructed me to stay with Mrs. Fain. He was very emphatic about this. I think he knew what had hurt his wife, what she had seen."

"Mrs. Fain didn't tell you what it was?"

"No. She seemed afraid to. I don't mean that anyone had threatened her, nothing like that. She seemed to fear that her sanity would be doubted."

"I see."

"Mr. Fain came back and told me he had sent you this telegram. He asked me to come to New York in the morning and bring you to him. Or rather, bring you to Mrs. Fain and Mr. McKim, and they would take you to Mr. Fain."

"Why that arrangement?" Doc asked.

"I'm not quite clear, but I think—" She fell silent. The waiter had come. She glanced at the menu, said, "I'll take the mackerel."

Doc was suspicious of the steak on the menu because it was called a steak *salmis*, and *salmis* in French meant hash, and he had never heard of a steak hash. He took the mackerel, too, and the consommé. The waiter departed.

"You think what?" Doc asked.

"I think Mr. Fain is worried about his nerves," Faye Linsky said.

"Nerves?"

"Two years ago Mr. Fain had a nervous breakdown. Didn't you know that?"

Doc said he didn't know very much about Mr. Fain. He hadn't known about any nervous trouble.

The girl said, "Well, Mr. Fain worries about his nerves. He watches his health very closely. For example, he had a gymnasium put in his home and takes exercises every day, and has a masseur come up three days a week for treatments."

"Sensible precautions," Doc said.

"I think Mr. Fain went into seclusion because of his nerves."

"Seclusion with his nerves?" Doc said. He contemplated the young woman. He added, "You're not saying what you mean, are you?"

She was uncomfortable.

"Not exactly," she confessed.

"You mean," Doc said, "that Fain's crazy."

"I mean that I don't think he knows," she explained. "I think he's not certain whether he is having hallucinations or not."

The waiter came with the mackerel, and Doc wished they had ordered the steak *salmis*, hamburger or no hamburger. The mackerel looked as if someone had prepared it for the purpose of half-soling a shoe. It didn't taste bad, though. It didn't have much of any taste.

Doc asked, "What about Mrs. Fain? She would know whether she saw something or not."

"She also seems to doubt her sanity."

"That's strange."

"I think they must have seen something quite terrible, both of them."

The waiter brought their coffee, although they hadn't ordered coffee. He went away.

Doc Savage asked, "What about Lys Smith?"

"The laboratory assistant?"

"Yes. Where did she turn up?"

The girl was looking intently at the back of the dining car.

"She hasn't turned up," she said.

"You mean she's disappeared?"

Still staring at the back of the car, Faye Linsky said, "Yes, no trace of her." Her eyes became wide. She asked, "Do you know a tall man in a brown suit? He's redheaded."

"Why?" Doc asked. He had taken hold of his coffee cup.

The girl suddenly put her hand palm down, over his cup of coffee.

"I think the man poisoned it," she said.

Doc Savage came to his feet, wheeled and looked. But he saw no tall red-headed brown-suited man.

"He left," Faye Linsky said. "Just a moment ago. I saw the waiter set the tray down on the serving table at the end of the coach, and that man got up from his table, stopped a moment at the tray, and went on."

Doc sat down again, picked up his coffee, sniffed of it. "Oh, oh."

"Poisoned?"

"Let's see yours," he said.

The girl's coffee had the same smoky odor.

"Nicotine," he explained. "They're not showing much versatility."

She was puzzled. "Nicotine? Could anyone put enough of that in to be fatal?"

"In concentrated form, it is one of the deadliest poisons," he said. "There's probably enough in here to kill a dozen."

Her lips seemed to get stiff. "In both cups?"

"Yes."

She thought that over. She looked at what remained of the mackerel in horror. But when she spoke, she surprised him with a question. "What did you mean, not much versatility?" she asked.

"Just a remark," he said.

He had meant that it was the same poison which the man who had said his name was François Chesler had used on himself—or had had used on him. There was still some doubt which.

Faye Linsky picked up her gloves and purse. Her fingers bit into the purse. "I couldn't eat another thing if I were starving," she said. "You—you don't think that the food was—was—"

"That they put poison in it? I doubt that. Here comes the waiter." Doc caught the waiter's eye and beckoned.

The waiter was a tall stovepipe-colored man with a nice face and a lot of grin. "Yes, suh," he said.

"How much did the tall red-headed fellow pay you to put our coffee down where he could get at it?" Doc asked.

The waiter was genuinely startled. "Boss, you got something wrong." He pondered. "I do remember puttin' the tray down for a minute, though."

Doc was quite sure the waiter was innocent.

He asked, "You notice a tall, red-headed man go to the tray?"

"No." The waiter thought some more, turned and examined the other diners. "Ah don't remember no such a man," he said. "Ah sure don't."

"You never saw him?"

"No."

Doc said, "All right. Thanks." He indicated the coffee. "Be careful where you pour this. There's enough poison in these two cups to kill twenty people."

The waiter's color changed from stovepipe-black to dust gray and he showed considerable eye-white. "Yassuh," he said. "You want me to call the conductor."

"We'll see him ourselves," Doc said. "And don't worry about it. It wasn't your fault."

The checks came to two dollars and fifty cents, an outrageous sum for what they'd had. Doc paid both, and they worked toward the rear of the train.

Faye Linsky said, "You seemed certain the waiter had nothing to do with it."

"He probably didn't."

"Maybe not."

Doc said, "We'll look this train over with a fine-tooth comb. You take the ladies' lounges, and I'll take the men's. One of us will stay in the corridors all the time so the fellow can't get past."

"Good."

But she didn't think there was anything good about it half an hour later, when they had worked their way the length of the train. They found no tall red-headed man in a brown suit. They didn't even find a red-headed man.

VII

Hammond City's Union Depot had been built of blond brick and shiny metal just before the war. It had a crisply new look and it was in a nice part of town. The station porter spoke to Faye Linsky, saying "You been away, Miss Linsky?" During the walk up the ramp to the station, others spoke to Miss Linsky and she responded with a voice and smile sufficiently convincing. She explained, "A small town like this, one gets to know so many."

"Lived here long?" Doc asked.

"Oh, several years." She waved at someone whom she called Irene.

Suddenly a man yelled, "There's the Linsky woman!" Doc saw that the fellow had a Speed Graphic camera and surmised that he was the newspaper photographer.

Doc wheeled away, intent on escaping. But Faye Linsky seized his arm, demanded, "What's wrong?" By that time, the photographer was on them, and Doc couldn't leave without causing excitement. He did say, "I want to get a newspaper," and went to the news rack about a dozen feet away.

The photographer's flashgun flicked light over the station.

"Oh!" Faye Linsky gasped. "What on earth do you want with my picture?"

"You don't mind, I hope?"

"No, but I—why do you want *my* picture?"

"On account of what happened last night, and today," the photographer explained. "Could you give us a statement, Miss Linsky?"

"Why should I?" The girl sounded puzzled. "I don't see why—"

The photographer, who seemed to be a reporter as well, was excited. He said, "We think this is going to be the story of the year. The way it's sweeping town is amazing. First, a guy named Blake is chased by something. And then two guys land at the airport, and go to talk to Blake, and they're kidnapped. And then a woman named Ginsmetz sees something in her front room."

"Something?" Faye Linsky stared at him. "What do you mean by that?"

The photographer laughed. "This Ginsmetz dame is a screwball. She says she saw a terrible little dwarf of a woman about two feet tall, and it tried to kill her. She ran into the street screaming her head off and having hysterics about it."

Suddenly both of Faye Linsky's hands went to her cheeks. She lost color. "That—that is insane," she said. But she didn't sound convincing. She sounded horrified. She wheeled, said, "Mr. Savage—"

The photographer nearly dropped his camera.

"Doc Savage!" he yelled. "My God! It was two of his assistants, Ham Brooks and Monk Mayfair, who got kidnapped!"

There was nothing for Doc to do but be photographed. He composed himself, blinked after the flash whitened everything briefly.

Excitedly, the reporter demanded, "Did Miss Linsky go to New York to get you, Mr. Savage?"

Doc asked, "What about this kidnapping?"

The reporter was full of information. Being a newspaper man accustomed to corroborating his facts, he had names and times and places exactly. The time Monk and Ham had arrived at the airport—they had signed the register, so their names were there—and who had been present at the filling station when they were kidnapped, together with the fact that they had been asking questions about the Fain mystery.

"Now," the reporter said, "you owe me some information. First, you are here to investigate the Fain mystery?"

"That seems rather obvious," Doc said.

"What is behind it?"

"I can't say."

"What do you think about this Ginsmetz dame and her terrible midget?"

"No comment."

"Is it possible for a human being to be only two feet high?"

"Nothing is impossible, but many things are ridiculous," Doc said.

The reporter-photographer had a notebook. "That's good." He scribbled. "What are your plans?"

Doc shook his head.

"You're not very free with information," the reporter said. He was displeased.

"Sorry."

"I've heard you are a tough guy to get information out of," the reporter said unpleasantly. "What's the idea?"

Doc took Miss Linsky's arm. "Let's go," he said.

"Here, you can't walk out on me!" the reporter said angrily.

Doc hurried the girl out of the station. There was a taxi in the street stand, and he entered. Doc was unpleasantly surprised when the reporter started to get in with them.

"What do you think you are doing?" Doc asked.

"I'm getting this story." The reporter was nasty. "You may be pretty hot stuff in the city, but around here we don't go for that."

"You're being unpleasant, aren't you?" Doc asked.

"My manners are my own business, brother."

Doc contemplated the man thoughtfully. He said, "So are an individual's photographs, in case you didn't know it." He reached quickly, slipped the two plateholders the man had exposed in the station out of the reporter-photographer's pockets, jerked out the slides.

"Damn you!" the man yelled. "You light-struck my negatives!"

Doc flipped the plate holders and slides out on the sidewalk. The man cursed him, scrambled out to get them.

"Get moving," Doc told the driver.

When he looked back, the man was shaking his fist after the departing cab.

Faye Linsky was nervous. "That was Carl Brunow of the *Tribune*," she said. "He throws a good deal of weight here in Hammond City."

Doc was not impressed. "He should throw his manners away and get some new ones."

*   *   *

The Fain home was a pleasant place in the late afternoon sunlight. The house was while and square, but with pleasant lines and nicely landscaped. Faye Linsky pointed out the laboratory, a small building, one-storied, white like the house, located about a hundred and fifty feet from the main dwelling. She also indicated the terrace where she and Mrs. Fain had been playing gin rummy the night before when John Fain came out of the laboratory and things began happening.

"Oh, there's Gard McKim," Faye Linsky said.

A man had been about to get in a car; now he came toward them. He walked heavily, with the tread of a bear, and in many ways he resembled a bear. His face was round and from a distance looked benign, but seen closer it was an intense falcon-like face. He was very flashily dressed.

Faye Linsky introduced him: "Mr. Savage, this is Gard McKim, general manager of the plant."

Gard McKim had a hard quick handclasp. He said, "Heard of you, Savage. Understand you were here about a year ago. Sorry I was in Washington at the time."

Doc said, "Have you any ideas about this thing?"

Gard McKim looked puzzled.

Faye Linsky said, "Mr. Savage received a telegram from John Fain asking for help."

"Oh," McKim's eyes widened. "I didn't know that. By George, old John does have a practical idea now and then." He looked at Doc Savage approvingly. "This is damned fine. It's okay. This thing needs your touch. I never saw a thing go with such wildfire."

"Go?"

"Over the town. Rumors. Wild stories." Gard McKim chuckled, added, "Reminds me of something that happened in a midwestern town." He pondered, scratched his head. "Name of the place escapes me. Anyway, the whole town got in an uproar over a phantom gas assailant."

Doc said, "You mean Mattoon, Illinois."

"Yes, that's the place. Got a lot of publicity. The whole town went crazy. I remember it now. There was a phantom who used a mysterious gas that put people to sleep without their knowing what had happened. They never did catch their phantom, either."

Doc shook his head. "There was no phantom, was the final conclusion. It was a case of mass hysteria."

Faye Linsky's eyebrows arched. "You mean to tell me a

whole town became upset over something that didn't exist?"

"They did," Doc said. "And it was rather terrible while it lasted, I understand."

Gard McKim adjusted his necktie. "You get a mob of people, you can't tell what they'll do." His necktie was a rayon and silk with all-over figuring. He added, "You'll want to meet Mrs. Fain."

"Yes, where is Grace?" Faye Linsky asked.

Mrs. John Fain was resting in a gloomy room which was made doubly somber by drawn shades and closed windows.

"Mr. Savage!" she exclaimed. "I'm so glad you got here." She indicated the room. "I was resting—resting my nerves."

The gloomy room, Doc Savage reflected, was a poor place for her to rest her nerves, if her nervousness was caused by fear. The somber place was an incubator for terror, in his opinion.

Gard McKim was registering astonishment. "Grace, you knew John had sent for Mr. Savage?" he asked.

"Oh, yes," Mrs. Fain told him.

"You didn't say anything to me."

"I know. But John said no one was to know but myself and Faye, here."

"I'll be damned!" Gard McKim wasn't injured. He was surprised.

Mrs. Fain said, "I'm sure John didn't intend for you to be kept in the dark, Gard. He just didn't think of telling you."

"Have you a telephone I could use?" Doc Savage asked.

"Yes, you can use the extension there." She pointed at an ivory handset.

Doc eyed the telephone. He recalled the phony voice which had answered his long-distance call from New York. He asked, "Are there many extensions in the house, Mrs. Fain?"

Mrs. Fain pondered. "There's—let me see, at least five. One in the laboratory, one in the gardener's cottage, and three, no four, here in the house."

"Who lives in the gardener's cottage?"

"Why, no one. Our gardener is in war work."

Doc picked up the telephone book under the instrument, thumbed through it and found the police station number. He called, identified himself, and was rather pleased that the chief of police—Tucker, the man said his name was—had never heard of him, except that he had learned that

Monk Mayfair and Ham Brooks worked for a man named Doc Savage in New York, Doc found out what he wished to know:

Monk and Ham had not been found.

"Let's take a look at the gardener's cottage," Doc said.

Mrs. Fain was surprised. "Don't you want to hear—"

"Later. After we look at the cottage."

The gardener's cottage was square and white like the main house, but much smaller, covered with vines, pleasantly shaded by a large American elm tree. Mrs. Fain had brought the keys, and while she was looking among them, she explained, "I suppose we really should rent this place to someone because of the housing shortage in town, but I can't bring myself to liking strangers around the place."

"We will not need the keys, probably," Doc said. "Just a minute."

He moved around the cottage, giving attention to each window, first examining, then trying the window to see if it was unlocked. The third window came open under his shove.

He indicated marks on the sill.

"Forced," he said. "And rather crudely, at that."

Mrs. Fain seemed alarmed. "Oh, my goodness! I'm going to see if anything was taken."

Seemingly nothing was missing, however. "I don't understand it," she said.

"Some bum," said Gard McKim.

"Why would a bum—"

"Hunting a place to sleep."

"Been any rain recently?" Doc asked.

"No. But—"

"Bums usually prefer to sleep outdoors during nice weather," Doc said thoughtfully. He had been scrutinizing the floor. "Notice the recent sweeping job in this room?"

They all noticed it now. Faye Linsky looked in some of the other rooms, said, "This is the only one that is swept. Isn't that strange? The floors in all the other rooms are dusty."

"Very strange," Gard McKim agreed.

"Unless the sweeping was done to get rid of footprints in the dust," Doc said. "The telephone happens to be in this room."

McKim looked astonished. "Eh?"

"I made a telephone call this morning," Doc explained.

"Man answered, said he was John Fain. It wasn't John Fain, because I happen to know Fain's voice. The faker tried to make me believe Fain hadn't sent a telegram which I had received."

Gard McKim blinked. "I guess I'd make a damned poor detective. You figure the guy waited here and took your call."

"It is possible."

Mrs. Fain was showing fright. "But the telephones in the house ring at the same time. How would this faker have been sure someone at the house wouldn't answer and—" She stopped. Her hands went to her cheeks. "Oh!" She was startled. "I see now! The telephone trouble!"

"What telephone trouble?" Doc asked.

"Why, our phone was out this morning. It wasn't ringing. The man came out and fixed it about an hour ago. I had forgotten."

Doc was satisfied. "That takes care of the telephone call," he said. "Now let's hear your story, Mrs. Fain."

Mrs. Fain's story covered about the same territory which Faye Linsky had covered with hers. She passed over the part about her scream on the terrace by merely saying she had shrieked. He was astonished.

"Why did you scream?" he asked.

The look she gave him was desperate. "I—do I have to tell that?"

"It might be important."

Gard McKim spoke firmly: "Grace, you must tell everything. Absolutely everything. Has what you saw any connection with this wild story that's sweeping town?"

Mrs. Fain nibbled at her lips. Her arms were down at her sides, her hands tightly clenched. An actress could not have done a better job of portraying frightened desperation.

"I was the first to see the horrible dwarf woman. She—the thing—attacked me. She had a chisel, a carpenter's chisel, and it was razor sharp when she struck me with it." She pressed her hands to her cheeks, squeezing. "Oh my God, it was awful!" She began to tremble.

Gard McKim jumped to her side, put his arm around her shoulders. "Get hold of yourself, Grace," he urged. "This is no time to throw a wing-ding."

Mrs. Fain moistened her lips.

"It was Lys Smith," she said.

Gard McKim jumped violently. "What the hell!"

"It was."

"Now wait a minute!" McKim didn't get it. "You said this was a dwarf. And now you say—"

"It was both."

"You mean the midget was Lys?"

"Yes. But not Lys like we knew her. This was a horrible shrunken thing, and it was insane, I know it was. A hideous, little, bloodthirsty horror!"

Mrs. Fain burst into tears.

Gard McKim had been the most incredulous, the most unbelieving, of the lot of them. But now, and this was surprising, he was the one who seemed to accept the goofy story as a fact.

"I'll be damned!" he said. His eyes, made round and porcinely predatory by nature, grew rounder from surprise. "I'll be damned!"

Doc Savage said nothing. He was watching them closely.

Faye Linsky moved back a step. She lifted a hand, but didn't finish whatever gesture she had intended to make. She said, "The story going over town—the man Blake, that Ginsmetz woman—they saw. . ." She did make a gesture now. It was of disbelief. "I don't believe it!" she exclaimed.

Gard McKim still had one arm around Mrs. Fain's shoulders. He used his free hand to give his jaw a vigorous rubbing.

"I wish to God we knew what happened in that laboratory last night," he said.

Doc Savage spoke quietly. He said, "Why couldn't we look in the laboratory. The setup of equipment might tell us what Fain was doing."

McKim shook his head.

"It wouldn't tell me anything." He was positive they wouldn't learn anything. "I'm a businessman, not a scientist. I don't know a positive electron from a negative one."

"I might be able to tell something," Doc said.

Mrs. Fain took hold of herself with quite an obvious effort. "We'll look," she said. "I feel we should look."

The laboratory was not locked. Doc shoved the door open, entered first. He saw that the place was excellently equipped, saw apparatus which he himself did not possess, but wished he did. But about a third of the laboratory was a ruin.

Gard McKim yelled. "Somebody's smashed the place to bits!" He pointed excitedly.

"Not quite to bits." Doc Savage eyed the damage thoughtfully. "But enough."

"So much is ruined that you couldn't tell what John Fain was working on?" McKim demanded.

"That's right."

Gard McKim said he would be damned, totally damned. He sounded as if a little more of this would start him screeching.

"No use wasting time here," Doc said. "Where is John Fain?"

Mrs. Fain wheeled suddenly, dashed out of the laboratory. Surprised, Doc ran after her, only to discover that she had stopped outside and was waiting. She looked ashamed. I couldn't stand it in there," she explained.

"Do you know where your husband is?"

She nodded. "The farm."

"Farm?"

"Well, it's really our place on the river. About ten miles out."

"Have you a car?"

"Yes."

Gard McKim asked, "Can all of us go along?"

Doc said he saw no reason why not.

VIII

Rural breezes, laden with the aroma of clover and wildflowers, stirred the tall hollyhocks that had overgrown what had once been a garden spot beside the farmhouse, making them bow gently in concert as if a day of mourning was in effect. This effect of sobriety was further carried out by the river, which now lay in deep shadow because the sun was behind a hill. It had a darksome appearance, as if the black ribbon from a funeral wreath had come untied and dropped there in the valley. The breeze, freshening now that the sun was going away with its stuporizing warmth, moved among the trees and around the clapboarded corners of the farmhouse, made sighing sounds that were remorseful. These sighings accentuated the stifled sobbing of the woman inside the farmhouse.

Mrs. John Fain did not cry loudly, but she cried with deep emotion and continuously, holding a dab of white handkerchief to her eyes.

Presently Doc Savage came in from outdoors and said, "He's gone. I think he has been gone three or four hours."

Mrs. Fain stopped her sobbing long enough to make an announcement. She said, "I know he's dead."

Faye Linsky said, "There's nothing to indicate any such thing, darling." Her sympathy did not sound quite genuine, probably because she was frightened.

Gard McKim rubbed his hands. "He's probably all right, Grace." His hands sounded like sandpaper.

Doc Savage did not join in the cheering-up.

He said: "He was gotten by two men."

"Yes, we could all see the signs," McKim said. He seemed to think it was unnecessary to discuss what had happened.

"Mrs. Fain," Doc said. "Stop that sobbing."

He had spoken without thinking, but his request got results that surprised him. Mrs. Fain ceased crying. "You must find my husband," she said.

"How was he dressed when you last saw him?" Doc asked.

She pondered. "A blue suit," she said. After more thought, she added a blue-striped shirt, blue-and red regimental tie, red handkerchief, black hat and black shoes to her husband's ensemble.

"And just what did he say?" Doc asked. "Before he left."

She fumbled in her purse. "Here, you can see for yourself."

Surprised, Doc wondered if she had taken the conversation down in shorthand or something. But it developed otherwise, because she handed him a slip a paper with typewriting on it which said:

Faye Linsky has gone to New York to meet a man named Doc Savage. She will bring him to Hammond City. When she comes, please fetch Savage to the farm. I will be there. Do not speak to anyone about this matter or what happened last night.

John

The signature was pencil-written.

"His signature?" Doc asked.

"Why, I think—" Mrs. Fain took the note, examined it. "Yes, I think so."

"Let me see," Gard McKim said. Later he added, "It's Fain's signature, all right."

"How was this delivered to you, Mrs. Fain?" Doc asked.

"By a taxi driver."

"Did that strike you as strange?"

"Why should it?" The woman seemed surprised.

"Then it wasn't unusual?"

"The note being delivered? No, John often did that." Her eyes swam with moisture, and she used the handkerchief again.

A shadow darkened the window.

Doc Savage sprang suddenly, wildly, knocking Mrs. Fain off balance, lifting her, carrying her to the other side of the room.

The suddenness of the move and its violence held everyone rigid for a moment, then Faye Linsky jumped also and screamed, not because she was scared, but because she thought something had happened and she should jump and scream. Gard McKim burst out laughing.

"Ho, ho!" McKim roared. "That was a hawk or something flew over. My god, you're jittery!"

Doc looked sheepish.

"Jittery is right," he said.

He went over and picked up Mrs. Fain's handkerchief, which she had dropped, and handed it to her. He then looked out through the door, eyed a circling hawk, said, "It was a hawk."

Mrs. Fain was pulling at her handkerchief, staring at it as she did so. "Can't we do something besides stand here and ask questions? Can't we find John?" She dabbed at her eyes with the handkerchief.

"Have you a suggestion?" Doc asked.

She shook her head.

Gard McKim stared at Doc. "Mean to tell me you're up a tree?" he demanded.

"Not necessarily."

"Then you've got a plan?"

"Not yet."

Gard McKim snorted. "I should think it's time you had a plan." He sounded disgusted.

Doc Savage rubbed his jaw thoughtfully, moved around the room, picked a kettle off the stove and looked in it. It was empty. He lifted a broom thoughtfully, eyed a pale scattering of white drops; spilled sugar he found when he tasted it. He kicked a slice of onion on the floor, noted potato peelings in the garbage pail and saw they were very old. He asked, "How long since you have used the place?"

Mrs. Fain pondered. "Weeks," she said.

Doc went outside again. He looked at the footprints.

The footprints indicated as plainly as signs could indicate that two men had dragged another man from the house. They had hauled him through the dust, his heels raking the dust, and put him in a car. The car tires had knob tread on the rear wheels.

"We might as well go back to town," Doc said.

Mrs. Fain became offended by the expression on Gard McKim's face. McKim's expression said he did not think much of Doc Savage. It said: This guy is a bust as a detective. He hasn't done anything yet but jump from a hawk's shadow.

Mrs. Fain said, "Gard, Mr Savage will solve this thing; I know he will."

Gard McKim grinned at Doc Savage. "Being big and bronzed and handsome always gets them, doesn't it?" he said.

Doc thought: I hope I get a good excuse to swat this guy on the nose.

Mrs. Giggins, the Fain cook, was a woman of girth and emphasis, gifted with a fire engine red face and a rafter-shaking voice. And a Swedish accent worthy of a radio comedian. She met them at the door, displaying indignation.

"Aye got fine yob," she said. "But aye tank it bane run me nuts." She settled lobster-colored fists on her hips. "Aye von't answer telephone no more, so help me Yoseph," she added.

"What's the trouble, Mrs. Giggins?" Gard McKim asked.

"Aye got enough vithout crazy peoples call," said Mrs. Giggins.

McKim made his voice soothing. "You mustn't get upset, Mrs. Giggins. A tragedy has befallen the household, and we must all be patient. Naturally there are going to be a lot of telephone calls from the newspaper people, from friends, and of course from a few cranks. But you'll have to be patient."

Mrs. Giggins didn't think so. "I yoost got about enough,"

she said. She snorted loudly. "Drawin' pictures bane last straw."

Doc's curiosity was aroused. "Pictures?" he said. "What do you mean?"

"Wait sax seconds, aye show you." Mrs. Giggins vanished into the house, returned with a sheet of tablet paper which she presented for inspection. "Dummoxes," she said.

The picture bore a crude drawing of two objects, only one of which Doc could identify. The one he made out was a picture of some kind of an animal. Mrs. Giggins spoke continuously while he was looking at the drawings. She said the person who had called on the telephone, a man, had sounded perfectly sane when he asked her to make the drawing. The second drawing was that of a line about two inches long with a crook on the end. What convinced her the caller was nuts, explained Mrs. Giggins, was his asking her to show the drawing to any and every man who visited the Fain house.

Gard McKim said, "That's crazy. That *is* crazy, isn't it."

"What kind of an animal is this supposed to be?" Doc asked.

"A vild dog."

"Wild dog?"

"Yas."

Gard McKim, looking over Doc's shoulder, demanded. "What's that line with a hook on the end?"

Mrs. Giggins didn't know. The man had told her how to draw the line, and that was all. "Aye tank he got nuts in head," she said.

"It seems silly," Doc said.

Mrs. Fain was puzzled. "But why should he want that shown to everyone who came here."

"Every man," Doc corrected.

"Probably a nut, as Mrs. Giggins said," McKim declared. "I think he bane got nuts in head too."

Mrs. Giggins took offense. "Aye yus don't speak English goot, but you don't need make fun," she said.

"I was just kidding," McKim said.

"Aye don't kid."

Gard McKim looked as if he was going say the hell with her then. But he didn't. He shrugged.

Doc Savage made an announcement.

"I am going to town," he said.

"I'll go with—"

Doc shook his head at Gard McKim.

"Alone," Doc said.

IX

Hammond City was a courthouse square town. The main business houses were on the square and the streets within three or four blocks of the square. On the north side were the theaters, the west side had the ladies' ready to wear and most of the drugstores.

It was now dark enough that the electric signs, bulb and neon, made a nice display, and early enough that the theater crowds were milling on the north side. The taxicab in which Doc Savage was riding made two trips north and south along different streets, after which Doc directed it to follow the east and west streets. Puzzled, the driver said, "Whatcha huntin'? One of the wee people?"

"Eh?" Doc was surprised.

"You know, one of them terrible little people they been seeing around town."

"Have more of them been seen?" Doc asked.

"So I hear."

"Do you believe such stuff?"

"I dunno," the driver said. "It's kind of weird. You take that guy Blake, I've known him for years. He used to drive a hack, too. Told me a while back he wasn't making no dough in the filling station racket and was going back to hacking. If he said it, well I don't know."

"You do believe it, then?"

"I said I dunno." But the driver did believe it, his tone proved.

"Just keep driving in the business section," Doc said. "I'm trying to solve a puzzle."

He resumed watching the signs on the streets, the names on the business firms. Presently he grinned at a sign that said JAECKEL DRUGSTORE.

"Jackal," he said. "A wild dog."

"Huh?" asked the driver.

"Talking to myself," Doc said. He was pleased with himself. "All right, I leave you here. What's the meter?"

"Two dollars ten."

The Jaeckel Drugstore was elaborate, probably the largest drugstore in town. Doc Savage glanced approvingly at the banks of fluorescent tubing overhead, at the neat displays. He walked past the long, pale tan fountain with the girl soda jerks in pale tan uniforms and slid into a blond wood booth in the back.

He said, "The straight mark with a hook on the end was easy enough because you always carry a cane. So I surmised it was you. But that wild dog business almost threw me."

Ham Brooks said, "You figured it out, anyway."

Doc examined him. "What parted your hair like that?"

"A bullet." Ham touched the arrangement of gauze and adhesive tape which angled across the top of his head from left front to right back. "Let's get going. I'll tell you about it."

He picked up his black cane.

Ham, it developed, was driving a small, black coupe with white sidewall tires and soiled upholstery that reeked of spilled whiskey and stale cigarette smoke. Doc commented that the car smelled like a honky-tonk. "Where did you get it?" he demanded.

"Found it in the brush near the quarry pit," Ham explained. "I think it belonged to one of the three fellows who tried to kill us."

"Maybe you had better tell me the whole story," Doc suggested.

Ham had dramatic inclinations, this being one of the things which had made him a great courtroom lawyer. He told the story of the flight he and Monk had made to Hammond City, how at the airport they had heard about Blake having been chased by something mysterious, and that a strange kind of story was sweeping the town. Rising in dramatic scale, he told how he and Monk had visited the filling station and had been kidnapped. By the time he got to the abandoned quarry, and Monk and himself about to be killed, he had Doc on edge. "And so the man who had driven their car shot Monk." Ham laughed heartily. "It was the funniest thing I ever saw," he added.

"It sounds very humorous," Doc agreed. He was shocked.

"Oh, this guy forgot Monk was wearing a bulletproof vest," Ham said. "That was the funny part. They had searched us a little before that, and found the vests, but this guy was so

excited he forgot about the vests. You should have heard
Monk yell. The bullet hit him in the bay window and made
him as mad as a hornet."

"What happened?"

"We cleaned house," Ham said. "Or rather Monk did.
As mad as he was, he could have licked the German army."

"You catch them?"

"Two got away. We've got one."

"Where?"

"Monk is holding the fellow in the woods near the
quarry. We're going to make him talk."

"Then Monk is okay?"

"Except for a sore belly."

Doc leaned back. He was relieved. Also he was amazed
by Monk and Ham, as he frequently was. They got into the
strangest scrapes, but managed to get out of them somehow
every time. This one was a little less zany than the ones they
usually got into, but the outcome was about the same. He
wished he had seen the fight that followed Monk getting
shot. It must have been worth watching.

Ham was driving with reckless abandon. He was pleased
with himself. He explained:

"We drew straws, and I got the short one, so I came to
town to hunt you up. Monk stayed with our prisoner. I
thought I might find you through the Fains, so I telephoned
out there. But I was afraid to let anybody know where I was,
so I used that drawing gag to tip you off where I could be
found."

"Suppose that I hadn't figured out the drawing?" Doc
said. "I might not have found you."

"Well, neither would the outfit that wants me and Monk
killed," Ham said.

"You two haven't got a monopoly on the killing attempts," Doc said. He described the trip from New York, and
the poison which he, or rather Faye Linsky, had found in his
coffee in the diner.

"Is this Linsky babe good looking?" Ham asked.

"Aren't you impressed by the fact that someone tried to
kill me?" Doc asked. He was disgusted.

"Sure. But what about the babe?"

"She'll pass inspection," Doc said.

Ham was suspicious. "She's not the mental type? I

notice you're inclined to look at their brains instead of their better points."

"She's moderately brainless," Doc said.

"Did you bring something to eat?" Monk demanded.

He was sitting crosslegged beside a tree to a branch of which the man named Charlie was hanging by his feet. Charlie's head was barely clear of the ground, his face was distorted and plum-colored, and he was gagged. He looked as if he had a rough time.

"Eat?" Ham said. "What do you want to eat for?"

"To keep alive," Monk said. "And don't try to be cute and ask me why, I'm starving."

"I forgot it," Ham said.

Monk was of the opinion that Ham had forgotten to bring food on purpose. He said so, and tacked on an opinion of Ham and his ancestors, all of whom were pork-eaters according to Monk. This form of insult always enraged Ham, because he had a mania against pork, one of his few peculiar traits.

Doc Savage asked, "Is this one of the fellows who tried to kill you?"

Monk nodded. "His name's Charlie."

"Charlie what?"

"He prefers not to tell us," Monk admitted.

Ham yelled. "You mean you've wasted all this time and you haven't got him to talk?"

"Maybe you'd like to try it," Monk retorted. "This guy is the original no-answer boy." He indicated Charlie. "I hung him upside down half an hour ago thinking it might make the words run out of him, but none have."

Doc removed Charlie's gag, said, "Listen fellow, don't you know you are going to have to talk to save your skin?"

Charlie thought deeply for his answer.

"No," he said

Gard McKim had changed to evening clothes, a tux and batwing tie, patent leather slippers. The black-and-whites of the outfit gave him a more predatory look than usual, made the eyes with which he was examining Charlie look dark and bright like a crow's

"There's something familiar about him," he said. "But I don't know him, I'm sure."

Doc asked, "Why the familiarity?"

"I've got a damned good memory for faces," Gard McKim said. "I think the guy must be a resident of Hammond City and I've seen him in the year and a half I've been here, but not to speak to or know his name."

Doc asked Charlie, "Is that right, Charlie?"

"No," Charlie said.

Monk Mayfair said, "He's a guy with a vocabulary of one word."

Ham said, "He had more words than that before we caught him."

Gard McKim consulted his wrist watch. "I have a Commerce Club meeting at nine," he said. Doc Savage was surprised to notice that McKim's wrist watch band was also black to harmonize with his monkey suit. McKim added, "What are you going to do with him?"

"Find out if Mrs. Fain or Miss Linsky knows him," Doc said.

"Oh."

Mrs. Fain appeared shortly. Doc was surprised to notice how much worse she looked than she had not much more than an hour ago. It made him realize that the woman was under much more of a strain then he had thought.

Faye Linsky didn't know Charlie. Monk and Ham looked at Miss Linsky, then looked at each other, and Monk said, "I think one of us should stay right here and guard Miss Linsky and Mrs. Fain."

"Why?" demanded Gard McKim.

"They may be in danger."

"Nothing of the sort."

"We don't know," Monk said ominously. "This is a very mysterious affair, and we don't know what its ramifications are."

"I'll stay," Ham offered.

Monk gave him a look that said: I thought of it first, you overdressed shyster, so don't try to horn in on my ideas. The look also said: I'll probably knock your block off if you insist.

Doc Savage had been thinking. "Maybe we had better have Mrs. Giggins, the cook, and Annie Rice, the maid, look at Charlie."

Gard McKim said angrily, "You're missing the main issue, aren't you?"

"Which is?" Doc asked.

"Finding John Fain."

Doc said, "Let's see what Mrs. Giggins and Annie Rice say about Charlie."

Mrs. Giggins was no help. "Aye don't know dot vun," she said.

But Annie Rice squealed at Charlie. "Charlie!" she cried "Whatcha doin' here, Charlie?"

Charlie was disturbed.

They didn't have as much as they thought they had. It seemed that Annie Rice usually made the local bars on her night off, and that she had run into Charlie a time or two and he'd bought her some drinks and taken her for a drive and they'd done some smooching. That was about all; she didn't know Charlie's other name, or where he lived or what he did. But she did know the bars where she'd been with Charlie, and remembered that they'd met men who seemed to know him.

During most of this, Charlie thought of things which he could call Annie Rice, a slut being about the mildest.

Gard McKim became angry at this profanity. He said, "I'll take you in the library, you blackguard, and kick your teeth in!"

"Just take him in the library," Doc said, "and keep him there."

McKim flung Charlie into the library, which was the adjoining room. "I'll keep him here," he said. "I'll leave the door open."

Monk said he would stand in the door, and would personally hold Charlie's head up like a teed golf ball so McKim could knock it off if the man didn't stop cussing.

Annie Rice stopped to give her opinion of Charlie, which about made them even, Doc thought. She knew a couple of words that surprised him, and he looked to see if the ladies were blushing. The Linsky girl was, but Mrs. Fain wasn't.

"He's just a fella around town," Annie Rice finished.

"Do you know any of his associates by name?" asked Doc.

"Nah, I don't remember."

"Thank you very much," Doc said. He was anxious to get the maid back to her job before she did some more swearing.

Ham Brooks said, "Now we're getting someplace. We'll take this Charlie around the joints and somebody's sure to know who he pals with. We corner some of the pals and we've opened up a line of investigation that'll lead to somebody."

There was a yell in the library. Gard McKim yelled, "Here! Stop that!" A blow sounded. "Ouch!" McKim howled. There was a falling noise. Rattle of feet. Glass breaking. Wood snapping. Glass falling jangling to a floor, and more hammering of feet.

Monk shouted, "Hey!" He whirled, dashed into the library.

Doc ran to the library door, through it, saw Monk going through the large French windows, saw Gard McKim getting up off the floor. McKim's nose was bleeding. He was angry.

There was a shotgun among several other arms in a gun cabinet beside the fireplace. McKim ran to that, yanked the cabinet open, got out a shotgun, scooped up shells from a box. He was remarkably fast about this, and had the gun loaded by the time he and Doc gained the terrace outside.

Charlie was taking long running steps across the lawn with Monk in pursuit. Monk was gaining.

McKim threw up the shotgun, aimed.

Doc knocked the gun down.

Gard McKim said, "I can blow the hell out of that Charlie!" He sounded bloodthirsty.

Doc said, "We want him in shape to question him." He twisted, got the gun. "Come on. He won't get away."

Charlie and Monk vanished into the shrubbery.

Doc took up the chase. McKim followed, making some specific remarks about what he thought of not being allowed to shoot Charlie. "The blighter hit me in the nose!" McKim complained.

Doc ran with all the speed possible, left McKim and his complaints behind. Sounds of smashing in the brush guided Doc; then this sound ceased. Puzzled, Doc called, "Monk!"

"Here."

"Where is he?"

"Right here."

Doc presently found Monk standing over Charlie, who was on the ground, his face congested, his mouth gaping, his hands clutching spasmodically.

"He don't feel so good," Monk said. "He just fell over."

Doc went to a knee. His examination was quick, and after he had caught the odor on Charlie's breath, he gave his opinion.

"Nicotine poisoning," he said.
Presently Charlie was dead.

X

Patrick Hennessy McGuire, Police Chief of Hammond City, was a tall sunburned Ulsterman with a stubby black pipe fixed in his teeth as if it had grown there, a pleasant voice, and a reasonable manner. He sat behind a golden oak desk marked with cigarette burns in his office at police headquarters, and carefully built a log cabin out of the kitchen matches in the ash tray on his desk while he listened to Dan Edgar, the coroner, tell what had killed Charlie. The coroner finished, "It was nicotine poisoning, as Mr. Savage said."

Chief of Police McGuire asked a reasonable question.

"Who the hell gave him the poison?" he asked.

"Maybe he took it himself."

"Why?"

"He was in a mess."

McGuire admitted, "Sure, and he was at that." He turned to Monk Mayfair and asked, "Didn't you search this Charlie?"

"I searched him," Monk said.

"You sure he didn't have this poison hid on him?"

"I didn't think he had," Monk said. "But only the Lord is infallible, and I haven't got any wings, so he might have had."

McGuire fiddled with his log cabin of matches. He was trying to make the roof. He made a bobble, and one wall fell down. He swore. "Well, it's damned funny," he said.

Doc Savage said. "A lot of strange things have happened, but one definite thread runs through them all."

"You mean somebody doesn't want you here in Hammond City?" McGuire asked.

Doc nodded. "Yes. First, the attempt to get us on a wild goose chase on a boat going to France. Then the attempt to kidnap and murder Monk and Ham. The try at poisoning me on the train. Then..."

"That thing on the train," interrupted McGuire. "That's screwy. Where did the tall, red-headed man go?"

"I didn't see him."

"This Miss Faye Linsky says she saw him."

"Yes, but I didn't, and we didn't find him on the train when we looked."

"Was the train going too fast for him to jump off?"

"If he jumped off, it didn't do him any good," Doc said. "The train was going about sixty miles an hour the whole time."

"He must've crawled on top of the coaches, or something."

"Something, all right."

McGuire looked at Doc. "I called the New York police about you," he said. "They say you're okay, and I won't lose anything by cooperating with you. So that's what I want to do."

"Thank you, Chief."

"You got any ideas?"

"Two or three," Doc said.

"Let's hear them."

Doc Savage said there were some people he thought they ought to investigate. One was the man called Alvy, the taxi driver who had picked up Monk and Ham at the airport on their arrival. "While we're at it, we might give the other men who were at the airport when Monk arrived a checking," Doc added. "The idea is that somebody tipped off the three men, Charlie and the other pair, when Monk and Ham arrived."

"That's a lead." Police Chief McGuire was pleased. He started rebuilding his cabin.

Another fellow they should investigate, Doc continued, was Blake, the man at the filling station. "The fellow made a telephone call while Monk and Ham were there," Doc explained. "He could have been calling the kidnappers. Monk and Ham seem to think there wasn't much time between the call Blake made and the appearance of the kidnappers, but they might have been in the near neighborhood."

"I already got a man on Blake," McGuire said. He placed two matches carefully. "Maybe it was him that did the tipping."

"Quite possible," Doc admitted. "The people behind this, knowing we would have to come to Hammond City to investigate the mystery of the little person, could have been reasonably certain we would question Blake about the first thing. So they could have had their ambush ready."

McGuire became enthusiastic. "Sure. They even could have had Blake lie about something getting after him and spread the story. That would have been bait to get you to the filling station where they could lay hands on you."

Doc was pleased also. He said, "Of course, it doesn't prove Blake is guilty. Blake could have been in earnest with his story, and the gang, hearing of it, could have had the ambush planted for us when we appeared, as they could have surmised we would."

Ham Brooks entered. He was wiping his forehead with an immaculate handkerchief. He said, "Well, I described Charlie's two pals until I got blue in the face. If they don't pick them up from that description, they can't be picked up."

"We're not infallible," said Chief McGuire modestly.

A uniformed officer entered. "Chief!" he said. "There's another woman seen it." He was excited.

"Seen what?" McGuire demanded.

"The wee person."

"The hell you say!" McGuire was amazed. "That's the third one already tonight." He turned back to the officer. "Who was it this time, Mike?"

"Old maid on Gale Street," Mike said. "We're going out there now."

McGuire looked at Doc Savage, Monk and Ham. "You want to go along and see what's what?"

They did.

The house was on Gale north of Fourteenth Avenue, a modest cottage among many flowers and vines. They could see a small crowd around the place when they were two blocks away, and Chief McGuire said, "It takes something crazy to get people excited."

Mike said, "I know this dame." He grinned. "Three times she's called us this year. Same thing every time. A guy under her bed."

"What was he doing there?" McGuire wanted to know.

"He wasn't. He was imaginary."

"The hell!" McGuire lit his pipe. "Old maid, eh? Must be a goony."

"Sure," Mike said. "Goony as they come."

The lady's name was Miss Tiller, and she could make a

great deal of noise. She had a shrill calliope-like voice and a
way of using six words to do the work of one. She didn't like
them immediately. "Well, you took your time getting here!"
she snapped.

"Lady," said Chief McGuire, "we got here quick, and
you know it."

Miss Tiller's opening accusation was the only short-
winded statement she made. It took them five minutes to
find out that she had gone out on her back porch to lock the
screen door and had seen a little fiend in the form of a woman
about eighteen inches high carrying a knife of about equal
length, and wearing an utterly fiendish expression. The general impression was that Miss Tiller had barely escaped back
into the house with her life.

"Only eighteen inches high." Chief McGuire was masking
a grin. "Surely you weren't afraid of such a little woman."

Miss Tiller said: "It wasn't any ordinary woman who
could move in an ordinary way because this thing could move
fast as a flash and jump higher than my head and wave that
awful little knife at my throat as if she were going to cut it if I
hadn't got away, back into the house and slammed the door
before she got at my throat and that made her mad so that
she jumped up and shot right out through the porch screen
tearing a hole right in the screen wire and the hole I can
show you."

The Chief wiped his forehead.

"Let's see this hole," he requested.

He was somewhat astonished when the aperture in the
porch screen was shown him, and further bemused when he
made a close inspection and ascertained, from the unrusted
condition of the places where the wire had broken, that the
break was recent.

Doc Savage pointed out: "Except for the broken ends,
the wire is rusty, and you can see where the rust, which was
knocked off the screen by the blow, fell on drops of dew
which had gathered on the railing. The rust specks are
floating on top of the dew drops, indicating the break was
made tonight."

"You trying to scare me?" McGuire demanded.

Doc said, "We both know there aren't people eighteen
inches high. Anyway, the other reports were of a wild girl two
feet high."

McGuire grinned. "The other one must have been a giantess."

But he was displeased with the situation.

Doc Savage said, "We had better look around some more."

They found there was a cement sidewalk under the hole in the screen, a walk about three feet wide which ran around the house, and on which dew had gathered. But it was impossible to learn anything from the tracks because there were too many. The neighbors had trampled all over the place. The excited shrieking of Miss Tiller had created plenty of commotion.

Doc listened to some of the talk. A fat woman was saying to a small man: "Dan, don't you dare go to work and leave me alone in that house. I won't stay there. I won't for a minute. I'll go home to Mama."

Dan was her husband, and he evidently thought that he would enjoy it if she went home to Mama. But he didn't say that. He spit on the sidewalk and said, "You women are nuts."

"I don't care," his wife said. "You're going to stay right with me. We're going to lock all the doors and windows, keep the dog in the house and load the shotgun."

"What about my job in the plant?" Dan demanded.

His wife spoke further, wishing to know which he valued more, his job or her.

Chief McGuire was disturbed.

"That's going on all over town," he said. "And that's bad."

Doc Savage observed a photographer taking photoflash pictures of the scene. He saw that it was Carl Brunow of the *Tribune*, the fellow with whom he'd had some trouble at the railway station.

"If the newspapers play up the goofy angle of this," Doc Savage told McGuire, "it isn't going to help the situation."

"That's right."

"Why don't you suggest to Brunow that they play it down?"

"That's an idea." Chief McGuire went over and talked to Carl Brunow. Presently their voices rose in an argument, and the reporter-photographer said, "You can go straight to hell! The press prints what it wants to in this town."

"He doesn't want to cooperate," McGuire reported when he returned.

"Who does that fellow think he is?" Doc asked.

"His old man owns the paper."

"Oh."

"He's a stinker from far up the creek."

When they were back at the police station, Monk Mayfair and Ham Brooks suggested that, if Doc didn't have anything else for them to do, they'd like to hang around the station and engage in wee people hunting with the cops.

"The Associated Press has got a man down here already," Monk reported.

Doc Savage frowned. "The newspapers are getting ready to make a Roman holiday out of the thing, apparently."

"You can't blame them much. Something as crazy as this doesn't happen every day."

Doc admitted this was true. "But it's going to affect absenteeism at the Electrar Corporation plant, and they're doing essential war work. This thing, if it really gets going, could shut the plant down."

Ham Brooks started. "Do you suppose that's the purpose behind it?"

Monk asked, "Who would do that?"

"Oh, Nazis or Japs."

Monk was skeptical. "It looks to me like burning down the house to get rid of one bedbug."

"Well, there's something behind it."

Doc Savage said, "Chasing around phantom hunting may entertain you fellows, but we really should be doing something constructive."

"For example?" Ham was curious.

"Well, let's go over the Fain ménage," Doc suggested. "For one thing, Monk, you investigate Mrs. Fain's past. Ham, you take Gard McKim. Don't be conspicuous about it, but don't miss anything for say, the last five years."

"I'd rather take Miss Linsky," Monk said.

Ham was discouraged also. "Gard McKim, eh? That'll mean a lot of work by telephone. I understand he hasn't been here over a year and a half."

Monk eyed Doc. "What are you going to do, Doc?"

"Take Miss Linsky," Doc said. "What do you suppose?"

XI

Mrs. John Fain was darkly dressed and her face was pale, but composed, set in the expression of a martyred saint made of plaster. She spoke in a voice surprisingly gone, milked of feeling.

She said "Miss Linsky? She's in the hospital."

"She is!" Doc was astonished. "What happened?"

"She says she was afraid she was going to collapse."

"Who took her?"

"She went herself."

Mrs. Fain looked startled. She put her fingertips against her cheek. "Why, it's—I've forgotten. Isn't that silly of me. I must be upset myself."

Mrs. Giggins had overheard. She said, "Aye took telephone call. She bane in Central."

Mrs. Fain was relieved. "That's right."

Mrs. Giggins said, "Aye wish cop was watch the telephone. All kinds noots bane call oop."

Doc inquired what kind of nuts were calling up, and it developed that they were Hammond City citizens who were disturbed about the excitement and were blaming the Fains. They wanted to *know* whether John Fain had accidentally released some kind of a horror on the town.

"I'm worried," said Mrs. Fain. "Gard McKim had to go back to the plant, and he'll have to get some sleep sometime tonight. That's going to leave me alone here. I'm afraid to be alone. Mr. Savage, you'll have to stay."

Doc said he had an idea. He said, "I'll call Chief McGuire and have him station a policeman here to take care of the nuts on the telephone and serve as bodyguard."

Mrs. Fain seemed about to object, but she didn't. "I suppose that would be all right," she said. "Yes, I'm sure it will. It'll leave you free to hunt my husband."

Doc telephoned McGuire.

"Sure," the police officer said. "It's a good notion. I'll have Bill Spencer up there in two shakes."

Two shakes proved to be about fifteen minutes. Bill Spencer was a fortyish policeman with cheeks the color of

Jonathan apples. He was no hick cop, his manners indicated. Doc was astonished to see that he had brought a recording machine, which he proceeded to attach to the telephone. He explained, "There might be some significance to one of these nut calls, and McGuire thought we might as well record them."

Central Hospital was located on the hill in the better north side residential district, a rambling two-storied brick building with a coating of Boston ivy.

After an extended argument, the receptionist called a doctor, who at first was obstinate. He said, "Miss Linsky is obviously suffering from strain, and she did the right thing in coming here. If more people would come to hospitals when..."

He stopped and pondered. He examined Doc Savage intently. "Savage," he said. "Did the receptionist say your name was Doc Savage?"

Doc admitted this.

The doctor flushed.

"Good Lord!" He was impressed. "I'm making a twenty-four carat ass out of myself, telling you what people should do about doctors and hospitals. You're the fellow who developed the new surgical method for paranoia, aren't you?" He conducted Doc to a room, explaining, "I examined Miss Linsky, and she shows signs of great nervous strain, although I'll confess I was surprised that she came to the hospital for treatment. Usually they wait until their physical symptoms drive them here, or until it's almost too late." He opened the door of a room, added, "Anything we can do, let me know."

"You give Miss Linsky nembutal?"

"Yes. Not a heavy dose, however. You can awaken her."

Doc entered the room, closing the door. Faye Linsky was breathing regularly and deeply, had her eyes closed, but Doc decided after he had watched her for a while that she was not asleep.

He said, "So you were afraid they'd kill you, too."

She kept her eyes closed.

"Cut it out," he said. "You're not asleep. It takes a thief to catch a thief and a doctor to fool a doctor."

She opened her eyes then. "You're talking strangely," she said.

"The truth sound strange?"

She didn't say anything.

He added, "I figured out why we didn't find the red-headed man on the train whom you said put poison in my coffee."

Fear made her eyes round and bright. She didn't speak.

"There wasn't any red-headed man," he said. "You put the stuff in my coffee yourself when you laid your hand over the cup to keep me from drinking it."

Her lips moved without sound, but he could see that she was asking, "Did you see me?"

He shook his head.

"Deduction," he said.

It was very dark outdoors, and the blackness gave the night breeze an animal breath quality which the warmth of the air enhanced. The milk-colored window curtains stirred restlessly, switched at the bottoms, and somewhere in the distance and the sky there was noise of a passing multi-motored airplane.

Faye Linsky began to sob softly, and for a while there was only the dry sounds of her sobs in the room.

Doc said, "What upset you? The murder?"

She covered her face with her hands, asked, "Was—was Charlie murdered?"

"Of course." Doc watched her. "You know he was."

"I didn't—" She hesitated, pressed her fingers tighter against her cheeks, said, "I didn't know that."

"But you thought so."

She didn't say anything.

Doc leaned forward. "Look, you're in this pretty deep, but possibly not too deep to keep out of the electric chair—or to keep your associates from killing you. They will kill you, you know."

He knew, from the flash of terror across her face, that she was afraid of being killed. He guessed the rest, added, "That's why you came to the hospital, to be safe. However, I doubt if that will guarantee security. Remember Charlie? Poisoned right under our noses."

This got no response.

He shrugged. "I have it fairly well worked out," he said. "We won't really need your help."

No answer.

He added, "Your job, or course, was to come to New York and meet me, get in my confidence. That trick on the train wasn't an attempt to poison me at all, but an attempt to establish yourself in my confidence. You had saved my life, so I would be grateful. As an extra touch, of course, you put some nicotine in your own coffee on the train."

She spoke. Again it was lip movements rather than words with sound. "Who told you?" she asked.

He shook his head.

"Nothing but the facts told me," he explained. "When my suspicions began to shape up, it was fairly evident that the only place you fitted was the part of spying on me and reporting what I learned and what I was going to do."

She was silent again.

"Your following me in New York," he added, "was rather fishy, too. And people trailing me as you described. I think I'd have noticed such a procession. There wasn't any, was there?"

"No."

He waited for a while. She was stewing, and it was doing her good. Finally he said, "How would you like to tell me where John Fain is."

"What good would that do?"

"It would wind things up, and you know it."

That scared her. It shocked her more than anything he had said previously. "What would happen to me?" she wanted to know.

"A minor accomplice." He shrugged. "You have a nice leg to show the jury. You might get off with a suspended sentence if you were of some help."

She thought about it for a long time. Five minutes at least.

She said. "I'm going to tell you just one thing. It's all I know, really."

"What?"

"Where John Fain is."

"Where?"

"At home," she said.

At the reception desk, Doc Savage used the telephone to call police headquarters. Chief McGuire was not there; he had gone home to get some sleep. Doc called McGuire's residence number, and his wife said she would call him.

"Something come up?" McGuire didn't sound sleepy.

"I wanted you to start your men doing something for me," Doc said. "And then you can go back to sleep."

"Shoot."

"I want to know all there is to be known about Faye Linsky's background."

"Linsky? Oh, that's the girl who is a friend of the Fain's. Just what do you want to know?"

"Her past," Doc said. "And I don't mean whether or not she has been in jail, because probably she hasn't. What I want to know is all we can find about her family, her relatives, her past associations, close friends at school and that sort of thing."

"She in this?"

"Up to her pretty ears."

McGuire chuckled. "She has got pretty ears at that." He spoke cautiously, as though his wife might be in the neighborhood. "I think I'll take that angle myself. I don't feel a damned bit sleepy. You know, this thing has got me upset. You've no idea how crazy this town is going. Everybody is beginning to see wee people."

"There is no justification for them seeing any."

"I know, but that isn't keeping them from seeing 'em."

Doc said, "I know that, with you on Miss Linsky's trail, we'll uncover something."

"Thanks."

"There's one other thing."

"There is!"

"Miss Linsky is in the Central hospital, and I think it would be a good idea to put a guard over her."

"What the hell's wrong with her?"

"A violent attack of conscience complicated by fear."

"Huh?"

"It doesn't make much sense yet," Doc said.

"Who's she afraid of?"

"The people who killed Charlie to shut him up. She's afraid she may know too much, too."

"I'll be damned," McGuire said. "I'll have a man right over there. If this keeps up, I'm going to run short of cops."

"It won't keep up much longer."

"Let's hope."

Doc Savage waited at the hospital until McGuire's officer arrived. He talked to the man long enough to decide that he was an alert fellow, and to impress on the cop that Miss Linsky's life might be in danger.

XII

Monk Mayfair said, "What've I got on Mrs. Fain? My God, you expect quick results, don't you?"

"What have you been doing, phantom chasing?" Doc asked.

Monk grinned. "Well, she came from Chicago. I dug that out of a member of her bridge club, and I got the Chicago police on the telephone, and sure enough, the lady's name was in the city directory of two years ago. From the directory, the cops were able to give me the names of some of her neighbors. Of course she was living there at the time under her maiden name of McKim and..."

"Wait a minute!" Doc was surprised.

Monk grinned.

"Yeh, it struck me, too."

"McKim, you say?"

"That was Mrs. John Fain's maiden name, yes."

"Any relation to Gard McKim?"

"That's what Ham is trying to find out."

"Oh." Doc pondered. "Did you ask Mrs. McKim's, or Mrs. Fain's Chicago neighbors anything about the lady?"

"Yep. They said she was okay. An average sort of a lively woman. Quite a lot of parties and that sort of thing, but nothing bad, particularly. She wasn't a working girl. She seemed to have a little money, and she didn't live on too flourishing a scale, although she did have a fairly snazzy medium-priced roadster, and she traveled in the better circles."

"What do you mean by better circles?"

"The circles where an unmarried gal her age would be likely to meet and fascinate a nice guy with quite a lot of money."

"Nothing against her, then?"

"No."

"Where is Ham?"

"In the room where the telephone switchboard is," Monk explained. He added maliciously, "They got a pretty telephone operator."

Doc found Ham. Ham looked guilty. He had been leaning over the board talking to the operator, and the operator was giggling.

292

"Working hard?" Doc asked.

With the bustling energy of a man trying to make it appear that he had been as busy as a beaver, Ham rushed into a report of his activities, making it as wordy as possible to give it more impressive substance.

He said: "Gard McKim came from Chicago, where he was in the airplane brokerage business. He bought and sold airplanes, and was what they call an airplane consultant, which I take to be more of a promoter than anything else."

The telephone operator, a honey blond, was looking at Doc Savage with interest. He was returning the inspection.

Ham continued: "Gard McKim's outfit folded up about two years ago, probably because of the war and what it did to the airplane business for civilians. Anyway, there was some money lost, but McKim straightened it out all right."

Doc asked, "Did you talk to anyone who knew him in private life?"

"Yes."

"What kind of a private life did he lead?"

"Okay, as far as I could learn. He's been married twice, but so have lots of other guys. His credit rating was okay, as far as I could learn."

"I see."

Ham said, "That's all I have dug up so far. Of course, I've only had a couple of hours to work." He sounded as if he, personally, thought he had done darned well. Doc thought he had too, so he said, "That's a lot of information for so short a time."

Doc Savage contemplated the windows absently. He wished they could get their hands on something definite. He wasn't entirely satisfied that his theories were correct.

They had missed a night's sleep, he saw. The window faced the east, and a flush of dawn was in the sky, suffusing a packed layer of stratocumulus clouds with the color of watermelon flesh.

Ham said, "Want me to keep at it?"

Doc consulted his watch.

"Yes," he said. "But I think it would save time if you would call Gard McKim and get his own story of his past, then check on it."

Ham grinned. "The guy's a big shot. He may not like the idea of being investigated."

"On the contrary, I imagine he will welcome it," Doc said.

"Yeah?" Ham was skeptical.

"Certainly. He won't want any suspicion attached to himself."

"Oh."

Doc buttoned his coat. "I'll see you later. I'm going out to the Fain home."

"Anything particular out there?"

Doc said, "You might call out there and check with me about once every hour."

Ham nodded.

A drop on the telephone girl's switchboard whirred. She inserted a plug, said, "City offices," and listened. "For you, Mr. Savage," she said.

It was the police officer Doc had left at the hospital to guard Miss Faye Linsky. The cop was as mad as he could be and still speak coherently.

"She got away," he said.

"Miss Linsky?"

"Yes."

"How?"

"Tied some sheets together and slipped out of her room."

"She left of her own accord, then?"

"Yes."

"In that case," Doc reassured the officer, "I don't think any harm has been done."

The cop thought differently. "Chief McGuire is going to eat a leg off me," he said gloomily.

Ham Brooks watched Doc Savage leave, and Ham was suspicious. "I think Doc's got this thing about cracked. I think he's maneuvering these crooks into stubbing their toes, and doing it so smoothly that nobody notices anything unnatural happening."

The phone girl said, "He's very handsome, isn't he?" Her voice was admiring.

Ham looked at the operator. He thought she was lovely. He decided this was the time for a good lie. He said "Doc's secretly married."

"Oh!" The girl was shocked and disappointed.

Ham thought he might as well toss in another one.

"That Monk Mayfair is married, too," he said.

"Oh."

Ham grinned. "How about that date we were talking about when we were interrupted, baby?"

The girl looked shocked. "Aren't you ashamed of yourself?" she demanded.

"Me?" Ham was surprised.

"I know all about your wife and thirteen poor children in a home for the feeble-minded," the girl said.

Ham turned somewhat purple. "You believe a yarn as goofy as that?"

"Why not?" She shrugged. "Anyway, my boy friend wouldn't like it if I went out with you."

Ham went hunting Monk Mayfair. "You got a nerve," Ham complained bitterly. "If you've got to lie about me, why does it always have to be that goofy yarn about me having a wife and thirteen children?"

"Half-witted children," Monk corrected. "I always put that in."

The two stared at each other bitterly. It was an argument of long standing, and they couldn't think of a fresh approach to it at the moment. Ham gave up and snorted.

"I got to go talk to Gard McKim about himself," he said. "You got time to go along?"

"I guess so," Monk said. "We've got to eat breakfast some time, too." They left the police station, Monk yawning and complaining that he wasn't the man he used to be apparently, because he certainly missed a night's sleep.

"Good morning, supersleuths," Gard McKim said brightly. "I'm sure glad you came here. I was just telephoning the police station, and they said you'd gone."

"We wanted to ask some questions," Monk said.

Gard McKim, neatly dressed but unshaven, looked excited. He said, "That'll have to wait."

"Eh?"

"I got a telephone call from John Fain," McKim said.

Monk and Ham were startled. Monk's mouth merely hung open, but Ham recovered and demanded, "What did he say?"

"I didn't talk to him directly," McKim said. "But I talked to his laboratory assistant, Lys Smith."

"The hell you did!" Monk was amazed. "The girl who is supposed to be the wee one that is scaring the hell out of everybody in town?"

"Exactly."

"How'd she sound?"

"Why, perfectly natural."

Ham became suspicious. "Are you sure it was Lys Smith?"

"I think so." Gard McKim pondered. "We'd better be careful, though. It might have been someone else."

"Well, it's an interesting development anyway," Monk declared. "What did she have to say?"

"John Fain wants to see us."

"You mean Doc Savage?"

"Yes."

Ham said, "Doc went out to the Fain home." He picked up the telephone, rubbed his nose until he recalled the Fain home telephone number, and put in the call. Bill Spencer, the cop who was stationed at the Fains, answered the telephone. He said Doc Savage hadn't put in an appearance. "You want him to call you if he does come?" Spencer demanded.

Monk pondered. "We'll call back," he said. "But tell Doc we've got a line on where John Fain is."

"The hell you have," said Spencer. "Sure, I'll tell him."

Gard McKim's car was a long convertible which looked as if it had just come out of the factory, although it was a pre-war model. Driving out of the parking lot, he said, "The car's not as good as it looks. Half the time I've got it in the garage and have to borrow one of the Fain's cars. John Fain is sure a nice guy about lending his car."

"Why shouldn't he be?" Monk wanted to know. "A man as rich as Fain is shouldn't bother about cars. He's worth a million or so, isn't he?"

"More than that," McKim assured them. "The plant is worth about four million, and John owns it, lock, stock and barrel."

Ham demanded, "Where's Fain now?"

"We go out in the country, place called Indian Woods, the girl said," McKim explained. "I guess he's got a cabin out there nobody knew about. Probably a hideout to go to when his nerves got the best of him and he had to have some real rest."

Monk was interested in John Fain's health. He asked, "What about this nervous breakdown Fain had some time ago?"

"Overwork."

"Was it bad?"

"It had people worried."

"Did he go dingy?" Monk wanted to know. "I mean, did

he blow his top, sort of, like people do sometimes when their nerves get to the ragged edge?"

Gard McKim looked uncomfortable. "I would prefer that you fellows didn't scatter it all over town, but Mr. Fain was very ill. It scared the devil out of him, and it scared all of us. Since then, he has had to be very careful. The doctors said that the least sort of worry might push him over the edge."

"Oh, John Fain was in danger of going crazy, then?"

"Well, that's what it amounted to."

Monk looked pleased with an idea which had occurred to him. "Maybe Fain went nuts, and the whole case is the result of his craziness."

McKim looked at them. He moistened his lips. "Boys, the same thing has occurred to me." He stared straight ahead at the winding country road. "Poor John. We're all very much his friends, and if this does prove to be the result of dementia, we'll carry on."

"Who will take charge in that case? Of the plant, I mean?"

"Oh, Mrs. Fain, I imagine," Gard McKim said. "To tell the truth, I hadn't given much thought to it."

Indian Woods was a stretch of thickly overgrown timberland, a damp and somber place that smelled of flowers and wet wood. They parked the car in a clearing where there were signs of picnicking in the past, and got out and looked around.

"John!" Gard McKim called.

His shout silenced the song birds who were noisy in the trees, but got no other result. Nor did three other yells.

"That's queer," McKim complained. "Let's look around."

They began wading through the undergrowth and the weeds, and discovered there had been an unusually heavy dew the night before. McKim complained, "A man needs boots."

"He needs a diving suit," Ham said.

Monk looked at the clouds in the sky. Monk was the old-fashioned type of weather man, and still clung to the conviction that there couldn't be any dew when the sky was cloudy. Clear nights, lots of dew; cloudy nights, no dew. But there was lots of dew this morning in spite of the cloudy sky. He complained about this contrariness of nature. "Something's screwy," he said.

The others thought he was referring to their inability to find John Fain.

"You're darned right something's funny," Gard McKim said. "I think somebody sucked us out here on a wild goose chase."

"But why would they do that?" Ham demanded.

They discussed this. They decided they didn't know. "But we'd better get back to town and find out," McKim said.

Monk was thinking about the deposit of dew in connection with their search. "There hasn't even been anybody around this clearing," he said. "The fact that the dew isn't disturbed on the leaves anywhere proves that. I've been noticing that." He added proudly, "I'm pretty good on woodcraft."

Ham snorted. "Come on, Hiawatha. Let's get back to town and find out what kind of suckers they've made of us."

McKim was disgusted.

"Maybe that wasn't Lys Smith on the telephone after all," he said.

"This is a funny time to think of that," Monk grumbled.

"How was I to know!" McKim snapped. "I hardly know the girl."

The road which they must follow out of the woods was narrow, rough, winding and rocky. They had covered a hundred yards bumping and jolting, when the wheels took on a different, but quite self-explanatory sound. Ham glowered at Monk, who was driving. "Your missing link!" he said. "You've got a flat tire."

Monk was enraged. "I suppose I punctured it myself!"

They got out to look at the tires. The one on the left rear wheel was flat.

"Dammit!" McKim said. "The jack is in the compartment, I hope. One of you get it and—"

He didn't finish when a voice advised him, "You won't need to fix anything, brother."

"Oh my God!" Ham gasped.

So many men had come out of the bushes around them that it looked as if the woods had turned into humanity. The men were all armed, and displaying their weapons prominently.

"I guess the phone call wasn't phony after all," Monk muttered.

He knew some of their hosts. He knew the two who had been with Charlie at the kidnapping. He would never forget their faces, he suspected. And he recognized François Chesler, the man who had appeared at Doc Savage's headquarters in

New York and tried to get Doc started on a wild goose chase aboard a boat bound for France. Ham was doing some recognizing himself. He pointed, said, "My, my, the fellows who rescued Chesler. The guy who was hiding behind the cigar counter in the lobby in New York."

"Old home week," Monk agreed.

The two who had been Charlie's friends were particularly ugly.

"Want to bet you don't get away from us this time?" one of them asked.

*The picture bore a crude drawing of two objects,
only one of which Doc could identify.*

Monk thought it would be a risky bet.

XIII

Doc Savage had finished his examination of the Fain laboratory, and having found nothing, was devoting his attention to the Fain home. From a distance. From the shrubbery

in the neighborhood, in fact. He had been doing that for an
hour, without discovering anything particularly interesting,
and now he had moved down to the gardener's cottage which
he had previously visited with Mrs. Fain and McKim in
trying to ascertain who had taken the long-distance call which
he had made from New York to Fain, the call which the
fake John Fain had answered. Now he was not interested in
research. He was interested in the telephone, which he wished
to use. He climbed through the window, which they had
found forced, and used the instrument. He found that
there was no ringer; in order to get a call back on the line,
or to the house, there was a push-button which probably
sounded a buzzer at the house. He didn't wish to use that,
because he didn't want it known that the call he was to
make came from the premises. He lifted the receiver, and
when the operator answered, said, "Will you ring back,
please."

He held the book down until the instrument rang, and
then listened again. Presently he heard the cop on watch, Bill
Spencer.

Doc changed his voice, making it sound as much as
possible like that of Chief McGuire.

He said, "This is McGuire, Spencer."

"Yes, Chief," McGuire said. "What have you got on your
mind?"

"Have you seen Doc Savage?"

"No, he ain't been out here."

"That's damned bad," McGuire said with Doc's voice.
"I'm afraid he's in trouble."

"What kinda trouble?" officer Spencer wished to know.

"I think he found out who is at the bottom of this case,
then made a misstep and they grabbed him."

Spencer was impressed. "The hell! Who's guilty?"

Doc swore disgustedly, as he imagined Chief McGuire
would have sworn. He added, "He didn't say."

"That's bad."

"You bet. I think they've either got Savage, or he's gone
to the place they're hiding out. In the latter case we'll hear
form him, if they don't discover he's around and put him out
of commission." Doc swore some more. "If you hear from
him, for God's sake let me know."

"Okay."

That terminated the telephone conversation.

Doc left the gardener's cottage hurriedly, left the grounds. He had a car, a rented machine, parked down the hill, in a side road. He had learned from previous examination of the neighborhood that cars leaving the Fain estate would have to take this road. He got in his machine, drove a quarter of a mile to the crossroads, took a right turn, drove another quarter of a mile, going slowly and always watching the back road, parked on top of a hill. He waited there, watching the lane to the Fain place.

Presently a figure appeared on the road, not coming down the lane from the Fain's, but appearing furtively from the brushland near the road. It was Mrs. John Fain.

Doc Savage started the motor of his car, got the machine in motion, and went on over the brow of the hill out of sight. He left the car there and ran back to take a cautious look over the top to see what Mrs. Fain was doing. She was plodding forward. In a few moments, when an automobile approached, she stopped and thumbed a ride.

The moment Doc saw she was going to be picked up, he wheeled and dashed for his car. He barely made it, and was inside the machine when the car passed him carrying Mrs. Fain.

She didn't ride far. To the nearest cluster of neighborhood stores, a grocery-, drug-, tobacco-, hardware-store setup on the four corners of an intersection. Mrs. Fain went into the drugstore.

Doc Savage parked when he noticed the hardware store had a side door and that he could watch the place Mrs. Fain had entered through the front window. What he really wanted was a telephone. "Of course," he was told.

He started breathing freely again when he discovered the instrument was located where he could watch the drugstore.

"Fain residence," said Spencer, the policeman on watch.

"Why did you let Mrs. Fain leave alone?" Doc asked.

"Oh, Mr. Savage!" said Spencer. "Say, Chief McGuire telephoned me a while ago and he wants you to..." Spencer was completely silent for a moment. "What did you say?"

"Mrs. Fain."

"What about her?

"Didn't you know she had left the house?"

"I'll be damned, no!" Spencer yelled. "What'll I do about it?"

Doc said, "There's not much you can do except feel embarrassed." He hung up, amused by Spencer's astonishment. He had made the telephone call to ascertain whether Spencer was uninjured. Apparently he was, and Mrs. Fain had merely slipped from the house after eavesdropping on the telephone call Doc had made.

He went out to his car.

He sat in the machine and scowled at the drugstore which Mrs. Fain had entered, wishing it would have been practical to call police headquarters and the telephone company and have any calls Mrs. Fain might make listened-in upon. But this was not practical. The sign on the place indicated there were telephone booths inside, which meant several instruments to watch. Too many.

Presently Mrs. Fain left the drug store, walking westward along a street that was not deserted.

The car that picked her up was a grass-green sedan.

North of town about fourteen miles on a blacktop road Doc Savage watched the green car turn into a farmyard. The farm did not look particularly prosperous, although the buildings were large and substantial. They needed painting. Hills shouldered up around the place, thickly forested. Doc drove on past, hat over his forehead, shoulders drawn up, hoping they weren't watching the road too closely.

He didn't drive on just a quarter of a mile or so and stop. He kept going for three miles, parked and waited five minutes, then drove back slowly, turning into a side road at least three quarters of a mile from the farm.

It was not the Fain farm where they had gone earlier.

Doc went toward the farm, moving through the woods, not trying at first to be particularly quiet or careful. A loud commotion, snorting and crashing of the brush, gave him a bad moment or two. But it was a cow. It went bolting off through the brush. He went ahead more cautiously.

Later he came to a hoglot fence, and beyond it was the barn. He eyed several sleeping pigs in the lot, decided to take a chance of not arousing them, and worked his way around the lot to the barn to a double door, the upper half of which was open. He decided not take a chance on opening the closed half of the door because the hinges looked rusty enough to squeak. He felt for the beam over the door, hooked his fingers over it, and swung over the door and inside. He was in a runway and hay crushed softly underfoot.

He saw Mrs. Fain a moment later. The man who had told Doc the French loot story in New York, François Chesler, was with her. They were not saying anything. They were just standing.

Finally Mrs. Fain said, "What's keeping him?"

"Everything is probably all right," Chesler said. "He went back to town to see how things were going, to get track of Savage if he could."

"Savage worries me." Mrs. Fain's fingers were working at her purse, digging at the fabric.

"He doesn't exactly ease the minds of any of us," Chesler said.

Nothing more was said for five minutes or so, then Mrs. Fain exclaimed, "There he is!"

Gard McKim had driven into the farmyard in a tan coupe. He drove straight to the barn, waited for Chesler to open the doors of the wagon shed section, then rolled his car inside.

"Shut the doors," McKim said. When Chesler had done that, McKim grinned at Mrs. Fain. It wasn't a very enthusiastic grin. "I didn't find Savage. Something screwy is going on. Somebody called Spencer, the cop at the house, and told him Savage had been seized, or at least had disappeared."

"What on earth!" Mrs. Fain was frightened.

A muffled female voice said angrily, "Let me out of here!"

Gard McKim went to the baggage compartment of his car, raised the lid, and let an angry young woman crawl out. She was stiff from her confinement and she stumbled a few paces, stamping the floor, knocking dust from her garments, straightening her skirt.

"Hello Lys," said Mrs. Fain.

Doc Savage examined the strange young lady. Lys Smith, he presumed. John Fain's laboratory assistant. She was a slender young woman with blue eyes and a baby face which wasn't kittenish or soft.

Lys Smith said, "When does this thing end? I'm getting tired of hiding out!"

Gard McKim looked at her unpleasantly. "You've got to stay out of sight quite a while yet."

"I thought you said it would only be a few days."

"That was before things got in a mess."

Mrs. Fain said, "Lys, I think you'll have to take a trip."

"Why?"

McKim answered her. He said, "Because you're supposed to be the terrible midget who's scaring the pants off the town."

Lys Smith pretended to think about this. "I wouldn't mind going to Yellowstone Park. I've always wanted to spend some time there." It obviously wasn't an idea she'd thought up on the spur of the moment.

"A damned good thought," McKim said.

Mrs. Fain thought so, too. "She should be out of the country. If John should happen to see her now, it would ruin the whole thing."

"It'd cure him of his jitters, all right," McKim admitted.

"Gard, what are we going to do next?" Mrs. Fain asked.

"The thing we've got to do," McKim told her, "is get John Fain back in town so he can see the uproar the town's in, and listen to those phantom stories that are going around. I think a little of that, and he will go satisfactorily nuts, and we can have him committed. Very sorrowfully, or course."

Mrs. Fain thought that was funny. She laughed and said, "With fitting sorrow, to be sure."

Lys demanded, "When do I get paid?"

"Right away."

"Good. But what about Doc Savage?"

Doc was an unpleasant topic. McKim scowled, said, "I've got to get hold of him like we did his friends, and get him out of the way."

"Going to kill him?"

"We'll have to, I guess."

"What about his two friends?"

"We'll have to knock them off at the same time," McKim said. He turned to Chesler. "By the way, how are they getting along?"

Chesler grinned. "Very unhappy."

"That's good."

Lys Smith was looking more composed. "Does anybody mind if I ask a question?" she demanded.

Nobody seemed to mind.

"What is an accomplice?" Lys Smith asked. "That's what I want to know. All this killing, will the law figure I'm guilty?"

"The law won't ever know about it."

"They know about Charlie." Lys Smith wasn't convinced. "What if they should find out the truth, Gard, that you gave Charlie that capsule of nicotine before you turned him loose."

Gard McKim stiffened. "Don't say anything about that!"

"I'm not, but—"

"Shut up!" McKim ordered.

"I—"

"Shut up!" Gard McKim was angry.

Chesler said dryly, "There's nothing to get worried about, Gard. Charlie isn't around to tell the cops you gave him the capsule and told him it was something that would make him sleep so the cops couldn't question him. Why worry?"

McKim glared at him.

Mrs. Fain was looking at Lys Smith.

"To answer your question, Lys," she said. "Yes. Yes, we're all accomplices. One hang, all hang. Remember that if you're tempted to talk."

Gard McKim raised his eyes. "Savage's two friends in the haymow?"

"That's right," said Chesler.

McKim put a hand in his pocket and brought out a small, shining revolver. He said, "I think I'll go up and look at them now." He moved toward a slanting stairway.

"Why not shoot them now?" Chesler asked.

"I may." McKim climbed two steps toward the mow. He added, "But I'm going to do some other shooting first." He turned, leveled his gun at Doc Savage and fired.

XIV

Doc Savage was moving down and to the side when the bullet reached him and he felt it strike his back. There was some shock, but he couldn't tell, couldn't tell at all, what the bullet had done to him. His next few moments were very bad, because he knew that spinal injuries would fool you. With some of them, you could feel fine, or at least no more than a little strange, right up to the moment you dropped dead.

He kept moving. There was nothing else to do. There were three pitchforks in a rack in the runway and he made for those. He could hear McKim clattering down the steps to get in a position to shoot over the runway sides at him.

How the man had seen him, he didn't know.

He got one of the pitchforks, listened for McKim's movements, then used the fork to dig up hay chaff and throw it several feet out and up. The stuff made a cloud of dust and hay particles in the air. Enough to mislead McKim in the dim light. McKim fired at it.

Doc came up. He had the fork gripped like spear, and he hurled it, wishing to God he had spent more time learning to throw such things. But he did fair enough. The fork tines impaled McKim's right shoulder and neck with eight inches of shining steel. Enough to make McKim lose interest in using his gun.

Doc got another fork, went lunging down the aisle, and tried to high-jump the mangers to get into the section where McKim lay, and where Chesler was trying to get something, undoubtedly a gun, out of his clothing. His jump didn't quite come off, for he hooked his toe and took a tooth-loosening fall on the floor beyond.

He got up from the fall feeling rather relieved. If McKim's bullet had really damaged his back, the fall should have finished him off. It hadn't. He was merely dizzy. He stuck his pitchfork into Chesler's right ·g.

Chesler screamed, began trying to pull the fork out of his leg. Doc set himself, yanked the fork free, and used the handle to whale Chesler over the head. The man was tough. Doc had to hit him twice more, then got Chesler down no farther than his knees.

Mrs. Fain was in the car.

"Get out," Doc said.

She surprised him by obeying instantly.

He added, "Lie down." He looked at Lys Smith, told her to lie down also. She complied.

Somebody in the hayloft shouted, "What the hell's going on down there?"

It was Monk.

Doc demanded, "Are you alone up there?"

Monk said he was alone, then changed it to say, "Ham and the Linsky girl are here."

"Come down, then."

"Can't. We're tied."

Doc used the pitchfork handle on McKim and Chesler. He knocked McKim senseless, but he couldn't do anything with Chesler. The man stayed on his knees, but he was dazed.

Doc collected what guns were lying loose, and flourished them at the two women. "Stay right there!" he warned.

He went up the steps. The mow was about half filled with clover hay, and at first he saw no sign of Monk and the others. "Where are you hiding?" he demanded. Monk assured him they weren't hiding, they were covered with hay. Doc ran toward the voice sound, stopped when a yell of pain came from underfoot. He had stepped on Ham Brooks.

He hauled Ham out and used his pocket knife, then when Ham's hands were free, gave the knife to Ham.

Doc went back and looked down the aperture where the steps came up. The women hadn't moved. He hunted for a crack which would give him a view of the house.

"Hurry up and get loose," he told Ham. "We have company coming."

Four men were coming from the house. They were running, and one of them had a rifle. Nearing the barn, they became cautious.

Doc wondered if there were more, if they might be covering the rear of the barn. He looked suspiciously, and discovered how Gard McKim had happened to notice him doing his eavesdropping. A beam of morning sunlight, slanting in through a crack in the side of the barn, crossed the place where he had been crouching and passed on to make a plainly noticeable pattern on the floor where McKim could hardly have missed seeing it. Doc knew he must have crossed the sunbeam without noticing it. It was a dumb sort of an error, but something that could happen under strain.

Monk joined him, rubbing his wrists. Doc indicated a crack, whispered, "Who are they?"

Monk looked.

"The two guys who were with Charlie, the one who was in New York with Chesler, and another lug," Monk said.

Doc nodded. He had recognized the one who had been in New York. He thought the other man had been there, too. He thought the man had driven the car in which Chesler and his friend had escaped.

Doc raised his voice, made it shrill, and spoke, hoping the men outside wouldn't recognize him for an enemy. He said: "That's a damn fool mistake, shooting that gun by accident."

Monk grinned, said, "I'm sorry."

"What if John Fain heard it?"

One of the men outside called, "What's going on in there?"

"Ah, we had a little accident." Doc tried to sound disgusted.

The deceiving was only half successful. Two of the men approached the barn door, but the other two hung back and one of the latter said, "Wait a minute, Bill. I don't like—"

Bill entered, and Doc slammed the pitchfork handle down on his head. Monk slugged the other one. They fell almost together, and Monk went over them, stooping to get the rifle Bill was carrying, going on to aim the rifle and shoot one of the remaining pair.

Monk jacked the bolt to get a fresh cartridge in the chamber, but the extractor didn't work. The fired shell remained in the barrel. Monk used his head, pretended nothing had gone amiss, pointed the rifle at the other man, and said, "Let's see them hands, buddy!"

Ham came scrambling down the steps. Faye Linsky followed him more slowly.

Ham demanded, "Where's a gun?"

Monk looked at him in disgust.

"You got here a little late," he said.

When Doc Savage entered the farmhouse five minutes later, he did so cautiously, harboring doubts. Monk and Ham had said this was all of the gang, but he wasn't too sure.

"Mr. Fain," he called.

"In here," a voice said. The voice was low pitched and nerve-tension crawled in it like snakes.

"You alone?"

"Yes. What happened?"

John Fain was in bed. He was propped up on pillows, but the covers were thrown back as if he had started to get up, but had changed his mind.

"Oh!" He was astonished to see Doc Savage. "I wondered why you hadn't come, or answered my telegram."

Doc was looking at a medicine bottle on a stand beside the bed. He lifted the bottle, looked at the label, sniffed of the contents. "Who gave you this?"

"Why, it's what the doctor gave my wife to quiet my nerves."

Doc shook his head. "No doctor gave your wife this to soothe nerves. It's a prescription that would fray the nerves of an iron man."

Fain moistened his lips, pondered a while, and didn't like what he was thinking about. He said, "So there *is* something queer going on."

"Your wife and Gard McKim," Doc told him, "have been driving you into a nervous breakdown."

"My God!"

"What happened to set this off? What about the laboratory thing?"

"You mean—" Fain pondered again. "Oh my God! Was I that much a fool?"

"They probably rigged it cleverly."

Fain sat up stiffly. "Tell me one thing—was Lys Smith in with them?"

"Yes."

Fain nodded slowly. "That would explain it then. I was testing a new type of radar projector, and I wished to learn whether it would have an unpleasant effect on the human body. I knew it wouldn't be harmful, but I thought it might make burns at close range. I turned it on Miss Smith to test it, and an incredible thing happened. There was a burst of flame and some colored smoke, a lot of it, and afterward Miss Smith was gone. There was just her clothing there, and some tiny footprints on the window sill, and the way the dog acted . . ." He stopped his explanation to shudder violently.

Doc said, "Rigged."

"I—I guess so. Dammit, my nerves must have been shot at the time or I wouldn't have fallen for such a thing."

"How long have you been taking this nerve medicine?" Doc indicated the bottle.

"Several days."

"No wonder you believed it. You would have been in a shape to believe anything."

"They were trying to drive me crazy?"

"It amounts to that."

John Fain lay back. "They would have done it, too. When I heard about the horrible little dwarf being seen in town, and attacking people, I began to feel I couldn't stand it."

"They rigged that town stuff, too," Doc said.

"How?"

"Very simply. They have four or five men working for them, and the fellows merely got very busy spreading wild stories."

"Why?"

"To get the town to thinking a phantom—"

"I mean, why did my wife and McKim do such a thing?"

Doc asked, "Who would take over your factory once you were committed as insane? An insane man is considered legally dead as regards his property, you know."

"My wife," Fain said.

He looked sick.

Chief of Police McGuire came bustling into his office about noon and grinned at Doc Savage, Monk and Ham. He said, "I think his wife is going to pop. I think she's going to spill the whole works."

"That would help," Doc agreed. "But we won't need it, probably."

McGuire nodded. "I know. But I want to hear her explain why the hell she did it."

"For money. The plant. Probably four million dollars, which is plenty of motive."

"I know," McGuire said. "But she was his wife. Hell, she had a wife's dowry in everything he owned anyway, plenty of money and all kinds of social prestige. What the devil kept her from being satisfied?"

"We think we're on the track of that now," Doc told him. "Ham Brooks is working on it."

McGuire scratched his head. "How'd you get next to his wife?"

Doc considered. "Two or three things," he said. "First, she was doing a lot of crying about her husband's disappearance, and shedding genuine tears by holding a piece of onion in her handkerchief. I found that out, found the onion on the floor after I purposefully shoved her around when the shadow of a hawk went past the window and caused her to drop the handkerchief. Then the note she told me came from her husband was a little far-fetched, because she claimed a messenger had brought it, and looked a little strange when she said that. That started me putting things together. Mostly it was that corny onion in the handkerchief."

"That would be hard to explain away," McGuire admitted.

Doc said, "They watched Fain send the telegram, slugged the telegraph office man and got a copy of the message. They came to New York to get me off on a wild goose chase, fell down on that, then put Faye Linsky in my lap. The Linsky girl lost her nerve after the killing and they made her a prisoner when she got out of the hospital and came to me. In the meantime they were keeping John Fain away from me by keeping him at the farmhouse. As soon as they disposed of me and my men, they intended to take Fain to town and finish driving him crazy. There's a lot of other detail, of course, such things as McKim leading my two friends into ambush and . . ."

Monk came in. He was pleased. "Got it."

"Got what?"

"Ham did it."

Doc said, "Will you talk sense."

"Ham'll be here in a minute."

Ham Brooks did come in shortly. He said, "I was on the long-distance telephone to my law connections in Chicago, and they dug up the reason for this. I mean, the reason Mrs. Fain had to work it."

McGuire hit his desk a fist blow. "Now that's what I want to know.

"She isn't Mrs. Fain," Ham said.

"Eh?"

"Mrs. Fain isn't Mrs. Fain."

"The hell she isn't!"

"She's Mrs. McKim."

McGuire was stunned. He didn't say anything.

Ham told him, "It was like this: She was McKim's second wife, and she didn't get a divorce before she married Fain. Fain applied for a heavy insurance policy on her about a mouth ago, and the insurance people were going to investigate, and she was afraid they'd uncover her bigamy. They would have too. The policy was so big they were going to go over her past from A to Izzard. So she had to get Fain committed to an insane asylum, which would make her his legal heir, and she could shut off the insurance investigation. It would stop anyway, because the company wouldn't issue the policy after Fain's legal death by insanity. He was going to pay the premiums."

Doc said, "She probably thought the truth would come out some time anyway."

Monk Mayfair was impressed. He said, "Whooe-e-e-e! You can't trust these women, can you?"

Ham eyed him bitterly. "I hear they're going to release Faye Linsky this afternoon and that you've got a date with her for tonight."

Monk grinned. "Sure. They're releasing her in my custody."

"Aren't you afraid?"

"Why?"

"You can't trust women," Ham reminded.

Monk grinned. "They can't trust me either," he said.

TERROR TAKES 7

1

The man from the American Express arrived about three o'clock bearing a skinny package about six feet long and wrapped in tough pigskin-colored paper. Monk Mayfair, the chemist, accepted the shipment, after inquiring cautiously whether or not it was collect. He carried in into the library of Doc Savage's eighty-sixth floor headquarters in a midtown New York building and showed it to his friend Ham Brooks, the lawyer.

"Look," said Monk, "what somebody sent us."

"What are you trying to pull now?" asked Ham Brooks, who felt that it was well to regard with suspicion almost anything Monk did.

"Don't be so suspicious. Somebody sent us this thing."

"What is it?"

"I don't know."

"Why not look and find out."

"It's addressed to Doc."

"Well, stop bothering me about it," said Ham, who thought Monk was probably playing a practical joke on him. He added, "Take it in and give it to Doc."

Monk was dubious. "Doc still working? I mean on that limit of compressibility for the air research job?"

"What if he is?"

"Yeah, you want me to get chased out of there, don't you?" Monk said.

Ham grinned. "I think he's going to run us both off anyway if his temper keeps getting worse. What have you got to lose?"

"I'll take a chance," Monk decided.

He went into the laboratory carrying the package, explaining, "This thing came by express, Doc."

The laboratory, which occupied most of the eighty-sixth floor of the building, had been temporarily crammed with air-compressors, wind tunnels and compression chambers. The current research job, which Doc Savage was doing for an aircraft manufacturer, concerned the behavior of air when it went past the so-called compressibility limit. The research covered a field of hitherto unknown phenomena, for it had only lately been discovered that when an airplane starts

315

traveling faster than sound, mysterious and unorthodox things happen to it.

Doc Savage was aggravated about the whole thing. It had been dumped in his lap after everyone else was stumped, handed to him along with a lovely speech how he was probably the world's greatest research scientist, that since his abilities covered a number of fields in addition of aerodynamics, he was the man most apt to strike a solution. This he didn't mind; it had been a lovely speech.

What he did mind was a story he'd heard, going the rounds of aviation engineering circles, to the effect that Doc Savage had the thing in the bag. He didn't have it in the bag; it had him in the bag. He wasn't sure who had started the story, but he suspected the plane manufacturer was using his reputation to scare a competitor. He didn't like that. This was supposed to be for the Army; he wasn't getting a commercial fee.

His mood was acid. When Monk unwrapped the package and Doc saw what was inside, he said several things, using plain words, about not being bothered again.

Monk retreated in red-eared haste, carrying the thing that had been in the package.

"I was spoken unkindly to," he reported to Ham.

Ham chuckled. "I heard."

"I guess he thought somebody was ribbing him when he saw what was in the package."

"What was it?"

"I'd call it part of a Daniel Boone outfit," Monk decided. "A flintlock rifle and a pair of buckskin leggings. Here, take a look."

The rifle was dilapidated and useless-looking under a coating of rust. It was over six feet long. The buckskin leggings were in somewhat the same condition.

"Why would anybody send us that stuff?" Ham wished to know.

The name of the sender was on the pigskin-colored paper wrapper:

P. ARGUS
NEW YORK CITY

Monk said, "Let's get his name out of the telephone directory, call him up and ask what's the big idea."

They spent some time with the telephone directory.

"I'll be damned," Monk said.

"There's no P. Argus listed," Ham agreed.

They were looking at each other, puzzled, when the telephone rang.

"Answer it," Ham said.

"Answer it yourself. It's probably that blonde babe you fed that line about being a millionaire. That girl will get your shirt if you don't watch out."

"Yes?" Ham said into the telephone.

A well-put-together female voice said, "I wish to speak to Doc Savage."

"I'm afraid that Doc—"

"It's important, please."

Something in the young woman's voice jarried Ham. A quality of urgency that was not normal. "Just a moment," he said, and threw the switch which connected the laboratory instrument. "Call for you, Doc!" he yelled.

Monk eyed Ham suspiciously. "Man or woman?"

"Man," Ham said, merely for the satisfaction of telling Monk a lie.

In the laboratory, Doc Savage listened to the very good voice of the young woman. Young? That was a guess, but he thought it was probably correct. She said her name was Paula Argus.

For a moment, Doc didn't remember the package that had just come. Then he asked, "P. Argus?"

"Yes, I—but I don't think you know me." She sounded puzzled.

"The name was on a deerslayer's outfit that came by express a while ago," he said.

"Oh! You got the rifle and leggings?"

"Yes. Did you send them?"

"I did."

"Why?"

"I want to talk to you about them," P. Argus said. "I want you to come downstairs, walk north on Fifth Avenue, and enter the small bar on the right side of the street just off Fifth. I'll be waiting in the first booth on the south side. I have on a brown coat, a mink."

Doc remembered he was trying to find out why air went crazy when airplanes when through it faster than sound traveled, added the thought that the young lady was probably a crank, and concluded he wanted no part of it. He said, "That is a very explicit set of directions, but it happens that I am infernally busy just now. I'm sorry." Then, because the girl might be in genuine trouble, he added, "Why not come here if you want to talk?"

"I'm afraid," she said.

He frowned at the telephone, wishing he could tell something about a woman's voice. He didn't think she sounded frightened: on the other hand death might be at her throat and he would have the same opinion. Every man in the world, he frequently thought, knew more about women than he did. Not, he suspected, that any of them knew very much.

"You don't sound scared," he said.

"What do you expect me to do, scream and faint?" she demanded.

He suspected, now, that she might be frightened. At least she was angry; if she were some silly fan after an autograph, or wanting to tell her girl friends she'd had a date with Doc Savage, she wouldn't flash anger probably.

He said, "I'm sorry, but this experiment of mine is in a critical stage. I can not come." The experiment had passed through series of critical stages, none of the productive, he thought. He added, "However, I will send one of my friends to talk to you."

He was surprised when this satisfied her. She asked, "You mean one of the five men who are associated with you? Mr. Renwick, Mr. Roberts, Mr. Littlejohn, or Mr. Brooks?"

She knew who he was, he thought, knew his friends by name.

"You left one out—Mr. Mayfair," he said. "I'll send him."

"The wolf, eh?" she said. "Well, all right. I'll wait."

Entering the library, concealing his impulse to laugh to Monk, Doc Savage said, "Monk, that was P. Argus, who sent the rifle and leggings. You are to walk north on Fifth Avenue, enter a small bar on the right side of the street just off Fifth, go to the first booth on the south side and meet P. Argus, who will be wearing a brown coat."

"Me?" Monk was disgusted. "Listen, I've got some work to do. Ham is loafing. Why can't Ham talk to this crank."

Ham snorted. "You haven't got any work. You noticed it is raining." The Ham remembered that P. Argus had been a female, and a pleasant-sounding one, and he pretended to make a great concession. "However, you manage to shove off all the dirty work on me, so I suppose I'll have to go see the crank."

Monk eyed him suspiciously.

"Yeah? I think I'll go," he said. "You sound too eager."

Monk got his hat and raincoat and departed.

Doc told Ham, "You're losing your technique with Monk."

"I should have kept my mouth shut and let him bulldoze me into going. The minute he saw I didn't mind going, he smelled a mouse."

Doc nodded. "The mouse sounded very nice over the telephone, too."

"You're a big help," Ham said bitterly.

Outdoors it was raining fat oyster-colored drops, and Monk Mayfair turned up his raincoat collar and wished he'd let Ham do this.

Monk was not a tall man, but he was very wide, and his hair was bristling, resembling rusty wires. His face was homely to such a degree that its homeliness was an asset; any and all expressions on such a face were amusing.

There was one hitch in the directions to finding P. Argus, he discovered; they didn't say how many blocks he was to go north on Fifth before he found such a bar. It proved to be some distance.

The place was small, done in chrome and shades of sky blue and royal blue, and with the customary inadequate lighting. Monk shook the rain off his coat and looked around.

A wild goose chase, he thought, discovering a girl in the first booth. He took a closer look and added the thought that it was just too darned bad she wasn't P. Argus. Wow, wouldn't that be something!

She was a long young woman; no, on second thought she wasn't tall, but she was built so that she seemed so. A pocket edition, seal-brown hair, blue eyes, a diamond ring of eye-popping size, but not an engagement ring, and a brown mink coat... Brown mink... Brown! Glorious angels!

"Are you waiting for someone?" Monk asked her.

"For you, Mr. Mayfair," she said. "I'm Paula Argus, and I sent Mr. Savage that devil-spear thing. Won't you sit down?"

Monk said, "Will I sit down! Would I like to look at a

million dollars!" He slid in on the other side of the booth. "This is a surprise, and I'm not easily surprised."

She looked at him intently.

"Not readily surprised? That's good. Because I want to talk to you about a murder."

Monk batted his eyes a couple of times. "What was that?"

"I didn't intend it to sound as if I was shooting off firecrackers." She stood up. "Will you come with me? I'll talk while we're driving."

II

They rode north through the oyster-colored rain in a cream convertible roadster that must have been listed at about four thousand six hundred dollars F.O.B. Detroit before the war. Monk Mayfair was thinking about Ham Brooks, Ham Brooks the dirty liar who had told him that P. Argus was a man. A great pal, that Ham Brooks.

P. Argus drove. She said, "I have an uncle, Carlton Argus. I have noticed him being scared for two or three days. This morning, I heard a noise in the orchid culture room and went in to investigate—"

"Pardon me, where was the noise?" Monk asked.

"Uncle Carlton raises orchids as an avocation. I heard a noise, and found that Uncle Carlton had fainted."

Monk liked her handling of a private orchid culture room as if it were nothing special.

She added, "He fainted when he saw that old flintlock rifle and buckskin leggings, which had just come by express."

Monk jumped. "The same rifle and leggings?"

"Yes."

"Why'd they shock him into passing out?"

"I don't know."

"Who sent the stuff?"

"There was no return address on the wrapper. I looked."

Monk rubbed his jaw. "Sort of got a mystery on your hands, haven't you?"

"I don't think I've impressed you with Uncle Carlton's condition, his complete, abject error. It's a frightening thing to see. There is something strange about it, because he doesn't want to talk to anyone. It took a great deal of persuasion to get him to consent to talk to Mr. Savage."

She turned the car left into the more expensive section of Park Avenue.

"Mind telling me how you thought of calling on us?" Monk asked.

"You know Patricia Savage?"

"Doc's cousin? Sure. Do I know Pat? Every once in a while she takes a notion to help us out on a case, and gives us fits. She likes excitement a little too much."

"Patricia is an acquaintance of mine, and I've heard her talk about Doc Savage. That's why I happened to think of asking him to look into this thing. It sounds like the sort of thing Pat says always interests him."

"You live at your Uncle's home?" Monk asked.

P. Argus nodded. "My mother and my father—my father was Uncle Carlton's brother—are no longer living. For many years Uncle Carlton lived with our family, and then he made a lucky investment with some money he borrowed from father during the war and cleaned up. He insists that I live with him, that whatever he has is mine." She looked sidewise at Monk, added, "Which is rather fortunate for me. I haven't any money."

Okay, so you're not wealthy, Monk thought. So what? So it's a minor matter, like a pine tree not having pine cones. You're very ornamental without it.

"We'll do what we can," Monk assured her.

She smiled. The world stood still, covered by sunshine, as far as Monk was concerned.

"I wish Doc Savage could have had time to help personally," she said. "Not that I don't appreciate your efforts, Mr. Mayfair."

Monk said, "When I telephoned him about it, Doc was awfully sorry but he couldn't possibly get away."

This was an inspired lie. The telephone call which Monk had pretended to make had been another. What was he, a dope? Call Doc and have the handsome Doc and the syrup-tongued Ham Brooks around for competition? Ho, ho!

"I'm sure I can take care of everything," Monk said, pleased with his chinanery.

The copper was named Clancy. Clancy Weinberg, and he happened to know Monk personally, and also happened

not to like Monk; the other circumstance, how Clancy happened
to be standing in front of the Argus apartment house, remained
temporarily a mystery. Temporarily was to be about fifteen
minutes, which was too fatally long.

"Well, well, the answer to the chorus girls' nightmares,"
said Clancy unpleasantly, scowling at Monk.

"Hello, flatfoot," Monk said, also with no pleasure.

"Get outa that car, Romeo." Clancy put his hand under
his coat tail, where New York policemen keep their guns.
"Start something if you wanta," he added invitingly.

Monk was amazed.

"What's got into you?"

Clancy wasn't fooling. "Come one, come on, get outa
that heap! Too bad I gotta pick you up for something as petty
as car stealing. But it's your speed, I guess."

"Car stealing?"

"Alight and relax in these handcuffs, brother," Clancy
said. "I got a telephone tip you were stealing this car and
would turn up here."

Monk's amazement climbed. "Who telephoned you that
lie?"

"Search me."

"Ridiculous!" P. Argus exclaimed, entering the argument. "This is fantastic."

Clancy took out his handcuffs and shook them and said,
"It's a damned great pleasure, though."

P. Argus said, "But this is my car!"

Clancy eyed her suspiciously, and with approval. "You're
a lovely babe," he said. "But it'll take more than your good
looks to prove it's your car."

"Would my license and certificate help?" P. Argus asked
angrily. "And the apartment house doorman's word?"

Clancy looked at her documents; he listened to the
apartment house doorman. He wasn't pleased. He was puzzled. He was angry. He grasped Monk's necktie and said, "If
I find out you caused that phony telephone call. I'll feed you
your own teeth!"

"Leggo my tie!" Monk said.

Presently Clancy departed, putting his feet down hard
on the sidewalk.

Monk placed a hand on his forehead and found perspiration thereon. He said, "Whew-w-w-w-w!" feelingly.

P. Argus eyed him dubiously.

"Just what," she asked, "was that."

Monk used a handkerchief to blot his forehead. "It was a cop giving a citizen a bad scare." He gave the distant Clancy a somewhat frightened look. "That guy's after my peace of mind. We—uh—we had a little trouble, couple of days ago. A kind of a fuss in a night club, mostly words, although Clancy took a swing at me and missed. A nosey newspaper columnist saw it and next day his piece carried a wisecracking squib about it. Doc Savage gave me a lecture, and Clancy nearly got suspended—would have, too, except I told his superiors I started it. Which was a lie, incidentally; I only did half the starting. His girl friend did the other half by sitting on my lap."

"Serves you right," said P. Argus, "for fighting over a girl."

"That was about what Doc said, too," Monk admitted.

"However," said P. Argus, "I don't think he was just riding you. I think, from the way he sounded, that he had really received a telephone call.

Monk pondered this. The same idea had occurred to him, together with another one—that Ham Brooks had pulled a practical joke. He suspected Ham.

"The rat!" Monk said feelingly.

"He seemed like a nice young policeman," said P. Argus.

"I didn't mean the cop." Monk was wondering how Ham had found out about his trouble with Clancy. Probably the same way Doc had found it out: the paragraph the columnist had printed. Convinced Ham had cause him the embarrassment. Monk said, "I'll look into the thing later. Right now, let's talk to your uncle."

The apartment would have been the latest thing in ultra-modern living back in the late twenties, when there were stock-market-millionaries and a penthouse on Park Avenue was the ultimate. It was rather impressive now. The furnishings weren't modernistic, Monk noted with pleasure. He had gone in for the very gaudiest form of ultramodernism when he fixed up his own place downtown, and he was getting almost as tired of its flash as he was of the mortgages he had on the place.

A tuxedoed old gentleman with a Scotch whiskey and sea wind complexion stood stiffbacked in front of them and said, "Your hat, sir."

"A butler, eh?" Monk said admiringly. "I thought they survived only in the history books and the movies."

"One of Uncle Carlton's little extravagances," P. Argus said.

Monk wondered what she meant by little. The salary of a genuine butler equipped with dignity like this one was probably something to raise your hat.

"Fifteen minutes till two, Miss Paula," the butler said.

P. Argus seemed surprised. "Why do you mention what time it is, Jonas?"

"Didn't you call by phone, Miss, and remind me to state the time to you when you arrived?"

"Certainly not!"

"I beg pardon, Miss." The butler seemed somewhat confused. He went away.

"I'll leave you in the armory," P. Argus informed Monk, "while I go hunt Uncle Carlton." She added vaguely, "I wonder why Jonas said that about the time." She consulted her wrist watch. "It is fifteen of two."

The armory . . . what's the armory, Monk wondered. He found out. It was the armory, a room for storing arms; pop-eyed, Monk eyed an array of hunting rifles, revolvers, modern and antique hand arms, knives and machetes, which adorned the place. There was an added collection of hides and mounted heads of such ferocious animals as tigers, lions and bears on the floors and walls.

"Some collection!" Monk waved a hand. "Uncle Carlton must keep busy hunting. It would take practically a week just to shoot all the guns in here."

P. Argus smiled slightly. "Uncle Carlton doesn't shoot anything but the breeze."

"Who's the nimrod, then?"

"I am."

"Hully chee! No kidding? You'll have me scared of you."

"I'll find Uncle Carlton," she said, and departed.

Monk, examining the stuffed animals, was impressed. The place looked like a taxidermist's shop. A remarkable girl, certainly a lovely girl; however, he was glad he'd found out she was adept with dangerous weapons.

He felt like grinning, so he hooked his thumbs in his vest pockets and grinned. The situation pleased him. The girl was beautiful. There was no Ham Brooks around to fly-speak the situation; there were a couple of interesting mysteries—

who had telephoned Clancy, and who had phoned the butler.
And Uncle Carlton's fright, of course, with his Satan's pitch-
fork. And I'm just the boy, Monk thought, to save Uncle
Carlton from his fears and receive P. Argus' gratitude.

He was feeling of the teeth in the gaping mouth of a
stuffed tiger to see how sharp they were when the butler
said, "He'll see you, sir." Monk only jumped a foot, wheeled
and demanded, "Whatcha mean, see me? The thing's stuffed,
ain't it?"

The butler bowed apologetically. "I meant Carlton Argus,
sir. He will see you now."

"Oh."

"This way, sir." The butler was holding open the door.

They walked down a hall, turned right through a door
into a room which was furnished as a living room, and the
servant stopped before another door, faced Monk, asked, "Do
you have a watch, sir?"

"Watch? Sure."

"Might I see it?"

Monk carried a pocket watch with a closed front; the lid
opened by pressure on the stem. It was old-fashioned. He
produced it, said, "Five minutes until two."

"Might I have it a moment?" the servant asked. He
accepted the watch with a polite, "Thank you. Just a moment." He turned and went back into the hall; in a moment he
returned and gave Monk the watch, saying, "I am sorry, but I
thought our clock was off. Thank you again, sir."

The butler went to the inner door, opened it a couple of
inches, stopped quickly as if he'd made an error, and rapped
the panel with his knuckles.

"Yes?" asked a gruff voice inside.

"Mr. Mayfair to see you, sir."

Louder, the gruff voice said, "Come on in, Mayfair, and
have a chair. Be with you in a minute."

Monk entered. The butler withdrew, closing the door,
possibly two seconds later, the lock clicked.

The butler had locked the door.

What the hell, Monk thought.

Apprehension came slowly to him; he was feeling too
good for it to grab him at once. He faced the door, put out a
hand. Locked, all right. He wheeled again slowly, now aware

of the stillness in the room, the utter abnormal stillness that stirred the skin along his nape unpleasantly.

He saw the clock, an electric clock lying on the floor, indicating two o'clock. It had fallen there; the fall had yanked its cord from the wall socket, so naturally it had stopped. Two o'clock, it said.

A chair was upset. The rug was crowded up in one spot, as if it had skidded under urgent feet. The room was a sort of an office, a record room; there was a desk, a swivel chair, and the straight chair that was upset. Books were on the desk, books about orchid culture. A few tools on shelves, and in a rack, tools for the care of flowers, Monk supposed.

"Mr. Argus!" Monk said loudly. "Carlton Argus!"

Stillness came to him, settled about him, as warmly moist as animal breath. It was greenhouse air, he supposed; this must be a part of the orchid culture room P. Argus had mentioned. There was a glass-paneled door through which he could see plants growing like a jungle. He had seen orchid plants growing, and these were orchids. But what bit into him was the sight of the broken glass in the door.

One pane was broken out of the door. The glass, in fragments, was scattered on the floor.

"Carlton Argus!" Monk said sharply.

He expected no answer. He didn't know why he hadn't expected a reply; he had just known there would be none.

Two o'clock. He was looking at the stopped electric clock. Two o'clock. It must be about two now; it had been five minutes to when the butler borrowed his watch. When the butler borrowed . . .

He got out his watch and looked at it and the face was smashed in and the hands had stopped at two o'clock.

I'm in something, he thought. In something, and in plenty. Good God!

Cra-a-a-sh! It came from the next room, the glassed-in place where the orchids grew in sickening sweet warmth. One crash. But loud. Something upsetting. Something made of wood, heavy; it made a great noise. Just the one noise and no other sound following it.

He put his smashed watch back in his pocket. A sweat drop, sliding down the line of his jaw, made a slight tickling.

The knob of the door rattled, the door the butler had closed. It rattled again, anxiously.

"Uncle Carlton!" called a feminine voice. "What was that noise?"

It was P. Argus.

She waited awhile for an answer.

Then she said, "Uncle Carlton!" Anxiously now. And she added. "Did you call the police, Uncle Carlton? They're here. They say you called them."

Monk went into the orchid room then, went quietly, avoiding the broken glass on the floor, trying not to let the orchid plants touch him. He hated the things, detested their fulsome greenness, their nasty, bloated look. He had always hated orchids for their abnormality, their difference from other flowers.

He supposed the man lying dead among the plant boxes was Carlton Argus.

III

Now fists were beating on the door, beating hard, and a voice was saying, "Open up in there! Come on, open up!" A man's voice. A policeman's voice.

Monk stood beside the body; without any awareness of doing so, he pressed the palms of both hands hard against his temples. He was strangely unable to think; if he ever needed to think, it was now. His mind was quite clear and receptive, but it wasn't generating anything. It was receiving impressions.

The dead man, Carlton Argus... The knife that had killed the man had an ancient-looking brass and wood hilt... It could have come from the armor room. Maybe it had, Monk tried to remember whether he had handled such a knife when he had prowled around the armor room, looking at things. He couldn't recall; not even that much could he remember.

He scowled at the orchids, wondering if the damned things were paralyzing his wits, a ridiculous wonder that seemed quite real to him at the moment.

There was not much blood around the dead man... The crashing sound... What had made it?... One of the orchid boxes was upset near the body, its rich earth, the rotten-rich looking earth in which the plants grew, was scattered over the floor. Okay, what had upset it? "What upset it?" Monk said, and the sound of his own voice caused him to dodge.

The police fists were beating the door again. "Open up for the police!" the heavy voice was yelling. It added, "Get a key. Isn't there a key to the door."

"He must have it inside," another voice said.

What upset the damned box, Monk thought?... Then he saw there was no other door into the orchid room. No other door... His mind wouldn't accept that.

He had heard a voice from the orchid room when he arrived. Presumably it was the voice of the man dead on the floor; the butler had said so, but it might not have been the same man. But there had been a voice. And then later, the plant box had upset. It took somewhat of a push to upset such a box. But no door... No way anyone could have entered or left the damply oppressive orchid chamber.

"Isn't there a skeleton key around here?" the policeman was demanding.

"There are spare keys to every room," a voice said.

This was P. Argus speaking.

Monk stood where he was. He wished he could think; he needed to think; he was finally getting his brains to mesh. The voice... the plant box upsetting... but no way in or out of the room.

Ridiculous. There had to be a way.

He heard P. Argus say she was going to get the key. And then he heard her again, coming back, saying she thought one of these keys must be the one. It seemed she had been gone no time, and he knew his brain must be working very slowly.

Presently the police came inside.

The moment when P. Argus saw the body was bad. She lifted both hands; her fingers tensed in a splayed, strained position. She said, "Uncle Carlton..." She didn't lose much color, but her eyes became stark. She started forward and Monk said, "No, no, please don't. He's dead." She looked at him steadily for a while, a long-seeming while that was probably not quite a minute, then her knees began to bend slowly. Monk thought she was going to faint. He started forward to catch her. She screamed.

A cop took her outside. She didn't faint.

Another cop put a hand under his coat tail and pointed his other hand at Monk and said, "Don't start anything."

The third officer was looking at the stopped electric clock.

The fourth said, "I'll call the doctor and the photog and the print man."

The one who had his hand under his coat began using his free hand to search Monk. He said, "Better call the Lieutenant, too." He was giving Monk a quick frisk, first for weapons. "Stand over by the wall," he said.

The officer who had been looking at the clock now went to the body, held the body's wrist, his face wearing an inquisitive expression. He said, "No dice," and dropped the wrist, fell to examining the knife, the inquisitive look again on his face. He turned the body. He hurriedly let it slump back. "Lord, still bleeding," he said.

The man who had taken P. Argus outside put his head in the door and said, "I think the girl is—"

"Stay with her!" ordered the officer who had charge of Monk.

"She's going to be all right."

"Stay with her anyway! We don't know what the hell this thing is yet."

Monk pointed at the orchid chamber. He said, "The butler let me in. I heard a voice"—he pointed at the dead man—"that I thought was his voice, telling me to have a seat. I saw the stopped clock. I heard something upset. I saw the glass broken in the door. Then the body." Monk scowled at the orchid room. "Somebody in there killed him, then got away."

The policeman who was giving orders said to one of his men, "Take a plant at the back door, if there is one."

Monk said, "Watch the front door, too."

"We left a man there when we came in."

"Oh."

The man who had looked at the body and the clock was moving around among the orchids, pushing the leaves aside with his hands. Awed, he said, "My wife would go nuts about these things, particularly these dark speckled ones." He disappeared and they could hear him moving about. He opened a window, the sounds indicated. "Whoeee!" he said. "Straight down." Presently he reappeared.

"There ain't no way in or out of here except by the door," he said.

They looked at Monk.

"I've seen better liars in my time," one of them said finally.

Monk was not particularly afraid of policemen, but he had always had the normal man's vague feeling of apprehension in the presence of a uniformed cop. His present sensation was mostly a sickness.

"Get the butler," Monk said.

The man who had searched Monk raised his voice. "Carl, send that butler in here."

"What do you want with the butler?" asked the officer who had looked in the greenhouse.

"He borrowed my watch, set it at two o'clock, and smashed the face in so it would appear to have stopped at that time."

"When was that?"

"A couple of minutes before he let me in here. He locked me in, too."

The officers exchanged looks. They didn't say anything. But they didn't believe it.

The butler came in. He was chewing on a handkerchief and crying, sobbing as a man sobs, mostly with a convulsing of his chest and shoulders, but now and then with a raucous appalling outburst of sound that was animal-like.

He wore a blue suit. That was the first thing Monk noticed.

"He hasn't got on the same suit," Monk said.

"Eh?"

"The butler wore a livery when he showed me in here."

They turned to the servant. "What about that?"

The butler kept the handkerchief to his mouth. "I don't know what you mean. I haven't changed, not since this morning."

Monk's mouth suddenly felt dry. He didn't believe this was the same butler. At least the man was dressed differently. It was hard to be sure. He realized, with growing horror, that he hadn't paid too much attention to the butler.

"Do you remember letting me in?" Monk asked.

The servant stopped biting that handkerchief to nod. "I admitted you and Miss Paula."

"I mean into this room—do you remember bringing me here?"

The man didn't reply at once. His eyes looked ill, his mouth twisted. "Yes," he said, and immediately made the weird honking sound that was a part of his sobbing.

"Okay," Monk said. "Now what about my watch? Remember borrowing it?"

Again the response was slow. Then the butler shook his head.

Violently, Monk said, "Don't lie about it! Your fingerprints will be on it!"

"I didn't borrow your watch," the butler said.

Now suddenly the terror broke loose inside Monk, flowed through him, made his breathing difficult, put numbness in his fingers. This butler wasn't the one who had brought him to the orchid incubator, or whatever the place was called. It might be the butler who had admitted him and P. Argus, but he wasn't sure about that. There might be fingerprints on the watch, but it was doubtful; if there were prints, they wouldn't be those of this man, because this wasn't the one who had smashed the watch.

Speaking with some difficulty over the fear crawling in his throat, Monk said, "I want to talk to Doc Savage. And to my lawyer, Ham Brooks."

One of the policemen swore suddenly. "I been trying to think who this guy is. . . . He's one of Savage's men."

"You're crazy!" said a second cop.

"No, no, he's the one they call Monk."

The one who had searched Monk cleared his throat. "They won't electrocute him any the less quicker for that."

The shout, reaching them suddenly, came from somewhere back in the apartment. The shout, at first a bellow of wordless surprise, became the policeman named Carl bellowing, "Watch out! Stop him!"

There was a shot. Feet hitting floors hard and fast. Furniture going over. Doors slamming. And Carl bellowing again, "Dammit, head him off!"

Now three shots in a row, the bullets smashing against the wood and metal.

The policemen with Monk were jamming through the door. In the hall, it was dark. The hall depended for its light on a central chandelier; there were no windows in the hall.

Because it had been quite light in the orchid culture room, here in the hall it seemed ink-black.

"What the hell's wrong, Carl?"

Carl said he had found a skulker. The so-and-so had gotten away through a door, slamming and locking the door. Carl said he was shooting the lock out of the door. His gun banged again, then they could hear him kicking the door. "Watch out for the guy," he warned.

Someone snapped a light switch off and on rapidly. "The lights are jimmed."

"Anybody got a flashlight?"

The man at the switch wished to know what kind of a guy would be carrying a flashlight around with him during daytime.

A new voice, Irish and policeman-like, yelled, "What's goin' on in there?"

"You stay at that door, Mike," he was told. "Somebody's loose in—oh! Oh, hell! Here—grab him! *Grab him!*"

Movement, blows, grunting, a man falling down, and feet scraping the floor came all together, like a single act. Monk thought it would be a good time to get away himself; on the second step he took, he was hit over the head and knocked flat, and the policeman guarding him said, "Try to lam, will you!"

The confusion subsided as unexpectedly as it had started.

Stillness flowed into the apartment, hung breathless and poised, until an officer broke it by coughing.

Carl demanded, "He get away?"

"Mike!"

No answer from Mike.

"Mike!" This time anxiously.

They found Mike, a round-headed apple-cheeked man, sitting on the floor beside the front door. Carl sank beside him, exclaiming, "Mike! My God, Mike!"

"Mother of heaven, my jaw!" Mike mumbled. "He kicked me like a mule."

"Who was he?" Carl demanded.

"I didn't see him. I just felt his fist," Mike said.

"You were in the hall. Didn't you see him when he opened the door?" asked the man who had downed Monk.

Mike grimaced painfully. "No, Thompson, I didn't. I had the door open and my head stuck inside to see what was goin' on."

Thompson said, "Where's the telephone? Maybe we can get him stopped downstairs. Carl, you and Joe grab an elevator down."

Carl was carrying a piece of cloth in his hand. He started to put the cloth in his pocket, changed his mind and shoved it at Thompson. "Here, hold this."

"What is it?"

"I grabbed at the guy and got hold of his pocket and tore it loose. That's it."

Monk wished his head would clear. The blow over the temple had done something to his eyes, crossed them or something, and made him practically blind. Actually he wasn't as blind as he had thought; there simply wasn't much light in the hallways. He realized this when they returned him to the small office portion of the orchid culture room. He was relieved.

"You guys let the murderer get away," he said.

Thompson ignored him. "Find what's wrong with the lights, somebody."

An Indian-head penny was what was wrong with the lights. Someone had removed a bulb from a wall socket and dropped in the penny, the resulting short-circuit blowing the fuse. Only it wasn't a fuse, but a circuit-breaker, and the lights came on when someone pushed the light knob.

"Is Miss Argus all right?" Monk demanded. His spirits were rising.

She was all right, except that she looked at Monk with horror, then buried her face in her hands. She believed Monk had killed Carlton Argus.

The telephone rang. Thompson picked it up, said, "Yes? . . . Did anybody see him? Well, ask around." He hung up.

"The fellow got away?" Monk asked.

"He got out of the apartment house, apparently," Thompson admitted.

Monk pointed at the room were the orchids grew. "How did he kill Argus in there, then get out without me seeing him?"

Thompson frowned. "You still say that's what happened?"

"Of course that's what happened."

Thompson went in among the orchids. He worked around the walls, tapping them with the barrel of his service revolver, listening. He opened one of the windows—one whole slanting wall of the room was windows—and looked out. "Straight down to the street," he said. Then he got down on hands and knees and began crawling among the plant boxes, looking for trapdoors in the floor.

Carl came in, breathing hard. "Nobody saw the guy downstairs," he reported. "What are you doing, Thompson?"

Thompson said he was looking for a trapdoor. He added, "I don't think there is one." He stood up and threw something he had found out on the floor of the little office, demanding, "What's that thing?"

For a moment, Monk didn't recognize the thing; when he did, his skin began to crawl.

"What's the matter with *you?*" Thompson's eyes were on Monk.

"Coonskin cap, isn't it?" Monk asked. His voice treated him much better than he expected. It was almost natural.

"What'd you look so queer for?" Thompson demanded.

"Did I?"

"Know what it is?"

"I never saw it before, if that's what you mean," Monk said. "It's a coonskin cap, like Daniel Boone and those old-timers used to wear, isn't it?"

The girl, P. Argus, did an unobstrusive job of fainting. She was sitting in a chair, leaning back; Monk saw her eyes roll and became all whites before they closed and remained closed.

The next thing, which had nothing to do with a deerslayer's costume, was the bit of cloth, the pocket which Carl had ripped from the coat of the man who had escaped. Carl said, "Thompson, what'd you do with that piece of pocket?"

"Oh, that." Thompson produced the fragment. "Gray tweed," he said. "Subdued pattern, but good cloth. Not so many men wear tweed these days, since the war shut off the English supply. This may be a help."

Carl extended a hand. "Let me see that. I got a brother who's a tailor. I know something about materials." He examined the piece for a while. He whistled "You know something?"

"Yeah?" Thompson was puzzled.

"I think we oughta be able to trace this material." Carl was elated. "It's a special weave, and I bet one tailor has an exclusive on it."

Monk Mayfair closed his eyes tightly. He thought: Oh, God! Oh God, I've got to do something, or they'll look at me and realize I've discovered something. . . . He pointed at the girl.

"She's fainted," he said.

That distracted their attention fairly well. There was a collecting around P. Argus.

"Poor kid."

"Fainted, all right."

"I wonder what caused it?"

Thompson snorted, used his jaw to gesture at Monk. "Maybe looking at this guy's phizz, but more likely the shock of her uncle getting murdered."

Carl shook the bit of cloth dramatically. "We'd better get after this cloth business before the tailors all close up for the day and go home."

Fright sat on Monk's brain like a buzzard. They would be able to trace that cloth all right, and when they did they would find it had come from a suit tailored for Doc Savage.

IV

Doc Savage used the basement garage entrance to the building which contained his headquarters. He didn't believe anyone had noticed him particularly, although the taxi driver might have. He wasn't sure. He had kept a hand over his coat pocket to hide as much as he could the fact that the pocket was torn away.

He rode his private elevator up, very glad he hadn't followed an impulse to eliminate the private lift to cut expenses. He could feel the perspiration on his forehead.

Ham Brooks, in the library, was picking out a brief on a typewriter, using his one-fingered system. He stared at Doc.

"You look funny as hell," he said. "Only funny isn't the word."

"Funny certainly isn't the word." Doc began taking money, keys, card case, out of his pockets. "You know how to work the electric furnace, the one on the south side of the laboratory?"

"I know how to switch it on, is about all."

Puzzled, Ham asked, "You got curious and followed Monk, didn't you?"

"Yes."

"Something happen?"

"Too much. Get that furnace hot, will you?"

Ham went into the laboratory. He got the furnace going, watched the gauge, and presently Doc came in with the coat, vest and trousers of his tweed suit, which he chucked into the furnace. Ham said, "My God, you paid two hundred dollars for that suit!"

"Yes, and from now on, I'm going to buy them where ten million men buy theirs, some place where you walk up and save five dollars."

Fancy clothing was Ham's hobby. He liked to maintain, probably with a good deal of truth, that he was one of the best-dressed men in the country. He was indignant. "Quality like that saves you money."

"It may very well get me in the electric chair, too," Doc said. "I got this suit from your tailor. How well do you know the fellow?"

"Know him? Listen, that fellow owes the success of his business to me."

"Can you get in his shop and see that he destroys any record of ever having sold me a suit made of that cloth?"

"Huh?"

"Put it this way," Doc said. "I went down to watch Monk meet that girl. The business of that flintlock rifle and leggings we received got me interested, but I didn't want to mix in it and waste time if it didn't amount to anything. Well, it amounts to something. It amounts to murder, so far, and almost the fastest frameup I ever saw."

"Who got murdered?"

"I don't know. All I know is that a man trailed Monk and this girl to a Park Avenue apartment. I spotted the shadow and followed, keeping out of sight. The man followed Monk and the girl into a penthouse apartment. He left the door unlocked. I went in. While I was in there, a rumpus started, and the police came. Monk was tagged for the murder. He had been framed. The only way to break up the frame to any extent was to douse the lights by blowing a fuse, and make a break, so the police would think the real murderer had been present and had escaped."

"Dangerous, wasn't it?"

"No. It happened fast. But one of the policemen tore the pocket out of my coat."

"Anything in the pocket?"

"No. But he got the cloth, and they can trace that if we can't get to the tailor's records."

Ham said, "I can take care of that."

He left, running.

Five minutes later Doc Savage opened the electric furnace, raked the ashes out of the interior, carried them in a tray to the sink, flushed them away, and washed the tray.

The laboratory was pretty much his living quarters also and he kept extra clothing in a locker. He put on a suit about the same shade of gray as the tweed he had destroyed, but of flannel and a pin-stripe. He hoped this would fool anyone who had seen him going around in a gray suit.

Doc went into the reception room, got out the telephone book and city directory and began learning what he could learn by telephone.

The tenant of the apartment was named Carlton Argus. He lived there with his niece, Paula Argus, and one servant, a house-man butler named Elmo Tollen. This information came from the building superintendent, and Doc was positive a policeman was listening in.

The Park Avenue address suggested money, so Doc tried a volume of credit ratings for Carlton Argus. The man's credit rating was respectable, two million dollars. His business was metals.

Doc called an acquaintance, Ted Lennings, with Central Steel Corporation. "I'm trying to get a line on Carlton Argus. Know him?"

"Slightly," Lennings admitted. "What do you want to know about him?"

"All you know."

"Well, it's not too much. Came into metals in 1941, with about a hundred thousand dollars, which I understand he had borrowed from his brother. The brother and his wife were later killed in a plane crash, leaving a daughter. Carlton Argus was a plunger, and it was a good time for plungers. He cleaned up."

Doc asked, "His reputation good?"

The steel man hesitated. "Well, he wasn't caught in

anything. That war boom was a wild affair, and anybody who really did anything made mistakes."

"Anything specific?"

"There was a landing craft construction deal that caused some talk. The Seven Companies Allotment, it was called. But the congressional investigating committee looking into it and put on an okay, so I guess there was nothing wrong. I understand Carlton Argus is taking care of his niece, so the guy's probably all right."

Doc made three more calls, all designed at finding out what he could about the girl, Paula Argus. She was twenty-one, a war-time deb, Red Cross worker, belonged to a college sorority group, and was quite a huntress. She held a record trophy for women in two types of game, and had placed twice in the women's nationals with the small-bore rifle. Intelligent, competent, good character, a sportswoman. Nothing very dark about her.

Ham Brooks returned.

"Got the tailor's records changed," he reported. "We just took your measurement and records card out of the file. There's no other trace that you ever bought a suit there."

"Good," Doc said.

"Any report from the police on Monk?" Ham asked.

Doc shook his head. "That isn't a good sign, either. In the past, we have worked with the police in harmony, and they should have notified us."

"What are we going to do?"

"Take the thing by the horns, and go to the apartment. That's about the only thing we can do."

Monk Mayfair was not in the Argus apartment, which was full of detectives from the homicide detail, an assistant district attorney, photographers, print men.

Thompson introduced himself. "I'm still in charge," he explained. "I was with the squad which came in answer to a call for help from Carlton Argus."

"This call from Argus—was it a telephone call?" Doc asked.

"That's right."

"Sure it was Argus?"

"I didn't take the call. But I checked with the man who did at headquarters, and the fellow who called said he was Argus."

"Which doesn't prove it was Argus," Doc said.

"It'll be up to your friend Mayfair to prove it wasn't," Thompson said dryly. "Unless he can find a phonograph recording of Carlton Argus' voice, the proving may be tough."

The assistant district attorney came over. His name was Wilton Ivans, and he was obviously out to make a name for himself by convicting a Doc Savage associate. He said, "Thompson, why are you letting Savage and Ham Brooks hang around here?"

Ham snorted. "Look, Ivans, we have special police commissions which entitle us to hang around here if we want to."

"Commissions?" Ivan's tone implied disbelief. "Let me see them."

Ham and Doc produced the documents, which had been issued for assistance rendered the metropolitan police in the past. They were, they both knew, quite in order.

Assistant District Attorney Ivans looked at them. "These are cancelled." He threw the documents on the floor.

"For God's sake!" Rage gave Ham's face a shiny hard look. "Nobody but the Commissioner can cancel those. Now, you bloated little pipsqueak, get on the telephone and tell your boss we're investigating this thing. See what he tells you."

Ivans retreated uneasily. Thompson shook his head soberly, said, "Ivans can make it tough. He's an up and coming young man in the D. A.'s office."

"He'll be down and crawling if he doesn't watch out!" Ham was angry.

When Ivans came back, he wore the air of a young man who had found a mouse in his hash. He said, "We're going to take that commission business up with the Commissioner in damned short order."

Ham laughed in his face. "Where's Monk Mayfair?"

"The hell with you," Ivans said.

Doc Savage turned to Thompson. "Those commissions are good until they are cancelled, as you know. Now where is Mayfair?"

Thompson avoided Ivans' scowl. "Downstairs."

Ivans shouted for a police stenographer, and ordered a transcript made of their questioning of Monk. With a suspicious eye on the stenographer, Monk left out some of the story. He didn't mention the flintlock rifle and the leggings, but the rest he told as it had happened up to the point where he omitted his recognition of the piece of cloth from Doc's suit.

At this point, Monk suddenly changed to the ancient Mayan language, a tongue he had learned in Central American on one of their earliest adventures together. It was probably one of the world's least-known languages.

In Mayan, Monk said, "There was a coonskin cap in the orchid culture room where the body was found. It ties up in a crazy way with that rifle and leggings, maybe. And get rid of that suit, because they're trying to trace the cloth—"

"Here! Here!" Ivans shouted. "Hells bells! Talk the England language!"

In English, Monk said, "Check the butler, Doc. The butler who showed me into the orchid place wasn't the one who let us in."

Ivans yelled, "What did you say a second ago?"

"I was clearing my throat," Monk said.

Ivans wheeled on Doc. "What did he say?"

"You heard it as clearly as we did," Doc said. "How do you know he wasn't clearing his throat?"

Wheeling on the stenographer, Ivans demanded, "Did you get any of that gibberish?"

"Some of the sounds," the stenographer admitted. "Hell, I never heard any language like that before."

They talked to the girl. The doctor had given her a bromide, and she was in her room. Doc narrowed his eyes warningly when Ham Brooks looked as if he was going to whistle his admiration.

"So you're Mr. Savage," Paula Argus said, extending her hand. "I'm awfully glad you came. I don't know what this terrible thing is all about, and I'm frightened."

"We wanted to ask you a couple of questions," Doc told her. "You see, our friend Monk is badly involved in this."

She made a distressed gesture. "Some of that is my fault, I'm afraid, because I was so shocked I didn't make it clear immediately that Mr. Mayfair was here because I had asked him, and that he didn't know my Uncle Carlton Argus, and couldn't have any reason for killing him. Now the police don't seem to believe me, or at least Mr. Ivans doesn't."

"Mr. Ivans doesn't *want* to believe you," Ham said.

"You won't mind a couple of questions?" Doc asked.

"I'll gladly do anything I can to help."

"When Monk got here, he walked into a frameup," Doc said. "That could have happened two ways. First, it might have been sprung on Monk on the spur of the moment. Or second, it was planned by someone who knew in advance he was coming. Now, who knew that?"

She shook her head. "Nobody could have been really sure. I didn't know myself whether any of you would agree to talk to Uncle Carlton."

"Then who knew about your plan to ask us to talk to your Uncle?"

"Elmo."

"Elmo Tollen, the butler?"

"Yes."

"No one else?"

"No one."

"Couldn't your Uncle have told someone of your plan?"

She looked uncomfortable. "I'm a fool to think no one knew but Tollen, aren't I? What I meant is that I know of no one but Tollen and Uncle Carlton who knew I was coming to you."

"Do you think your Uncle would tell anyone?"

She shook her head. "Uncle Carlton was in the strangest state of mind. He seemed to have two kinds of fear. First, fear of an actual menace to himself. Second, the fear that someone would find out he was scared and start investigating."

"Then he wasn't likely to have told anyone, you think."

"I don't think he would, no."

"We'll talk to Tollen," Doc said. "Now, about the deerslayer outfit, the rifle and leggings. You say that your Uncle became very upset when he received them by express?"

She nodded. "But I'm not sure, now, that the package came by express. I just know it came."

"Any idea whether the wrapper is still around?"

"It might be in the trash box in the orchid room," she said. "I'll gladly help you look."

Doc said that would be a good idea. He told Ham Brooks, "Get hold of that butler, Elmo Tollen. See what you can find out."

Ham said, "I'll put the suction to him," and went out.

Assistant District Attorney Ivans had been keeping his mouth shut, but he had been listening. He barked at Thompson,

"Go along and see what he asks the butler." Ivans' tone implied that he was dealing with a bunch of crooks.

In the small office adjacent to the orchid culture room, they dug brown paper and string out of a large trash can. Once the paper was flattened out on the floor, they could tell that it had once been wrapped around something the shape of the long flintlock rifle and the leggings.

"No express company tag," Doc said.

Ivans was stalking around with his jaw thrust out. He said, "I want that rifle and leggings. Produce them."

"Why," Doc suggested, "don't you let the police do their own investigating? They're trained for it, and they know their business."

Ivans snorted. "The things I do, I want done right."

Doc noticed one of the listening policemen stiffen slightly with anger. He knew the news that Ivans didn't think the police could do this case up right enough to suit him would get back to Thompson and to whomever was over Thompson. It would not make them love Ivans, although Doc doubted if anyone loved Ivans to begin with.

"I have respect for the police," Doc said, hoping to goad Ivans into doing himself more damage.

Ivans didn't take the bait. He merely scowled.

Doc said, "If you're going to mastermind this case, you had better go in the orchid room and find out how the murderer escaped without passing through this office, where Monk Mayfair was waiting."

Ivans laughed with insulting loudness.

"The murderer was Monk Mayfair," he said. "And he didn't escape. We got him."

"The police got him," Doc corrected.

The listening cop grinned slightly at Ivans' expression of rage.

Doc asked, "Where is the coonskin cap?"

It was on the desk in the office. Without touching the thing with his hands, but turning it with a pencil, Doc learned that it was genuinely a raccoon skin cap, that it wasn't modern. The condition of the hide and fur told him the age. It was thoroughly worn. The sewing was done with a buckskin thong thread, and it was a hand-made job, not too expertly turned out.

"About the same age as the leggins," Doc said. "Possibly part of the same outfit."

The police photographers and fingerprint men had finished in the orchid culture room. They came out now, and were followed shortly by men bringing Carlton Argus' body on a litter.

Gray-faced with shock, but not sobbing, Paula Argus watched them take the body of her uncle outside. Doc Savage went to her, and led her to a chair; she held one of his hands with both of hers and said, "I—I feel as if I could go all to pieces, as if I can't stand it." He patted her hands reassuringly and said, "Turning loose hysterics doesn't help and it's messy. Try mechanical methods of relieving your mind by thinking about something entirely different that you have done or planned to do. It won't work magic, but it will help, and occupy time. One of the greatest gifts God gave the human mind is the power to forget. Time will do that."

Doc started into the orchid culture room, the greenhouse, and Ivans objected. "You stay out of there. I won't have you messing up clues."

This was ridiculous and Doc told him so. "The police have photographed and printed everything and gathered all the clues."

He went into the place. The jungle-like heat still filled the room, mixing with the peculiar presence of the orchids and the moist earth, making Doc think of a warm, moist, gaudily colored toad. The inside of such a toad, really.

He was interested in one thing: how had the murderer escape without Monk seeing?

The other possibility was that the murderer actually hadn't been in the orchid room, but had made it seem this was the case.

Ivans followed Doc around for a while, presently grew disgusted when Doc dropped a plant box and splashed mud on his trousers, and went to the door to wait. Ivans wiped at his trousers with a handkerchief. Doc concealed a grin, because he hadn't dropped the box by accident.

The plant growth in the place was rank. Obviously Carlton Argus had taken pride in a spectacular background, since there were plants other than orchids which reached nearly to the ceiling.

The point, though, was that anyone a few feet inside the greenhouse-like room couldn't be seen from the door. Right now, Ivans was standing in the door, but Doc couldn't see him. And Ivans couldn't see Doc.

Doc examined the roof. It was about half glass, but the glass was solid, the panes too small to permit a man to pass. It had to be the side windows, then.

The side windows opened. He swung one open, being careful that there was no noise Ivans would hear, and looked down. There was about thirty floors of straight drop below. He eyed the window framing, the deposit of dust, the places here the dust had been rubbed off, all places where paint had been disturbed.

"Finding anything?" Ivans called.

"Not particularly," Doc replied.

"How much of my time are you going to waste at this?"

Doc made a disgusted noise. He hoped the noise would keep Ivans away a few moments.

From his coat pocket, Doc took a hank of silk line to the end of which was attached a folding grapple hook. The line and hook, which he usually carried around with him, was a keepsake from the past. It had saved his life once, and been quite useful a few other times, and he still carried it out of sentiment.

He climbed out of the window. It was simple. The window, about forty inches square, was hung on axis hinges located about half way down each side. The hinges weren't quite half way down, though, because the window would slam shut of its own weight unless held open by a chain arrangement. Doc didn't fasten the chain. He did loop an end of the line over the window so that he could hold it open while he slid down the cord.

He went down the cord. He didn't look at what was below. Thirty stories of drop. But he was perfectly safe. The silk line, stronger than parachute shrouding, would hold a half ton, more than four times his weight. There were large knots for handholds, and wrist loops if he got tired.

He was quite glad when he had descended to the first window below, however.

There was one hitch. The window he had reached was locked on the inside. He studied the lock, tried his knife blade on it, had no luck. He broke the pane with his fist, reached in, turned the lock, raised the window. This window was not like those in the greenhouse; it was metal-sashed and slid up and down. He went inside.

The room was completely bare. An unoccupied apartment.

Now he did the business of closing and locking the greenhouse window. It was simple. First, he shook his grapple hook free, and it came swishing down. Then he pulled his cord off the top of the swinging sash above, and listened to it slam shut and automatically fasten. The fastener was a spring lock.

He had thought the spring lock of the orchid room window looked as if it had been carefully oiled at some recent date.

Coiling the cord around the hook, he went to the apartment door. It was also spring-locked, and he went out into a rich looking apartment house hallway. There were elevators to the left, and he laid a thumb against the call button.

Waiting, he wished he could be around to see Assistant District Attorney Ivans' face when that officious young man began searching the orchid room.

V

There were no police in the elevator, so Doc uncrossed his fingers. "First floor," he said, then asked, "What's all the excitement around here?"

The elevator operator was conscious of the dignity of being employed on Park Avenue. "I don't know, sir, I'm sure. Some trouble in the penthouse apartment, I understand." Some fifteen floors down, he relaxed enough to add, "I think they are questioning the penthouse butler in the superintendent's office."

"Thank you," Doc said. He was very grateful, too. He hadn't known where they were quizzing Elmo Tollen.

There was a policeman at the apartment house door, but he was facing the street, not the lobby, which was an impressive as a cathedral interior.

The superintendent's office was easy to find. It was labelled OFFICE.

He didn't enter immediately. The officer at the entrance

couldn't see him there. So he bent an ear to the door, listening.

He could hear Ham's voice, solidly wrathful, at its best witness-cross-examining volume. Thompson. And another voice he hadn't heard before, but which belonged to the butler, no doubt. Surprisingly, he heard Monk's rather juvenile sounding voice. He hadn't imagined Monk would be present.

Doc started to open the door, didn't, fell to pondering. The case, he felt, wasn't going well. He hadn't, actually, unearthed anything tangible to help Monk, although he had given Ivans some confusion, he hoped. Confusion might not be enough. It was frightening to face the fact that Monk might be tried and convicted for murder, but it was something he knew he had better face. The fact that Monk was a man with a substantial reputation wouldn't help, because a prosecutor of Ivans' turn of mind would use Monk's fame to crucify any attempts to use Monk's reputation as character evidence.

Monk could easily be tried and electrocuted for murder. That was a fact.

Doc decided to go to extremes. It had always been his belief that something that was too fixed, too ironclad, could best be blown apart with dynamite.

The result of his pondering was that he dug out of another coat pocket a flat metal case containing more gadgets. Grenades, in this case. Smoke, tear-gas and straight explosive types. They were quite small, smaller than eggs, but in a restricted area they were effective.

There were two smoke grenades. He took them both, flipped the discharge levers, opened the door, and rolled them inside. He closed the door quickly, listened.

He heard Thompson yell, "Hell! What's that thing!" Then Thompson cursed.

Doc waited through a thirty second count. Under his breath: ". . . thousand twenty-eight, thousand twenty-nine, thousand-thirty." He opened the door and went into a room fairly well filled with smoke.

"Tollen?" he called. "Where are you?"

"Here," Tollen's voice said in the swirling blackness.

"All right. Stay right there," Doc said. He wanted the man to stay placed, so that he could find him. Moving rapidly, Doc made for the butler's voice. Nothing got in his way, although there was excited movement in the room, and some profanity. "Tollen?" he whispered.

"Yes?" Tollen said loudly.

"Whisper, you fool!" Doc whispered. "Listen! You've got to get away from the police! They've found out too much. So scram. When you get out, go to the boss."

"Right now?" Tollen gasped.

"Sure. Get going. And see the boss right away, you hear!"

"Okay. But how'll I go—"

Doc wished to get away himself without doing too much explaining to the police. He gripped the man's arm, breathed, "This way."

They did it by opening one of the windows and dropping out. The windows, he surmised from the location of the superintendent's office, opened into a court or a service alley.

For two reasons, he let Tollen go first. He wanted the man ahead of him where he could be followed. And he didn't want to be the one who fell into an areaway and broke a leg if there was too much of a drop below the window. He was convinced now that Tollen was a crook, so if any legs were broken, he preferred they be Tollen's.

"Don't wait. Keep going," he warned. "Go to the street and walk north, then turn right at the first corner. Don't run. Walk. And don't look around. Go into the restaurant at Third Avenue and Sixtieth and have something to eat. Then leave and take a cab to the boss."

"That's a lot to—"

"Get going," Doc said.

He listened to Elmo Tollen land, decided it was no drop. The smoke was pouring around his head, and he knew that Tollen hadn't seen his face. He waited, hoping the police didn't find him. He could hear Thompson in the apartment house lobby, talking loudly to God and Satan about the situation. Thompson was mad. Out of Monk and Ham, he had heard so sound. Monk and Ham would know what the smoke was. He supposed they were remaining motionless, probably quite puzzled.

Doc went out of the window himself, hoping Tollen had gotten to the street. The brick paving in the service alley was rough. Doc worked along it, out of the smoke which poured from the window. He took a chance on the door guard having gone inside to see what the rumpus was about, and moved out on the sidewalk.

He was not bothered.

Elmo Tollen took his time eating in the restaurant, staying there nearly an hour. It was a nervous hour for Doc, because he was not able to learn whether Tollen was actually in the place, and he didn't dare go in personally for an inspection.

Darkness was smudging the streets when Tollen did come out. Doc, waiting down the street some distance in a cab piloted by a very puzzled driver, said, "There's the fellow we want to follow."

"The red-faced old guy in the monkey suit?" the driver asked.

"Yes."

Tollen showed some nervousness. He looked around, then came toward them.

"My God, he's comin' to this cab," the driver said.

Doc slid off the rear seat, down on the floorboards, made himself as small as possible. He said, "Don't let him look in here! Get out. Tell him the cab is engaged."

The driver had brains. Probably the ten-dollar banknote Doc had shown him earlier helped his thinking.

"Okay," he said. He got out hurriedly, stood beside the cab on the sidewalk, and presently said, "Sorry, this one's taken, buddy."

Doc did not know immediately what had happened. But there was a startled silence.

Then Tollen's voice said, "What's the matter? Don't you know when you've got a gun in your guts?"

The driver made a frog noise.

"Now get in there and drive," Tollen said. "I'm going to keep this thing in your ribs, and blow them out of you if you make a funny move."

Doc braced himself. But Tollen got in front with the driver.

"Head her over on the west side, off Central Park West," the Argus butler ordered.

The cab began rolling.

Elmo Tollen, Doc reflected, couldn't have a gun. He must be using a finger in a coat pocket... Again, maybe not. Maybe the scheme had blown up. Maybe Tollen, from the restaurant, had made a telephone call to someone, and the someone had sent him a gun . . .

Doc began to perspire. If Tollen had used the telephone, he might have found out the escape wasn't what Doc had told him it was. Logically he would realize that Doc imtended to follow him to whoever was giving orders. The next natural step would be to let Doc follow, and be led into a spot where they could finish him off. Tollen might, as a matter of fact, know Doc was in the cab.

"Turn left here," Tollen said. And a moment later, "Pull up. And get this, friend: You drive on and forget this, see."

The front door on the left opened and slammed; the cab jerked into motion. When it had gone a few yards, Doc said, "Turn right at the first corner. Did he have a gun?"

"Sure he had a gun," the driver said bitterly.

"You see it?"

"Nah, he had it in his pocket. But I could feel it."

Doc shoved a ten-dollar bill over the partition. "Here's your money. And thanks." The driver was swearing when he opened the door and got out, then ran back to the corner.

There was no one in sight on the street.

It had started raining again, but softly, a thin mist that moved lazily with the wind, stirring and shifting like fog. Doc Savage looked down at the sidewalk, back at his own tracks. The moisture on the concrete retained his footprints very vaguely, and if he moved fast . . .

It wasn't necessary. He saw Elmo Tollen. The man appeared suddenly, crossing the street, going into a brownstone house. He moved fast, went up the steps and through the door. If someone didn't open the door for him, he opened it quickly himself.

Doc began at the corner and counted houses. Seven. Tollen had gone into the seventh house from the corner. Doc decided to go into the same house by the back door.

Tall apartment houses, dignified in the gnat-like rain, filled each corner of the block, and the brownstones were sandwiched one against the other with no passageways between. But behind the brownstones must be what New Yorkers call "gardens".

Doc decided to try a delicatessen in one of the apartment houses. The only clerk in the place, a fat man in an apron, eyed him suspiciously. "Back door? Wathcha want with tha back door?"

"Police investigator. Plain clothes," Doc told him. "If you want to see some credentials, here they are." Doc showed him the special commission which had aroused Ivans to a rage. The card was impressive enough for the fat man. He jerked his head. "Through the back, take a door to the right."

The "gardens" were satisfactorily dark. The man in the apron followed Doc, asked, "How ya gonna get over them fences?"

Doc decided the fences wouldn't bother him. "They won't be too tough," he said. "Thanks."

There was noise from the front of the store, a customer. The man hesitated, torn between the customer and desire to see the excitement, if any. The customer won, and he disappeared.

Doc began climbing fences. Three wood, one brick, one what he thought was privet hedge, only it wasn't privet, but thorn bushes, and gave him a worse time than any of the others. He moved quietly, kept in the shadows.

The back door of the seventh house was locked, which was to be expected. He tinkered with the lock silently, without success, then tried to decide whether any of the windows were open. None on the ground floor were, and they were barred anyway. But a window upstairs was open. He got out the cord and the hook.

Twice he threw the hook at the open upstairs window, but jerked it back before it hit when he was sure he had missed. His third throw put the hook through the window. He waited fully two minutes, which seemed a long time, before he pulled on the cord until the hook hung on the sill. After testing the fastening by jiggling his full weight on the silk line, he went up.

Climbing the cord wasn't as easy as descending, but presently he hauled his head inside the window and listened. He could hear an electric clock running, smelled perfume. A man's perfume, though, probably cologne or shaving lotion. And tobacco odor.

He went inside, pulled in the line and coiled it. He was doing this when he heard the man whimpering.

He opened the door quickly, because the whimpering was downstairs. Down in the darkness somewhere, in the blackness and the odor of good tobacco smoke, the stillness. He stood and listened. He was suspicious. Finally he went down.

The man was hanging from the stair bannister. His feet were roped to the bannister, his hands were tied at his back, and he was gagged. His best noises, and he was trying hard, were nasal whimperings.

Doc turned on the light.

The man was tall, about fifty, gray-haired, wore slacks and sport shirt. His watch, which had slipped out and was dangling by its chain, was edged with small diamonds.

Doc gave him only a look, then went to other rooms and turned on lights, leaving the man hanging there. Doc didn't find anyone. What he found was a fine bachelor's house, three floors, good rugs and elegant paintings. A rich man's house, and what was more, the house of a man who had been wealthy for a long time. There were things, mostly things of taste, which told him that.

He went back and ungagged the man.

"There seems to be no one else here," Doc said.

"No, they left," the man said. Considering he had been hanging upside down and his face was the color of a salami sausage, he spoke calmly.

Doc had some trouble untying him and lowering him to the floor. "One man didn't tie you there," Doc said.

"No, there were two."

Doc said, "My name is Savage. Doc Savage." He freed the man's wrists.

The man rubbed his wrists, but looked at Doc. "Savage," he said, pondering. "I believe I've heard of you. Didn't you develop the thermoelectric bonding process for plywood that came out a few months ago? Or was that you?"

"Evidently you're in the plywood business," Doc said. "No one outside the industry would be likely to know about such an obscure thing."

The man grinned faintly. "Obscure? I wouldn't say so. That process scared hell out of the plywood industry until they found it was going to be made available to all manufacturers."

"Who are you?"

"Holland. John Holland," the man said.

"Of Holland Wood Plastics?"

"Yes."

Doc extended a hand. "Glad to run into you, Holland." He knew of the Holland concern. It had made plywood glider parts for the army during the war.

"The pleasure is mine, damned plenty," John Holland said. "I thought I was going to hang there until I died. The couple who takes care of my place has the day off, not due back until tomorrow. I don't think I would have lasted that long."

Doc said, "Let me look at you." He tested the man's pulse, and found it all right. "Just stay quiet for a while," he advised. "But it won't hurt you to talk. What's going on here?"

"Thieves, I guess," Holland said. The doorbell rang, and I found two men at the door. They pretended not to speak English, but they had a paper with what they made me believe was an address on it. I know they were pretending, because later they spoke damned good Bronx English. I started to look at the paper to tell them where the address was, and *bang!* Right over the head. I don't know what it was, but it felt like a locomotive. I woke up tied to the stairs, the way you found me."

"How long ago was that?"

Holland flashed for his expensive watch, growled, "The damned crooks!" Then he found the watch dangling and looked foolish. "It's seven-ten now," he said. "This was a little before six. Say an hour and a half ago."

"Were they still here when you woke up?"

"Yes, but I didn't see them."

"You didn't see them?"

"They were in the front hall. I could hear their voices. The door was closed. Later, there was some kind of a commotion, and after that they left."

"What kind of a commotion would you say it was, from the sounds?"

"I figure that they were waiting with their loot, and a car came for them. They made the commotion when they carried their swag out to their car."

"When was this?"

"The commotion? Not over fifteen minutes ago."

That, Doc Savage thought, would be after Elmo Tollen, the Argus butler, had entered the house.

Doc asked, "Do you know the Argus family?"

John Holland made faces while putting his watch back into the pocket of his slacks. "Who?" he asked.

"Argus. Carlton Argus. Or Paula Argus. They live at the Northern Arms on Park Avenue."

Holland shook his head. "Never heard of them." He sat up. "Say, can't I move? I'm damned anxious to find out what they took."

"Go ahead," Doc said. "I'd like to know, too."

"They didn't take a damned thing!" John Holland said.

They stood in the downstairs living room, on a vermillion rug that buried their shoe soles, and Holland stared at Doc in amazement.

"I don't get it!" Holland added.

Doc said thoughtfully, "Two men knocked you out and hung you from the bannister, waited around a while, had a commotion, and went away."

"Yes." Holland rubbed his jaw. "Damned senseless, I'd call it."

"And you don't know anyone named Argus?"

"No."

"This Carlton Argus was in war work, like you were. But in metals."

"I don't know him. The whole nation was doing war work."

Doc said, "Then it goes back to Elmo Tollen."

"Who?"

"Tollen. Elmo Tollen. A heavy, middled-aged man with a red face."

"I'm damned if I know him either," Holland said. "Say, what the hell is this thing, do you suppose?" He grimaced angrily and added, "It's getting me dizzy."

Doc said, "You'd better let me look at that bump on your head."

"Oh, that knock was nothing. I'm all right."

"Best let me look at it anyway."

Holland hesitated, looked as if he was going to refuse, but shrugged in the end. "Oh, all right."

The bump was there. Doc had wondered if it would be. It was, as Holland said, nothing very bad. Just a small knot, but such a blow could readily have stunned the man. "They knew where to hit you to lay you out for only a short time," Doc said.

"They were efficient as the devil," Holland agreed. "I'm going to call the police."

"I have a police commission, so it's the same thing," Doc told him. "I'll call in the description of the pair, though, if you'll give them to me."

The two men Holland described were strangers to Doc. One thin, one wide, both dark, both wearing tan corduroy pants and dark coats. One gray hat, one black cap. "Will that help any?" Holland finished.

"Not much, I'm afraid," Doc said. "Too general. What about their voices?"

"I'd know them if I heard them again," Holland declared. "Or I think I would."

"Nothing peculiar there, then?"

"Only the squeaky-voiced one. He had kind of a shrill voice, and that might help."

"It might," Doc agreed. But he didn't think it would particularly. He was feeling thwarted again. At the Argus apartment, he'd had the same sensation of getting nowhere, of knowing damned well that there was a web of plot, but unable to put his finger on a thread leading anywhere. He put his mind back over what he had asked Holland, and realized he'd left out one thing.

"By the way, you haven't been getting any Daniel Boone clothing recently?" Doc asked.

Holland's eyes went round. He seemed to freeze.

"What's wrong?" Doc asked.

"My God!" Holland said. "Here, let me show you!"

It was a shirt. Buckskin, fringed, ancient and much worn. No buttons, but with strings for tying, and ornamentation that had once obviously been pretty loud.

"How the devil did you know I had gotten it?" Holland demanded.

Doc said he hadn't known. "When did it come?"

"This afternoon. It was in the package container. You see, the house has one of those package chutes where the deliverymen leave groceries and things. After you open it once from the outside and close it, it locks itself. I found it there."

"Mean anything to you?"

"Good grief, no! Why should it?"

Doc said, "Carlton Argus, whose name you don't know,

got a rifle and leggings that would go with this outfit. He was killed this afternoon. And a coonskin cap, also part of such an outfit, was found near the body."

Holland looked as if he wished he could laugh, but could find nothing to let him give way to mirth. He ended by moistening his lips, asking, "What does it mean?"

"For one thing, it means a link between you and Carlton Argus."

"But damn it, I don't know the man."

"It's a link, anyway," Doc said.

Holland showed some resentment, started to speak, then faced the front of the house, said, "Isn't that someone at the door."

There wasn't any doubt about someone being at the door. A fist beat on the panel thunderously, a voice roared, "The police! Open up, or we'll smash the door in!"

Astonished, Doc Savage thought: That sounds like Thompson!

It was Thompson. Also two other officers. And Assistant District Attorney Ivans.

Thompson went straight to Doc Savage, put a hand on Doc's arm. Not gently. "You're under arrest, Savage," Thompson said.

Doc knocked the hand off his arm. "Don't be a fool! I didn't touch Argus and I can prove—" He went silent, astonished by the suddenness with which the policemen had drawn guns.

Assistant District Attorney Ivans came forward putting his feet down hard, jaw out. "We're not talking about Carlton Argus," he said. "This one we can hang on you, and plenty!"

Doc didn't say anything. He didn't feel like it. He was looking beyond them, at the vestibule entrance, which consisted of an inner and outer door and a space of perhaps six feet between the two. In this space lay the body of the Argus butler, Elmo Tollen, who could hardly be anything but dead with the knife in his chest where it was.

VI

Doc Savage tried to get a closer look at the knife, but Assistant District Attorney Ivans moved in front of him, saying,

"Get the bracelets on him, Thompson, before he pulls another Houdini."

Thompson told Doc, "Yes, let's not have any more vanishings."

Loudly, angrily, John Holland said, "What the hell do you cops mean busting into my house, and arresting my friends?"

Ivans looked startled. "I would advise you—"

"When I want advice, I'll ask my attorney, who makes two hundred thousand a year as against the five thousand you make, sonny," Holland said. "Now let's understand each other. Savage didn't kill that fellow. And Savage did save me from dying of strangulation, or whatever you get from hanging upside down. As for who killed that man, I can describe them to you."

Ivans was displeased. "Better be sure of your information. And attend to your own business." The last spitefully.

Doc told Holland, "Thanks for the good word. But don't get into trouble with the police yourself."

Holland snorted. "I don't like high-handed methods."

One of the policemen removed the knife from the body, drawing the wrath of Ivans, who told told him, "You should have left that there until the medical examiner came."

Doc noted that the knife was a broad-bladed affair with a crude hilt wrapped with some sort of thonging, possibly rawhide. It looked, he reflected, something like the kind of a knife the Indian fighters carried more than a hundred years ago.

He wished this deerslayer stuff would stop turning up. It was absurd. But it must have some meaning.

Thompson used a fairly civil tone to ask Holland, "You say you can describe the murderers?"

"That's right!" Holland snapped, "They were—"

"Wait a minute. Are you sure they're the killers?"

"Of course I'm sure."

"Did you see them do the killing?"

"I heard them."

"Okay. What did they look like?"

Holland proceeded to describe his two assailants again, but this time he said he thought one of them, the thinner one, might be a little taller than the other one who had the small, child-like voice. Otherwise his description was the one he had given Doc, and he did not add more to it. He finished, "The commotion at the door, when I thought they were packing off their loot, must have been when they were killing this man—Elmo Tollen, you say his name is?"

Ivans, who was listening, let out a gasp of surprise that was like a whistle.

He yelled, "Monk Mayfair and Ham Brooks!"

Doc Savage had been coldly afraid of that. The description of sizes did fit Monk and Ham, and Monk had a small voice. "Why be ridiculous?" Doc asked. "You have Monk Mayfair under arrest, so you know he couldn't have done this."

"Like hell we've got him," Ivans said bitterly. "He got away from our knot-headed police force."

Thompson's neck darkened. He didn't say anything, but he looked as if he would like to.

"When did that happen?" Doc was curious.

Ivans didn't tell him. Ivans jammed his fists in his coat pockets and asked Holland, "I suppose we'll have to get a search warrant to search your house."

Holland sneered at him. "Go ahead and search it."

They climbed the stairs together. Holland wearing the expression of a man with something sour on his mind. He told Doc, "This is the damndest outrage I've heard of. They're going to lock you up, did you know that?"

"So it would appear," Doc admitted.

Holland lowered an eyelid slightly, and turned to Ivans, asking, "Do you speak French?"

Ivans batted his eyes. "No."

Looking steadily at Ivans, pretending to speak to him, Holland said in fair French, "I am going to let you in the back room, then close and lock the door so you can escape, if you wish."

"I don't speak French," Ivans snapped.

"Okay," Doc said, and added, "An Assistant District Attorney doesn't have to speak French."

"Very funny!" Ivans said. But they had fooled him.

John Holland took about five minutes to perpetrate his trick on the police, in the end managing it so that he seemed an innocent victim, which relieved Doc's concern about the man getting himself in trouble. Holland merely shoved open the bedroom door, saying, "I suppose you'll want to look in here." The police were busy elsewhere, and Thompson said,

"In a minute, in a minute. One thing at a time." Doc went through the door and closed it. A heavy door with the key on the inside. He locked it, knowing they wouldn't smash it open easily.

He didn't use the silk line. It was a second-floor window and he knew there was level ground below. He hung by his hands, let go; a moment later he was sailing over fences. They were yelling and beating on the door.

In the delicatessen store, he stopped for a talk with the fat man in the apron. "Did my friends, the police, get there?" he asked.

The fat man was dubious. "They didn't sound like your friends."

"They were kidding you," Doc told him, and added a resounding laugh which didn't come from his heart. "I suppose you told them you saw me climb into the window of that house."

"That's right." The man was wiping his hands on his apron. "Wasn't it okay?"

"Sure, it was swell," Doc assured him. "What did they do with the taxi driver?"

"Oh, him. I heard 'em tell one cop to wait in the cab with him."

This cleared up the question of how the police had happened to turn up at the Holland home: The alarmed taxi driver had called the officers, as he had good reasons for doing, and he must have also watched Doc enter the delicatessen.

Leaving the store, Doc tacked a revision on his long-held opinion that there was a general inclination on the part of New York cab drivers to get as far away from trouble as fast as they could.

No one bothered him in the street, but he wasn't there long.

The Hidalgo Trading Company warehouse on the Hudson waterfront below Fiftieth Street was a frowsy looking mass of red brick with boarded-over windows and an air of uselessness. The rear was built over the river, or rather into the river, where the rat-gray, rubbish-laden river water swirled around the foundations. Age had rendered the sign, *Hidalgo Trading Company*, harding readable, and the only regular visitors seemed to be the harbor seagulls which liked to perch along the riverward roof edge between glider-like trips over the river.

Doc Savage took no chances on cab drivers this time. He walked from the subway, several blocks.

He also took the precaution of hooking a ride on a truck four blocks up the waterfront street, and dropping off under the pillars of the elevated highway in front of the building. He made the warehouse door with a feeling that he had done a good job getting there without being seen.

The steel door had no lock and no evidence of a keyhole. He put the heel of a shoe against the door near the bottom, about the center. He frowned. Frowned at himself, for feeling foolish about using another gadget. There had been a period when he went in enthusiastically for gadgets, and this door was one of the many. There was a fragment of radioactive material in the shoe heel, an electroscope gimmick inside the door; the radioactive stuff made the electroscope leaves separate, close a contact and the door would open. Presently it did open, and he entered.

For all his pains, he got a gun jammed in his ribs.

He was sure his hair was on end for a moment. "Take it easy," he said.

"Oh!" Ham Brooks' voice said. "I didn't know who it was." The lawyer raised his voice, yelled, "Let's have the lights, Monk. No—wait until the door is closed."

Light, following the closing of the door, came in a blinding flood. The interior of the warehouse, except for a long shop room, was a hangar for a seaplane, a helicopter equipped with floats, a speedboat and a larger express cruiser. The collection gave the place a crowded, spidery look.

"Is Monk here?" Doc demanded.

"Over here," Monk called. He sounded nervous.

Disturbed, Doc said, "The police know we use this old warehouse for a hangar and boathouse."

Ham nodded uneasily. "But Monk has some different clothes here, and I was going to pick up some makeup stuff somewhere and see if we could change his looks." Ham grinned faintly, added, "Change him into something more human, I mean."

Monk had reached them. He let the insult pass, which was proof that he was worried. "Doc, I made a bad move, didn't I?"

"You got away from the police when I put the smoke into

the superintendent's office at the Argus apartment, did you?" Doc asked.

Monk grimaced. "Hell, I was scared. I didn't think. I figured the smoke was so I could escape, because I knew it was the kind of stuff you carry around. So I beat it."

"Ham go with you?"

"Yes."

"I made the same mistake Monk did," Ham admitted. "I thought he was supposed to escape."

They both sounded worried, and Doc tried to ease the situation by saying, "It was dopey on my part not to give you fellows some kind of warning, because skipping was the logical thing for you to do. So let's not fret about who pulled the bone."

"Did you rig it so the butler led you to anything?" Ham asked.

Doc Savage said dubiously, "I rigged something, but I'm still not sure what it was."

"What happened?"

Doc gave them the story, and when he came to John Holland's description of the two intruders who apparently had murdered the butler, he asked, "Now, can you prove you weren't there?"

"My God, no!" Ham gasped. "We weren't, of course. But we were getting to this place, and I don't think anyone saw us." He turned to Monk, demanded, "Can you think of any way of proving where we were?"

Monk shook his head. "We tried to keep out of sight."

Ham was alarmed. "This means the police have me on their wanted list! Not for helping Monk escape, but for murder! It means I can't get around town and work on this thing."

Doc Savage said, "I'm going to get the Police Commissioner on the telephone and see what can be done."

"They'll trace the call!" Monk exclaimed. Then he remembered, and added, "Oh, just to headquarters, is all."

In the beginning, in order to keep unknown the fact that the warehouse was used by Doc Savage, they had arranged the warehouse telephone circuit themselves so that it tapped, unofficially, the headquarters phone hookup. This was not by authority of the telephone people, either, and was not according to rules. But it was effective. The wire could be traced, but it would take the police a couple of days to do it.

The Commissioner sounded uncomfortable. He said, "To begin with, Savage, I want to assure you that I have complete faith in the integrity of you and your men. But there are some things I haven't the authority or moral right to do, and one of them is to tell murder suspects they can walk around free. But if you could produce satisfactory evidence of innocence . . ."

"We need some time to do that, Commissioner."

"I know, and, I can't do it. Don't get me wrong. I'd like to."

"What about this Assistant District Attorney Ivans? Can you get someone else in charge of the case?"

"Lord, that's out of my pasture."

"Can you delay suspension of our commissions?"

"Naturally I will not cancel them without proof and testimony submitted in proper form. That might take a day or two." The Commissioner sounded pleased with this idea.

Doc assured him it would be a big help.

Next, Doc called the District Attorney's office. He ran into a snag there. The D. A. was on vacation, and his office didn't know where. Who was in charge? Assistant District Attorney Wilton Ivans.

"That tears that," Doc said, and hung up. He informed Monk and Ham, "We've got to stay underground and do what we can."

Ham Brooks shook his head slowly. "That makes it tough. Where do we start?"

Doc Savage contemplated the murky girder-netted upper regions of the warehouse thoughtfully. "One thing the police are going to do is come here looking for us. So we can't stay here."

Ham indicated the seaplane. "What about hopping in a plane and going some place where we'll be safe."

"No good," Doc decided. "There's no such place, I think we'd find."

"Another angle would be to get hold of our friends, Renny Renwick, Long Tom Roberts and Johnny Littlejohn."

Doc shook his head. These three, the other members of the group of five who frequently worked with Doc, were widely scattered at the moment. Renny, the engineer, was in Russia; Long Tom the electrical expert was in China, and

Littlejohn, the archaeologist, was in occupied Germany. "Take too much time to get them here," Doc said. "And anyway, they're doing important jobs where they are."

Monk grunted loudly. "I got an idea. Call on Pat."

Doc winced. "You know what that'll mean. She likes excitement too well for her health."

"She might help, though."

"I guess we'll have to try Pat." Doc said reluctantly.

Patricia Savage was cousin to Doc Savage, and she had Doc's unusual bronze coloring of skin and hair, but without the peculiar flake gold eyes which were Doc's outstanding feature. She had Doc's liking for excitement, though, but with the difference that she frankly admitted she had, whereas Doc usually proclaimed a strong aversion to trouble while always seeming to wade deeper into it.

Pat, on the telephone, was suspicious. "Listen, what has come over you? Did you fall on your head, or something?"

"All we want you to do is furnish us with a little hideout," Doc explained.

"Hah! Usually you break both legs to keep me from enjoying a little break in the monotony. How come the sudden change?"

"We're influenced," Doc confessed, "by the fact that we're practically in jail."

"I can hide you out in my apartment."

"Oh, fine! It will not take the police more than an hour to think of looking there."

"They're already thought of it," Pat said. "They just finished searching and left."

"Have they got the telephone wire tapped?"

"Probably."

"Goodbye."

"Wait a minute," Pat said. "Do you remember the little man with the green suit?"

Doc didn't get her meaning for a moment. Then he did. "Oh! Oh, sure," he said. He had been walking with Pat one day and they had seen a man in an atrocious green suit, had mistaken him for Monk Mayfair, and Pat had swatted him with a snowball with embarrassing results.

"Meet you there in forty minutes," Pat said.

"Well, it's against my better judgment," Doc told her. "By the way, do you have a friend named Paula Argus?"

"Yes, I know Paula. And the police asked me a lot of questions about her when they were just here."

"What kind of interest in her do the police have?" Doc asked, surprised.

"A pup of an assistant D. A. named Ivans did the talking, and although he naturally didn't tip his hand, I got the idea he was trying to build a bulletproof case against you and Monk and Ham, and he wanted to make sure that Paula didn't turn out to be a crook who had led you innocent lambs into a trap."

"The part about the innocent lambs had occured to me," Doc said.

"Well, better dismiss it. My okay is on Paula. You know where I'm going to meet you?"

"Yes, I know the spot."

"See you there, then."

Pat met them at the corner of Forty-eighth and Ninth Avenue and they stared in amazement at the vehicle she was driving, a panel delivery truck marked JOE'S DIAPER SER-VICE. "My God, when did you go into that business?" Monk demanded.

"Oh, I borrowed the truck." Pat was wearing a white smock which went well with the vehicle. "Don't you think I look innocent?"

They climbed inside the panel body of the truck in haste. The spot was fairly dark, it was raining again slightly and the streets were deserted, so it was not likely they had been seen.

"Anybody follow you?" Doc asked.

Pat nodded. "Yes, they had a plainclothes detective watching my place."

"Blazes! did you—"

"Oh, I gave him an empty bag to hold. I got in a cab, and he followed in a car, and I made a quick shft to the subway and lost him. You can lose any kind of a shadow in the subway if you know how to do it."

"What kind of car?" Doc asked.

"Eh? What car?"

"What make of car did the shadow use?"

"A Packard. One of the small ones."

Doc leaned back. He looked pleased. "I think we've got something," he said.

Pat turned her head, puzzled. "How?"

"I don't think it was a cop shadowing you," Doc told her. "And here's why: I've had enough dealings with the police to know what kind of cars the detective bureau uses, and they do not have any small Packards."

The hideout Pat had for them turned out to be the apartment of a girl friend. "It belongs to Thelis Van Zeltin, and she's in Lake Placid for a month," Pat explained. "She won't mind your using the place."

The house was a gray stone one in the Sixties slightly east of Fifth Avenue, and it had a private drive-in garage which made their entering the place much simpler. Pat merely unlocked the door, opened it, then drove insde.

"You've got the whole house," she explained.

"No servants?"

"They're in Florida, with Thee's parents."

There was a telephone, too, Doc found, and it was connected. He had been afraid service would be discontinued.

"Pat," he said. "Can you go back to your place and let this shadow get on your trail, then lead him around to where we can put our hands on him?"

"Sure."

"Call us before you start out with him," Doc said. "We can make arrangements about a spot to take the fellow."

"You still don't think he is a policeman?"

"The chance that he isn't is worth looking into."

Pat left on foot, saying she would take a cab to her place. Doc Savage told Ham, "The goofy touch to this thing is the parts of the deerslayer outfit that keep turning up. I want you to do some checking on that by telephone. Call the theatrical costume house and see if they have sold or rented such a costume. And try the museums, too."

Monk asked, "Want me to help in that?"

"Better not. That gravel voice of yours is going to be one of the things the police emphasize in their descriptions of you."

"Dang it, I don't want to just stand around here and have cold chills," Monk said.

"You can come with me," Doc said. "Providing Pat calls in that the shadow is still around."

Pat called about ten minutes later.

"Lead him into the driveway into Central Park, east side, farthest south," Doc directed.

VII

Monk Mayfair had discovered that when he pulled his chin down and thickened his neck and spoke with the accent of an Italian comic, the effect was impressive. He was practicing. He said, "Mucha better we catcha the fish, make wit' tha vino, no? Betcha Mexico gotta tha fish, no? . . . Say, Mexico isn't a bad idea at that, until this thing blows over."

"Mexico isn't like the old days," Doc told him. "The Mexican police would catch us as quick as the American police, and their jails aren't as comfortable."

Monk shivered. "I ain't kidding you, I'm a scared boy. Did you know that Ivans made them put the handcuffs on me? Handcuffs, when a cop puts them on your wrists, aren't a bit funny."

Doc Savage consulted his watch. "I wonder what has happened to Pat?"

"How late is she?"

"It has been an hour since she called. She should have made it." Doc got out of the baby service truck, which they were using. He added, "I think I'll watch the entrance to the park where she was to appear. That will put me where I can let this fellow who is following her pass me, then come up behind him."

"What'll I say if a cop asks me who I am?"

"Spika tha Italian to him," Doc suggested.

Monk didn't grin. He had darkened his skin with a mixture of cold cream and mascara, and blackened his eyebrows and hair with mascara, but he did not feel that he had changed his appearance enough to fool an alert policeman.

"How'll we grab this guy?" he wanted to know.

"I'll close with him when he's about fifty feet from the truck. You get out and help."

"Okay."

Doc Savage went back toward the entrance to the park. There was plenty of shrubbery, so he left the sidewalk and moved quietly, a wet business because the rain had soaked the grass and the leaves deposited spoonfuls of water on him frequently.

He waited near the park entrance. It was not raining at the moment, but probably it would start again. It was about ten o'clock and the streets were rather deserted. He contemplated the lighted windows in the tall buildings around the park, impressed, as he always was, by the majestic wonder that was New York at night. There was probably no other place, he thought, quite as reassuring as this part of New York City at this time of the evening. If you were low, if your belief in the capacity and integrity of the human race was far ebbed, standing here looking at the city at this time of the evening was good medicine. It would do a lot toward restoring faith.

Presently his relief became even more tangible, for he saw Pat coming. She was afoot, walking rapidly, swinging along in a blue satin raincoat which caught and reflected rays from the street lights. She entered the park.

The tall man was not far behind her.

As Pat was passing, Doc asked softly, "That the fellow?" He did not show himself.

"That's the one," Pat said.

Doc set himself. He was behind a bush at the edge of the sidewalk. This should not be difficult; about all he would have to do would be to step out and collar the tall man.

The man approached. Doc prepared to step out quickly behind the man. But the man suddenly came up on his toes, dashed toward Pat. He was past Doc, racing toward Pat, before Doc could do anything about it.

Doc came out on the sidewalk himself, called urgently, "Pat! Watch him!"

Pat wheeled. She made a sound, a gasp with fear in it, when she saw there was no time to run, no chance to escape. Then she was fighting the tall man, crying, "Oh, be careful! He has a knife!"

Doc was running toward her. So was Monk, but Doc got there first, coming in carefully. The tall man wrenched away from Pat and wheeled, holding a long-bladed knife ready in front of his stomach.

"Put it down!" Doc warned him. "Don't try to use that thing on me."

The man said, "Yah, hell!" He lunged, digging out and up with the knife. Doc got away from the blade, struck down hard with his fist at the man's forearm, and landed the blow. The impact numbed the man's arm and he lost the knife, but went down on his knees, trying to get it with his other hand. Monk was racing toward them.

Doc chopped at the side of the man's head with a fist, missing twice, then sending the fellow to the sidewalk. The man rolled after he landed. Doc stepped on his wrist, trying to pin the man down. Monk came up saying, "A tough nut, ain't he!" And immediately got both feet kicked out from under him.

Falling on the man, Doc got the fellow's coat, hauled it over the man's head so that his vision was shut off and his arm movements hampered. That way, he restrained the fellow enough that he was able to rap him twice and bring on a certain amount of dazed quiet.

Monk got up, quite made, and hit the man twice in the middle section, a right and a left, hard blows. Doc partially blocked the last one.

"You can stop a man's heart hitting him there," Doc warned.

"I would be a pleasure," Monk said violently. "You saw what he was trying to do, didn't you? Trying to kill Pat."

Pat said, "How can he talk if he's dead, you idiot?" Then she looked past Doc Savage and said, "Oh, great grief! Here comes a policeman."

Doc hauled the man off the walk, and dragged him toward the panel truck. The policeman, a park patrolman, yelled, "Here! What's going on here?" They could hear his feet hitting the sidewalk toward them.

Doc told Monk, "Get in that truck and get it going." Monk swung around to the front of the machine. Doc piled the tall man in the back, got in himself, and the truck began moving as Pat was trying to climb in. Pat gasped, "Help me!" and Doc gave her a haul inside.

They heard the policeman yell again, and shoot once, and from the sound of the bullet he evidently tried to hit a tire and missed. Then they took a corner, the swing piling Doc and Pat against the side of the van and rolling the tall man over against them. The tall man made sick noises.

Pat said, "I don't understand why I couldn't climb in here a minute ago. I just went all weak. I don't understand it."

Doc saw the way she was trembling, and thought it was no mystery.

"You're scared," he said.

"I never get *that* scared," Pat argued. "I don't know what happened."

Doc pounded on the front of the panel body and told Monk, "Get this thing back to where we're staying the shortest way possible. In a few minutes, the police are going to be grabbing diaper service trucks all over town." He turned and asked Pat, "Did you have any advance warning that the fellow might try to... Pat! Pat!"

"What's wrong?" Monk demanded.

"She's fainted, or something," Doc said.

"If we weren't in so damned much trouble, that would be funny," Monk said. "She's always so anxious to barge headlong into—"

"I have not fainted," Pat's voice said faintly. "Can't I close my eyes and just be really scared for a minute?"

The tall man had in his clothing two five-dollar bills, three ones, a dollar eighty-three in silver, two cigars, a paper book of matches which was no clue because it came from the largest tobacco chain in the city.

Monk finished searching and said, "He went at it with foresight. Nothing on him to identify him. Probably means he has a police record."

Doc told Pat, "Clear out of here, will you. Go upstairs and help Ham."

"Why can't I—" Pat began.

"Because you can do more good helping Ham," Doc said. "He's working his head off trying to find the source of that Buffalo Bill outfit."

Pat was suspicious, but she moved to the door.

Doc added, "In case you come back, knock before entering."

"Why?"

"Because we're going to take this fellow's clothes away from him."

Pat said, "Oh," and went away.

The prisoner was awake. His face was the color of zinc that had been quite a while in the weather and he did not have an optimistic expression. He demanded, "Whatcha takin' my clothes for?"

"So there won't be any bullet holes in them," Doc said.

The man didn't like that, but he didn't know exactly what view to take of it.

"Of course," Doc added, "you might talk your way out of it."

"How you mean?"

"Well, you might begin on the Daniel Boone suit, and tell us what significance it has. We're quite curious about that. And we would also like to know who killed Carlton Argus and his butler and why, and why you were going to kill Pat."

The man gave them a round-eyed look. "Pat? She the babe who was just here?"

Monk snorted. "If you're going to play dumb, at least don't overdo it."

"I didn't know her name."

"You kill them without troubling to learn who they are, usually?"

"Look, pal, I wasn't gonna knock her loose." The man sounded frightened. "I was gonna throw the fear of God into her, and let it go at that."

Monk said, "It didn't look that way."

"Sure it didn't look that way," the man said. "Whatcha think I am, an amateur? When I scare them, they stay scared."

Monk finished yanking off the man's clothes. The man's skin was pale, the hair on it sand-colored. He was in fairly good physical condition. He said, "Cripes, don't I get anything to wear?"

He was terrified. The terror was a gravelled harshness in his throat. Monk looked at Doc Savage and said, using the Mayan language, "I think he will split at the seams if we work on him at little."

Doc, in the same tongue, said, "Go ahead. Try making him think we are going to kill him."

Monk told the man, "Don't worry, we'll fix you up with something to wear." Then he balled the man's garments together, looked at Doc and asked, "What about the buttons and the belt buckle? They won't burn."

"We'll cut them off," Doc said.

The man eyed them. He didn't ask why they were going to burn his clothing, but he seemed to be wondering.

Monk said, "I'll be back in a minute." He left the room, went down a flight of stairs, and into the furnance room. The furnace was a coal burner, stoker fed. He went back and told Doc, "I think it'll make a hot enough fire."

Doc hauled the tall man to his feet, shoved him to the steps and down into the basement. He looked at the man intently, with no pity. "Look, brother. The young lady you tried to kill was Patricia Savage, and she's Doc's cousin, and she's one of us. If you think anyone can get away with a thing like that, you're crazy."

The tall man tried to make a break then. Doc, expecting that, was waiting, and he hit the man, knocking him to the floor. The man got up, and he knocked the fellow down again; the man began to scream in terror then, until they jammed a gag of old rags into his mouth.

Monk said, "I'll start the fire."

The tall man watched them build the fire. He saw nothing in their faces to show that they were not in earnest, that they had any intention of relenting. Monk fiddled with the stoker, got it operating, and the grinding sound as it fed coal, like bones breaking, was an excellent background for terror.

"What about the ashes?" Monk asked Doc. "Any chemist worth his salt can take ashes and tell whether they're human or not."

"We'll flush them down the sewer," Doc said. The tall man began to sob.

Pat Savage looked up when they brought the tall man, now dressed in his own clothes again, into the upstairs room where she was looking up theatrical costume firms and museums in the telephone red book, and where Ham was using the telephone to check them. After she had seen, with shock, how the tall man looked, she asked, "What did you do to him?"

Doc, without explaining the means, gave the results: "He says he was hired to kill you."

The tall man mumbled, trying to insist he had intended only to scare her, but his words were not very intelligible. Doc said, "Ham, have you learned anythng?"

Ham shook his head. "Nothing definite. There's one lead. I got hold of an outfit named Thesp-Theatrical, a costume outfit, and one guy said he thought they peddled a deerslayer suit a month or so ago, but he didn't know for sure. He's going down to the place to check the records, and I'm to call him in an hour."

"Then it may be a lead."

"Well, it could be."

Pat pointed at the tall man. "Has he told you who hired him?"

"Yes. Jeff Morgan."

"Jeff Morgan? Who on earth is he?"

"The name means nothing?"

"Not a thing."

"It means nothing to me, either," Doc told her. "Here's an idea. Suppose you get hold of Paula Argus and see if she knows Morgan. By telephone. I think it'll be safe to telephone her."

Pat nodded, and used the telephone for a while. They were listening, so she didn't need to tell them the results. Paula Argus didn't know any Jeff Morgan. Or said she didn't.

The tall man said, "I told you where he lives. Why doncha go talk to him."

"Suppose you take us," Doc said.

The tall man didn't like the notion, but he didn't have much choice. As they were leaving the house, he consoled himself by muttering, "The guy got me into this, so why should I give a damn what happens to him?"

Their transportation was a fresh problem, for the police would undoubtedly be watching for the baby service truck. Pat thought the best bet was her own car, which was parked in the same block. Maybe she wasn't on the police wanted list yet. Doc wasn't sure about that, but he decided they would take the car. There wasn't much else they could do.

"Why," Pat asked as soon as they were driving, "did this long drink of water try to kill, or scare, me?"

"He was hired."

"I know, but why? What's the motive?"

"He says he doesn't know."

"Does he know anything about what is behind this?"

"Claims he doesn't," Doc said, and then added in thoughtful state of mind, "Who knew you were involved in this, Pat."

"No one, as far as I knew," Pat said. "Except you fellows, of course."

"Paula Argus? Did she know?"

Pat's gasp came, shocked. "Yes, Paula! Paula would have known. That is, she called on you for help in the first place because she had heard me talk about you. And she would be reasonably sure you would have called me to check on her. . . . But Paula wouldn't have known I was really active in the case." Pat eyed Doc, bewildered. "Anyway, why should anyone want me killed?"

"Scared," the tall man mumbled. "I was to scare you."

"Okay, why scare me?" Pat demanded.

"You must know something," Doc suggested.

"I? Know something? But I don't know anything."

"Think," Doc directed. "Think hard. Maybe you've got something you don't know you have."

At City Island there were many boats. Doc Savage had not been there for a long time, and he was surprised at how little the place had changed. It had always been a yachting center, and apparently still was. It was now about midnight, and still raining a little, and quite dark away from the street lights; but he could tell there was lots of yachting activity, although now, because of the war, it was mostly small stuff.

The tall man had his head thrust out of the car, like a turtle sticking its head out of a shell, as they drove along. "Hey! Wait! Back up!" he said. "I think that's the name of the place there."

They reversed the car, and presently distinguished a bar which bore the name of *The Mast*. "That's it," the tall man said. "We turn here, go down to a dock, and find a boat named *Samothrace II*, and this guy will be aboard."

"You don't seem too sure of the way," Doc said suspiciously.

"I ain't never been here before."

"You haven't!" Doc was surprised. "Then why on earth are you bringing us here?"

"Look, I meet this Morgan guy downtown, see. Once at the Pirate Club, once the Ritz, once a bar on Fifty-second. He tells me where to find him if I need him, see, and where he tells me is right here. Says he lives on a boat."

He sounded so earnest about it that Doc was inclined to believe him.

Pat said, "I can't think of anything I might know that would give anyone reason to scare or kill me."

"Come on," Doc said. "We had better walk."

They passed, going quietly and cautiously, between two buildings, through a gate in a tall board fence, then between the grotesque-looking humps of shadow which were boats, sailboats, and power boats, hauled out on land for what was called dry storage. Now there was stillness about them, and odor of the sea at ebb tide, barnacles and shellfish and exposed beach.

"A dock," Pat breathed, catching Doc's arm.

The dock, narrow and spidery, appeared faintly outlined against the bay. There was, Doc decided, only one boat of any size tied to the piling. "Wait here," he said. "*Samothrace II*? You say that's the name of the boat."

"Yeah," the tall man said. "Morgan said something about an express boat. Know what that is?"

Doc knew. Express cruiser. The kind of a boat that cost a lot of money, had some living accommodations aboard, and would travel like hell. He thought the boat at the dock was that sort.

"Keep your eyes open," he warned.

A voice, a pleasant voice that was not trying to sound pleasant, addressed them, saying, "Good advice. But a little late."

They froze.

The voice added, "I've got a shotgun here, and I'm as nervous as hell."

"Watchman?" Doc asked. He didn't think it sounded like a watchman. Watchmen as a rule didn't have Harvard accents.

"Watchman?" The voice was coldly deliberative. "No. That is only in the sense of watching out for my own welfare."

"Morgan? Jeff Morgan?" Doc asked.

"That's right." The voice was surprised.

VIII

Light suddenly sprang the length of the dock, so sudden and bright that it was hair-raising. The stranger had thrown a pole switch, and the light came from three floodlamps along the cock, on poles.

Doc looked for the shotgun. And the man had one.

The man was young-looking, big-mouthed, red-headed. He probably wasn't as young as he seemed or acted, which was about twenty-five. No doubt he was nearer forty. But he was a rowdy figure in corduroys, sneakers, a flannel shirt of bull-frightening red color.

The tall man was staring at the rowdy young one. "You Jeff Morgan?" he asked.

"Jeffrey Joseph Morgan." The shotgun, an automatic, looked well used and in good shape.

"You ain't the Morgan I know," the tall man said.

Doc wheeled on the tall man. "What's that?"

"This ain't tha guy."

"He isn't the one who hired you to kill Pat?"

"Scare her," the tall man insisted. "Nah, he ain't tha one."

"Who'm I supposed to be?" Jeff Morgan demanded.

"Jeff Morgan."

"What's who I am."

Doc indicated the shotgun. "What's the idea of greeting us that way?"

Jeff Morgan contemplated the bronze man thoughtfully. He seemed to be digging around in his recollection; then he said, "There's something familiar about you. You wouldn't be a fellow named Savage? Doc Savage?"

Doc admitted he was.

"I'll be damned." Jeff Morgan sounded genuinely astonished. "That's quite a coincidence. It sure is."

"Why?" Doc asked suspiciously.

"Two reasons," Jeff Morgan said. He gestured with the shotgun. "Let's go aboard my vessel. I'm amazed for two reasons. I'll show you them both." He noticed that Monk was working around to the left, obviously planning to get in a favorable position for attack. He told Monk, "Let's not start any rough stuff without reasons. Let's hold it a minute."

They went aboard the boat. It was an express cruiser, all right. About forty-two feet on the waterline, twenty-odd thousand dollars worth of mahogany, chromium and gadgets. There didn't seem to be anyone else aboard.

Jeff Morgan turned on the broadcast radio receiver in the cabin, let it warm up, then turned in three or four different stations, not getting what he wanted.

"Maybe it'll come on in a minute. No, wait." He changed a switch, and tuned it again, this time getting the police radio. He listened for a moment. "They've been broadcasting pickup orders for you," he told Doc Savage "And for you two." He looked at Monk and Ham.

Doc said, "That isn't news to us. Is that one of the coincidences?"

Jeff Morgan nodded. "One of them. It's the one that got

me upset." He eyed them again. "That, plus the guy you sent out here to get the powder horn."

"The what?"

"Powder horn."

"You mean one of those things they used in the old days for carrying powder for muzzle-loading rifles?" Doc asked.

"That's it."

"Who came after it?"

"He said he was a friend of yours. I threw him out, after he got to talking rough."

"Where did you get this powder horn?"

Instead of answering, Morgan eyed Doc narrowly. "Did you send somebody to get it?"

"Certainly not. I never even knew of your existence until an hour or so ago."

"Well, somebody left it in the boat," Morgan said.

Jeff Morgan added that he hadn't thought particularly much about the powder horn, which was made of a genuine steer or ox horn, carved with a design and mounted with some kind of metal, probably silver. He'd supposed someone had left it lying on the galley table where he'd found it, but he couldn't imagine who it could have been. As a matter of fact, he said, he had taken the horn ashore and asked some of the loiterers in the neighborhood, other boat owners and boatyard employees, if they had seen anyone walking around with the thing. They hadn't.

"That was along this afternoon, about two o'clock," Morgan explained. "And then, right after dark, in walks this tough looking cookie, and says Doc Savage sent him, and he wants the powder horn. I didn't go for his manner, frankly, and he became quite rough. But not rough enough. As a matter of fact, I kicked his stern and put him ashore."

"Where is the powder horn?" Doc asked.

"I've got it."

"Let's see it," Doc said.

Jeff Morgan shook his head slightly. "Not so fast. Maybe what I should do is telephone the police."

Ham Brooks looked at him intently and said, "Maybe you could try it, but I don't think you would get the job done, shotgun or no shotgun."

Morgan pushed his lower lip out a little, said, "You begin to sound like the other guy."

"Cut it out. Shut up, Ham," Doc said. "The man is being reasonable."

"I'm not so sure I believe his story about a Daniel Boone powder horn," Ham said.

Morgan snorted.

Doc Savage told Morgan, "Here is, roughly, the set-up. There has been an epidemic of parts of an old-time frontiersman's outfit reaching people who profess not to have expected the items and not to know what they mean. Simultaneously there have been two murders, an attack with intent either to murder or terrify, and an extremely clever job of framing us with the murders."

Jeff Morgan's eyes popped a little. "The hell! Why'd you come to me?"

Doc pointed at the tall man. "This fellow said Jeff Morgan hired him to kill, or terrify, Pat."

"Me! My God! I never saw the lug before!" Out came Morgan's eyes still more.

"He led us here, though."

The tall man said, "This ain't tha guy, I tell you!"

"You're damned right I ain't the guy!" Morgan exclaimed. "Whoeee! What is this, anyway?"

Doc asked, "Know a man named Carlton Argus?"

"No! He's dead, isn't he? Murdered?"

"How did you know?"

"The radio. Police. You're accused of killing him and another man named Elmo Tollen."

Doc asked, "Know Paula Argus?"

"No."

"John Holland?"

"No."

Now they stopped, all of them, and looked at the radio as if it was a snake. The police announcer was giving their description, first Monk, then Ham, then Doc, and adding each time that they were wanted for murder. The surprise came when Pat heard herself added to the list, wanted for questioning. "Why, that's outrageous!" Pat gasped.

"Nice publicity you're getting," Jeff Morgan said dryly.

Doc Savage said, "Where's that powder horn?"

Morgan scowled. "I don't know why I should give it to you." But after he had looked at Doc for a while, he shrugged, said, "Oh, all right."

The horn was in a seat locker. He handed it to them. Doc said, "I suppose you've mauled over any fingerprints," but took the precaution of not touching the thing. It was unquestionably very old, but not a particularly fine nor expensive piece.

Ham asked, "Is there a telephone aboard?"

"Sure. All the conveniences of home," Morgan said. "There's water and telephone connections on most of these docks."

"Where is the instrument?"

Morgan pointed.

Ham said, "Vandergrift 3-9720," into the instrument, then told them, "That costume company where the fellow was going to look up the deerslayer outfit they thought they sold to somebody."

Doc Savage wheeled on the tall man suddenly, "This fellow who hired you, the one who said he was Jeff Morgan. . . . What did he look like?"

The tall man must have been expecting the question, because his answer was fast. "Gray-haired, over fifty I would say. Kind of tall, red face, kind of a smooth customer. The sort of guy who knows his way around, if you know what I mean."

Monk said, "That sounds like John Holland."

Doc turned to Jeff Morgan. "What business are you in?"

"Aluminum for airplanes," Jeff Morgan said. "Why?"

Doc didn't answer—he was listening to Ham Brooks saying, "Willis? This is Smith, calling about the Daniel Boone outfit. . . . You did, When? . . . Five weeks ago, that would be, wouldn't it? . . . Yes, thanks. Said his name was Bamburg, eh? What did he look like? . . . That's good enough. Thanks, Willis."

Ham hung up and turned to them. "Fellow who bought the frontiersman's outfit said his name was Bamburg. He bought a whole outfit—rifle, powder horn, leggings, coonskin cap, blouse, trousers and a knife."

Ham paused, looking at them dramatically. Then he demanded, "Who do you think this Bamburg looked like?"

"Stop playing!" Monk growled.

"Elmo Tollen," Ham said.

Doc was surprised. "The Argus butler?"

Jeff Morgan swore loudly. "Tollen? Elmo Tollen! For God's sake!" He stared at them blankly. "Butler? That guy wasn't any butler!"

"What do you mean?" Doc demanded.

Morgan said, "Wait a minute. Let me describe this Tollen I mean." He proceeded to describe the murdered Argus butler with unmistakable accuracy.

"That sounds like the Tollen we mean," Doc said.

"Well, get rid of the idea of his being a butler. That bird was worth a million at least. He should be. He owned E.T. Tollen, Incorporated, and they were the go-between for more war business than you could shake a stick at."

Doc turned to Pat, but Pat was ahead of him. She said, "All right, I'll get Paula Argus for you."

"Bring her here. Don't let the police follow you. And don't alarm her by asking her about her millionaire butler. We'll do that here."

Pat went out.

Monk began scratching his head, said, "You suppose that babe led me into a frame after all?"

"Led you!" Ham said, and snorted. "I'll bet you fell over yourself. I saw the girl."

Jeff Morgan showed some interest. "Good-looking, eh?"

"Like a picture on a wall," Ham said.

"On a magazine cover," Monk corrected him. "If she was bait, she was damned good-looking bait."

Jeff Morgan watched them, grinning. Then suddenly he lost his grin, and his eyes narrowed. He was watching Doc Savage. Presently, as he continued to watch Doc, a sheen of perspiration appeared on Morgan's forehead. He looked entirely placid, except for the sweat, which was the sweat of terror.

Doc Savage had intended to search the boat. To avoid a row, he had started unobtrusively, opening up a photograph album which he had noticed. It was a good leather-bound album and the pictures inside showed signs of some photographic skill. Mostly they were boat scenes, although there were some country shots and groups. Doc turned the pages slowly. He said, "You spend a lot of time on the water, don't you?"

Jeff Morgan didn't answer, and Doc glanced up curiously, whereupon Morgan nodded agreement. Doc noticed the sheen of perspiration on the man's head, but did not comment.

He went back to the album. Something in the album was working on Morgan's mind, striking Morgan with horror. Doc turned more pages, searching the faces and scenes in the snapshots. He hadn't found anything when Morgan began to swing slowly toward the shotgun. He had put the gun down, but now he started reaching for it.

Doc yelled, "Monk! Watch his gun!" And dived for Morgan.

Morgan made a barking sound of frenzied excitement, a rather strange noise to be coupled with such desperate movement. He got his hand on the gun, but didn't get it lifted before Doc had hold of the weapon also. Morgan shoved violently against Doc, used the shove to propel himself backward through the deckhouse window. It was a window, not a porthole. Large and square, and the glass went out, letting Morgan through.

He knew what he was doing. He went on over the rail, over the side of the boat. But not clumsily. He grasped the rail with his hands and straightened out so that he landed on his feet in a small boat. They could tell by the noise that he had landed in a dinghy.

Doc said, "Get him! Head him off!"

Monk and Ham were on deck a moment later. It seemed blackly dark. Probably it was no darker than it had been, but their eyes were accustomed to the light in the cabin.

Ham said softly, "I don't hear him!"

The stillness and the blackness was hair-raising.

"There should be a boathook somewhere," Monk grumbled, and made some noise moving about. Presently he said, "Here it is!" Monk brought the boathook back and jabbed it over the rail. The end splashed in the bay. Monk said, "Hell! Where'd the boat go?"

"Maybe there wasn't any boat," Ham suggested.

"Sure there was. He didn't splash when he hit the water."

"Jove! Maybe he's hanging to the rail by his fingers somewhere!"

Ham began exploring the rail, and he was doing that when an outboard motor started violently. It was a big four-cylinder job, and it took off at wide throttle. They saw flame spill from the exhaust stacks, for the motor was the type that exhausted above the surface; the drooling fire went away.

Doc wheeled, dived for the express cruiser controls.

"Get the springlines off!" he said urgently. "Maybe we can overtake him."

But when he put a thumb on the starter buttons, there was a dead lack of response.

Monk scrambled below and looked. "The starting batteries are gone. Probably ashore being charged."

Ham yelled, "You dope, we've got light."

"Different batteries."

Doc Savage listened to the outboard motor sound departing. It was, he decided, doing around forty knots, and its doubtful if the express cruiser could have overtaken the little craft anyway.

"We might as well relax," he said.

Monk came slamming out on deck and dived into the owner's cabin, saying he was looking for a rifle. He didn't find one and reappeared, demanding, "What lit that guy's fuse, anyway?"

"I think it was something in that album of photographs," Doc said. "Let's take a look."

They turned four pages, and found it. Jeff Morgan must have known Doc was that close to finding the photograph, must have realized too that Doc couldn't very well miss it.

"Blazes!" Monk breathed.

". . . five, six, seven, eight." Ham said, coutning the figures in the photograph. "I'll be damned! Everybody has been lying to us!"

The photograph was a yachting group, eight persons gathered on a power boat, an express cruiser. This particular cruiser, in fact. In the background was a rickety pier and a bleak looking bit of land which Doc, from the general appearance of the terrain, decided might be one of the islands off the Maine coast. The photograph was remarkably sharp.

The fact which amazed them was that included in the picture were the two dead men, Carlton Argus and Elmo Tollen, and also John Holland, Jeff Morgan, their prisoner the tall man and Paula Argus. The two others were little more difficult to make out.

Suddenly Monk pointed. "Hey, I know that guy!"

The man was chunky, rather dignified, about the same size as the murdered Argus butler, Elmo Tollen.

"Who is he?" Doc demanded.

"The phony butler. Remember, at the Argus place, I told you I didn't think the butler who let me in was the one who took me to the room, that orchid place, where the body was?

Well, this is the phony butler, the one who took me to the room."

"Who is the other man? Any of you know him?"

The stranger was taller than anyone else in the picture, lean and pole-like, a gaunt frontiersman type, a man who could have been a woods ranger during colonial days.

None of them knew him.

But he seemed somehow quite familiar to them because of the buckskins he was wearing, the coonskin cap and buckskin shirt and trousers and leggings, the long rifle he was carrying, the powder horn slung across his shoulders.

Monk brought the powder horn over and compared it with the one in the photograph. He moistened his lips. "They're the same."

IX

Doc Savage straightened and began getting gray-faced. He had thought of something, and it had shocked him so badly that he had trouble getting his voice to say, "Pat! They tried to kill her once!"

Ham, not getting the thought, said, "But Pat's all right now. She'll get Paula Argus—"

"Morgan knows where she went!"

Monk Mayfair said, "Oh, hell!" in a frightened voice.

Ham understood. "If Morgan tips them off—" He wheeled for the companionway.

"Wait! Where are you going?" Doc said sharply.

"Pat went to get Paula Argus. Maybe we can head her off before they have time to pull anything—"

"Let's try something first. Where would Pat logically go to find the girl?"

"Her apartment, I suppose—"

"All right," Doc said. "Let's try the telephone. It won't do any harm—" He went silent, jumping for the tall man.

The tall man—they had been keeping a close watch on him throughout—had thought there was a chance to make a break. He had started silently for the companionway. Doc came toward him, and the man tried kicking. He was slow and Doc got his foot, yanking him off the companion steps

and the man slammed down hard on the floor. Monk hurriedly stepped on the man's neck.

"Brother, you've got a rough time ahead of you," Monk
told him, and threw weight on his foot.

The tall man twisted on the floor, made painful noises
with his throat, looking up at them with eyes that for the first
time were genuinely frightened.

Doc picked up the telephone. He remembered the
Argus apartment number and gave it. Presently a man's voice
answered, a gruffly confident voice that Doc decided must
belong to a policeman or the family doctor. The latter, he
hoped.

Doc changed his voice as completely as he could, made
it important, demanding, asked. "Who is speaking?"

"Doctor Abrams," the other said. "If this is the newspapers, I'm sorry but you'll have to—"

"Put Patricia Savage on the wire," Doc said.

"Who?"

Doc said, "This is Captain Clements of homicide. I want
to talk to Patricia Savage. Put her on the wire."

"Just a minute," the doctor said.

Monk and Ham were holding their breathing. Doc nodded slightly, and they exhaled noisily with relief.

"Hello," Pat's voice said presently. "What do you want?"

Doc changed to French, whcih Pat could handle fluently,
and said, "You're fooling around with dynamite, we've suddenly discovered." Still speaking French, he told her about
the photograph. "Everyone connected with the case so far is
in that picture, which proves they've been lying when they
told us they didn't know each other." He added the information that Jeff Morgan, who was one of the men in the picture,
had escaped, and that in view of the earlier attempts on her
life—or to scare her—Pat had better be careful.

"What shall I do?" Pat asked.

"Is Paula Argus with you?"

"Yes. Doc, I don't think that girl is guilty of anything.
Really I don't."

"You stay there—wait, are the police there?"

"No."

"Who was the man who answered the phone?"

"Their family doctor."

"Don't trust him too much," Doc said. "In fact, don't
trust anybody, and don't leave. Don't let anyone come in.

We'll get into town, get the place covered, then telephone you when it's safe to come out."

"Okay," Pat said. "And I don't think Paula is a crook."

Monk was looking on the back of the photograph which he had removed from the album. "Boy, we're lucky," he exclaimed. "Look what's on the back. Their names." He ran down the list of names, added, "The fake butler was named R. E. McFellen." Monk pointed at the tall man. "And you're C. Allen Culteel."

The tall man showed his teeth unpleasantly. "The name is Cultell—tell as in you *tell* someone something. Not teel."

Ham demanded, "Who's the guy we don't know, Monk?"

"R. Jones-Field," Monk said.

Ham showed surprise. "I've heard that name. . . . I think it was in connection with some kind of law business. . . . Let me think."

Doc Savage was eyeing the tall man. "Cultell? You head a big industrial engineering firm specializing in metals, that right?"

The tall man tipped his head slightly, assenting. "That is correct."

He was not using his former lowbrow manner or tone, a fact which Monk noticed with astonishment. "All of a sudden, you sound pretty highbrow," Monk said suspiciously. "What were you doing before, putting on an act? Or is this the act?"

The tall man said nothing.

Doc told Monk, "If he is Cultell, it was an act. C. Allen Cultell is quite a prominent industrial engineer in the metals field."

Ham snapped his fingers loudly. "Now I remember who the eighth man is! Jones-Field! With the government, or rather the army. One of those agencies that handled airplane contracts."

Doc Savage said, "Come on. Let's get going. I'm still worried about Pat."

The matter of transportaton gave them some trouble. Pat had taken her car, which was the machine they had been using, and a taxicab seemed too risky. But they finally had to take a cab. They took two, to lessen the chance of the police bagging all of them.

Doc rode in the ead cab with the tall man, Cultell. Cultell was surly. He kept kneading the back of his neck where

Monk had come down hard with a foot, and when they passed under street lights, Doc could see the man was scowling.

Doc asked, "Care to talk about this?"

"The hell with you!" Cultell said bitterly. "Why couldn't you have attended to your own damned business?"

"Why was Jones-Field wearing that deerslayer outfit in the photograph?"

"You're supposed to be quite a buzz-bomb, aren't you? The great Doc Savage!" Cultell said.

"That attitude won't help."

"Maybe not," the tall man said sourly. "But I'll tell you this much: You haven't got me in a spot where I have to tell you anything."

"Perhaps not. But it's all going to come out, you know."

Cultell laughed, not very pleasantly. "You think so? You've learned a hell of a lot so far, haven't you?"

"Not enough to brag about."

"You haven't learned a damned thing, as a matter of fact."

Doc shrugged. "At least we've got all of you tied together. The photograph did that."

"So what?"

"Which part of the Daniel Boone suit did you get?" Doc asked casually.

"The sh—" Cultell began, and stopped. His laugh came again, edged with strain. "Never mind."

"The shirt, eh?" Doc said.

Cultell didn't answer.

For a while Doc watched the rear view mirror to make sure that Monk and Ham, in the other taxi, were coming along without mishap.

"We have you all tied together in another way," he told Cultell finally. "Metals."

The tall man didn't entirely keep emotion off his face. "That's your imagination," he muttered.

"No. I think not. Metals. All of you are in the metals industry in some form or other. That helps make a package of a lot of you."

"Imagination. You heard Brooks say Jones-Field was with the army handling contracts."

"Airplane contracts. They make airplanes out of metal."

Cultell didn't say anything.

Doc Savage watched the tall man closely, presently concluding that the man was quite frightened.

"Why were you going to kill Pat?" Doc asked suddenly.

"I wasn't," Cultell said briefly. "She was to be scared. That was all. I've told you that."

Whatever the man is scared of, Doc reflected, it isn't fear of being held accountable for what he tried on Pat, whether it was murder or not. Doc tried again, saying, "Of course you're all going to jail together for the murder of Argus and Tollen."

"If you only knew it," Cultell said, "that proves how wrong you are."

The thing he is afraid of isn't the murder charge, Doc reflected.

He remarked, "That deerslayer outfit was well scattered, wasn't it."

Cultell gave back a wooden, gray-faced silence.

He's in terror of that buckskin outfit, Doc decided. What the devil?

They paid off their cabs two blocks from the Argus apartment house and collected in a doorway for consultation. Cultell said, "I've a damned good notion to yell for the police."

Monk told him, "You do, and you'll be a dead body in about two seconds flat." Monk sounded so utterly in earnest that Cultell's lips loosened slightly with terror, and his belligerence subsided.

"Ham, you work around the block and get on the other side of the Argus place," Doc said. "I'll scout this side, and we'll meet back here in fifteen minutes."

"What's the idea of all the phenagling around?" Monk wanted to know.

"If they have any kind of a plant waiting for Pat, I'd like to grab the fellows," Doc explained. "Maybe he would be more communicative than Cultell, here."

"Oh."

Ham drifted away. The lateness of the hour, far past midnight now, made their presence more conspicuous, but at the same time it would make it easier to spot any other skulkers in the neighborhood. "Watch Cultell," Doc told Monk. "I will," Monk said. And Doc moved away himself, cautiously, but not so that he appeared to be cautious.

There were a few places open, a very few, but almost no

one on the streets. He spotted Pat's car, crossed over to it, and made sure the keys were in the switch. They were. He went on, passing the Argus apartment house, wishing he could go inside, but not daring to. There was no doorman now; probably there was none after midnight. He went back to Monk, and presently, Ham joined them, saying, "Coast seems clear."

Doc said, "You make the telephone call. I would do it, but I'm a little conspicuous. Try that lunch room over yonder."

Ham went away. He was gone quite a while. Time dragged, and they were sober with their thoughts, their eyes probing anxiously at each walking figure which appeared, lest it be a policeman. Cultell breathed noisily, in short jerks, ridden by his own nerves. There was a continual film of perspiration on Cultell's face. He was not enjoying this.

Worried, Ham came back. "Doc! There's no answer! No one answers at the Argus number!"

Doc had the feeling that his skin had gotten tight all over.

"We'll go up there," he said.

There was, they found, but one elevator operator on duty in the building at this time of night. A young man, he was evidently a student, for he was reading a text on toxicology. A student chemist, obviously. Monk, who was a famous chemist, showed alarm lest he be recognized, and was first out of the elevator cage when they got to the top.

"Hold the cage here," Doc told the boy.

"I'm sorry, I—"

"Only for a moment," Doc said. He wanted the elevator handy in case they had to make a quick escape. He told Ham, "You wait here," and Ham nodded.

The door of the Argus apartment was not locked. It stood partly open.

There was a dead man spread out on the floor inside. A thick man, rather elderly, who had died from having the front of his skull bashed in.

Doc pulled back. "Keep your hands off things," he said. He lifted his voice, called, "Pat, Pat!"

No answer came.

He went back to the elevator, told the operator, "You'd better see this." The operator, he was glad to see, had been standing in the cage door watching them. The operator could testify that they hadn't had a hand in the death of the thick man. "How's your stomach?" Doc said. "It had better be good. There's a dead man in the Argus apartment."

The boy became wide-eyed. "Jesus! Another murder in here!"

"Looks that way." Doc led him to the body, asked, "Know the man?"

"That's Doctor Abrams," the boy said.

"The Argus family doctor?"

"Yes."

"We want you for a witness," Doc told the boy. "We want to search the apartment. Come on."

The search did not take long. Pat was not there. Paula Argus was not there. And there was no sign of violence other than the slain doctor.

"Miss Argus," Doc said to the boy. "When did she leave?"

The young man had been staring at them. He said, "I—I think I know who you are. Aren't you Doc Savage?" He looked at Monk. "And Mr. Mayfair?"

"When did Miss Argus leave?"

"About, I would say, forty minutes ago."

"Was another woman with her?"

"Yes."

"Who else?"

"A man. One man."

"Know him?"

"No, sir, I didn't."

Ham had the group photograph they'd found in the album on Jeff Morgan's boat. Doc said, "Show him that picture, Ham." And then, after the operator had examined the photograph: "Was the man one of that group?"

The boy was distressed. "I don't know, sir. To tell the truth, I don't recall seeing his face. He was tall and wore a raincoat, as I recall. He could have been any one of those men.

Cultell said bitterly, "Well, it wasn't me, thank God." His voice had a hoarseness that caused them all to stare at him. Cultell was deeper in terror.

The boy was nervous. "I've got to call the police. I'll get in trouble if I don't."

"We're clearing out," Doc told him. "So go ahead and

call them. Better use the telephone downstairs, in case there might be fingerprints in the apartment."

The boy looked uncomfortable. He spoke to Monk, for whom he apparently had the most awe. "I can refrain, if you wish, from telling the police you were here. I—ah—am aware that the police are searching for you gentlemen."

Monk was pleased. "No, thanks. Don't get yourself in trouble. Go ahead and call them. Tell them just what happened."

Doc added, "And tell them the murderer kidnapped Paula Argus and Pat Savage."

Eyes made round and staring by astonishment, the boy watched them leave.

X

They rode north in Pat's car, turned left to catch the cross-town drive through Central Park. On a deserted part of the drive, Doc pulled in to the curb, told Monk, "Will you get out, grab a fistful of mud and smear a little over our license plate. The police may have the license of Pat's car. Probably have." Monk did this. They got rolling again.

Cultell stirred his tall form angrily. "What the hell do you plan to do with me?" he demanded.

Monk said, "Brother, your friends have got Pat Savage. We think a lot of Pat. So what—"

"They're not friends of mine!" Cultell snapped.

"—what we'll probably do is cut you up and feed you to fish," Monk finished. He sounded earnest. Cultell eyed him, moistened his lips, moved his shoulders wearily.

Doc said, "Cultell, you're pretty scared, aren't you?"

"With three murders? Why not?"

"The murder of the doctor wasn't scheduled, was it?" Doc asked.

Cultell jumped visibly. "What the devil do you mean?"

"I'm beginning to get an idea of the shape of this thing. My advice to you would be to come clean."

"You willing to make a deal?" Cultell demanded.

"The deal would be for us to drop everything?"

Cultell jumped again. He hadn't expected that. He rubbed a hand against his thigh nervously. "Damned if I don't believe you do know quite a lot. . . . Yes, drop it. That would be the deal. Get your friend Pat free. Then drop it."

"We can't drop murder," Doc said.

"Why not? The police will go ahead and take care of that."

"The police," Doc said grimly, "will hang it on us if we don't turn up somebody else for them."

The truth of this silenced Cultell for a while. He continued to rub his leg, fell to coughing. He sounded somewhat ill, so rampant was the fear inside him.

Monk said, "Friend, if anything happens to Pat, I wouldn't want to be in your shoes."

Cultell said nothing.

Doc Savage was driving. He made a left turn, coasted in to the curbing and stopped.

"See any signs of police?" he asked.

They were half a block down the street from John Holland's house. They searched the vicinity with their eyes for a while. "I'm going in," Doc said. "If he's there, I'll bring him out, and we'll pry some truth out of him."

Cultell cleared his throat. "He won't be there."

Monk made an angry growling noise. "Brother, if he isn't you'd better wish you hadn't been born—or talk."

Doc went to John Holland's house.

Holland wasn't there.

There was a metallic cast of fury on Doc Savage's face when he came back to the car. He got into the machine, looked at Cultell intently for a while. He said, "Monk, there's a psychiatrist on Central Park West. Doctor Wilfred Bedell, a friend of mine. I hate to pull him into this mess, but I think he will be willing to let us use his office and his equipment."

Monk nodded. "Now you're talking."

Doc started the motor.

"Wait a minute!" Cultell mumbled. "You figuring on pulling something on me?"

"You're going to talk."

"The hell I am."

Doc told the man unpleasantly, "We've fooled around with you too long now. There are perfectly feasible methods of making you talk, whether you wish or not."

Cultell sneered. "Truth serum? I've heard of that stuff. It's not dependable."

"This isn't truth serum, exactly. I take it you've not familiar with some of the new methods psychiatrists use?"

"Psychiatrists? They're the guys who doctor your mind, aren't they?" Cultell settled back, added smugly, "It'll take a hell of a mind-doctor to get anything out of me, I'm telling you."

Monk laughed unpleasantly.

"What's so funny?" Cultell demanded.

"You—not knowing what's going to happen to you," Monk told him.

Doc believed Cultell felt none of the confidence he was voicing. He thought Cultell was in a state of mind where the application of a little terror might save them considerable time and effort; also there was always the chances of failure when they did start working on the man with drugs.

"Cultell," Doc said. "You might as well know what we're going to do with you. It will make no difference. But to understand it, you'll have to keep in mind what you doubtless already know about psychiatric difficulties. You know, of course, that individuals are rendered neurotic by the appearance of something or other in their minds which creates an anxiety. This anxiety, which has an effect on the mental system of the individual as real as the effect of an infected wound in his physical body, isn't always something of which the victim is aware. He is aware of such things as trouble with his wife, danger of being fired from his job. Usually he is aware of these obvious mental anxieties, but usually these are not lastingly serious, because when you know what your trouble is, you can always do something about it."

Cultell looked puzzled, said, "This doesn't have any connection with the wild and wooly stuff we've been having. What are you leading up to?"

"I'm getting to that. In psychoneurosis, the patient does not consciously know what is causing his disturbances. The job of the psychiatrist is to work with the patient until the hidden cause is found, then dragged into the open; and the patient, when he once sees what is wrong, usually cures himself. This is called psychoanalysis. The war has broadened the use of one tool of psychoanalysis which was hitherto to regarded with some doubt. Drugs."

Cultell grinned uneasily.

"You're getting back to that truth serum business," he said.

"The drug," Doc said, "induces a mental condition where the patient talks without any inhibitions whatever, and naturally most of his talking is done about the things which are bothering his subconscious the most."

Cultell shuddered. "That stuff makes you sick as the devil, don't it?"

"Not necessarily. But you already knew about the method, didn't you?"

"I've read about it in magazines."

"Well, that's what we are going to do to you. And I can assure you that you'll tell everything you know."

Cultell sat very still for a while. There was not much color left in his face. "I'm afraid of drugs," he muttered.

Doc concealed his elation. "Meaning you would rather talk without it?"

Cultell moistened his lips.

"That's right," he said.

"Let's have it."

"They're out of town, Cultell said.

"All of them?"

"Yes."

"Where did they go?"

"Jones-Field's summer home. On one of the Maine coast islands."

"How do you know they're there?"

"Because that's where we all agreed to go and settle this thing . . ." He went suddenly silent, and stared with fright at a car that had slid up silently and halted in the street beside them.

There was one man in the car, and he leaned over and rolled down the side window and stared at them.

"It's that snotty Assistant D. A.," Monk breathed.

It was Assistant District Attorney Ivans. He eyed them in astonishment. Then he did something that was typically Ivans. A man with less ego would have driven, and driven like hell, for police assistance, Ivans didn't. Ivans got out, said, "You're under arrest."

Doc Savage looked at Ivans, and Doc was impressed. Ivans was overbearing, a bore, unreasonably ambitious, but he had an ample supply of the quantity called unadulterated guts. Ivans was scared; he couldn't quite keep his hands from shaking. He didn't have a gun. But he said firmly, "You're my prisoners."

"For God's sake!" Monk exclaimed, and stuck his head out to see whether the neighborhood was swarming with police. It wasn't.

Ham said, "He hasn't got a gun."

Doc eyed Ivans and demanded, "What on earth are you doing here?" Normally Ivans might not have answered that, but he was scared, so he said, "I came to see Mr. Holland. He does not answer his telephone." He moistened his lips, added, "If you have weapons, you will please toss them out in the street."

Doc opened the car door. "Get in."

Ivans drew back. "I'm damned if I—" He began to struggle as Doc got hold of him, and he yelled once, violently, before Monk was out and had a hat jammed over his mouth.

Monk cocked a fist, asked, "Shall I put him to sleep?" He sounded hopeful.

"Take it easy," Doc said. "The guy has a lot of nerve, along with his bad manners."

"What you gonna do with him?"

"Why not carry him along with us?"

Monk didn't think much of the idea. "Why?"

"Maybe we can talk him into thinking we're innocent," Doc suggested. "Which isn't likely. But if he is along when we straighten this out, if we do, it might be a big help with the police."

"Well—okay." Monk helped jam Ivans into the car. The Assistant District Attorney fought with considerable violence and not much dignity. Finally Monk said, "I'm gonna have to choke him a little."

"Go head. I would enjoy doing a little of it myself," Doc said.

He started the car and drove toward their delapidated warehouse-hangar on the Hudson waterfront. He asked Cultell, "You can point out this island to us?"

"Sure," Cultell said.

When they were on the superhighway headed south in the sixties, Doc asked Ivans, "Are the police watching our Hudson River place?"

Monk released Ivans' mouth, and Ivans said, "How the hell would I know! I'll see you electrocuted, so help me God!" Ivans sounded as if he considered the police somewhat to blame for his predicament.

Cultell told him, "It's your own fault."

"Who the hell are you?" Ivans snarled. Then he tried to yell for help, but Monk clamped his hat over Ivans' mouth again, and kept it there.

There did not seem to be a police guard at the warehouse. But Doc was cautious, and drove on down the street, made a turn into a side street, circled and came back. He saw nothing alarming, but was not reassured.

"I have a hunch this will be fast going. The police aren't fools enough to leave this place unwatched," he said. "So hold your hats."

He swung the car toward the warehouse entrance. The door of the place, the big one, was operated by a radio control, the only hitch being that this was Pat's car and there was no transmitter of the correct frequency. Doc slid to a stop in front of the big door, said, "Drive it in, Ham," and ran to the small door. Across the street, a man came out of a store and yelled, "Here! Here, now!" A cop.

Doc got the small door open with the gadget control, jumped inside, threw the switch which opened the big door.

As the big door raised slowly, Monk got the car in motion. He drove inside. The policeman was crossing the street. He bellowed angrily, lifted his gun, began shooting. But the big overhead door, of steel, was now closing. The policeman's bullets made loud drum-tap sounds against the panel.

Doc got the lights on. "The seaplane," he ordered. "and move fast."

He had decided by now that the police hadn't been inside the warehouse. They were merely watching the place. Outside, he could hear the officer yelling, and getting an answer. Evidently there were other police in the neighborhood.

Ham ran to the seaplane.

Cultell and Ivans both picked this time to try to escape. Monk, trying to control both of them, made angry noises, finally was reduced to yelling, "Hey, Doc! Help me!" Doc joined the mêlée. He used his fists, for he was angry, and helped Monk haul the victims to the seaplane.

Ham had the seaplane engines filling the interior with thunder. The big doors at the riverward end were lifting slowly, rumbling. Doc fought the springlines which held the plane in the slip. They were getting one lucky break—there was nothing in front of the plane that had to be moved before they could get the craft outside. Doc got into the cabin as the ship began moving away from the work floats in the slip.

They were well out in the river before there was any shooting at them, and then the firing was ineffectual. Presently they were in the air.

Ham flew. Doc Savage went back into the cabin, turned on the lights, and met Ivans' baleful stare. "Feel all right?" Doc asked.

"Kidnapping and murder and God knows what else!" Ivans said violently.

"Don't get too mad to listen to this fellow's story," Doc said, indicating Cultell.

Cultell scowled. "I didn't agree to tell anything in front of an Assistant District Attorney."

Doc Savage studied Cultell's face, adding to his earlier belief that physical danger wouldn't be a very great factor with this man. The fellow was a thinker, a planner, and the dangers that were most real to him were dangers to the mind.

Doc, having eyed him intently for a while, said, "I was afraid we made a mistake not shooting you full of that drug. But it's not too late. And this time, God help you."

Fear lifted Cultell's lips enough to show his teeth.

"I guess I'm stuck."

"I guess you are. How many of you are involved in this?"

"Seven."

"There are eight in that photograph."

"The girl isn't in it. Paula Argus. She doesn't know what it's all about."

"What started it."

Cultell squirmed. "That goes back a little."

Doc turned to Ivans. "You'd better get this. Move over here where you can hear." And Ivans scowled at him, but changed his seat. There was a normal amount of motor roar inside the ship. Ham, handling the controls, had lined out across northern Manhattan Island and the Bronx.

Doc told Cultell. "It goes back to the war, doesn't it? To some kind of a deal you seven were involved in? A deal concerning metals?"

Cultell nodded. "Mind telling me how the hell you figure that out?"

"All of you were in the metal business in some connection. All of you were active on the wartime industrial stage."

"Well," Cultell said, "it doesn't go back that far. It only goes back six months ago, to a house party we all attended on that island. We were Jones-Field's guests. Jones-Field put on that frontiersman's outfit as a gag, which was supposed to invoke a curse. Well, since then, attempts have been made at various times to kill all of us."

Doc looked at Cultell intently to see if the man was lying. It was hard to tell.

"What do you mean, curse?"

Cultell shrugged. "That buckskin outfit belonged to some old guy, Jones-Field's great-great-somebody or other, a relative. Somebody put a curse on this ancestor. The curse was supposed to ride with his outfit, forever. A story like that."

"Oh."

"I know it's nuts. Anyway, strange attempts have been made to kill us, and before each one, the victim got a part of that deerslayer suit, as you call it. Finally Carlton Argus was killed, then Elmo Tollen, and we decided to go to Jones-Feild's island, all of us, and see what on earth was back of it."

"That the story?" Doc asked.

"Yes."

Doc caught Monk's eye, and Monk proceeded to make various grimaces conveying that he didn't believe a word of it.

"Hah!" Ivans said explosively.

Doc asked Ivans, "Don't you believe it?"

"It's a bigger cock-and-bull story than anything you've told me." Ivans said angrily. "And that's going some!"

XI

The island was an island by grace of a stretch of water five feet deep at low tide and a hundred yards wide, which was all that separated the crooked-thumb of a neck of land from the Maine coast. The result in all was not bad, since five feet was not deep enough to allow much of a tide rip and as a result there was a partly land-locked harbor about half a mile long and up to a hundred yards in width. The wind was just right; they came in from the sea, dropping down in an easy normal glide, and touched water. Ham called back, "Do we go right ashore?"

"Why not?" Doc asked. "We have an Assistant District Attorney of the City of New York aboard for protection."

Ivans said, "Don't be funny!" He didn't sound as sure of himself as he had.

Ham sent the seaplane in toward shore, keeping enough speed that he could nose up into the wind and keep off the rocky beach. It became clear that they would have to anchor offshore, and Doc climbed out on the nose. There were four mooring buoys offshore a few dozen yards, and he picked up one of those, made their mooring line fast and gave Ham the throat-cutting gesture which silenced the engines.

Fifty yards away was the dock which had been the locale of the photograph they had found on Jeff Morgan's boat.

Beyond, slightly higher, was a lodge of some size. Not a yachting place, but a rustic looking structure of stone and logs.

A splash caused Doc to wheel nervously, but it was only Monk putting over the rubber boat. The inflation gadget hissed, and the boat squirmed and grew into shape. Doc turned his attention back to the island. He had already decided that he didn't like the quietness of the place, the look of stillness.

"Cultell and I will go ashore first, alone," he said. He was watching Cultell's face, but it told him nothing.

The rubber boat, or raft, was a G. I. job which did not respond to oars with any special grace. Cultell sat in the stern and watched the island fixedly. Doc rowed backward, facing the island himself, and tension made a stiffness in his arms, a tightness in his hands.

Then a figure appeared on a path. It was the boisterous looking Jeff Morgan, hatless, his hair a red blaze in the very early morning sunlight.

Morgan kept walking until he was on the dock, and stopped there to watch them. His expression was unpleasant.

He threw an angry question at Cultell. "What the devil did you bring them here for?"

"I had to. I told them—"

"Shut up!" Doc said.

Ignoring the order, Cultell said, "I told them that the—"

Reaching forward, Doc struck Cultell above the ear with his fist, putting some steam behind the blow, upsetting Cultell unconscious in the raft.

Morgan scowled. "You're not welcome here, Savage."

"I did not expect to be," Doc said, and ran his eyes over the island, gripped by the feeling of being watched, perhaps menaced. He added, "We're coming ashore."

"Come ahead," Morgan said after a while. "I don't believe the mess can be made worse."

"Is Pat here?"

"That bronze-haired girl? Yes."

"Is she all right?"

"Mad as hell," Morgan said. His lips twisted in the ghost of a grin. "She's quite a ball of electricity, that girl."

Monk and Ham and Ivans came ashore, Doc rowing back after them. Cultell was still out from Doc's blow, and Monk carried him up the path toward the log lodge.

Doc told Morgan, "The fat is in the fire. So if you are planning to start something, don't!"

Morgan indicated Cultell. "He talked, did he?"

"Yes."

Sober-faced, Morgan said, "That surprises me. I didn't think he would."

Doc walked warily, for his feeling of danger was strong. He was not sure of himself. He was bluffing, letting Morgan think that Cultell had told everything, whereas all probabilities were that the man had told little but lies. Some of his suspicion of danger might come from his own uncertainty, but he was inclined to put more trust in his feeling for trouble.

They reached the house, though, without incident. The door was closed, but Morgan went to it, announced wearily to someone within that, "The whole thing has blown up. They got Cultell to talk."

Presently the door opened.

The man who had worn the buckskins in the picture, Jones-Field, was inside, and two other men. One of the latter was John Holland. The remaining man was recognizable from the description Monk had given, and from the photograph, as the fake butler, McFellen, who had led Monk into the murder frameup at the Argus apartment. They were placed at widely separated parts of the room, near doors or windows. Doc, sweeping them briefly with his eyes, did not like the way they were standing, nor the way they held their hands. They were not holding weapons, but he suspected weapons were close.

"Pat?" Doc called. Strain made his voice louder than he expected.

"In here," Pat's voice answered from another room.

"You all right?"

"I'm tied up. So is Paula."

"Take it easy," Doc said quietly. "This thing is about over."

"Watch them," Pat warned uneasily. "I think they're all dangerous."

Doc thought so also, but he kept the alarm out of his voice and said, "The have nothing to gain now." He had not taken his eyes off the men. He indicated Ivans and said, "This is Assistant District Attorney Ivans of New York."

They didn't like the presence of Ivans, their eyes indicated.

"Mr. Ivans wants your statement," Doc said. "Briefly now. More fully later."

"What statements?" Holland demanded.

"Corroborating what Mr. Cultell told us."

Doc Savage was sure, for a moment, that they weren't going to talk, that violence was going to explode. But Ivans saved the moment.

Ivans said, "The District Attorney's office has no desire to be particularly tough on you, providing you are cooperative."

It was John Holland who said, "If you expect us to confess that seven of us got together and swindled the United States government out of several million dollars, you're crazy. For my part, you can talk to my attorneys about that."

Ivans batted his eyes, startled at the discovery of a sordid wartime scheme of graft. But he handled the find nicely, and much better than Doc thought he would. He said, "Suit yourself. That will be a federal case, and out of my hands." He levelled his arm at them. "But those murders! They're my business!"

Holland, pleased by his little victory, spoke more freely. He said, "The same thing happened to all of us. We all got a demand for a half million dollars. Blackmail."

Ivans glanced at Doc Savage. He didn't want to handle the questioning, his glance said. He didn't know enough about it.

Doc thought: You probably know as much as I do.

"What was the threat if you didn't pay?" Doc asked.

"The threat was to give the government proof of this imaginary—mind you, I say imaginary—fraud which—"

"It wasn't imaginary," Doc said.

"The federal government will have to prove differently."

Doc said, "You were going to be turned in if you didn't pay?"

"That's right."

"Did you pay?"

"Naturally not."

"Then what?"

"We started getting parts of that frontiersman's outfit by way of warning—"

Doc lifted a hand. "Just a minute. Why would a flintlock rifle, or a powder horn, or buckskin leggings, be a warning?"

Holland turned to Jones-Field. "Tell him."

Jones-Field hesitated, and Doc saw menace radiating from the man, and indecision. He saw Jones-Field control a frenzied desire for violence, with considerable effort.

"That part is silly," Jones-Field said. "My great-great-great grandfather was Cultus Field, a notorious forest pirate in the lower Mississippi river country back in the primitive days. He had, as a matter of fact, quite a bloody career, through which he led a charmed life. His good luck he attributed to that outfit of buckskins and his flintlock rifle. He died a natural death, and the clothing has passed down as a sort of family heirloom, together with the story of it bringing good luck to any rascal who wore it."

Doc asked, "Why did you wear it that day for the photograph?"

"A gag."

"What do you mean, gag?"

"There had been some drinking and kidding that day, and I said I would put on the outfit and it would bring us good luck. I was a little tight, and it seemed a funny idea at the time."

Doc asked, "Did you send the parts of the outfit to these different people?"

"Certainly not!"

"Who did?"

"The blackmailer, whoever he is."

"As a matter of fact," Doc said, "aren't you quite sure the blackmailer is one of your own number? One of the seven?"

No one answered.

On the floor where Monk had put him, Cultell opened his eyes. He kept them open, listening, not saying anything. He had not, Doc was sure, just regained consciousness. He had been awake some time.

"Suppose you give your version of the murders," Doc said.

Holland looked at Morgan. "Suppose you tell that, Jeff."

"Why the hell should I tell it? I don't know anything about it." Morgan nodded at McFellen. "You were there, McFellen."

McFellen scowled, hesitated, then said, "Carlton Argus called me and told me Paula had gone to get Doc Savage. Argus said he didn't like the idea, and would I come over and help him figure out some lies to tell Savage. I went over. I found Argus dead. Murdered."

He scowled again, this time at Monk, added, "I got the not-so-good idea of framing Savage, but you turned up instead, so I framed you. I led you into the orchid culture room—"

Monk was batting his eyes. "Hell, wait a minute!" he said. "You weren't the guy who opened the door and let me in when the girl brought me to the apartment."

"No, I was the second butler. Remember, you were looking at a stuffed animal head in the armory? Well, I rushed you into the orchid room quick, so Paula wouldn't see me, and hoping you wouldn't get suspicious about two butlers."

"Paula didn't know you were in the apartment?"

"Of course not."

"How'd you get around in there like that without her seeing you?"

"I knew the family habits, and the real butler was helping me."

"Oh, Elmo Tollen was helping you?"

"Yes. I put you in the orchid-culture room, and Elmo Tollen was in the greenhouse part with the body, and it was his voice which spoke to you to make you think Carlton Argus was alive. Then Tollen slid out of the window on a rope he'd rigged, got to a window of an apartment below and pulled in the rope. I understand Savage did the same thing later to fool the police. I guess he saw enough signs to know what had happened."

"That's right," Doc said. "There were marks on the window sill and frame."

Monk frowned. "Somebody told us Tollen was a millionaire. That right?"

"No. He has a distant cousin who owns a company of some sort, but there was no financial connection. No, Tollen had merely accepted money in the past to help us. In other words, for a little pay, he was one of us."

"Then who killed Tollen, and why?" Doc Savage asked.

"The murderer killed him," McFellen said sourly. "Why, I don't know. But it could only have been because Tollen had found out who the murderer was."

"Where did you go after you left the Argus apartment?" Doc asked.

"I got a train and headed here," McFellen said.

"Can you prove that?"

"You're damned right. I met two bankers I know and we played poker on the train. Want their names?"

"Later," Doc said. He turned to Jeff Morgan, said, "How long had you been aboard your boat before we got there?"

"All evening."

"Was the story about someone claiming to be one of my men coming for the powder horn a lie?"

"It was a lie. I wanted to confuse you."

Doc swung on Jones-Field. "Where were you about the time Argus was murdered, and Tollen also?"

"I have been right here on the island the whole time," Jones-Field said emphatically. "I can prove that, also, by long-distance telephone calls I received from Morgan, Holland and McFellen. The toll slips will prove it. Furthermore, I had friends out here last night for cards."

John Holland growled far down in his throat. "I can prove where I was all the time, and I'm damned glad of it."

Doc turned to Cultell. "What about you?"

Cultell's face had become gray again. "I was at my apartment when Argus and Tollen were knocked off. McFellen called me there. He told me you were mixing in the case, and for me to grab your cousin, Patricia Savage, so we could use a threat to her safety to make you drop your investigation."

McFellen nodded. "That's right. I did. I told him to scare hell out of the girl, and we'd work out a way of having her convince you her life was really in danger."

"You've all got alibis, so somebody is lying," Doc said.

Ivans grunted loudly.

"The doctor's murder!" he exclaimed. "That's going to crack it!"

Jeff Morgan's eyes grew roundly frightened. "Wait a minute! I was at the Argus apartment when the doctor was killed, but I was with the girls. I didn't do it."

Doc lifted his voice. "Pat?"

"Yes?"

"You hear that?"

"He didn't kill the doctor," Pat said. "The big bum came in and chased the doctor out of the living room, talked to us for a while about what he'd do to us if we didn't come with him quietly, and then we started out and found the doctor dead."

Morgan blew out his breath. "That poor old Doc thought the murderer was with me, probably, and tried to grab him. The murderer brained him and left in a hurry. That's the way it had to be."

Doc looked at Ivans. "You see who it is?"

"Now I do," Ivans said. "Yeah, it's the guy who can't prove where he was when the doctor was killed. I'll be damned! Just like in the movies—"

Cultell, on the floor, yelled suddenly, "You damned fools! Why didn't you keep your months shut! I never told him about any government swindle!"

Silence, as brittle as glass, hit the room.

Cultell broke it.

"Do something!" Cultell said. "They came here alone! Nobody knows they're here. Nobody—"

Monk kicked Cultell on the jaw, silencing him. But the damage was done. The room filled with violence.

XII

Doc Savage had been expecting fury all during the questioning. His expectation had stretched until, now when the thing happened, his readiness was like a rubber band that had been overstrained until it had little snap. For a moment the fight smashed around him without his being able to take part, and not until he saw Morgan coming up with a gun did he move.

He came down hard on Morgan, fought the man with growing freedom and fury. Morgan was tough. He hung on to his gun for dear existence until it was torn from his fingers.

The room had been a trap. Each of the men had a gun concealed where he could reach it. None of them had the guns on their persons, probably because they had known it was a serious matter in the eyes of the law to carry concealed weapons. But they had them hidden close at hand.

McFellen had his revolver in a desk drawer. He got to the desk. Monk, rushing on from kicking Cultell, hit the desk, heaved it over. There was large pottery lamp on the desk, and McFellen snatched this as the desk was going over, struck Monk with it, brought it down on Monk's head and shoulders. Monk seemed not to notice. McFellen began to run. Monk pursued him. They left the room.

Ham and Jones-Field had hold of each other, grunting and straining for possession of a stubby double-barreled derringer pistol which Jones-Field had plucked out of an overstuffed chair.

Ivans fared the worst in the fight. Physical violence did not seem to be his meat. He was hit in the face by John Holland, hit very hard, so that he fell backward stiffly. Holland kicked him in the face quite callously, went on toward the door.

Doc Savage threw Morgan from him, threw him so that he crashed against Holland, and Holland was unfooted. Holland was quickly erect again, and making for the door. Doc lunged and seized him.

Holland fought with a demon fury. A knife was suddenly in his hand, and he struck outward and upward with the blade. Doc drew away. It was never wise to take on a man with a knife when emptyhanded, no matter what your skill. But the best of weapons to cope with a knife fighter was a chair, and there were plenty of those. He retreated until he could lay hands on one, then made for Holland, pinned Holland against the wall. It was then simple to kick Holland's kneecap, breaking it, draw back and use the chair to break the man's knife arm.

Holland fell at Monk's feet as Monk came back into the house, hauling McFellen by the hair.

"Kinda rough on him, aren't you?" Monk said.

Doc rested, blowing out some of his hot violence in hard breaths. Holland moaned and whimpered at his feet, but he felt no pity for the man.

He said, "Holland's it."

"The hell he is!" Monk said.

Monk had thought it was Cultell, because Cultell had started this fight.

"Holland had no alibi for the time of the doctor's murder. All the others had ironclad ones." Doc's voice was tired and pitched in lower and lower tones. "And remember that Tollen was killed at Holland's house. Holland probably did it because Tollen knew who the blackmailer was. Then Holland tied himself to the stairs. He could have managed that himself."

Monk scratched his head.

Quiet had fallen in the room, except for Holland's whimpering, which was an ugly guilty sound like a beast in a trap.

"A mixed up mess," Monk said.

Ivans sat up, feeling of his bruised face. He began swearing presently, and while he might not be able to fight well, he swore with great facility, much depth of feeling.

"Not as mixed up as it was," Doc said.

Pat was calling anxiously. Doc went to the door. He looked in at Pat and Paula Argus, tied to chairs. "It's all right," Doc said.

"Oh it is, is it?" Pat said, and proceeded to tell him what she thought about being left tied to a chair during the excitement. "Suppose you had gotten licked?" she demanded.

Ivans had stopped swearing suddenly when he heard Pat's voice. Now he appeared in the door, bowing, saying, "I wish to apologize for my language."

Pat laughed. "You were expressing my feelings exactly. I thought of joining you."

Ivans advanced into the room with a flourish. He produced a pocket knife, began cutting the girls free, at the same time delivering sympathetic words.

Doc watched Ivans in surprise. Ivans was a ladies' man!

Monk Mayfair stood in the door and scowled, irked by the attention Mr. Ivans was paying Paula. "Who stepped on his face?" Monk wished to know.

"Holland," Doc explained.

"That's too bad," Monk said unpleasantly. "It should have been a horse."

DON'T MISS
THESE CURRENT
Bantam Bestsellers

BANTAM
SHOP-AT-HOME
C·A·T·A·L·O·G

Special Offer
Buy a Bantam Book
for only 50¢.

Now you can have Bantam's catalog filled with hundreds of titles plus take advantage of our unique and exciting bonus book offer. A special offer which gives you the opportunity to purchase a Bantam book for only 50¢. Here's how!

By ordering any five books at the regular price per order, you can also choose any other single book listed (up to a $5.95 value) for just 50¢. Some restrictions do apply, but for further details why not send for Bantam's catalog of titles today!

Just send us your name and address and we will send you a catalog!